SUMMERLAND:

THE GOSPEL

OF LEVI

*"And the sword of your lamb shall pierce
the womb of my daughter"*

TONY SOSA

a novel

Summerland:
The Gospel of Levi

Copyright © 2022 Tony Sosa

adevilreads@gmail.com

First paperback edition 2022

Cover and Interior design by CoverKitchen

Edited by Sasha Boyce

Published by Tony Sosa Publishing, LLC
in the United States of America

To the African Diaspora. Wherever across the seas, we were scattered, to settle in lands where we were told our lives never mattered. To the spirits of the ancestors, who endured by riding hope's distant gleam. We are their faith made flesh, where once we haunted their dreams.

"Never regret thy fall, O Icarus of the fearless flight, for the greatest tragedy of them all, is never to feel the burning light."

Oscar Wilde

CHAPTER 1

The Abyss

I was born dead but still born.

Imagine the chord of your soul severed from the husk of your flesh before the first breath. I was born in the darkness, a child of the void. I was christened by the abyss and made holy by the shadows that wound up and cradled my existence. I was kissed by the cold lips of death before I even entered this life. The same way God lingered in the darkness before He spoke the light.

That's a true god.

I was the light of the world conceived in shadow. A hidden word.

I was dead like the hopes and dreams for my life that my mama carried up until the moment I came out of her. I must've revisited this memory a thousand times. My screams as a baby waking to the cold world around me were replaced by silence. I was catatonic and ice cold, like my Pops's heart when he realized that his first experience with a new life, was death. I was ripped out of the ether, nursing on the breast of the pit instead of a mother who waited for a first breath that never came.

It was the memory of Immortal Records I've watched most. If I wasn't allowed to know my first life, I wanted to know as much as I could about this one. I wanted to see what I did to live a life so cursed. I wanted to know how I became so calloused to this world and humanity and yet be crowned the Prince of Life.

The first emotions my mama felt toward me were loss, like a horrible vomit that tasted of fear, regret, and pain, which were all the things I spent my entire life running away from. I wasn't always the monster mistaken for God, blameless and without blemish. No matter how scarlet red the sins that stained my hands were.

No.

I was made somewhere along the lines between divine ecstasy and the depths of human depravity. It's just the way things were when you were chosen. My birth was just the beginning of the suffering. And here I was again, sitting in the cold chambers of Cyprian's Cathedral, gazing into the Holy Grail of Immortality. These records belonged to the Church, and they dictated what knowledge was allowed.

Even to me. Also the Church's property.

As was every Nazarene before me.

The vision always began the same way. The doctors were baffled. Mama's screams of anguish were met by the doors of the hospital flying open and a group of men entering the room. The fabric of their suits was as fine as the thread from Minerva's loom, and they circled the hospital bed. The doctors were frozen in their places. Their eyes flickered back and forth in a frenzy, paralyzed by an unseen force. As they watched the group of men form a wall between them and my parents, one man stepped forward.

He was tawny, long, and lithe with a well-trimmed and peppered beard, and tight curls he kept just as neat. His eyes were small but calculating, and his almost timid nature defied his height.

"Father Enoch?" Pops recoiled.

"Forgive me, Daniel, I know this is a difficult time for your family. But you knew this day would come," he said.

Pops's dark skin glistened with sweat that now started to drip from his brow. He clasped onto Mama's hands, her face still wet and contorted with pained tears. One of the magicians snapped their fingers, and in the twinkle of an eye, my lifeless body appeared in the arms of Father Enoch. Mama screamed, using what was left of her strength to lunge forward. Enoch waved his hand, and she was instantly struck by his magic and forcefully held in place.

"I'm sorry, June," Enoch said. "You knew. You both knew."

Pops held her back.

"Hush now, June, baby. It'll be alright," he said.

"No..." Mama weakly struggled against the grip of Enoch's magic.

"It had to be this way. The stillbirth... It's part of the process,"

"T-The process!" Mama winced in pain.

"Daniel?" Mama said, her voice breaking.

"Shaddai came to you, June. Come on, now," Pops said, laughing wistfully. "The Good Lord's gonna dwell with us..."

"Would you like to come with us? Might ease the wife's mind," Enoch said.

Terrified, Mama watched on as Pops's lips met hers.

"Don't worry, June Bug," Pops said.

Enoch carefully handed my body to him. Pops shuddered as he held me in his arms.

"It'll all be over soon."

Mama screamed and begged for help, but the doctors remained frozen in their places, stiff boards under the grip of Enoch's power. They led me away to the bowels of their church, a bleak and cavernous underground cave with an expanse of water. The Abyss.

In this place, life and death become only dreams. It was a place of dimensional twilight, where even death can die. The black surface shimmered with the golden-orbed reflections of the candlelight that encircled us, glowing along the rippling onyx depths.

At the center of the cave was a long, marble dock forming a circle at the end. At the West, a mammoth cross that stood upside down towered over us all, inscribed with glowing, ceremonial symbols of death and resurrection. The pallid marble altar was set in the East, inlaid with 12 stones, lined with golden, ancient Aramaic inscriptions.

Pops stood beside Father Enoch with my tiny, frail corpse in his hands.

"Consider it a great prestige that your bloodline was chosen for this," Enoch said.

"You're the first Judge since the time of Elijah to enter this space. Shaddai has typically come through... priestly, more *noble* bloodlines..."

Pops ignored him, keeping his eyes instead on the appearance of two flickering torches growing closer just ahead. On each side of the looming fires were two boats churning and trudging through the water, like Charon ferrying souls across the river Styx. Two black hooded figures stood at the bow; their cloaks caught in the gentle breeze as they glided across the water. As the boats drew closer, the fires that seemed to float through the darkness cast an infernal glow on an old man's sagging and wrinkled skin.

He walked across the inky surface on his bare feet between the two boats. It was my predecessor, the outgoing Nazarene. God needed a new body. And I was the new host.

They unloaded the boat, surrounding Pops and Father Enoch. Pops clutched onto my body even though I couldn't feel the warmth and safety of his comfort.

"What're y'all gonna do with my boy? Enoch, you better be straight with me!"

Enoch smiled reassuringly and held his arms out patiently until my Pops placed me in his hands. Father Enoch led me to the altar and laid my body down. The old man shed his wine-colored robe. He stood now in a white undergarment and was led quietly to the cross by the two hooded magicians. Two more on either side awaited him.

The one on the left murmured chants, delicately holding the Crown of Thorns. Together with another magician, they drove the crown through his temples. He resisted screaming as long as he could until the pain became unbearable. Red, fresh blood ran down his face as he cried out to the God of the Garden. The other priests that arrived in the boat divided themselves, one half surrounding the altar and the other around the old Nazarene.

By the magic of the magicians, the symbols on the cross glowed brighter now, a shimmering gold. Together they uprooted and gracefully rested the cross onto the ground. The old man took one final, valiant breath and silently laid himself down for his death.

"All things must come to an end, Daniel," Father Enoch said.

"Where one cycle comes to a close, another can begin."

Relentless wailing pierced the open air, echoing and carrying across the water. His hoarse voice was closer now to a bleating as the old man was nailed to the cross. The Order coldly watched, chanting deeply in focus. The old man now choked on his saliva, gagging and gurgling on his blood. The magicians raised the cross back up together; the old man dangled upside down still hollering.

"Begin," Enoch said.

The magicians began to chant. The air was vibrating with a power that shook the water beneath them. By the collective power of the Order, the waters themselves rose into the air, almost seeming to dance as the inky waves gushed and stood on end. Then they stopped.

The waters fell with a thunderous crash. The eyes of the old man burst forth with a light that rivaled the sun. The magician to the right was handed a spear with a golden head. The magician signed the cross, and he mercilessly thrust the spear into the old man's side. Instantly, the old man's eyes burst with a blinding radiance, filling his entire body with light until every bone and organ inside his body was visible through his now transparent skin.

Blood and water poured from his side wound, and the magicians were handed the copper chalice, the Holy Grail of Immortality. They filled the cup strewn with onyx stones to the brim while another magician laid my body onto the altar. A fine-pointed ritual dagger glinted against the light shining on the old man's body. The magician dipped the dagger into the cup and placed a single drop onto their tongues. Their eyes glowed white, filled now with the power of the God of the Garden.

The old man's eyes started to flicker, slowly depleting until they went dark, and he took his last breath.

The shrouds of darkness above them parted open, and radiant blue skies and white clouds began to appear, swirling into an infinite and endless dome. Golden, translucent beings vibrant with colors unimaginable flapped their wings, descending on the space below.

An otherworldly sound filled the room. Choirs of angels sang and lifted their voices to the highest heaven as they raised my lifeless body from the altar. Gusts of wind filled the room, blowing the priests down onto the ground. Pops kept his teary eyes on the Heaven's opening before him, smiling and laughing incredulously.

A shimmering beam of light touched down onto me. The light was vibrant and alive, fluctuating like great wings and descending over me like a dove. My eyes opened, and the light rushed into my eyes and mouth. The magicians held me tightly, chanting fervently. All of Heaven opened before them and funneled downwards, surging and coursing through my frail body.

Pops was lost in the glory of the sight. A voice like a raging storm spoke from above, shaking the ground beneath us.

"*Behold! The dwelling of God is with men!*" it roared.

Pops gasped, rushing towards the altar. He held me to his body. I was alive with the fresh flame of a new life. My eyes were alight, glowing with the power of the spirit that now flowed inside me.

I was alive.

I was born.

But I should've stayed dead.

Pops returned home after that, presenting me to Mama and jumping with joy. But Mama was so destroyed by the stillbirth that she was beside herself. She couldn't even manage to break a smile; she only stared blankly in shock. Pops thought it was just the trauma and that it would wear off, but Mama only seemed to get worse. One day she tried to drown me in the tub. I was barely even a month old. Mama got put away after that, and that's when Grannie came in to take care of us.

He couldn't handle raising my brother Ezra and I alone, so he didn't fight when Grannie came in and took over, and we all moved back in with her. While she kept us busy with church and chores, Pops did everything he could to forget my mama. When Pops wasn't drinking himself to sleep or gambling himself into debt, he was taking us away on certain... excursions.

I wasn't proud of the things that Pops made us do at first, but as a man, I now understand that they're necessary. I've seen hell. Figuratively and literally. God is real, Hell is real, and so are all the angels and demons that go along with it. You see, atheists like to sit there and play the game of God when all they're good at is besting the game of fraud. We like to worship ourselves and put ourselves at the center of everything. That level of arrogance is good for societies that exist like ours, but that's why we're not built to last.

Just because you don't believe in rain doesn't mean you won't get wet. We can sit here and philosophize the afterlife all we want, but at the end of the day, we all know we're going to have to answer for what we've done eventually. That cross the old man died on, he was also inducted on. Initiated and killed, born and slain. A tradition for which I was chosen for. That cross was both a womb and a coffin, a place between life and death. One day I'll take that old man's place, dying so that another may live on. It was the fate of all like me, and I had to come to accept that.

I'll never forget the day they brought me down into that room for my initiation into the Mystery of Death. It was the way of every Nazarene before me that was brought into the Order. You must die in the way the Christ did, who then passed it onto Peter the Apostle. Shaddai continued his reign through Peter after the death of the first Nazarene. Without him, this power would cease to be.

On the day of the yearly Great Descent, they nailed me to an upright cross and speared me, letting me slowly bleed out and choke on my blood. The pain was excruciating, beyond anything I could put into words. I knew I was dying when I started to catch the whiff of burning flesh. It's a stench that lingers. The smell was mingled with sulfur. I opened my eyes and found myself surrounded by a blazing inferno.

Hell.

I was caught in a flaming storm that melted the eye sockets of everyone around me. Their skin was black and covered in boils, popping and oozing with pus. Others around me had their eyes sewn shut and their faces backward, wandering off cliff sides into molten magma pits. They screamed in ways that made my skin crawl, covering their faces in shame and despair. They hid behind large rocks that turned to ash, exposing them to the searing winds.

Fires surrounded me, burning high into the atmosphere without end. New, earthly souls caught on fire like flaming meteorites and plummeted into an eternity of torment.

For three days, I experienced the total wrath of the God of the Garden upon his enemies. I saw things that I'd give anything to forget, things that cost me so many sleepless nights. There was no end in sight. I banged my head against the wall some nights, driven mad by the souls in Hell begging for mercy and the prayers of those on earth pleading for help.

The God of the Garden entrusted me with power beyond human comprehension but also showed me what awaited me should I stray. The real secret to life is that none of it matters. The God of the Garden already knows who belongs to him and who doesn't. He already decided who his chosen people were from the beginning of time. And if you're chosen like me, then there truly is no wrong that you can do. Especially when you're still being controlled by an ancient society of elites that dictate your every move.

Every miracle I've done, every wonder I've performed, each disease I cured and healed, was all at their direction. And every life I've allowed to slip through my fingers was also at their word.

How can I not be fucked up living this way? I'm never my own person. Not even the life I have now was ever truly mine. It's just something borrowed. No matter how powerful I was, they never saw me as their equal. I was only a pawn in their agendas. This institution has used the name of God to enslave, kill, coerce and torture.

And yet, serving Shaddai showed me that they were truly carrying out His will. All my life, I've told myself I'm following the right path, fighting the good fight. But these days, deep down, I'm scared because I can't tell the difference between God and the Devil. Shit, even good and evil. I've seen what this being can do. He devours worlds and souls. By giving yourself to him, you sign yourself over, committing yourself to an eternity either in Heaven or Hell. But no one will ever know. Faith would take the place of asking difficult questions.

I gauged my eyes out to see myself in their Christ. The entity whose feet I knelt at for centuries and cried, "*Oh, God! Oh, God! Forgive me of this sin.*"

My power would only be respected as long as I knew my place. Mindless obedience, that's what God wants. But I couldn't be that. After all the people I've killed, and despite every battle to resist, I still find myself being just like Him.

I hated that I loved to kill, and I hated everything I did to maintain his power throughout all my lives. I knew there were things hidden from me. If Shaddai was allowed to have secrets, so was I.

I didn't even know where my loyalty lies, only where my fears did. I was never cherished by the God of the Garden, only needed. I was never loved, only necessary. I could never bring myself to love him, only fear and resent him. I feared him too much to ever stand against him. But as time went on, the brewing of rebellion only stirred stronger within me, simmering with thoughts of treason.

The martyr.

The savior.

The saint.

All roles more than they are titles, and that's fine by me.

I don't mind playing along.

CHAPTER 2

Benediction

Killing is an acquired taste, it turns out.

The first time, Pops made me watch him do it. Next time, he made me do it myself. Before I came into any of my power, I thought he was downright the vilest type of man. The kind who stalked and preyed on innocent people and talked about it like it was an art. He spoke about what to look for and how to know for sure I found the right one.

Sick.

But genius.

I'll give him that. Pops always said hunting was a craft, there was certain finesse to it. witches were powerful creatures, and there was an exhilarating rush that came with making a predator your prey. I was 10 years old when he took me hunting for the first time. There was a woman who settled in town and mostly kept to herself. Pops stalked her for months.

One evening, when he watched her emerge from the woods, he said the voice of God spoke to him clear as day with one simple command: *kill her.*

She had the Hell-given power to conjure powerful and terrifying hallucinations. Pops nearly died trying to capture her. That's when he took us to see her. He led us down to the basement of the house, which plunged deep into the ground like ancient catacombs. My brother Ezra was 16 then, and he held me by the hand with a blazing torch held in the other. At the time, I didn't know where I was being taken, only that I trusted my brother and Pops with my whole heart. They and Grannie were the only things I had in this world since Mama had been locked away at the psych ward.

Once we got to the bottom, there was a woman whose stringy, dirty blonde hair hung in a mangled mess. Her hair was cemented to her face with blood and tears. She struggled frantically against the glowing golden chords that bound her to the chair in place. Pops walked around a large circle, engraved with words of power in Coptic. At the center was a large triangle with a black, hollow interior. It was created to be the womb in which the ritual pyre would burn. I was shaking. Ezra's chestnut skin glowed almost gold against the flickering torch. His eyes were alive and bright with a dutiful dread.

I trembled behind Ezra as Pops approached the woman. She fought and resisted the grip of his hand across her face, forcing her to look at me.

"This way, boy," Pops said, gruff.

I looked back at Ezra but felt only his rough hands against my back pushing me forward.

"Do you know what this is?"

I glanced at the woman, whose eyes now flickered black. I shuddered, jerking away quickly. Pops struck her in the face so mercilessly I could hear the bone in her jaw crack. A tooth flew out of her mouth and slid across the floor. Oozing globs of bloody saliva ran down her cheek. She spat, heaving.

"That there's a witch, boy," he said. "She can conjure all kinds of trickery by the Devil's hands."

The woman cocked her head up suddenly, and her gaze pierced into me directly. I could feel her eyes penetrating the depths of my soul, shifting through my spirit like a filing cabinet. It felt like fingers digging into my brain as she searched for fears I buried deep inside and pain I never knew was there. The sensation was awful and invasive, but I was too rigid with horror to move.

"Son?" Pops said.

The woman was muttering something low when, from the dark depths of the shadows behind her, I saw a woman emerge. She was a lovely sight, with golden brown skin with thick coils down to her shoulders and big, welcoming eyes. She smiled at me tenderly and held out her hand.

"M-Mama?" I gasped.

"What!?" Pops exclaimed.

"Come on now, baby... You don't gotta do this," Mama said.

Her voice was distant like an echo, foreign and familiar all at once. Pops struck her again and pulled her back by the hair.

"You *bitch*." Pops's voice trembled. "H-How dare you play with my boy like that?"

The woman's shoulders bounced; a faint chuckle began to fester into an uneasy, disgruntled laugh.

"You see, boy? I wanted you to see this with your own eyes. So that you don't go thinkin' your Pops is some kind of monster," he said. "Remember, these ain't people. These are *witches*. They're demons dressed up to look like us. Nothin' more."

Pops drew a copper blade from a sheath around his waist. He kissed it, praying quickly over it before he showed it to me. Its metal body glinted against the flames as he approached me.

"Don't you worry. She can't hurt you. Them chords around her wrist are blessed by the most powerful magicians; she ain't gettin' out those. As for what you saw..." Pops knelt to look me in the eye. I met his dark, grey eyes that were clouded with zealous rage. "Don't you believe anything she tried showin' you. Your Mama's locked away, bless her heart... It wasn't real, you hear? It's more of the Devil's tricks."

He held out my hands, placing the cold metal blade in them. It felt like it must've weighed 20 pounds in my tiny hands, but it was vibrating with power. The blade was alive, charged with a sublime energy that I could only describe as electric. It was engraved with strange symbols and left a tingle against my fingertips as Pops smiled at me fondly.

"This here's been in the family since the days that Elijah first walked with us. It was my Daddy's once. It has the power to sever the witch's ties to their god, which spares 'em from facin' judgment…"

Pops turned back towards the woman. The moment her eyes caught sight of the blade, she screamed, flailing in place, mortified and desperate to escape the bonds. Her mascara ran in clumpy black globs down her cheeks while she begged for her life. It was ugly. Snot flew out in strings of saliva, forming webs, weeping and wailing. Pops laughed provokingly.

"Ain't nothin' funny now, is it? I'd say by the looks of it, you know exactly what this pretty little thing does, don't ya?"

Pops pulled her hair, forcing her head back and exposing her neck. "Ezra, hold him."

Ezra's big hands grasp my head firmly, forcing my eyes to stay open.

"Now, son, this is your first time, so I'm gonna make this fast."

"Pops, please, I…" I stammered.

His blade tore open a clean gash in her throat, spraying crimson blood across my face. I tasted iron as it seeped through the crack of my lips and onto my teeth. The warmth oozed down my face. The woman's body convulsed as Pops carved her open ear to ear. He held her by the hair, letting her bleed out, choking and gagging on her blood.

Her body convulsed before slumping over with her hair cloaking her face from view. Pops pushed her body back up against the chair.

"Now, this next part is very, very important son. In times of battle, this can't always be done, but when you can… seize each opportunity and cherish it…" he explained.

I tried to tug away from Ezra's grip, but he held me in place.

It wasn't over.

Pops thrust his blade into the woman's chest and slashed down as if he were cutting open a box. He dug into her chest, his arm squished and mushed around her insides as he dug through her freshly made corpse. A thrilling smile drew across Pops's face, and his eyes sparkled as he ripped her heart out of her chest. Blood ran down his hand as he approached the unlit pyre. Pops began praying in an ancient tongue, calling down blessings from the God of the Garden. Voices and hisses flooded the room, and ethereal notes rang down from unseen places, filling the dark space we stood in.

Shadows moved along the walls, and a sound like fluttering wings circled us. Ezra followed Pops, lowering himself down now to light the pyre with his torch. A tall, blazing flame fanned into life, shooting high into the air before settling into a pulsating pile of sparks and golden fire. Eyes slowly started to cover the walls around us, even the floor beneath my feet. I jumped, backing away from the eyes that appeared and looked down at us from the ceiling. Pops opened his arms, breathing in the ecstasy of a successful kill.

"All of heaven is watchin' us, boys,"

I stood close by Ezra, horrified at the blinking large eyes that watched our every movement.

"*Thy kingdom come, thy will be done, Lord…*" Pops said.

He raised the heart into the air, presenting it before the unseen throne of God.

"*On earth, as it is in heaven,*"

He cast the heart into the fire, and the flames exploded, blowing back gusts of violent fires and winds. A ferocious howl from the fire filled the room. Pops laughed, lifting his hands into the air and shouting praises of thanks. The flames settled into place, and a solemn silence hung in the air, broken only by a strange clinking against the floor. The eyes fluttered, blinking and twitching, following my every move. Hushed voices coming from invisible heavenly hosts filled the room, and a reverent silence fell over us. It was a silence so suffocating it sucked the air out of my lungs, and the walls seemed to breathe with the air it snatched out of me.

I looked up, and the ceiling was translucent, blended with a crystal blue sky filled with luscious clouds raining down gold coins. I watched, awe-struck as God himself rewarded the murder of this woman. This was his will made perfect in my weakness to comprehend how a loving God could demand something like this.

But it wasn't my role to question, the first Nazarene was no different. My duty was to the crown of heaven and to follow his perfect will.

To obey.

It's what God loved most of all.

Now, when I remembered the lifeless, hollow expression on that woman's face I don't feel bad about what Pops did. If I could go back in time, I'd help my younger self take that knife up and carve out her heart myself. I don't feel bad. She was a witch. My Pops was a hero in his own right, ridding the world of such inhumanity. They're demons guised in flesh. Some magicians say when witches receive their pact for power, they're no longer themselves. An agent of hell assumes their bodily form and takes their place, walking the earth in the body and experiencing all the earthly delights they so desperately want to indulge in.

Demons will do anything to enter our bodies, seducing us with powers beyond human control. That's what makes them so dangerous, they're the worst kind of people. The type that would do anything for power. Sacrificing babies, eating children, and drinking blood for promises of transcending their earthly bodies.

If it were up to me, I'd line them up and have them butchered. I'd watch all their heads roll to the ground and let their cold, dead lips kiss my feet as the soil became drenched with their blood. I may have been born dead, but that was the day I truly died inside. Life didn't matter, I was just numb to it all.

I used to feel when I thought of him. Hatred, disgust, confusion… But the thing that I remember most about my Pops was how afraid I was of him and that look in his eye. The furrowing of his brow in the quick flash of rage that traveled across his stare like lightning across the sky. He was a force to be reckoned with. Because of him, I was no stranger to killing. At first, I thought he'd just lost his goddamn mind. But this is the result of generations of Beaumont men being bred to kill. And we did it well.

Pops had a particular set of beliefs engrained in him. They controlled and steered every move and decision he made. If he wasn't looking over his shoulder, he was looking over someone else's. As horrifying as Pops's rage could be, there was only one thing that ever put the fear of God in him: witches. They were savage and unpredictable, worshiping feral gods of nature and commanding infernal forces at the cost of their own souls. Answering not even to God.

Years after he was gone, I was working closely alongside the Order down in Georgia when they got a lead on where the Summerland coven was hiding. There were rumors that the Man in Black had chosen an heir, and that their Madonna lived again. When Nero Wardwell killed Adora Scott, it was a celebration of the ages. The witches were driven underground, and we hadn't heard from them since. But like the roaches and vermin that they are, somehow, they managed to find a way to slither their way back into the earthly paradise that the Order and I have worked so hard to preserve.

When they said that the Madonna returned, I didn't believe it... until I turned on the news one night three years ago. I remember still the goosebumps running down my neck, the sense of fear and dread was like a blade through the heart. Every TV station in town was blaring with the incident in Georgia.

FIRE IN THE SKY

It was the headliner across every anchor on any channel you can find. The footage showed the Sheol forest in a ruddy glow against the illuminated, fiery sky. It was swirling out of control. It was a mortifying marvel, flames raged from heaven before scorching the ground beneath it in a whirlwind, unlike anything the world had ever seen before. They called it fire, but the substance was beyond this world. Professionals and Conspiracists theorized everything from aliens to naturally occurring phenomena. But those of us on the inside knew what they really were.

Angels.

And not just any kind. What the world witnessed that night was the heavenly army led by Michael himself. No one had ever seen that kind of power, not since the days of Pentecost, and should never be seen until the final Trumpet sounds.

The night after the news, Father Enoch and I traveled to Summerland ourselves. We could feel the ground vibrating and alive with the dark forces that built that town. Even angels feared to tread that space, to pass through that awful door from the ordinary world of men and into that Dread Lord's blackest outer spaces. The Bloodwood circled that town, acting almost like a fortress of trees to keep everything else out. I had to travel deep into the belly of Sheol, past the sounds of shrieking specters and disembodied spirits that wandered the wooded darkness.

The ceremonial archway where magicians had performed their sacred rites for centuries had been reduced to nothing but rubble, and all that lay around it was scorched earth. The marble altar carved by the hands of Elijah himself now laid split down the middle, shattered into corroded scraps on the ground, still blackened by the fires that destroyed it. Bones were scattered, snapped in half, and forgotten like twigs now a part of the landscape.

I'll never forget the way Father Enoch fell to his knees and wept. He cried like he'd lost a child, clasping onto the stone as snot ran down his nose. Once again, the witches had desecrated something hallowed and sacred.

I thought Father Enoch brought us to investigate the scene where everything happened. But there was a truth he brought me to discover. A terrifying truth I wasn't yet ready to face.

CHAPTER 3:

Blasphemy

That was the night everything changed. After exiting the woods, we arrived at Summerland, the unholy town that had drawn us to Dev's den. Slumbering on the edge of the Bloodwood Forest was the house of old man Abertha, still standing tall. Knots filled my stomach, tugging and wrapping themselves around so badly my breaths were starting to suffocate me. Then I heard a trembling humming, like a eulogy for the dead that was carried along by shaking voices.

"What's gotten into you?" Father Enoch asked, disapproving.

I shook my head dismissively. I hated showing any sign of weakness or discomfort. I am God walking on earth; there's nothing more powerful on this plane than me. But the humming that began didn't concern my ego or the fortress of emotional impenetrability I'd created. My heart couldn't help but wrench when I saw what started to form. Beyond the chasm of darkness illuminated by only the dimly glowing yellow windows of the mansion, shades and emaciated spirits began to appear before me.

The Abertha family was the first to come and settle this land and profit from the Georgia peach. But a little-known fact about Ewen Abertha was that he was the cruelest, most sadistic slave owner the South had ever seen. My Grannie used to tell me that the E his name stood *evil*. As the shades started to form, so did the wetness of their tears. Their droplets of pain fell against my skin. For a brief moment, their suffering became mine, and I could no longer tell the difference between theirs and my own. This wasn't the first time I'd come across wandering spirits, especially not back home in Florida. But I'd never encountered spirits in this condition.

The depth of his inhumanity was actualized at that moment. There were souls with eyes gauged out, mouths sewn shut, breasts and genitals mutilated, and others lacerated beyond human recognition. Their pain was still as fresh as the tears that filled my eyes. Everyone spoke so highly about the wealth and opulence of the Abertha fortune. Unfortunately, our desire to be dazzled and adored by displays of wealth helped us blind ourselves to the bloodshed and torture it was built on. When I looked at all the suffering souls around me, the Abertha mansion still so pristine and white despite the buckets of blood it was painted with, all I could do was weep.

"What is it?" Enoch said. "You've never done this before."

"Enoch," I said, "Look at 'em… how can you ask me that?"

Enoch looked around, removing a handkerchief from his breast pocket and gagging into it.

"Come on now, boy, wasn't you in hell itself for three days? You've seen sufferin' souls before. Now, you tell me why this should be any different?"

I laughed off the anger I could feel heating up in my cheeks.

"They were godless," he said.

I was dazzled by his indifference. Enoch grumbled, a haughty expression growing across his face. I wondered how anyone could hate their own humanity that much. Enoch was so lost in his worship of God that he lost sight of his mortal condition. Suffering was just a part of the grand design for him. Nothing more, nothing less.

He stared back at me quietly. The car was still parked outside the gate. I wanted to turn around, too nauseous to even begin to imagine the horrors that awaited me inside. The infernal glow that lit the windows painted Abertha mansion like a kingdom in hell. The air was foul with the smell of seared flesh, and the air still vibrated with reverberating screams that echoed throughout eternity. There was nothing but the taste of ash and soot in my mouth, and the air was so thick every step I took felt like trudging through water. I took in every smell, sound, and feeling of the tormented ghosts that wandered this land.

The spirits gathered around me like moths to the light, hovering in frantic swaths. As they laid their hands on me, I saw flashes in my mind of the final blow that killed them. Spirits that die under these circumstances like these are doomed to repeat the trauma like a broken record, their agony continuing for eons. It's a kind of hell that exists because they're still so caught in the moment of suffering that they could never see it was over. To leave this world as they did here was the peak of human depravity. It was inflicting suffering on innocent people for the sheer enjoyment of it.

"We can't keep on like this, E," I said. "This ain't right," I said.

I opened my arms and laid my hands on them. One by one, they came. The moment I touched the coldness of their skin, their eyes opened and looked up at me like a newborn, bright and filled with the light of life. The whole of their forms quickly shimmered a golden light before fading into the darkness. Spirits like these remained with their eyes closed; they couldn't see. That is why they wandered and wallowed in their suffering; they couldn't open their eyes to see the light. Anguished souls seeking deliverance followed us as we headed toward the mansion.

"I ain't comin' back here again," I said.

Enoch gave me a solemn pat on the back before turning to face the door. Before he could knock, a statuesque maid with a long face and streaks of silver through her hair opened the door. Her icy blue eyes watched over me cautiously.

"Evenin', ma'am. I'm Father Enoch, and this is Levi Beaumont. Mr. Abertha requested to see us?"

The woman stood aside.

"Yes, he's been expectin' you. Mr. Abertha ain't been... right since the incident," The maid said.

Her voice was frail and unsure, fading away as she trailed away from us. She stopped, fidgeting in place.

"He's just up them stairs in his den. He don't like to be... seen. So pardon my ill manners for not escortin' y'all to the door myself,"

I gave her a nod, and she turned away. The house was dark and dead. There was a coldness through this cemetery of memories. The house was beautiful from the inside, but with a kind of forgotten luster, like ruins of a castle. I saw fleeting shadows from the corners of my eyes, dispersing before I could get a good eye on them. The spirits' eyes were on me. A long strip of golden yellow light ran down the hallway leading to the den.

As we passed through the door, the crackling of the fireplace fell to the background of labored wheezing. Sprawled onto the couch was a bloody, eviscerated stub of flesh gasping and moaning in pain. Its skin was singed and burned nearly down to the bone, baring not even eyelids or lips. Instead, his eyes were bulging and wide, having the skin around them burned down. As we approached closer, we started to see more clearly it was a man, at least what was left of one. He flapped his jaw, gurgling, and coughing. Enoch covered his mouth, heaving behind his hand.

"Is this where I tell you to get it together?" I said.

He glared at me from over his hands.

"No, this is the part where we introduce ourselves," another voice said.

It had a raspy-like growl, almost predatory. The man stood to his feet. He was tall and possessed a kind of regality that you'd expect from old nobility. His smile was mischievous like Loki was grinning back at me from behind his eyes. His beard was trimmed cleanly, and his suit looked like a single thread on it cost more than someone's house. His dark, olive complexion glowed almost gold against the crackling flames from the fireplace.

"Thomas?" I said.

The man laughed. He slowly rotated the whiskey in his glass and took a drink.

"No, no, Thomas is… incapacitated," he said. "As you can see for yourself,"

"It can't..." Enoch gasped, horrified.

His legs trembled as he approached the mutilated stub lying on the couch.

"I can't believe this..." Enoch said, breathless.

Thomas's body continued to moan and struggle to breathe.

"Who did this? And who are you?" I said.

"Well, to answer your first question... witches, undoubtedly," he said. "As for the answer to your second question? Well, I'm just a friend... Business partner, really. But our families go back quite some time,"

"Holy shit," I said. "I know who you are,"

"Ahh... But I know you, Mr. Beaumont. And what an honor, I must say it is, to meet the Hidden Pope," he said winking.

"Hannibal Castillo," Enoch said in a panicked clarity.

"I should've known..."

"You ain't got no business in none of this," I spat. "So what're you doin' stickin' your neck around here?"

"Ohhhhh...." He grumbled, amused.

"That's where you're wrong. You see, my business partner's hanging by a thread and that jeopardizes my dealings. In other words..."

He stood almost nose to nose with me now, smugly grinning.

"This has now become my business. Besides, have you seen Thomas? Does it look like he was the one who placed the call to bring you here?" Hannibal said.

I glanced back at the blubbering mess Thomas was on the couch, and Hannibal was right.

"Listen, this whole Rico Suave thing you've got goin' on might impress the folks back in Miami. But all this suit and whisky get up is tired. So, my man, why don't you just cut the bullshit and get right to it?"

Hannibal chuckled, then stood beside Thomas.

"You know my Abuelo Miguel never trusted witches, he'd seen what magic can do. And looking at Tom now... I see why he was so afraid. But I'd rather let Tom tell you all about how he was raised from the dead and all,"

My heart fell to the pit of my stomach.

"Say that again?" I said.

Hannibal nodded.

"Fa...ther..." Thomas groaned.

He took a deep, sharp breath that came out as a raspy wheeze. Enoch and I stood by Thomas, leaning in closer to hear him.

"He... B-Brought... Me... B-B-Ba-Back...." Thomas strained.

"Who did?" Enoch said.

"N-N-No-ah...." Thomas said.

"His son?" Enoch shuddered.

"Not possible." I scoffed.

"No, no, no..." Enoch stammered, shaking Thomas.

"How did he do this? How!?" I shoved Enoch away from him.

"Take it easy," I said. "This guy's on death's doorstep already. You really think shakin' him around's gonna get you anywhere?"

"Y'all got any idea what this means?" Enoch said, pacing the room.

"Gerald was right, his bastard was the heir. And now, the essence of Roshana has been unlocked..."

"Look, relax. Wasn't y'all the ones who told me the Devil could only ever mimic power? If I'm really Christ on earth, ain't nothin' to worry about," I shrugged.

Enoch looked at me gravely.

"But that don't mean it's unparalleled. The Madonna alone is a deadly force. But if she's become Roshana... then that means the witches have come to full power... Everywhere." Enoch said.

"So the Devil's returned to earth through Noah..." I said darkly.

"So what does this mean?"

"It means we better be fast about findin' and killin' the Madonna. The witches will start a war..." Enoch said.

"But this don't make no sense! I thought y'all said Nero killed Adora... how? How can there still be a Madonna in place?" I said.

Enoch paced the room for a moment. Hannibal smirked at us as he took another puff from his cigar, blowing O's as if he were savoring the scene.

"The woman... always like the serpent- *cunning*," Enoch said with revulsion.

"This is bullshit!" I said. "I knew somethin' was up the first time we'd caught wind of a Madonna in Summerland."

"We were handlin' the situation," Enoch said firmly.

"This shit look handled to you?" I snapped back.

I scoffed, stepping away from him because I just wanted to make him swallow his teeth.

"If you'd have just let me go down there, I would've ripped that bitch's throat out myself!"

"I told you Gerald was takin' care of it!" Enoch said.

His brows furrowed, his forehead morphing him into a nightmare creature. I laughed off the tension.

"Nah, of course. 'Cause the Wardwells do everythin' better, don't they?"

Enoch's eye twitched.

"Sorry to interrupt," Hannibal said. "I know I don't know much about witch wars and all that. But where I'm from, what happened to Thomas is called... *sending a message,*"

"What're you tryna say?" I said.

"That these witches already started the war by delivering up Thomas to you this way," he laughed.

"It's a threat and a warning. Well... More like a promise, really."

"Well, they've got another thing comin'. Don't y'all worry. If the Witch Queen wants to go this route, then let's fuckin' run it. I won't even need no Transfigure,"

"Let's not rush ahead of ourselves, Levi. Use your head for a moment, you can't solve every problem by bulldozin' your way through it," Enoch said.

"Besides, as much as I'd hate to admit it, the witches are worthy opponents. They'd never step out into the open, especially not now,"

"Then what do we do?" I said.

"Durin' your first lifetime on earth, you came for the lost sheep of Israel to gather your flock... she will do the same and return to Florida to collect the rest of the Summerland descendants."

"So, in other words, wait until she comes to us?"

"Exactly right," Enoch said.

"And when she does, we'll be ready for her. And you can finally rip the heart out of the Witch Queen yourself and put an end to this satanic savagery once and for all,"

Hannibal slipped on his coat and placed his fedora back on his head before he headed for the door.

"There is... one last thing he asked me to call you here for, Father. But such a request I'll allow him to make himself..." he said. "Give him some dignity in all this,"

"Yeah? And where you goin'?" My question firing out more as a demand.

"Some things are better left unsaid. I'll leave you two to handle the supernatural issues. It was a pleasure doin' business with you two gentlemen. Not every day one gets to meet the Son of God. Say, put in a good word with the Big Man for me, will you?"

He patted my shoulder and slipped out of the door. He truly didn't give a single fuck about who I was or what I could do. Oddly enough, and I'd never admit it out loud, but it made me respect him. To knowingly stand before the Son of God and shrug him off like a bum was both offensive and impressive.

I'd only ever heard stories about him; even back home in Florida, he was folkloric. But having a brush with Hannibal Castillo even left me feeling a little secretly star-struck. He's the most wanted man in the world, the biggest kingpin since Escobar. People talked about Castillo with bated breaths; they say he's got eyes and ears everywhere. I'd heard rumors about Castillo being involved with the Abertha's, but people down South love to gossip, and I tried not to believe everything I heard.

But now I know it's undoubtedly true, and he knows of the existence of witches. Real witches. Although he may not have seemed it, I had to consider him an ally. Anyone who supports eradicating the existence of those hell spawns has a friend in me. Besides, drug dealing and murder wouldn't be the worst thing the church has turned a blind eye to.

"Enoch?" I said.

He turned around, his eyes were heavy with regret, and he hung his head defeatedly.

"Gerald Wardwell asked for our help, and we denied him... We didn't believe him when he said the Madonna and Son of Promise were amongst us. And now look at the price we paid. That our Brothers in the Art paid," Enoch covered his face shamefully.

"They're dead now and at peace. But you know who isn't?" I said.

Thomas turned his head, slowly flapping his jaw to speak.

"P-Please," he said. "P-Please..."

Enoch and I approached Thomas.

"K-Kill... me..." Thomas begged.

His chest bounced as he struggled to cry. His words were strange and garbled. I could only imagine how difficult it must be to talk without a tongue.

"Kill me... please..."

He looked disgusting, sniveling there on the couch. He was barely human in any sense of the word. Hannibal was right. Thomas was a message to all of us. He could barely speak, was missing his limbs, and was so badly burned I had to hold down vomit every time I looked at him. He wasn't alive, at least, not in the sense that anything would want to be. Although looking at Thomas, all I could think about were the horrors of Ewen. I know children shouldn't suffer for the sins of their fathers, but I felt more disgusted than empathetic. I wanted to kill him because his sounds were starting to annoy me, not out of mercy.

"They won't get away with this," Enoch said. "Gerald was like a brother to me. He warned me so many times, but I just wouldn't listen..."

I sucked my teeth, annoyed.

"We start losin' hope now, then all this really would've been in vain," I said

"You're right," Enoch said. "And now, the difficult part,"

He looked down at Thomas, who groaned and cried to himself.

"Nah," I said. "This won't be hard at all."

I passed my hand over Thomas's face, and the essence of his soul escaped from his mouth. I could feel his soul passing through my hands like a gentle breeze. Thomas sighed long and deeply as his spirit drained from his body. His head rolled to the side, mouth hanging open and lifeless. Thomas was truly dead now, and there was no bringing him back.

For as long as I can remember, I'd been the most powerful force on earth without a rival or match, and suddenly, this was challenged. But I wouldn't let it phase me. I wouldn't be bested.

Father Enoch and the other magicians raised me to believe that I was unstoppable, I was their God, made flesh and living on earth alongside them, and now I felt weak.

I was the only one able to raise life back up from the dead, and now a counterfeit power has emerged that has allowed the witches to do the same. And if that was true, what else are they capable of?

CHAPTER 4:

The Myrrhbearers

It all seemed like another lifetime. But today I lived it again. I was almost late today for the Sunday church service, lost in the murky and brooding waters of the swamp in front of me. The wafting heat and moisture in the air were only made bearable under the shade of the magnolia tree. One of the only things not draped with moss. The fresh scent of the flowers nearly masked the putrid smell of rotting eggs from the swamp. This is where everything started. Cicadas in the air hummed, and I lost myself deeper in the pool of my mind and the memories that haunted me still.

The bloodline began here, sailing over these same waters. A place called Serpent's Swamp. Grannie told of her earliest ancestor, Tituba, who came with three Marys from the New World. Before I was old enough to walk, I learned that witches were the most horrifying creatures ever created. The elders of Grannie's choir called them *Iyami*. *Witches* in their purest state, harrowing spirits of primal nature without body or form. Once passing through Sheol, the Summerland descendants had to cross this swamp.

My family's story is interwoven with shame, glory, blood, faithfulness, and downfalls and triumphs. Tituba arrived here, traveling across the dark waters. With her magic, she wove boats made of reeds and bald cypress, and together she and the other women of the Pact arrived in this town. My Pops comes from a long, line of judges who swore to hunt down and kill the hell spawns of Lilith and Eve. But his Mama, Grannie Tamar, comes from the *Mother of Blood*; Tituba Parris.

I wish I could say I knew anything about my mama's side. Pops says she was a woman he met at the church, but it was nearly a sin to ever ask about her. I know she's a mental patient kept at St. Hildegard's, but other than being out of her mind, she was a mystery to me. I almost went looking for her, especially as a teenager. But I just couldn't bring myself to see her that way. I didn't want to remember her in that state, especially if I couldn't save her. Mama was inflicted by madness at the hands of God himself, and if that was His will, then there wasn't shit I could do about it.

My thoughts were his thoughts.

His ways were mine.

He was like a shadow, forever entwined.

The God of the Garden controlled my every action and almost all my thoughts. If He wanted to kill, then so did I, and I was the vessel He'd use to do it. I felt at odds with myself, between what I wanted and His voice inside my head. I had to learn to push aside guilt, shame, and regret; if not, I'd have drowned in the emotions that followed His orders. There was still a voice inside me that urged me to resist and follow my desires. As badly as I wanted to listen to it, I knew I had a duty to uphold. To redeem my family from the Summerland Pact by serving the God of Heaven.

I was feeling doubtful again, but I had to remember this was all just a part. A role I had to keep playing. I'm sure there were other Nazarenes before me who experienced the sting of doubt, but it was their actions that determined who they were. Despite the spirit of the God of the Garden dwelling within us, we were still *men*. Rebellion doesn't begin until an action is taken.

Or did it begin first in the heart?

A thought?

If it did, then I've already taken the first step.

The thoughts churned in my stomach. I anxiously flicked the cigarette I puffed into the swamp and watched it slowly drift across the shrouded waters. I had to get to the church service. Maybe being surrounded by those who prayed and placed all their faith in me would restore what I'd lost in myself. I didn't know much longer I could hold onto being a prisoner in my own body and having my thoughts spied on by this other entity living inside me. The years of being a host have worn me down, and at this point, I was looking for a way out.

I didn't need a miracle.

I needed a fucking exorcism.

It took everything in me to get to church today, but I'd finally made it. I managed to sneak in before the service began. *Will Be Done* was the first church built in this town, long before the sun shone through the stained-glass windows of St. Cyprian's Cathedral that now towers over everything in sight. It was a homely church; you'd miss it on your drive through town if you weren't looking for it. It was nestled within the ruddy trunks of Sheol, a beacon of hope in a place named after Hell. The free folk that found solace in these lands built this place with their own hands, forming a place of worship from the bloody red bark of this forest.

One night they prayed for a miracle, and the witches who lurked in their trees answered their prayers. The Three Marys granted their desires of prosperity, and the first act of the divine to the settlers of this town was born: The Miracle of Blood. The trees oozed a bloody maple from the rust-colored forest and red bark, and their crying turned to laughter. It was the sweet blood from the body of the earth. From the veins of Mother Nature, they were fed. Syrup became Tophet's greatest treasure.

Ecstatic shouts echoed throughout the forest as I stepped out of the car and quickly joined the waves of people that poured into the church. Some looked for a divine connection, and others hoped for an excuse to justify their behavior. All were equally deluded. The truth was, God, didn't care much for the prayers of His people. They were food for him, an energy source that continued to feed Him and sustain his existence. Without the faith of the people, He would cease to exist. We were just energy sources for these beings, meals for a cosmic vampire that saw us as nothing more than something to fill their stomachs. We were bred for consumption like rats dropped into the den of a hungry snake.

I was greeted by women wearing wide-brimmed hats in every array of colors beneath the rainbow and men in suits that their wives picked out for them. Like any church, image was everything. Even if you were a sinner, you'd better look like a Saint. And be the best dressed in the congregation. That basically made you close to godliness, as far as anyone else was concerned.

"Levi," A voice called out over the crowd.

A woman stood, brushing the finger wave curls that hugged her dark brown face with shining amber eyes.

Bonnie Eastey.

Amma, Bonnie, and Rita lead funerary services here at the church. But it was mostly Bonnie's bread and butter. I'd never spoken to her much, but she was fiercely loyal to Amma, regardless of the odds. Not only did she descend from one of the Three Marys, but she was the heiress to the entire Eastey maple fortune, the first family present for the Miracle of Blood. And the only ones to survive the Great Cleansing.

She didn't care who she had to go up against, not even Reverend James when he spoke out of line towards anyone in the choir. Bonnie was old money, just as rich as any Abertha, only better. It was a legacy not founded on cruelty.

"Bonnie," I said. "Happy Sunday,"

"Happy Sunday, Levi. You lookin' for Amma?"

I blushed.

"You caught me,"

Bonnie smirked.

"Where's Ezra? Rita and me was just talkin' about him," She said, coquettish.

And when weren't they? It was no secret that Bonnie was long after Ezra. I thought Rita did too, but she just liked to flirt. Although Ezra was the church favorite since we were kids. Everyone loved him, especially any girl who met him.

"Haven't seen 'em," I shrugged.

"Anyhow! Did you hear the news? The Elders is congregatin' again tonight, but it looks like Amma's gon' be Queen!" She squealed.

Bonnie quickly covered her mouth excitedly.

"I'm sorry— I know Nita's gonna throw a fit. But I'd be lyin' if I said she didn't deserve it."

My stomach was in knots.

"You sure?"

Bonnie nodded excitedly.

"We'll know for sure after tonight. But Miss Tamar's announcin' her as head of the choir today, so I know she's got more than an itch."

"That's great." I feigned excitement.

"You alright?" Bonnie said.

Her face soured.

"What is it? Y'all think the power should stay with Tamar or go to Nita? The descendants of the Three Marys have every right to the crown as any. And Amma's one of them."

"Bonnie, Nita's the last person I'd wanna see inherit a power like that."

Bonnie rolled her eyes, glaring back now at Grannie Tamar that fanned herself, her stork-like neck towering over the crowd and watching disapprovingly.

"Miss Tamar should count herself lucky Eastey wasn't in line this time. First I'd do is send her on her way."

I grumbled.

"I think I'm gonna go ahead and find a seat."

She folded her arms watching me closely, as I pushed past the crowds of people shuffling towards the pews to find a seat. This would mean the world to Amma, but it felt like the end of mine. The Nazarene and the Witch Queen were forbidden from joining in any kind of union, lest the blood be *tainted,* so they say. As much as the Magdalene witches loved their power, they hated themselves just as much for having it.

Not even the Witch Queen was worthy enough to be with the Son of the God that they claimed to serve. It was an honor to be in service at all to Him, and that was their reward. God can have no equal, so that meant for me there was no wife. No love. Only him. I could have no other. Especially not the Queen of Florida.

I sat down in the furthest row from the stage and nearest to the door, drowning out the sound of the excited congregation with the grinding of my teeth. I buried my face into my hands, feeling the anger build up inside me. I knew I shouldn't be feeling this. I was supposed to be happy for Amma, I'd known her all my life. Amma was always destined for greatness, I just didn't think it would be something like this. Even if I couldn't marry her, I thought I could've at least had her, but now that she was possibly to become Queen, that was all gone now.

"I like when the light hits your eyes like that,"

I looked up, the blinding lights from the ceiling were blocked off by a beautiful silhouette. It was Amma, smiling down at me like a heavenly vision.

"Amma," I said, choking on my saliva.

"They're usually so dark. But here... there's a honey color to them. Who knew?" She grinned.

Her smile was intoxicating. It was like it came from her soul, lighting from within her body and shining out. She sat down beside me, laying her hand on my lap. I shuddered, averting the gaze of her upturned, cognac eyes. I pulled my hand away.

"How you doin'?"

She brushed her hair behind her ear.

"You feelin' alright?" she said.

Uncertainty clouded her face now. I cupped her cheek, shocked that I didn't slice my palms against her chiseled cheekbones. She laid her hand over mine.

"You've got a big day comin' up, I hear," I said.

Her Senegalese braids curtained her sable face as she hung her head bashfully.

"Finally... a Putnam woman to wear the crown... after all these years. It could've been Eastey or Warren, but... They chose me. The spirits, they chose *me,* can you believe it?"

"I do…" I said, longingly. "You deserve the world… And beyond," She groaned quietly.

"You've got a darkness in you. I can see it," she said. "I know what it feels like to have somethin' inside you that you feel… dirty for… But a bane can be turned into blessin' through Shaddai. Right?"

"What if He is the bane?"

Amma gawked.

"Fuck. I'm sorry. I— I shouldn't have said that."

"We've all got demons we wrestle with inside, Lee. But you're stronger than them. You've beaten the Devil before, and you can do it again."

"What if there's no beatin' him this time?" I hung my head. "Or worse yet… What if He's inside of me?"

She leaned in and pecked me on the cheek.

"The Devil's inside every man. And you're still a man, ain't you?"

Amma stood up, trying to iron out the wrinkles in her choir gown with her hands. Bonnie came to her side.

"Amma, we best get goin', the choir's all ready to start."

Bonnie tried to rush her off. I grabbed Amma by the hand.

"Amma, wait," I said.

A solemn expression glinted in her eyes.

"I'm happy for you. Really."

"I know, Lee. I just hope you find that same happiness within yourself."

Bonnie tugged at her arm again, and they made their way up to the stage. I sighed, watching her pass through the crowd and join the other choir members on stage.

I slumped into my seat, folding my arms, aggravated. The service began, and when the choir sang, angels leaned in through the walls to hear them closer. The organist slammed onto her keyboard and clapping mingled with shouts of praise vibrated from the entire congregation.

After a moment, the anger started to melt away, at least a little. As I watched them twirl and dance up and down between the pews,

I felt a fondness. The bliss on their faces was palpable like every worry and trouble didn't matter anymore. Nothing did. Just their spirits laid bare, leaping with joys buried so deep inside them they didn't know they were there. Time seemed to stop when they danced, but their raving states were soon tamed now by the appearance of the Reverend's wife. They all fanned themselves, applauding her arrival and shouting proclamations of praise.

"Praise Him!" they'd shout.

If only they knew the God they worshiped. Knew him the way I did.

"Let me hear the Saints say hallelujah!" she shouted.

Hallelujah! The congregation shouted back, cheering and clapping.

"Yes, Lord... Yes, Lord..." Sister Cheryl said, her ivory teeth flashing over her ruby lipstick.

"Now, church, I have a special announcement. Sister Tamar, as much as it breaks our hearts, has decided to step down as head of the choir..."

Gasps and whispers filled the church, everyone chattering amongst each other. Amma stepped forward, looking back at Bonnie who beamed with pride for her. Grannie stood tall from the pulpit. She smiled through the rage that I saw swelling behind her eyes. She gave a queenly wave to the crowd, careful not to let the cracks show. "And our very own Amma Putnam is going to take her place."

Applause boomed from the congregation, standing to their feet. Amma's full lips were alive with a smile now that was nearly blinding from where I sat. Grannie was even more terrifying when she smiled, and although she was pushing 90 years old, the Power that flowed through her made her half that.

"Now, Sister Tamar had a voice that could make the devil tremble and bring down the holy spirit. Those are big shoes to fill, you sure you can do live up to the legacy she left behind?" Sister Cheryl asked, laughing.

Grannie looked like a ruby amongst the rough. She was draped in maroon that glowed against her dark brown skin, with fresh roses in her hat and not a single hair in her victory rolls out of place. She coughed over her handkerchief, gawking at the napkin before she took her seat. I could smell the blood in the fabric from here. She was deteriorating. The new Queen was ready to rise and take her place.

"I'm honored. Although I don't think I could ever surpass Sister Tamar... But I still hope to leave behind a legacy that's wholly mine. Mama always said to be yourself, 'cause there's only one you."

The crowd screamed and shouted praises, and Sister Cheryl clapped alongside her. Amma gave a quick nod to the organist, who began to play a morose and sweet melody.

"Church, I wanna see you come together. Give us your sick, give us your broken, and let them be brought to the stage to feel the healin' power of the Lord!"

Gradually, people approached the stage. Men in wheelchairs, women who were terminally ill, and anyone with any ailment that was beyond medical. Amma began to sing, her voice raising the hairs on my arms and lifting the darkness that hovered over my spirit. It was like sun rays pushing aside a cloudy sky after a storm.

"*Soon... I will be done...*" she began to sing.

Sister Cheryl began praying over a man in a wheelchair, who gasped ecstatically as his wobbling legs found strength, and he began to stand from his seat. The congregation shouted and cried out glory to God's name. But it was all a lie.

Will Be Done may have been a church hidden in the trees, but its power lay in its miracles. People from all over the world flocked to the Miracle Crusades put on by the Leadership for centuries, but little did they know the source of their healings wasn't a miracle, it was witchcraft. The Deborahs were the town coven. They wove their magic into sound and song, performing wondrous acts under the guise of the Pastor's healing hands. As people stood from their wheelchairs, and the sick found remedy, it was witches whose hands worked their miracles. Proof, that the more things change, the more they stayed the same.

I watched on as Amma enchanted the crowd with her song, and scores of people were healed by the sound of their collective voices.

At that moment, under the spotlight that she stood, she seemed to shine with celestial radiance. She was like an angel, brilliant and beautiful. But despite the light she brought with her, all I could feel was the darkness taking over again and the looming eye of Shaddai over me.

I knew He heard my doubts.

He was watching.

CHAPTER 5

Mother Superior

The desire for blood since then has been nauseating. I've become addicted to it. My senses were enhanced, like being able to smell blood or sweat from miles away. It's almost predatory, it's all I've ever been able to think about. Especially when Shaddai's voice comes to me in moments of crisis or questioning.

'Kill' the voice of God would say to me. And I happily obliged.

I would never seek or attack innocent people, though. I don't have the heart for it. Despite everything I've done, sometimes for pleasure and other times for justice, I wouldn't consider myself an evil person by any means. Have I done questionable things? Sure. But I've always had a just cause. I'm willing to fight for anyone in the world as long as there remains goodness in them. Well, at least to what I deem to be good.

I'm the judge, jury, and executioner in this life, after all. Until the day they hang me back up on that cross, and I give up my crown to the next in line, I'll continue to judge as I see fit. I'm supposed to be morally superior. Though, if I'm being honest, I find that hilarious. God really does have a sense of humor. It was like this since the very first time I came to earth all those eons ago under that Bethlehem star. But I've changed, through many courses and lifetimes, and things are different now. That meek sheep hippie shit isn't going to cut it in this kind of world, and I've long run out of cheeks to turn.

When the priests were training me in the Ceremonial arts, they kept shoving humility down my throat, and to always choose the path to peace. They taught me to be harmless. But let's get real for a moment here: Does a person who has the power to command life and death, or determine eternal destinations of immortal souls, sound harmless to you? Peaceful, maybe, that's their goal. And even that, I'm not. But harmless? Now they're just kidding themselves. There have been many who learned that the hard way, and I say that with a smile. Their attempts to make me docile and controllable were in vain, and fruitless.

There's a secret to me that they never quite understood. I was like trying to hold water in your hands, to be able to cup me in your hands is to conceive me, but squeeze too tightly and I'll slip from your fingers. I hate to be controlled in any sense of the word. I wanted no shackles, and as the most powerful man on earth, I wasn't about to spray paint mine gold and call it power. They always said to *choose* peace, not that peace was the way. *Choosing* implies another option. Choices. Humanity was put here to continuously choose their making or undoing. That's called Eden. And even to that I wasn't immune.

I choose vengeance. Every time. The role of the Christ is to maintain peace between heaven and earth, and to continuously act as the bridge between the dwelling of God and this world. And I refuse to maintain peace without seeing to it that justice is served. There's a reason why the Pope himself gets on his knees and kisses my feet each time I meet with him. People don't quite grasp the concept of what it means to be God on earth. I am the Christ, those who have seen me have seen God too. I was him, hidden behind a shroud of flesh.

I am the vessel by which he exercises all his power, like a cosmic conduit for him to act and move through heaven. To sever the Christ's ties to God would be to remove his access to this world. Our mind is one. It would keep him from acting and protecting the people against the dark forces that seek to seduce and ensnare their souls to damnation. And the greatest temptation of the Devil's power? witchcraft.

I've studied the Art and trained with Masters, to who eventually I became a teacher. And over the years, I've secretly been unable to tell the difference between what we do and the witches. I didn't really get how we've each made pacts with our gods, and in turn, we receive and can channel powers beyond human comprehension. I should've known this feeling would creep up on me again, this lurking monster beneath the waters of my mind: doubt.

I've always lived without question to the God of the Garden's orders, and before three years ago, there wasn't anything that could have convinced me otherwise. But on that night, I was losing the fight against myself. The cannibalistic sense of fear that devoured me. The fear that I was wrong.

It's been three years since the night we met with Castillo, and not a day goes by that I don't think about those words. *Fire in the sky.*

It was disgusting to think that witches could have attained such a sublime power. And the worst part about it was that I wasn't even angry at the Queen of Georgia for making such a power grab. I hated only myself for failing my Order, and the world. The feelings of failure descended on my soul like night, and I lost myself every time in the crushing feeling of ineptitude.

Why can't you do anything right?

I could just hear my Pops now. I tried not to let the feelings get to me, but today was different; it was the anniversary of my Pops's death. I stood underneath the towering banyan tree in our backyard, looking off into the sherbet sky and the sun melting into the horizon. The cool shade offset the blistering Florida heat as I sucked down my saliva, salty from the sunflower seeds I chewed on. It would probably be easier for me to avoid thinking about my Pops if I stopped doing things that we used to do together.

We used to sit underneath this tree when he was in good spirits and eat these together, and he'd tell me stories of his ancestors. He told me one about a boy who was bullied for being the color of night was actually the spirit of rain, and he destroyed his enemies before joining his place in heaven as the god he was. And even now, when I hear the sky grumble and teardrops from the sky fall to earth, I think of him.

The air today was muggy and humid, like sitting in someone's mouth. But there was a crispness to the breeze that swept over the green pasture beneath my bare feet. I eyed the horizon, and despite the facade of a beautiful canvas, I could see a storm brewing up in the distance. There was a deep groan and rumble from the sky that made me flinch in a bittersweet fondness. I never told him he reminded me of the rain, but I wonder if in heaven God told him my secret.

I spat out the empty seed shells and cleared my throat from the knot that started to form.

"Lee!" A voice called from afar.

I turned to see the towering, husky, bearded shape of Ezra. His eyes were barely slits as he squinted to make out my form under the beaming sun.

"Grannie's been lookin' for you!"

I shook my head, strolling back towards the house. I could see Ezra's thick eyebrows furrowing deep creases into his forehead, frustrated.

"The hell you doin' way out there?"

His chestnut face twisted, and his wide square jaw was crooked now with a confused grin.

"I was just bullshittin' there… thinkin' about Pops, won't lie,"

Ezra's dark eyes rolled to the side.

"Yeah, you got so lost in thought out there you left me to do all the shit you was supposed to do," he said.

"Sorry," I shrugged, staring vaguely away from him.

"I got caught up."

"Look, I miss Pops too. This day kills me every year. But you know how whacked out Grannie gets when this day comes."

My smile was more of a grimace as I thought about how right he was. I didn't just lose my Pops. Grannie lost her son, and he was her everything. It's been 18 years since he died, and every year she cries again like she'd just found out about it. But there was a strange cadence to the way she'd wept. I'd heard that kind of cry before seeing so many give bitter words at funerals. Things they'd always wished they could say. It was regret. And most times, that was even stronger than grief, or death.

But what could Grannie regret so deeply?

We were all she had other than that old house. It was built around the Antebellum period and stayed in Grannie's family since her great-grandmother, Minerva Parris, poisoned the entire household and freed herself. It wasn't too long after that Confederate soldiers heard rumors of a free family living in the home of one of their fallen generals. But anytime anyone came, all they'd see were the hungry eyes of gators lurking through the swampy marshland that lay ahead of them; no house in sight. They called it the *Place of Hidden Color*, cause any Black man that disappeared into those swamplands could never be found by those who came looking.

We stepped up onto the front porch and past Pop's old rocking chair, swaying in the wind now creaking lightly. The door swung open, and out emerged the tall, menacing face that Ezra and I both revered and feared. Grannie Tamar. She held between her hands a fussing chicken, who beat and flapped its wings frantically in her arms. Her nostrils were flared wide, and her eyes were bulging out of their sockets. A dark strand of her salt and peppered hair dangled just between her two fine eyebrows. It was the most undone I'd ever seen her. She seemed to be unraveling.

"Boy, where have you been all this time?"

"Sorry, Grannie, I-"

"Have you lost all sense? You had your brother doin' all the things I asked you to do," she said as she coaxed the chicken.

"What do you think of yourself? 'Cause you a king in heaven that you're a king in this house too? You got maids?"

She glared at me with her same icy expression, almost floating away from us back and inside, an ancient ghost disturbed from its slumber. Ezra closed the door behind us, shaking his head. Grannie Tamar was frigid winter winds wrapped in skin and bone. She hardly ever raised her voice and was known to have said the cruelest things far too calmly. Grannie gave us everything we needed, except the warmth of affection. If there was anything you learned quickly growing up, it was that love wasn't something freely given; it was earned. And it was not unconditional.

Sometimes I preferred her to yell, but instead, a simple glare or turn of her head with pursed lips was enough to terrify you. I feared her more than God himself sometimes.

As we followed behind her, I noted that the house was laced with the smell of sweet potato and cinnamon. She was laying out all of Pop's favorite foods, sparing no cost or detail. She acted as if he was gonna walk through the door any minute now.

That woman didn't know how to stop moving, she was a shark, and in every sense of the word. One thing Grannie never played about was her kin. Family was always the most important thing, and it's all we've ever had. Grannie took care of me and my brother when our Pops passed away, and this house is plenty big for all of us. I know she can take care of herself, but she's getting along in years. And Grannie's kind are regarded as traitors.

"Am I goin' to have to repeat myself? Or are y'all waitin' on an invitation to help here?" Grannie said, peeking her head from behind the kitchen wall.

She caught me looking at her framed pictures, I was lost in the photos of her youth, where she was the leader of the church choir, the Deborahs.

"I'm sorry, Grannie Tamar…"

"Mmm…" She grumbled; her eyes were like two drawn, serrated blades.

The Summerland descendants that settled here in Tophet changed their allegiance to the God of the Garden. In truth, before it became the way of their generations, it was to spare their lives from the Order. Unfortunately, Grannie's sisters couldn't hide their magic behind their complexions like the Summerland witches. Anything they did was suspicious. So they agreed to use their power in service of the True God, for the Devil is cunning and gives Gifts that can never be returned.

Grannie stood with her arms behind her back as she watched me carefully move past her and into the kitchen. The back door was open, letting in an iridescent glow from the sunlight striking the mahogany floors. I could hear the pigs oinking from the farmhouse outback.

This house may seem luxurious, but you'd better believe it was me and Ezra that Grannie had scrubbing these floors and cleaning this place up. Grannie made us get down on our hands and knees, clean tubs, the yard, the kitchen, you name it.

If my sole purpose was to reign as Prince of this World, it was her job to see to it that I remained humble while I was here. A rooster ran past my feet from the black cat that chased after it. The cat stopped for a moment from its feathered pursuit, and I locked eyes with it. Its gaze lingered on me, and there was a strange sentience that came from its eyes that struck me. I stepped towards it, and it quickly scurried off across Ezra's legs.

"God, *damn it!*" Ezra yelled, almost tripping over it.

He grunted, frustrated, then approached me with a box full of peaches. He set the box onto the back of Pops's old pickup truck and quickly snatched up a peach for himself. His beard dripped with the juices that ran down from the peach as he tore into it like his last meal.

"Oh, so you wanna come lookin' for me for sittin' by that tree, but what's Grannie gonna say when she sees you eatin' them peaches meant for the cobbler?"

Ezra wiped his beard, glaring at me defiantly.

"She don't need 'em all. Besides, she got these straight from Georgia. These are Abertha peaches! You think I'm gonna pass them up?"

"That old plantation owner?"

"Liar."

"On God,"

"Don't say that!"

"I can say whatever I damn well please," I snarked.

"You always gotta throw some dark shit out there. Why can't you just let me enjoy this damn peach?"

"'Cause I been there myself! I saw all them spirits... all of 'em. They was there just... terrified and *stuck*. I don't know how that mother fucker slept at night all I could hear was them howlin' and hollerin'..."

"Well, shit..." Ezra said.

"I tried tellin' you," I said.

I snatched the peach from his hand, and he gave me a pat on the back. Even though Ezra was my older brother, his mission always seemed to be to make sure I wasn't a snitch and took falls with him rather than steering me in the right direction. It was never anything too serious, although by the time I was 15 we turned getting Grannie angry into a full-time sport.

"She's gonna put us both in the ground if she catches us out here instead of in that kitchen," Ezra said.

I laughed.

"*I'm my brother's keeper*, right?"

"Damn… you serious about that plantation though?"

I nodded.

Ezra sat back in an aggravated silence.

"You told Grannie yet?"

"Nah," I said. "Just leave it be…"

"Oh, so I gotta live with the guilt of knowing what I ate now?"

My phone vibrated in my pocket. It was one of the magicians calling. Every time I saw his name I was reminded of our sordid history.

"Just don't have no cobbler tonight," I said, tossing his half-eaten peach at him.

He used his brawny shoulder to block the hit.

I picked up the phone.

"Levi," the voice said.

It was Craven. Unlike his usual aloof and detached nature, he sounded breathless and frantic.

"I just sent you my location. Get down here… Now."

"Uh? Okay… on my way then?"

The line died. My heart was racing out of my chest. I turned to Ezra, who still stood in front of the box of peaches with a look of moral disappointment as he looked down at them.

"Tell Grannie I had to step out for work," I said.

"You'll be dead before dawn," Ezra said.

"She'll be alright." I shrugged.

"All good?"

"I don't know yet."

I dug my phone into my pocket and ran towards my car. There was a visceral and unnatural angst that came over me. I could feel it in the pit of my soul. I couldn't overcome the feeling no matter how brave I tried to convince myself I was at this moment. My mouth soured, and my stomach withered up inside me as I got in the car. Something evil was here.

No. Not evil.

Something worse.

CHAPTER 6:

Sacrifice

People liked to imagine Florida as having constant sunshine and clear blue skies. But here, the weather was more foul than friendly, and home to the nastiest tempests you'd ever seen. I drove down the coast, the sea and swamps being the only thing that ruled this place more than any forest. Tophet was birthed among the trees; they reached high to the heavens to hear the messages from angels, and they had roots that reached deep into the belly of the earth. Their secrets were just as deep and dark.

I tried to distract myself along the drive, riding the sky's waves of hues, the clouds churning and twisting like my mind. I felt it the moment I'd gotten off the phone with Craven, there was an uncertainty in his voice that I couldn't shake. If he was scared, that meant I needed to be. Craven, if anything, was always confident in his knowledge; he prided himself in it. During our years training with the Order, he'd have his nose so far down a book he could probably tell each apart by scent. But not this time. Now, Craven's voice was sullen and frail, his words carried on his breath like wilted flowers, just barely a scent of life.

He would never show fear in the face of anybody, especially not me. Craven was constantly trying to prove himself better than every magician in any way that he could, either by his "noble" blood status or by upping anything I did. It was like the successes and happiness of others were always a threat to him, never allowing a compliment to bloom fully before his disdain swept away any kindness that could escape his lips. Craven was perpetually dissatisfied and underwhelmed by his achievements. Even when he was at his height, it was never good enough, he always wanted more. He always wanted to surpass or break some unknown glass ceiling he'd conceived in his mind.

And yet, I respected him. Even looked up to him at some point when we were younger. Or even still. He knew it all, every angel there was to conjure and each demon to repel and counter that. But as the days wore down on our skin, and as summer's rays had cast their familiar glow each year, things started to change. His eyes once filled with so much care had become jaded.

I'd always thought he hated himself. Many magicians that descend from the Summerland bloodlines did because their source of power would always come from the Man in Black. He used to say it was like the morticians that try to cover the rot of bodies beneath beautiful shades. Decay was still going to do what it did, and death was stronger than the will to be accepted, the most beautiful illusion of all.

The car's wheels slid against the dirt road as I brought the car to a stop. The ash from the end of my cigarette fell onto my lap, giving hot kisses to my arms before I swatted the chalky remains off. I took one more burning drag before tossing the ember out the window. As I stepped out, I threw on my jacket and adjusted my tie. If there was one thing I wasn't going to be, I wouldn't be wrinkled. It wasn't so much about image as it was—Well, okay, it was about image. But it was so everyone knew I was meticulous, paying attention to everything. Like God watching above I was down here below, scrutinizing the tiniest detail; all-seeing. Being the Son incarnate came with things I deeply resented. However, always being dressed in the slickest designer suits and free designer was one hell of a silver lining.

But there were things I'd have traded Montblanc and Prada for. Like how my free time was spent learning to conjure and bind demons to serve you and commanding fleets of heavenly armies, when I could've been like other guys my age drinking, partying, and chasing sex.

The former, in the long run, is extraordinary, but what I would give to just have some kind of a life. For ordinary.

I looked over the hedge of gently swaying trees. The humidity was disgusting, a typical day in Florida. The sky gently beat the drums of its chest, and the wind thickened, rain was coming again; you could smell it.

I walked towards the house, swatting horseflies that circled me. There was a squad of Sheriff vehicles glaring their lights, and uniformed officers barricaded the area. I ducked under the neon border where officers stopped me.

"Whoa, whoa, now, no trespassin,'" the officer said.

His pig face twisted into an ugly satisfied grin that made me want to punch him in the mouth. And I almost did.

"You sure this a crime scene and not a circus?" I said.

His mouth quivered as his face flushed a deep red. I flashed him my badge.

"Because I've never so many fuckin' clowns in one place,"

I shouldered past him towards the house. I worked under Jasper Lodge, who was head of the FBI and their Shadow Department, the Watchers. They handled phenomena that don't have natural explanations. So little did these punk-ass sheriffs know I could make one call and have them all fired. But then, how else would they sustain their glamorous lives of Nascar TV, mayonnaise, and canned beans for dinner? I had to think of the greater picture.

The front porch was made of old, rotted wood and hosted a creaking rocking chair. The screen door had holes in it, and the evergreen paint that I'm sure once glossed the door was now chipped, fading away like a memory.

There was something about this house that was desperate to be forgotten. Hopefully, the memory of the people who once lived inside surpassed the perished wood and worn paint.

A tall, lank figure with short, tight curls filled the gaps in the screen door. He raised his eyebrows in shock.

Craven Good.

"You'd be late to your own funeral," he said.

Craven stood there with a smug grin on his face. His glasses hid the snarky squint in his eyes. There was always an elephant in the room between us, but I never knew what. I rubbed down his hair as I brushed past him.

"Be glad I'm here at all, don't forget what today is,"

Craven pursed his lips shamefully, nodding a kind of apology.

"Might be time for a lineup. We're lookin' a little rough." He jabbed.

"Get your dusty ass inside and quit worryin' about my hair." I said.

Craven and I always had our differences, and I always seemed to be the bad guy in his mind. Which, at some point, I just had to make peace with. You can have all the justification and reason, but there will always be people who can't face their own darkness and seek to project them onto you. Even angels become demons, depending on who's telling the story.

The house was ripe with the smell of blood, so strong that inhaling all the iron could be a vitamin. Entrails hung from the light fixtures on the wall, draped over decoratively like there was thought put into its placement. The floors were black and tarry with a syrupy texture that clung to the bottom of my shoes. Even the walls were drenched in an amount of blood you'd think it was the original coating.

"Fucking Christ… What went on in here?" I asked.

"It gets worse," Craven said.

He pulled out a white handkerchief from his jacket, covering his umber face beneath the snow-white fabric. Flies flew past the cracks of the door, expanding into a thick swarm as he pushed past the wooden frame. The cloud of flies parted like a curtain to reveal the bloody scene. I've worked many cases for Mr. Lodge, but nothing I'd seen until that point could've prepared me.

I covered my mouth to gag. Craven smirked. I could tell he was pleased with himself for not reacting. I retched. My stomach shriveled, and my guts bubbled inside. I kept fighting back the bitter vomit rising in my throat.

"You'd think you've seen worse things in Hell," Craven said caustically.

I cleared my throat, feeling the dizzying sensation leave me.

"Yeah," I said. "That time you came with me."

Craven rolled his eyes, fighting the smirk that grew on his face.

I fixed my gaze on the swaths of flies that continued to buzz around the bodies. There was a teenage boy, who couldn't have been any older than 15, kneeling with the knife still wrapped around his fingers. His back was arched, allowing his chalky white face to dangle with his head back. He was sitting in a pool of his blood with his throat slit from ear to ear. The gash in his throat continued to gurgle fresh blood onto the black, tarry substance that was now dried onto his skin. His eyes were wide open with a smile as big as the laceration on his neck. His teeth were stained with blood, and his expression was in this eerie state of absolute and sublime bliss.

Beside him were two disemboweled bodies lying on their stomachs. Their heads were severed, you could see the jagged ends of skin around the neck and blood pouring out from the fleshy crevice. As I looked up, I realized that the heads were sitting atop a brown dresser, flanked with blazing candles atop their heads. Their blood ran down the dresser flowing into a small ceramic bowl below. I wondered what kind of God this could possibly be for.

Craven pointed atop the altar, and painted in their blood was only one word in what looked like Greek:

EKSTASIS

As I read the word, I could see the murder happening. I saw him massacre his mother and drag her out of the shower, driving the knife into her so many times I lost count. His eyes were frenzied and unbridled. His little brother tried to fight against him, but even he succumbed to the vicious stabbings, and he was the first to be dismembered. The images poured into my mind in a relentless stream of violent images. I saw him begin to saw with the blade into their necks as he laughed hysterically all the way through; then, finally raising the knife to his own throat, he started to carve into himself.

Craven's hand on my shoulder jolted me out of the visions.

"If it makes you feel any better," Craven said. "I can't figure out what this is about either,"

"I've gotta say," I said.

I stood back, trying to take in the scene like some kind of sunset.

"I've seen and brutalized mother fuckers worse than this. But somethin' about this energy…"

"It's dark," Craven said.

"No."

I walked up to the wall and examined the writing in Greek.

"It's somethin' beyond that."

Craven scoffed. Completely on-brand for him. He knew everything, of course.

"Oh, *really*," he said. "What is it, then?"

All I could think of were the wild handmaidens of Dionysus, the Raving Ones who became drunk on the very essence of this force they honored.

"Remember when we studied the Fallen Angeles of mythology? The consorts of Dionysus,"

Craven laughed mockingly.

"As *if* some mortal nothin' could conjure up an Old One. They're long dead, anyway."

"The Old One's ain't dead. Only their followings."

"Which is just as good as."

Craven crossed his arms, looking away from me.

"If not that, then what? Maenad spirits came to him? Again, what business would they have with some mortal?"

I shrugged.

He was right. As annoying as he was about it. A mortal couldn't possibly have the power alone to conjure something like this. Even old man Wardwell warned against any magician even thinking about summoning them. Not even I've been allowed to attempt it. None of the Petrams ever have; it's considered a Forbidden Art to us and a perversion of the body. For anyone to attempt to do so, their very nature will slowly become corrupted to the point of rot. At which point, the Order will be forced to kill you. These are powers only witches would be perverse enough to trifle with. They live to be seduced by the darkness.

"How do you think this all went down?" Craven said, breaking the tense silence.

I grumbled as the images came pouring back into my mind. All I could think about was the crazed look in his eyes and demented Joker smile.

"I saw it all when I read the writin' on the wall," I said. "It was raw... ecstasy."

"Well, shit. This is takin' Crime of Passion to another level, wouldn't you say?" Craven said.

"Human passions can only carry you so far. But if this is what I think it is, then somehow, he tapped into the Passion of Creation. Mortal bodies just ain't fit to contain things like that," I said

Craven huffed, pacing the room for any new details.

It was the sheer, divine bliss that permeated and transcended mortal experience, and ecstasy in excess only leads to violence. Even Shakespeare said love and murder go together. The bloodshed doesn't happen right away with these Forces. It slowly slithers its way into your heart until your desire becomes so consumptive you can only destroy it to gain release. It was the same madness Heracles was stricken with, a kind that only clears in the ruins of everything you love, including your own life. It was such a thin line between absolute passion and violence. Ecstasy needs to consume. It's like a burning fire that begs to be destroyed by passion. Becoming the focal point of such a powerful force only makes you a candle yearning to be consumed by its own flames.

I sighed, digging my hands into my pockets.

"Any survivors or we lookin' at a family annihilation?" I said.

"No, no... there's one survivor, the father. He's with the paramedics out back."

"Lucky guy," I said, grimacing.

"Yeah, not too bad for being stabbed 17 times."

Craven led me toward the paramedic's truck. As we approached, they frantically tended to the man's wounds.

"He needs to get to a hospital!"

A freckle-faced paramedic shouted.

"Pardon me y'all, I know how pressin' this is and all, but we're gonna need some time alone with him," I said.

"What?" A big man with a thick neck and beady eyes retorted. "You ain't doin' no such thing! This man needs intensive care,"

I rubbed my eyebrows, frustrated.

"Trust me, he's in better hands," I said

"This man is dying! What the hell is wrong with you?" the man bellowed.

Hell.

This guy might be onto something. But I guess even a broken clock is right twice a day.

"You ever been to Hell, my brother?" I said.

"Levi, don't." Craven urged.

I smirked.

Instantly, their eyes inflated in their skulls with horror, screaming until their voices became hoarse. They fumbled onto the ground, covering their eyes and heads as they squirmed. I laughed as I inflicted them with gruesome visions of Hell, minus the actual pain in suffering. I liked to think of it as a 4D tour of the infernal layers.

The two of them scrambled to get to their feet and sprinted away. Craven hopped inside the van, and without missing a beat, I followed behind him, shutting the doors behind me. I kept trying to keep myself from laughing, but Craven glared at me.

"You ain't shit. You know that?" he said.

I shrugged, snickering. Craven approached the man still caked in so much blood not even a sliver of his skin escaped the crimson dye. His eye twitched.

"What... What are you?" he asked breathlessly

"I'm with Law Enforcement, sir. Do you think you can answer some questions for me?" I said.

He strained to form the energy to gawk at me.

"Law... Heh," he said gruffly.

His face grew with revulsion as he looked at the both of us.

"They let y'all be cops, now?"

"Remember this day. This moment. Those words," I whispered to him.

I could feel his essence slipping and fading, inching closer toward the great white throne of God, where he was to be judged. And I couldn't wait to make that deliberation.

"'Cause you're gonna have a lot of time to think about them,"

I patted him on the head.

"Fuck 'em, he's a lost cause. Worst comes to worst, we conjure up his spirit, and I force him to talk," I said

Craven flicked his hands at me, shooing me away from him.

"Let me talk to him," Craven said.

I sneered.

"Go ahead, he'd like *you* much better, wouldn't he?"

Craven stood over his body and cocked his head. He groaned, uncertain.

"God damn it," Craven said through gritted teeth.

"What happened?"

I approached the body to see the man's hollow-eyed and vacant expression.

"Ah, fuck," I said.

He was dead.

CHAPTER 7

Exorcism

The canvas of his body was eviscerated. I hovered my hands over his chest, sensing for the current of life within him. If he needed to be raised from the dead, no problem. But if I could save myself the time and the experience of absorbing what killed the person, it was better for me. My fingers started to tingle with hot energy that ran down to my wrists.

"He's alive," I said, quickly pulling my hands away.

"Bullshit," Craven said.

His body was cold, and there was no detectable heartbeat, but his essence was somehow still trapped inside. While his body continued to rot away, his soul was caged within a prison doomed to collapse.

"Somehow he's still in there… his soul," I said.

The body smiled.

I took a careful step back.

"Tell me you saw that shit," I said.

Craven's brows were arched in surprise. He blinked as if trying to wake himself from a dream.

"Yeah…" Craven said.

The pallid white lights in the back of the truck began to flicker like a strobe until we were plunged into sudden darkness. Craven ran for the double doors.

"We're locked inside!" Craven shouted, panicked.

The doors rattled firmly in place as he tried to shake them loose. He performed the Hidden Hands and muttered his incantations, but nothing happened.

"The Power doesn't work in here," Craven said.

An icy coldness crept into the room, making its way up the hairs on my neck. I pulled a lighter from my jacket pocket. It was filled with the Cruse of Oil, capable of sustaining and creating fires that would last 8 days. I flicked on the golden lighter, and a warm glow cast a hazy ring of light around us.

It shimmered and shone a soft amber light, the flame itself no bigger than a wisp, a breath at best; but its light illuminated the space like an open campfire. Bending, crooked shadows flickered alongside the walls, and the enclosed space soon looked like the mouth of a cave, dripped in jet shadows. Everything was now shades of black and red, cold enough now to see my breath.

"What're you doin', Levi?" Craven asked.

Slowly, the man's body wound itself until it sat upright. Fresh blood ran down his hanging mouth, pouring into his lap in dark pools seeping into the pockets of the sheets.

"Stop worryin' about me and pay attention,"

Craven stiffened and pushed his square glasses tighter onto his nose. The man's throat contorted, moving rigid and stiff, less like a person and more like a sock-puppet. The unnatural cracks and joint movements made him look like a marionette. The head turned straight back and curled its cracked, blue lips into a wicked smile.

"*Son of man,*" it said.

Its voice sent chills down my neck. It was profound, a rolling wave that rippled throughout time.

"*Have you come to torment me before the appointed time?*" It laughed, wheezing and forced.

"What have you done to this family?" I asked firmly.

"*I, answer to you? You may have been the first spoken word, but I was there when your God was but a breath in the starry pit, stirring in the pool of cosmic thought…*"

"Shaddai created the heavens as we know them."

It laughed raucously; its chest rose and fell with a tremble.

"Prove your might then, Son of man! Bend me to your will!"

I planted my feet on the ground and quickly formed the Hidden Hands, drawing on all the power of the Petrams gone before me. A glowing seal formed a six-rayed star beneath my feet, flaring into a bright white light before vanishing.

"Christus, Eikōn, Kyrios, Logos, Eklektos! By the Crown of heaven as the authority of God on Earth, I command you in my name! Speak your intentions on this plane!"

Nothing.

No sputter or flame of any power came from me. My throat tightened, choking on my disbelief. Craven slowly turned his head at me, his eyes wide with fear.

What was this? Every knee is supposed to bow to my authority. There wasn't a spirit I'd come across in all my lifetimes that could blatantly refuse my authority, and by extension, Shaddai, the God of the Garden.

I backed away, uneasy. It cackled mockingly.

"This is the King of Kings?" it jeered.

"Y-You have no authority over us, Demon…" Craven said.

He stepped in front of me, holding his hands together, ready to form Hands.

"You speak against me when you know me most of all? For it is each time you look upon your reflection you feel the most. When you feel the truth!"

"Shut your mouth," Craven said, his breaths beginning to tremble.

"Don't engage it with, Craven," I said.

"Last child forever forgotten… You are… the moon…brilliant and bright, but cursed to forever yield to the light of day, shining only when the world sleeps…"

"SHUT UP! SHUT YOUR MOUTH!" Craven screamed with a shaking uncertainty in his voice.

His body trembled, and his breaths were rapid and sharp as sweat rolled down the side of his head.

"YOU KNOW NOTHING!" Craven spat venomously.

"Hey, hey, take it easy," I said.

I took Craven by the crook of his arm. He tore himself away from me.

"*That's it… yes… let my essence flow through you.*"

"Craven, don't feed him your energy. Think of somethin' else," I said.

This being seemed to feed on the passions of man, warping what stirred their heart into a state of hedonistic savagery.

"What are you?" I said, holding my ground.

"*Ask he who is called 'Father'.*"

Its eyes glowed a brilliant white, and then flickered out like dying embers against the ashy, black hollows of his face. The man's body collapsed back against the stretcher. A static image formed in front of his body, and his mortal spirit stood naked and afraid.

"Well, how 'bout that?" I said. "Ain't you a sight for sore eyes?"

"W-What is this?"

"You're dead, of course," I said. "And the Second Death awaits,"

He looked between me and Craven, hoping to strike pity within the both of us.

"N-No, please… I didn't…"

"Remember, *what you have done to the least of these… you have done to me also*," I said.

I waved at him sardonically as a flaming hole opened beneath his feet, and billowing hot winds flooded the space. Agonizing screams tore out from the crevice beneath him, tears filling his eyes as he looked at me in horror. Before the scream escaped his lips, large, black arms pulled at his legs. He wriggled and writhed, wailing and begging for mercy as the spirits of the damned dragged him beneath the surface.

The rift shut as quickly as it opened, and a serene silence took the place of agonizing screams. Craven cleared his throat as he wiped his glasses with his shirt.

"I'm sorry about that," Craven said.

"It… It was lyin'."

I smiled, chagrin.

"Thing is, Craven... The shit that gets us that angry is usually true. If you'd confront that, it would have no power over you."

He glared at me.

"Comin' from you? You've never loved anyone but yourself. You even have standards?" he said.

"See... It's that. That right there. This is why I've always kept my distance from you," I said coolly.

"I've died for you and served you a thousand lifetimes..." He laughed bitterly. "And other times, we was more than that. But each life you've always been the same. About you. Everythin's gotta be about you."

Craven's nostrils flared as he drew a deep breath.

"All you give a shit about is yourself," he said.

And there it was. I finally understood Craven's resentment towards me. Not unfounded, of course. I was definitely self-centered. I couldn't blame him for the things he said. Some of it, anyway, because he was always sour even before we got intimate.

"Look, Craven, I've told you this a thousand times. If you gotta paint me as the villain in your narrative to sleep better at night, go right ahead," I said. "You've got a lot of shit about you too. But you know what's the difference between you and me? I always stood by you. Damn near feelin' sorry for you in every one of those lives. Includin' this one."

He winced. I could tell I hit a nerve.

I signed the Hidden Hands and pushed outward. The van's doors were ripped off their hinges and flew in either direction, allowing daylight to burst into the dark space.

"Call me if you find anythin' else out," I said.

I lit a cigarette and took a long drag before walking off.

Our relationship has always been competitive at best and violent at worst. He and I even fought a few times here and there. We'd gone from friends to lovers, then into other shades of grey. He was also the greatest magician the academy had seen since Father Enoch. I hated to admit it, but he was brilliant. I looked up to him in many ways, but that never mattered. It was always the same with him: do well, just never better than him. And that went for anybody. He'd never see the greatness I did when I looked at him.

I walked through the clouds of smoke, puffing out my cigarette when I noticed a man approaching me. He was fit, but not very muscular, with a handsome face and thick eyebrows. His ivory skin glistened against the sun, and he removed his sunglasses to reveal his almond-shaped eyes, which were like honey amber.

"You Mr. Beaumont?" he asked in a thick, New York accent.

He had a whole James Dean look going on with his leather jacket, pompadour hairstyle, white tee, and jeans.

"Mind if I borrow one of those?" he said, pointing to my cigarette.

I was taken aback by his forwardness, but I respected it.

"Nice kicks," I said.

He looked down at his boots and smirked. I handed him the cigarette. He held it to his lips. As he inhaled, embers and fire crackled at the ends, put out by the smoke that emanated from the end now.

"Menthols. Good shit."

"You a magician?" I said.

"Ehh," he said. "Nah. But a friend to you, nonetheless. You got somewhere we can talk?"

I looked back at Craven, who was stepping out of the van and began walking before he could get involved in my business.

"Sure, this way to my car," I said.

I followed beside him, quietly taking drags from his cigarette. His I.D. glinted gold, revealing the prominent eye with the one 'W'.

"You must work for Lodge," I said, breaking the silence.

"What gave that away?" he asked.

I laughed, leaning against the car.

"So, what can I do for you?"

"You familiar with an Agent Bryson?" he asked.

"Abel? Of course."

"Good. Well, he wound up taking the Castillo Case."

"He's been sharkin' that case for months. Good on him," I said. He nodded, half interested.

"So, you probably figured out by now, I didn't come down here for that."

"What you want around here, then? Watchers ain't got no business in a town like this," I said.

"Let's just say there's certain… anomalies that have gotten our attention. Can't say much. But there's someone who can."

He tossed the cigarette aside.

"Belladonna Hooper. She wants to meet with you tomorrow night,"

"*Hooper?* Well, shit. Ain't she Lodge's right hand?"

He nodded, haughty. Hoopers make the Rothschilds look broke, and she was among the oldest American Ruling Bloodlines. Her family had wealth like Mithras, and they had the respect that would only rival it. In all my years working with the Watcher Department, I'd never seen her only heard whispers and the mention of her name; she was almost folkloric.

"Must be important if she wants to see me,"

"You don't think the Son of God's important," he asked snidely.

"Yea, yea. So what's she want with me then?"

He stood up and gave me a pat on the back.

"That's the only message I've got for you, Mr. Christ," he said.

He dug into his jacket and handed me a clear, thin square that felt like glass.

"Meet us here, and we'll discuss all this somewhere more private. Though, can't say I don't *love me some of that country air!*" He emphasized in a butchered southern accent.

"Who do I say sent me?"

"Just follow the map," he said with a wink.

He had a whimsical air about him, and I watched as he happily strolled away. I looked down at the card, and it illuminated with sky blue light that formed an eye at the center. The shape then morphed, and a red blinking dot appeared. I placed the strange map into my jacket pocket and took one last look back at the scene.

All I could think about now was the entity that refused to obey my command. If God's word was ultimate, and it didn't matter a lick to this being, then what did that mean for me? I've never been put in a position where I had to question my power before because nothing around me could ever compare. I was the most powerful being in the known universe.

So I thought.

Turns out, there was something stronger and older than me. And not only was I wrong, but for the first time in my life, I had to admit…

I was scared.

CHAPTER 8:

Contrition

The rain stopped halfway back into town, releasing muggy air into the car as I rolled the windows back down. I wanted to drive back home, but strangely enough, I needed church again. Or was it home? I could never tell the difference, I spent so much of my life there. The steeple was as familiar as my bed.

Tophet was a strange town, especially when one really got to know the area. When the first Summerland bloodlines arrived here, they built a twin town similar to the one they came from. It wasn't long before the witches that founded this land began to rival their motherland, and quickly, tension grew between the two.

I asked the Deacons and Elders of the church and every Magus from any Order I came across, and no one knew what really happened to the original settlers after the fire that destroyed this town. They vanished one day, every last one of them. It was like another Roanoke, a colony lost to the mysteries of history. Or so they said. But something about the bones of this town told me there was something more.

As I drew closer to town, the skeletal figures of the buildings emerged over the horizon, jaded fragments and dust ready to be blown away by breaths of time. There was nothing remarkable about this place; it seemed to just be a shell of something greater. Part of me feels as though this town lived another lifetime, and this was the carcass left behind. The energy was barren and stale. Even the town of Summerland had more life. This place was dead, just like all the people that inhabited it.

I pulled onto the gravel of the only notable structure in the town. The church. Compared to everything else made of rotting wood and worms, the titanic stone beast towered out of place. Its stained-glass windows depicted flights of angels and dazzled with life. Church services were always in full swing, but upstairs, in the heights of heavenly archways and painted ceilings, the Order gathered to teach and preserve the Art Magical.

I stepped out of the car, watching big-haired mothers walk alongside their toddlers carrying cotton candy or ice cream. Despite the deathly appearance, there were still traces of life. I imagined this is what divers felt like when they made discoveries in the ocean's depths.

Here, in this very church, I was taught things that mankind would never dream of, descending into the farthest regions of the heavens and down to the most frightening hells. I met beings more ancient than the stars and learned deep magic from God himself. I also learned about suffering. To them, suffering brought one closer to God, and it was the only way to learn. Which means they were doing their jobs, exceeding expectations of cruelty.

I'd had to kneel on nails to push certain powers. I died a thousand different deaths to gain mastery over what killed them, dying the way each Saint was executed. I was boiled in tar, buried, and burned alive. I was shot with arrows, ripped apart by lions, and beheaded. All this was done before I was 11 years old, culminating in my 13th year. That would mark the first of endless Equinox rituals of being Crucified and speared for Good Friday. It was to give me power, they said. But there was a sadistic pleasure in doing it all to me. I could see them wrestling with smiles as they killed methodically.

The only people I could confide in were the people who tortured me, and their students who, in turn, became my peers. A prophet had no respect in his own home. For years they thought I was weak, but enduring everything I had bred a special kind of callousness.

It brought a new level of brutality, consuming everything inside me until I lost control.

There was a terrible storm that night, as was common during Summer seasons. But the skies were as black as night, and winds howled like shrieking banshees. There was a warning for a tropical storm that night, and the Order decided to gather inside the church to conjure Hadad and trap him in the circle to absorb its power. The magicians frequently summoned the old forces by instruction of the angel Azrael, who showed them how to transfer power to themselves and enhance their abilities. It was also the night after my Pops died.

Some of the Order members decided to keep taking cracks at me and calling me the *Only Begotten*. Gerald Wardwell was visiting our branch of the Order that evening, and when it came time to draw the circle with the sword, something came over me. My eyes felt searing hot, and I screamed in what I knew was ancient Aramaic. I took the sword and slashed everyone that stood around me. Their screams sang for me while I hacked away, spilling their blood against the old seals along the ground, and they glowed with life.

The attack was so vicious that when I came out of my trance, all I could see were dismembered body parts and a few heads on the ground, still with frozen expressions of horror. It was also the only time I'd ever seen Gerald Wardwell smile. The Order ruled it an act of divine justice and believed Christ's consciousness possessed me involuntarily. They still use that sword for conjuring circles, believing it to be imbued with the bloody life force of the slain magicians who died standing within the circle. The Order worshiped power, even violent displays of it. It was the God of the Garden's capacity to kill and destroy that they admired most.

I took a deep breath as I stepped inside, bowing my head and signing the cross. I wasn't sure which part of my story made people think that I loved the crucifix. It was horrifically painful, absolutely brutal. I had to endure the scene on every Good Friday, being nailed and speared to death so the Clergy could drink the blood and water that ran down my feet. Pope first, of course. The best part of having to die every year and spend three days in Hell was that I was away from them. They were sadistic and wicked, and I was bound to serve them.

All this power, and it was created to serve man and the god he forged in his own image. It was a crown of thorns that reminded me each day that I was just a conduit. The only reason the Order even tolerated me was because of what I was.

The Gothic-style church was beautifully crafted. Stained-glass windows depicted scenes like the Last Temptation. The poignant aromas of Frankincense and myrrh filled the halls in a faint, smoky cloud, still fresh from the earlier service. People with their hopes and dreams gathered along the pews, like ants forever trying to gain the attention from a human being. As I passed down the rows, I could hear their prayers passing through my mind like garbled whispers, a barrage of desperation and selfish desires all clouding my mind.

They prayed in my name over and over. To give them power, money, and love. And I never minded answering their prayers if they put in half the work. But you see, that's the problem with prayer. It's people hoping and wishing while they do absolutely nothing to change their circumstances.

Father Enoch was the church Deacon. His robes danced as he moved about, closing his Bible and shaking hands with people approaching him. In this light, he looked like a humble man, but deep inside, Enoch was capable of many things. One thing I did admire about him was his willingness to get his hands dirty instead of sending cronies. If there was a job to get done, Enoch would be the one to do it. That is when he's not kissing up to the Summerland Order. Like Craven, their admiration for their privilege blinded them and stagnated them of their own greatness.

They so desperately wanted to emulate the Summerland Order. That's why they allowed all the bullying during my early training. If I was going to be great, I had to pay triple to be it. Enoch looked up at me through the smoldering smoke from the golden incense holder. His dark eyes lit with surprise.

"Well, I didn't expect to see you here... Considerin' your feelings about church functions," he said, leaning against the pulpit.

He wiped his glasses with his robe, inspecting them carefully for any smudges.

"Did you kill someone again?" he asked, eying me carefully.

"Nah, I did send another racist to hell again, though."

"Boy, I told you that you can't keep doing that," he said.

"Not like it was unmerited," I said.

Enoch rolled his eyes.

I walked towards the pews and took a seat. I sat down beside him. I clapped my hands together with a shrug.

"There are still people in there from past Petrams for 'excessive masturbatin' from the 1500s. At least one of them was actually harmful," I argued.

Enoch glared at me with a tired, dazed expression.

"Look, last I checked, the judgment of souls was a right I reserved, am I wrong?"

Enoch shook his head.

"This what you came here for, to clear your conscience?"

"Me? My conscience is good. It was the most fulfillin' thing I've done all day," I said.

"What all you want, then? I've got another service in fifteen." He flashed his watch, annoyed.

"Look... I got approached by some bigwigs in the FBI. The Watchers," I said.

"The hell kinda business they got in a place like this?" Enoch said. His eyes were big with shock, but there was a veiled sense of nervousness inside him.

"That's what I'm tryin' to find out. A teenage kid wiped out his entire family. But his dad was alive long enough for some kind of... spirit to puppet him," I said

"Demonic possession?" Enoch said, aghast. "And you stopped it, right? Once they drain the life force of the host, they just find another body."

"Well, I…" I scratched my head, trying to find the words. I never thought I'd have to say what I did.

"I couldn't."

Enoch's brows curled into a confused expression.

"You… *couldn't?*"

"I know," I said. "I… I can't explain it, E. It just don't make no sense."

"Every spirit has to bow and confess to the Christ. It's written!"

"Yeah, right… Well, I thought so, too. This one only laughed at me when I did. It said it's older than our God."

Enoch's eye twitched. He turned away.

"Oh," he said, anxiously. "Did you get a name?"

"It sent me to go fuck myself. All I've got to go buy is the writin' on the wall that kid drew."

"What did it say?"

"*Ekstasis.*"

"He said….To ask you," I said. His face was as dark as a grave now, and he fixed his gaze on me. "You're the priest of this church. So, tell me, *Father*. What should I know?" I asked.

Enoch adjusted the collar around his neck.

"It's a Primordial," he confessed.

I knew it.

"Primordial or not, you said every spirit must obey me."

"And they do!" Enoch snapped, frustrated. "But this ain't exactly a spirit, you see? It's… a force. A raw, ancient power that helped to forge creation. Beings that only God the Father got business dealin' with,"

I laughed off the tension. "But I'm his vessel on earth," I said. "I should have the power to stop this."

"There is power that mortal bodies just ain't meant to hold to that capacity… You are the *Son*. You are his *likeness* as sunlight is like the sun, but not the sun itself. It's an extension of its power. That is what you are."

I stood up, rubbing my face in agitation. My neck was hot, and I could feel my palms pulsating and throbbing. There was never a limit to my power before this. I was the end all be all; there was nothing that could stop me. I was taught that I had unlimited access and boundless potential and power. I suddenly felt so small.

"Not even Glorification? If I perform the Rite of Transfiguration?" I asked.

Enoch shook his head regretfully.

"Only God himself can stop somethin' like this. But you have the power to summon His council. You can stand before God and not die."

"This is fuckin' bullshit. I don't need to go runnin' to Daddy when shit gets real; that's never been me. I'll go to the library and find somethin'. There's gotta be a Miraculous Art performed by one of the past Nazarens!"

Enoch stood up and put his hand on my shoulder.

"I'll assemble the Order and we'll perform the Rite to summon his council. The Lord *will* prevail, Levi. Always. Remember, without you as a link, he cannot act on earth. This doesn't make you any less powerful…" Enoch explained. "Do you remember the words spoken to you on the night of your first Glorification?"

I sighed, frustrated and trying to find faith in those words.

"*What you bind on earth shall be bound in heaven, and what you loose on earth shall be loosed in heaven.*"

"Remember that," Enoch said. "And all the world will be at your feet. Don't lose faith."

He picked up his Bible and began to walk back towards the altar.

"Wait," I said, bolting up.

"When I went down there with Craven, even he said a mortal couldn't possibly conjure somethin' like this, and I agree. How is this even possible, E? Make it make sense, please, I'm goin' crazy here in my head!"

Enoch turned to add more incense to the smoke. He looked up at me and smiled kindly. The madness from his eyes gave way to clarity. Seeing Enoch remain calm reminded me of being still. God was ultimately in control, and by extension, that meant *I* was in control.

"It definitely exceeds mortal capabilities… Something or someone is acting in the shadows, and God as my witness, they will be brought to light. Like all things that hide in the dark."

"Like witches?" I asked. "What if the Madonna and her witches have come to Tophet?"

"Then we'll be ready."

"No, *I'll* be ready," I said.

I left Enoch and started to make my way toward the garden to clear my head.

And to smoke a cigarette.

My head was an endless echo chamber that affirmed my worst thoughts. There was always the possibility that I'd be defeated at the hands of Satan. But now wasn't the time for self-doubt. Not with our most ancient enemy lurking amongst us. witches couldn't resist the urge to cavort with darkness and to stir the cauldron of chaos wherever they want. They were children with boxes of matches setting their perversions and blasphemies ablaze. Only a witch would be destructive enough to bring a Primordial onto the mortal plane.

The Primordials were destructive forces, the powers of Creation itself. The God of the Garden fashioned the dome of the Earth to be a boundary, a fortified barrier against such raw powers that would rip the earth apart. But through centuries of treachery, the witches put cracks in that wall, allowing small essences of these energies to seep through like air coming in through the crack of a window. But cracks in a wall wouldn't appease them any longer. They wanted to bring down the walls of the Jericho we'd built.

And I wasn't going to allow it.

CHAPTER 9

Guardian Angel

The church garden was my favorite place, mostly because I used to sneak off during lessons to come smoke weed here. The garden was more like a maze, just hedgerows forming pathways winding down for at least a mile. The humidity was starting to shy away from the coming intense heat. I underestimated how hot it suddenly could get, and I lived there my whole life.

I walked through the endless greenery, lost in the streaks of shrubbery and looking for the bright red roses that usually freckled this place. But instead, all I saw were tiny bursts of fragmented sunlight proudly spreading their golden pedals against the cracks of blue in the sky. I reached out, touching the sunflower. I'd never seen them before growing in this garden, but they were more beautiful than any rose ever planted here. The sweetness of their scent was broken by the burning, ashy smell of a cigarette.

A nun emerged from the row of flowers behind me, her face half obscured by the honey petals.

"I can see you, you know," I said.

She stepped away from the mask of flowers that hid her face. She wore a cheeky smile, creating pronounced crow's feet in her eyes that dug deep crevices into her pale blue eyes.

She laughed, raspy and with a rugged smoker's cough.

"Well, looks like you caught me," she said.

She wore a rosary strung of white pearls, and strands of her sandy hair poked through her habit. She had a kind charm that transcended her age, and an energy that bordered on intimidating. I snickered, removing a fresh pack of cigarettes from my jacket.

"I won't tell if you won't?" I asked. I sparked my cigarette and exchanged relieved smiles.

"Can't say I've seen you here before, ma'am,"

"Oh," she said, breathless. She brushed her cheek, if I didn't know any better, I'd say she was flirting with me.

"I ain't from around here, darlin', just payin' a visit."

"What a shame. Usually, around this time of year, they've got the most beautiful roses... But someone's put sunflowers here instead."

"Well, these are much lovelier, ain't they? They just bring new life into this place," she said dreamily.

"So where'd you say you was from?"

"I didn't. But I'm from a quiet little town in Georgia; you probably wouldn't have heard of it."

"Oh, well, I'm a southern boy myself. I've been to just about every town you can think of," I said.

"Summerland," she said.

My eye flinched. It wasn't too strange to have people come into town from Summerland, but I never saw this woman before, and her appearance in proximity to a Primordial revealing itself was enough to put me on edge. There was something about her eyes too. Like gazing into the eyes of an owl in the dead of night, a piercing stare that seemed to know what I was thinking. And judging by the way she was looking at me now, I knew she could feel the tension.

"What're you doin' comin' from on that way?" I said, breaking the silence.

"Father Enoch works closely with the church. He requested extra help for the homeless drive, and I was more than happy to help," she said without missing a beat.

I took another drag from my cigarette. "Well, I don't want to scare you," I said, passing the heat from the smoke through my nose. "But this town ain't too safe these days."

She flicked her wrist, chuckling. "I may be old, but I long ago mastered the art of danger. Not much can scare this bag of bones," she said, winking.

Despite that part of myself that wanted to mistrust her, I liked her. I could've been paranoid. As much as I wanted to believe that witches were behind this, I started to doubt it. Maybe amateur magicians tried summoning more than they could chew and didn't want to own up. witches knew Tophet to be a stronghold for the Order. It would be like walking into the lion's den. But even still, I couldn't let my guard down.

"I'm sorry, I didn't catch your name,"

"Sister Agnes," she said.

"Levi Beaumont," I said.

I shook her hand.

"Are you a member of the church, Levi?"

"You could say we're all one body," I said.

She smiled playfully.

"How many Our Fathers that gonna cost you?" she said, gesturing to my cigarette.

"Ha! Only ask forgiveness when you feel guilty."

She laughed heartily.

"I'm takin' a likin' to you already, Mr. Beaumont," she said, taking a deep puff. "'Course I like to say *I only ask for forgiveness, never permission*. But I'll leave the askin' for when I get caught."

"I think you and I are gonna get along just fine, Sister. I'm happy to have you here with us."

She nodded. I finished the cigarette and tossed it into the bushes. I did enjoy her company, but that didn't mean she was immune from any digging. I've never heard of no Sister Agnes, but I was going to find out what she was doing here.

"I've got work to catch up on. It was nice meetin' you, Sister," I said

"Pleasure's mine. Oh, and Mr. Beaumont?" she said.

I stopped before I turned to take my leave.

"Promise you won't tell Father Enoch of my little... habit?"

I shrugged.

"Aside from the one on your head? As long as you won't tell him it's me leavin' all the cigarette buds in the garden," I said

She signed a lock and key against her lip. I smiled at her and turned away, making my way out of the garden. Father Enoch was in the middle of a Mass now, so I couldn't ask him about anyone named Sister Agnes. Tophet's become a snake pit, and anyone new cast doubt in my mind.

I looked at my watch, and a jolt of realization hit me. I'd been so driven to find answers I'd forgotten about my own Pops's memorial service. Grannie was going to murder me. And so would Ezra for leaving him alone to deal with all her neuroticisms.

By the time I'd made it home, the sunset was already dripping streaks of honey and blood across the sky, saturated with soft magenta that poked through the trees. I got out of my car and saw the pale yellow candlelight glinting through the frames of the window with silhouettes hurriedly moving back and forth. From where I was, I saw Grannie's form waving her finger at Ezra, and another figure slowly drifted past them. I knew this was all about Pops and honoring his memory, but all today ever made me do was want to tear my heart out of my chest so I didn't have to feel anymore.

I stopped at the entrance of the house. I could hear Grannie's voice loud and clear barking like a dog at Ezra. She was more disheveled, with hairs out of place and stained clothes. There were even traces of forming wrinkles. Grannie also had a maddened look in her eyes, like she was trying to fight other voices in her head. Ezra hung his head, taking more verbal cuts from her razored tongue. Though, I'd rather hear that than the desperate gasps and howling she did every night since the day Pops died.

Her cries were nothing more than background noise for the hosts of heaven. It was like someone had been ripping her in half every day, and I knew that was how it felt to lose someone. I'd always believed that grief was love with no home and nowhere to go. But why cry for the dead if they can't hear you?

Truth is, I had no more tears left to cry. There wasn't any more left in me. I could've been the God of the Nile, for the tears that flowed from my eyes could make the earth spring to life. Maybe something beautiful could come from my pain.

It all happened one hot Summer night. The stars were partially hidden, and the moon was barely a sliver in the sky. Pops had taken Ezra and me out to track a witch that he'd been following for some time. She had to have been from the Summerland bloodline because the only witches around here had color. Grannie had been working long nights with the church for a while, which left us with more time alone with Pops. We snuck out that night after she left for the evening because there's no way in hell she would have let him go alone otherwise.

The Magistrate of the judges ordered Pops not to hunt without an equipped partner, but there wasn't anyone trained better in the art of killing than my old man. And Pops couldn't be swayed. He had a fixation, a strange compulsion for this specific witch. He rarely hunted without the help of other judges, but for some reason, he was driven damn near insane following this one. The Order was always cunning and careful not to be caught. Magicians also typically came from upper-class families and worked from afar. The blue-collar killing was left to the likes of judges, who more than willingly got their hands dirty.

Pops was confident he had his two sons with him, and it wasn't anything he couldn't handle. But this night was different. On that night, Pops unloaded the truck with his axe in hand, ready for his prey to let their guard down. There was an old farm on that road and nothing else for miles. The cloaked figure entered the barnyard, and we followed behind her. There was only the glow of a lantern hanging in the barn, casting pallid yellow light through the cracks of the door. Pops and I crept in and saw the hooded figure disrobe itself.

"I don't think we should do this..." Ezra said in the car that night. "You always said don't go Huntin' alone,"

Pops snapped, slamming on the steering wheel.

"THIS IS DIFFERENT! SHE NEEDS TO BE STOPPED! DON'T YOU QUESTION ME!" he screamed.

For as tall and brave as my older brother was, I saw him shrivel back into his seat. He looked scared for the first time in my life. Even I didn't understand it. I couldn't begin to count the number of times he'd wake up in the middle of the night to go stalk this witch. He had become fixated with her like he alone had to be the one to kill her. And if there was any demon to be afraid of when angry, it was Pops. It was always best to just do what he said.

I still remember her long, silver hair falling to the curve of her wrinkled, sagging back. The old woman's frail, pale body walked ahead, crouched over she fumbled on her own feet. She seemed ashamed, as she approached an otherworldly figure. She lifted her head and held up her trembling arms in salute. Perched at the top of a wooden beam, cloaked in a canopy of shadows, was a great horned owl, whose slick black feathers reflected blue. The witch held the baby up before the creature and began to speak in a strange language. It had a serpentine cadence, with hissing and shushing sounds that sent the hairs on my neck standing up.

And I understood.

I should've known then. Something was wrong with me. Deeply wrong. But I swore I'd never tell anyone.

"*You stand before me as you soon shall be, as you go to the grave.*" it scolded her,

"Please, my Lord," she begged, "let me return to the bloom of youth." The old woman wept mournfully, covering her face. She went on until the owl hooted.

"*Do you have the offering?*"

"Eagerly awaiting,"

I quietly tugged on Pops's arm.

"We have to go," I mouthed.

Pops snagged me by the shirt, holding his fingers to his lip with a deep, furrowed brow and stern eyes. Suddenly, she raised her face to the creature again, and her cries turned into relieved laughter. The owl spread its great, black wings and flapped, blowing an unnatural gust of wind through the barn with a terrifying shriek.

The old witch began to holler and scream as if she were just being born. And she was. Again. The witch cried, lifting her shriveled, veiny arms, and watched in tearful awe as they rejuvenated before her eyes. She kissed her hand, feeling the smoothness of her skin again as she rubbed down her body.

She was lost in admiring her new form, still sighing and cooing. Pops knew this was the time to strike.

"The offering, my Lord..." the witch said

Wasting no time, he quietly opened the barn door and crept behind the woman, who pressed the horned, winged beast. I clutched onto Ezra, covering my mouth as hot tears rolled down my cheeks and onto my hands.

"Is blood."

Pops lifted his axe, and with a swing that you could hear cut through the wind, he brought down all the rage and judgment of God Almighty upon her.

The offering was made.

It was him.

Serrated blades of glass shattered against the end of Pops's axe as a violent gash appeared across his chest, severing his neck from his body. He was split nearly in two before I could even get a scream out. I fell onto the ground, and Ezra wailed with a ferocity I swore shook the ground as he ran towards Pops's body. In the place of the witch was a mirror with shards of broken glass.

Ezra gathered the severed halves of Pops in his arms, cradling them as he wept. Rivers of blood ran down his body until he sat in a pool of maroon. My eyes were blinded by tears, and no matter how hard I tried to scream, no sound would come out. As I looked up, I saw that red-haired devil woman watching coldly. The shadows behind her wrapped around her bare body, and she vanished into a shroud of darkness behind her.

Life for life. She must've already known that we were following her. In their corrupted ways, witches had to repay life with life if they wished to bring back the dead or restore their own. And while Pops thought himself to be the hunter, he was actually the prey. He went to be slaughtered, to be sacrificed to the horned beast that sat above us. The owl turned its head, forcing me to fix my gaze on its massive yellow eyes.

We must've been in shock because after we'd run clear out of the Bloodwood, we didn't talk at all again. Not the entire way walking back to the barn, not even on the drive back with Pops's body in the backseat of his old pickup truck.

The silence. That's all I could think about when I remember that night all those years ago. It was absolution. It was final.

The Son of God was able to save his mortal father from such a bitter end.

I stood on the porch, staring at the bronze doorknob of Grannie's house. I knew all I had to do was turn it and go inside, but I couldn't. I hated having to relive the night of my greatest failures in this lifetime, a guilt that I couldn't even forgive myself from. He wasn't the greatest Dad in the world, and in many ways, he contributed to the monster that I'd sometimes become, but I loved him anyway. Fresh, hot tears burned my eyes as I reached for the doorknob to the house, and my throat tightened. I clasped the bridge of my nose, frustrated. But it had to be done.

I opened the door as quietly as I could, stepping inside to the smells of freshly baked lamb, sweet potatoes, green beans, and corn. Nina Simone played over the old radio coming into view as I entered the kitchen. The sweet and savory aromas of home cooking gave me bittersweet hints of nostalgia, like gathered family meals around the table when Pops was still alive. It didn't help she was preparing all his favorites. But I should've been ready for this, it was the same every year.

A slim figure skirted past me. She hurriedly slipped on her mitts and reached inside the oven.

"Ezra, I need you to hurry on down to Mr. Carter's for some jam," she said, focused on the hot pan in her hands.

"You know your Grannie likes—"

She stopped, sneering at the sight of me. My stomach was in knots at the sight of her. I tried taking deep breaths to slow my racing heart. The corner of her mouth curled into an arrogant and smug smile. She delicately removed the oven mitts after setting down the ham, chuckling provokingly.

"Look who it is," she said.

She held her head high and stared down her nose as she looked at me, patting the sweat off her copper skin with one of the kitchen rags. She had a long neck like Grannie, and she was just as lithe and graceful. She approached me, allowing her wrist to dangle in front of her to reveal perfectly done nails.

"Aunt Nita," I said, standoffish.

Nita twirled her mane of thick, oily ringlets between her fingers. She was Pop's sister, Grannie's second child, and the only girl. The former Witches Society passed power from mother to daughter, usually. Unless you were one of the unlucky men to be cursed by the Summerland Pact. Either way, their matrilineal system meant that Nita got her way in everything. Whether you liked it or not.

Nita sighed as if annoyed by my presence even though I lived here.

"That ain't no tone to be takin' with your Auntie, now..." she said.

On the surface, Nita was honestly a beautiful woman. She turned her hubris into charm when she wanted, and despite her arrogance, she did carry an air of refinement and poise, a Lynn Whitfield type. She was a work of art.

She was also the ugliest person I'd ever met.

CHAPTER 10

Holy See

There was this uniquely awful, internal dread that happened every time I saw Nita. It was like she just sucked the life out of every room she walked into. Everything about her was unnerving, from her scowl to the up-and-down glances she gave you as she talked to you. She had a horrible talent for getting inside your head and under your skin. My family line was ripe with vain and beautiful women, and Nita was no exception.

I liked to think Nita was born with acid in her veins, but the truth was that it had more to do with the denial of a birthright. Grannie Tamar was a descendant of Tituba, and for generations, all the daughters of Tituba reigned as Madonnas, Witch Queens by blood—except for Nita. She was sure it was going to be next in line for the crown until she wasn't. Grannie broke the news that it wouldn't be her, despite nearly 300 years of Tituba's descendants with that scepter of power. It was yet to be announced who the new Madonna would be, but Nita knew it wasn't her.

Tituba founded Tophet in her image and even named it after an ancient Pagan god, who hungrily accepted the blood of newborns. She then wove a wall of magic. It was a guardian and protection that preserved all the power she would raise within its form.

The barrier's strongest hold was at the home she had built. But she assured it encased the entire town, cloaking it away from the prying eyes of magicians and any other person that would bring harm to them. But somehow, the magicians found it and cut through the barrier. Our house was all that remained of the Veil, the heart of the magic.

And to this day, no one has ever found out where we lived.

Nita turned the sink on and ran her hands under the water, flicking her wrists as she sneered at me. Her smile was unnerving and predatory. It was terrifying how insignificant and small she could make one feel. She looked God in the face every day and mocked him. Nita wasn't scared of anyone, and as much as I hated her, it was a level of daring I don't think even I had.

"You didn't think I'd be here to leave your Grannie all by yourself now, did you? Some of us do remember important days like this," she said, now delicately buttering the biscuits. "Or did you have somethin' more important you had to do?"

My throat tightened. "I had to investigate a murder," I said.

"Ohhh…" She said sardonically.

"Aint' you the big man in town?"

"Some of us work, yeah. But what would you know about any of that?"

Nita's eyes glinted with anger, but she breathed deep and slow. A devious smile etched across her face.

"Boy, you think you some type of special, don't you? But don't you go forgettin'— all of us gonna have to answer someday. And I reckon that day's just around the corner."

"You know, I didn't see you at last Sunday's service, Nita. That ain't like you," I said

Nita whipped me with the kitchen linen, feigning playfulness.

"Oh, you darlin' boy. You know it ain't polite to be in a lady's business," she said. "But, since you *must* know, I was arrangin' your daddy's memorial service."

"Hmm… It wouldn't got nothin' to do with Amma bein' chosen to be head of the Deborah's choir, would it? I know what that means."

"Last I checked, it ain't final. We'll know by tonight."

"I just couldn't imagine how you feel, Nita. 200 years of Parris women as Queen all endin' with you. I mean, how do you even sleep?"

She laughed and bopped my nose with her finger, patronizing me. No matter what I did, I'd always be a little boy to her. She walked away, humming *Sinner Man* by Nina Simone to herself, looking back at me as she returned to preparing the dinner. The mutual disdain was palpable between us, and always has been. Well, at least for most of my life. I never knew where things went wrong.

It wasn't always this way, not in the early years. When I was a kid, Nita used to buy me gold jewelry and take me rollerblading around the neighborhood. She used to take me to gas stations and get jerky or pickled eggs, but all of that stopped one day. After that, it was nothing but snide remarks and condescension.

When I was about a month shy of 10 years old, Nita cornered me in the living room one morning while Grannie sat up on the couch, smoking her cigarette. I don't remember the words she said, only the shrieking sound of her voice as she grabbed and screamed. She spewed residual hatred in a shower of venom and spite. All I could remember was the feeling of helplessness and my heart pounding with the shrinking of the room. It was the first panic attack I'd experienced, and all of it unfolded as Grannie callously watched the entire thing, not even flinching as she puffed away on her cigarette.

The worst part of it all was telling my Pops, only to be forced to apologize to Aunt Nita for upsetting her. He said if I broke down and cried like a bitch over that, then I'd never be able to handle the weight of the world. The funny thing is that the weight of the world was bearable. I still couldn't stand the weight of Nita's scrutiny.

"Why don't you go run along and make actual use of yourself somehow instead of runnin' around town playin' God."

"I ain't playin'," I said, tensely.

She smirked. She loved when she struck the right chords with me. It was like I was her own personal instrument of torment; she'd play all of my emotions until the right sounds of my suffering appeased her. She was sadistic in every way.

"Right… What did I say?" she said, snarky.

I balled my fist, shaking.

"Hey." Ezra's voice boomed.

His broad, massive body pushed passed me down the hall. He set the grocery bags on the table, breathless.

"Hey, baby," Nita said, doting.

Ezra leaned in for a kiss on the cheek from her. I gagged.

"Good timin', Lee. I just got back from runnin' to the store for Grannie after I told her about them peaches. You could help Nita make the cobbler."

Ezra looked back and forth between the dirty looks between the two of us.

"What's goin' on?"

"Oh, now, it ain't even a thing. Levi and I was just discussin' your daddy's memorial dinner. You know that kind of thing can always be sensitive… ain't that right, Levi?" Nita said.

I smiled, passively as I kept my eyes on her.

"Yeah," I said, turning to Ezra, "and Nita's nervous about who the new Queen's gonna be. I would be too, wouldn't you?"

Ezra's face morphed into uncertainty with his twisted eyebrows and curled lips.

"Alright… So, I'm gonna just leave this here for y'all."

Ezra stopped on his way out of the kitchen and laid his paw-like hand on my shoulder.

"Come see me in Pop's secret place. I need to show you something,'" he said. He gave me an assuring pat and left me in the kitchen again with that devil of a woman.

"I can take care of this cobbler, I'm sure you've got more important things to be doin' with your time, Officer Christ," she jabbed.

"That's right, he does," another voice said.

Grannie's silver streaked hair shone beneath the kitchen lights. Nita and I stood at attention while Granny slowly paced the kitchen with her hands folded behind her.

"Nita, you get to fixin' that cobbler, we don't got much time. Levi, why don't you come follow me into the next room, here?"

Nita shot me one last antagonizing glance before I lost her eyes in the living room.

The room was inlaid with dark red carpet and mahogany furniture. Paintings hung along the walls of the Madonna's of her family throughout the decades, standing together with a church choir. The paintings transitioned into black and white photographs of the group, all meeting at the base of a painted tree that formed a crucifix. From the base of the tree sprouted intricately entangled branches, depicting silhouetted, profile faces of women, forming the matrilineal downline.

Grannie sat down, resting her hands against the armrest of a velvet chair. Behind her was a large, framed portrait of Grannie's Mama, Miss Loretta. It looked to be from the early 1900s, and Miss Loretta's eyes gazed down at us, a faint but present sense of life still lingering.

Grannie took out her pipe, flaring her nostrils with a snort. The contents of her pipe ignited into flames, and she puffed out clouds of smoke.

"I see you got into my stash again," I said.

"This my house, boy. Everythin' in it belongs to me," she said, scowling. "Even you."

I sighed.

"What's goin' on here, Grannie?"

"Listen," she said, trying to compose herself, "I'm sure you've had a long day, and you're feelin' all the stress of work and your duties to the Order... But... I ain't the one."

"Grannie, I—"

"Ah—Ah. Don't you talk over me. This ain't no open mic night. I said... I ain't the one, you hear? Now you sit down and don't open your mouth again when I'm speakin'."

There was never any need to have God present when the fear of him was always so constant in Grannie. She commanded not only deep respect but fear. And, I didn't want to admit it, but I hated her a little bit too. So many times, she'd taken Nita's side against me in her senseless abuses.

Grannie was a very black-and-white kind of person. There weren't ever any shades of grey. Whenever I'd challenged her, I'd bought myself a one-way ticket to villainy.

I sat down, trying to suppress any outward signs of frustration with her. "Yes, ma'am," I said," I settled into my seat, "I'm listenin'."

"Hmmm." She groaned, watching me carefully.

A suffocating silence stretched between us.

"You just missed her," she said finally.

"Who?"

The red sparks burned bright in her pipe; her head now split the fumes that formed as she inhaled.

"Amma,"

My heart fluttered.

"What was she doin' down this way?" I said, trying to keep my cool.

Grannie smiled curtly. She could read me like a book. She knew that no matter how nonchalant I acted, it was Amma that drove me crazy, the Delilah that could bring me to my knees.

"She got a big day comin' up," Grannie said.

Amma was more beautiful than heaven, everything about her made my body sing. Since I was a kid, I felt like I was looking for a pair of eyes that I couldn't remember. I didn't know who they were, I just knew I had to find them. And I knew my search ended the day I met Amma. It was her smile that lit up my life and caused the sun to re-cede with shame. I couldn't have been older than 8 years old when her at church one day.

"What's that?" I said coyly.

"Oh, now… seems like you've forgotten our ways. Our tradition."

She was a love that haunted me like a ghost. I'd seen many men and women come and go, but Amma was the one that I was always holding out hope for. I loved everything about her, from the velve-teen smoothness of her voice to the softness of her caress. There was a love that burned for her so brightly that I know a thousand lifetimes I must've spent fanning its flames.

"You mean…"

"Mmhmm," Grannie mumbled. "I'm gettin' along in years now, Levi. It's time I pass the torch on… these old bones is givin' way to time… they ain't what they used to be…"

"But Grannie, how many times you come upside our head within the last week?" I said. "Is it really goin' to be Amma?"

She laughed, but it seemed painful to her. She laid her hand across her chest and sighed, laced with bitterness.

"She performed the 13 Pillars... and the spirits have spoken. It's time... the crown is hers."

She looked back at the portrait of her mama on the wall. "Soon I'll be just that right there. A pictur. A memory..."

"Grannie, don't say that,"

"It's time. Much... to Nita's despair, the ancestors ain't choose her to carry the legacy. So, it has been decided that Amma will be crowned and made Madonna. The Witch Queen of Florida," Grannie said.

"So, that means..."

"That means whatever business y'all got together? Consider it done and over."

"But Grannie—"

"What was that?" she threatened.

I settled back into my seat.

"Grannie... I... I love Amma," I said.

She smirked, taking another deep drag from her pipe.

"You know... I've never found you good-lookin'," she said coldly and factually. "You're average lookin' at best. There really ain't nothin' special about you. Why God chose you is beyond me, to be honest, I'll never know."

"Grannie," I said, wincing.

She shrugged.

"The spirit livin' inside you is the only thing that makes you special, really, but Amma? She's beautiful, intelligent, and powerful. A true leader. You never asked yourself, why in God's green earth she would be with someone like you?"

I was falling apart inside; she was always so casually cruel it was even more painful. Her words weren't made to be cruel; she was simply stating facts. But I was falling apart inside; she was always so casually cruel it was even more painful. Her words weren't made to be cut; she was simply stating facts.

"Besides… Even if you'd been a judge, a magician, or a witch like us… you know the rules. Why get your hopes up?"

"But Grannie…"

"No. The Son of Shaddai cannot taint himself by lyin' with a witch. Nor can he produce children."

I jumped to my feet.

"You're makin' a mistake!" I shouted.

Grannie slammed her fist onto her open palm, and with that, my body violently smashed down onto the couch, pinned down under an iron grip. Her fist wiggled and trembled as she struggled to hold me in place.

"Now I already done told you I wasn't the one. I said what I said, and I ain't gonna repeat myself. Amma will take her rightful place, and you ain't standin' in that girl's way," she said.

Grannie separated her hands, and I was broken free with a shaking gasp of air. I flopped off the couch and landed on my stomach, desperate for air. Even if I wasn't the Son of God, Grannie's power hold over me was indistinguishable from the grip of Shaddai. There never seemed a way for me to do anything to defend against it. I wobbled back onto my feet, trembling with each breath and shaking with rage as I stared her down.

"Get out," she said. "Ain't nothin' left to be said."

I stormed out of the room and past Nita's snarking face in the kitchen.

"Aw," Nita mocked. "What's the matter, bad news?"

I snatched my car keys off the holder and grabbed my jacket.

"For both of us. But at least one of us won't mind callin' Amma the Queen." Nita's eyes glossed over.

"All hail," I said, winking.

The door in front of me was pushed shut. I looked up to see Ezra's figure looming over me. I jerked back from him.

"What are you doin'?"

"Nah, what are *you* doin'? You walk out that door right now, and that's gonna be the end of both of us!" Ezra said.

I grunted, rubbing my face.

"Take it easy. Besides, you about to run off when I told you I had somethin' for you to see."

"It gotta be tonight?"

"Yeah," he said. Ezra's entire frame blocked the door now, and he took the keys out of my hand. "It does. You got somewhere else you gotta be?"

"Matter of fact, I do. I gotta meet with someone important, it's for work," I said.

I tried for the door again, but Ezra blocked my way with a single step. I bounced back off his chest after running into him.

"Yeah, so you can text your little work friends that you runnin' late tonight. This can't wait."

I threw my hands up, surrendering.

"Alright, fine," I said. "What is it?"

Ezra gestured for me to take his lead. I followed behind him down the long, dark wooden hallway and down into the cellar. Ezra picked up a lit torch from the wall.

"Father Enoch came down to the church today," Ezra said.

"He recruitin' more of y'all on another death mission?" I said.

Ezra laughed.

"We make do. Just 'cause we can't do none of that fancy work y'all be gettin' down with don't mean we can't take care of ourselves...."

"Yeah, Pops was a real match for the witch that took him out."

The wind was knocked out of me with the force of Ezra's punch.

"Pops was the best there was. You hear me?" Ezra said.

The fire in his hands flickered against his face, creating twisting shadows that deepened the furrow of his brows, making him look to wear of mask of anger and darkness. I proceeded quietly behind him, rubbing my chest from the dull throb he left behind.

"Enoch came down to the church because he says he thinks witches might be fuckin' with shit they ain't got no business in."

Ezra stopped at the door on the cellar floor that led down to the Secret Place.

"And I think I've got somethin' that'll give us some answers."

He opened the door and descended deeper into the dark precipice.

"What you got down there?"

The darkness around us scattered from the fire flickering from the torch.

"Why don't you get in here and see for yourself?" Ezra said, sly.

He laughed, leading me down through a valley of shadow until we finally reached the bottom. The muffled screams instantly filled the room, mixed in a stew of rattling chains and clanking metal.

Ezra held his torch above the form of a woman with blood running down her neck from the iron gag placed firmly on her head. Tears streamed down her face, too terrified to speak at the cost of her tongue.

"I've been followin' her and two other women," Ezra said. "I snatched 'er up the night before those murders happened. Then when Enoch came in today, it all fell in place."

I turned pitilessly towards the woman struggling for her life, bound to a metal execution-style chair.

"So," I said, clapping my hands together. "You better start tellin' me what I wanna hear, and I'll think about makin' your exit from this world as quick as possible."

The woman stared at me defiantly.

"What's the matter?" I laughed. "Tongue-tied?"

CHAPTER 11

Advent

It was karmic, cathartic even, to have a witch in my hands. I knew that there was a cloud of darkness looming over this town that only could come with the Devil's riders on the storm. They were his valkyries, charging from a realm unknown to collect the souls of those dead in their sins. Those dead enough to become ensnared by something so utterly wicked. Power, when you have none, is the ultimate offer, who in that moment of dire need can turn away from it?

I knelt in front of her, getting at eye level with her on the chair. She was trembling, but she retained a proudness in her eyes that I was eager to snuff out.

"Alright now, listen good 'cause I ain't repeatin' myself. Especially not to no witch," I began. "Now, I'm gonna remove this bit from your mouth. And when I do, those lips are gonna get to movin' and tell me everythin' I need to hear. Clear?"

Her eyes screamed at me in defiance but wavered with compliance.

"Good," I said.

I removed the Bit from her mouth, she winced in pain as more blood ran down her mouth from the spike that was latched to the Bridle. She gasped, hanging her head and breathing long, shallow breaths.

"You save up that energy now, 'cause we're far from done,"

What started as wheezing breaths slowly became a laugh that made my blood run cold. She laughed in such a way I half expected that dark spirit to return. But there was none, only hers, and all the corruption and deceit that was her own to claim.

"You think this shit's a game?" I snapped.

"What?" she said between her breaths of fitted cackles. "You don't? Darlin' if you ain't realize that the game's begun, then I've got news for you."

I rushed towards her and crushed her jaw within the grasp of my fingers. All it did was tickle her.

"Ooo..." she said coyly. "You's mighty strong, Mr. Man, how could someone like me compete with you?"

"You disgust me," I said. She snapped her teeth at me, fixing her eyes deep into mine as she glazed the surface of her teeth with her tongue. "Tell me your name."

"What's in a name?" she toyed.

"Answer me."

She spat. Her warm, frothy saliva ran down my cheek. I wiped it off with the end of my sleeve, laughing.

"I see you plan on revealin' no secrets," I said. I jerked my hand away from her, angrily. "But baby, you see the thing is... we've got... *different* plans. So, I'd advise you to cooperate before things start gettin' ugly."

The creases of her eyes folded as her smile nearly reached the ends of her ears.

"Say, now... whatever happened to not repeatin' yourself?"

I snatched the copper blade from Ezra's sheath.

"Girl, so help me God, once I sever your ties to the evil you serve, I'll see to it you get a VIP pass straight to Hell."

"You can go ahead and kill me, Son of *Man*. But my Queen holds the keys to the fiery pit."

"The Devil's deception. Only Shaddai has such a power."

"Oh... bless your heart. You've got it all wrong." Ezra looked at me tensely from the corners of his eyes. "I know it, and you know it, too. I can see it inside you. The urge to waver, to forsake your God."

"Shut up,"

"There is one comin'... *prepare the way*. Greater works than even you have done the child will do... wonders not seen since the days the Goddess walked the earth."

"Liar."

"And she *will* walk again. They both will, and you're goin' to be the one to help us do it."

I laughed.

"Y'all have already done the work for us. Your greatest mistakes will become our greatest weapon. *You* will be the final tool."

"I would never."

I hated to admit it, but the pangs of doubt started to slither through me. The strands of her hair were stuck together with blood and tears, hiding parts of her face that made her look more like a vengeful spirit than a woman. She shook her head, smiling incredulously.

"Christ almighty, here he is in the flesh and still fallin' for it."

"What are you runnin' your mouth about?"

I pressed the blade deeper against her neck. She fell into another ungodly spasm of laughter. All Ezra and I could do were watch on. I fought the knots that formed in my stomach. There was something different now. The air felt like it was vibrating with an unseen, sinister force. My heart skipped a beat; lightheadedness rushed through me as I tightened my grip on the blade.

"Every single step you take," she said, abruptly stopping. Her eyes were like an owl, round and penetrating. "Y'all are playin' right into our hands, and all we had to do was show up."

The voice of Shaddai came over me in a reverberating, painful chime.

"*Smite... Her...*" he demanded.

My heart raced.

"We'? There're more of y'all?"

"*Destroy her in my name*," he urged.

She smiled back at me, her teeth tinged with blood.

"We are legion."

"*KILL HER!*" he bellowed.

I rushed her with the copper blade. Her eyes hollowed black, and she cocked her head and hissed like a snake. Ezra clasped his head as the iron gag instantly appeared, wrapped tightly around his head.

"DON'T SCREAM!—-" I dropped the blade.

Even as I yelled for Ezra, he still shrieked, blood running down his face as he collided with the ground. Even his arms and legs were suddenly bound by the fastenings of the chair that once held her. I turned to face the witch, and she gave one final jeering laugh before flipping backward into the darkness with an unreal swiftness as if carried by the wind itself.

The blade clanked against the ground, slipping from my fingers in sheer disbelief. Ezra's fumbling on the ground quickly snapped me back out of my daze, and I rushed to his side to remove the bridle. As I unfastened the headpiece, my mind veered in a thousand different directions. What the fuck did I just see? Even I was shaken. Never in my entire life had I seen a witch do something like that. Something was wrong, and I feared she was right. I was late to the game. And at the rate I was going, not knowing what I was up against could cost me.

I quickly undid the bindings on his feet and wrists. Ezra's breaths were fluttering faster than the beat of a hummingbird's wing.

"D-Did—" he said, raising a shaking finger, pointing to the darkness ahead of us.

"I know."

"H-How?" Ezra said.

"Don't talk," I said.

I laid my hand against his cheek, feeling the healing warmth permeating from the palms of my hand, a heartbeat alive with divine power. I removed my hand, and Ezra flicked his tongue around his teeth. He punched me on the shoulder affectionately.

"Thanks, lil' kid," he said, afflicted.

"When they learn to do shit like that?"

I scratched my beard, sighing defeatedly.

"I don't know… but we got played."

"What? H-How? This shit far from bein' over!" Ezra said, slamming his fist against the ground.

He got up, picking up the burning torch, whose glow couldn't shine past the void beyond our faces.

"It's a game to them, and we played right into it."

"We'll find her again," Ezra said. He paced in place, mumbling angrily to himself.

"She let you catch her, don't you see?"

Ezra looked away; I could see the ego take a blow in the slump of his body.

"Nah... you're wrong."

"Ezra... ask yourself, if she could've done somethin' like that this entire time, how could you have caught her?"

Ezra's blank stare and silence admitted his realization to me. "Damn," he said. "So what's the move?"

I shook my head, pensively.

"Make sure everyone's on the same page. Includin' y'all... you heard her. There's more of them. Witches are walkin' these lands,"

Ezra's lip quivered, turning away trying to hide the grim expression on his face.

"She wasn't alone when I followed her..."

"How many?" I pressed.

"Three, maybe four?" Ezra said. He stopped, exasperated. "I caught them at the old barn house... Same place Pops died all them years back,"

"You went there *alone?*"

"I had to." He shrugged. "The women kept comin' and goin' from that barn for a week. And they wasn't Magdalenes. Not one of our witches is that pale, not even if they was knockin' on death's doorstep,"

"How did you do it?"

"This one came wanderin' out... I was covered by night, and asked a magician to cover me with Angel's Robe to make me invisible... The moment she got far enough away from that barn door, I snatched her."

"We need to tell Grannie... Big wigs from the Order and the Society is comin' tonight. I'll let everyone know. If witches are movin' the way we seen tonight, we need to step up our game. There's too much to lose."

Ezra gave me a firm nod of agreement, and we returned upstairs. As we approached the surface of the ground floor, booming voices and heavy chatter quickly circulated. Moving forms, returning from the memorial services in their Sunday bests.

"I'mma go run and change before Grannie throws a fit," Ezra said, holding out the blood stains on the fabric of his jeans overalls.

"That ain't a bad idea," I said.

I looked down at the blood on my hands smudged against my shirt from healing Ezra's wound. Grannie was obsessed with image and appearances, so there was no way in hell we could let her catch us dressed down and dirty like this in front of everyone she knew. As we shut the door behind us, two figures approached us.

"Wellll now…" The lively voice said. "What y'all gettin' up to down there?"

It was my twin cousins, Titus and Jonah, Nita's kids.

"Probably havin' a taste of them special collard *greens*," Jonah said to him. "What you got there, cousin?" Jonah reached his long arms over towards me.

"You always on the prowl," Titus said. "Ain't nobody got no weed."

He folded his arms. I finally overcame Jonah and shoved him off me.

"Well, I ain't say all that…"

Jonah playfully hit Titus across the chest, bouncing on his heels with excitement.

"You see? I told you. What you waitin' for then, cousin? Why don't you share some of that burnin' kush? I'm tryin' to talk to God too."

Their ruddy brown faces showed opposite expressions. Titus's eyes rolled from his raised eyebrow. Titus and Jonah were Nita's kids and were the only good thing about her daily visits. It made her presence just a little bit more bearable.

"Look, I'll smoke y'all out later," I said

"All jokes aside, cuz', you need our help?" Titus added.

Their dark grey eyes were wide open, alive, and ready for a fight. Titus and Jonah, I elected as my Sons of Thunder. Every living Christ must identify his Apostles, and failure to do so would not only bring great shame but create weakness. The purpose of the Sons of Thunder was to act as bodyguards for the living Christ.

"Ain't no trouble yet, not if we get our act together. Quick," I said

"You know I've been fixin' to flex some of these new moves on one of them demons. You just say the word." Titus said.

Jonah and Titus were two sides of the same coin. Jonah was the loudest out of the two, and most eccentric with his array of rings and button down shirt to reveal dangling necklaces with strange symbols. Titus was a no-nonsense type with a primed and neat style. Dress shirts, straight-legged pants, and shoes so clean you could eat off of them. They tried their hardest to be different from one another, as many twins do, only seeming to agree on the same medium-lock hairstyle that they both accused each other of stealing. Titus also had a thirst for blood that even made me blush at times. Together, though, they were exactly what I needed. They had a relentless taste for battle and laughed in the face of evil.

"Not yet. But trust me, you'll be the first to know," I said.

Not every magician was born with the tinge of the Summerland pact. The Might, the Gift, some called it. But it was a curse more than anything, and we all knew it. Fortunately, God is a God of mercy, and he allowed them to use their power to glorify Him. It was a mercy that was extended to the witches of this town, and they came to be called Magadelenes.

"And trust, y'all ain't gon' be waitin' around long neither."

Blood-born witches needed to know their place of subservience. It was the New Covenant, to use their own Curse of Eve to advance the newfound cause of the Order. Magicians were trained in the Sacred Arts, learning the proper way from the God of the Garden through the Prophets. They had no unearthly touch but instead made pacts with otherworldly beings and subdued inferior ones to absorb their abilities. It was the proper way.

Power was earned.

Never given.

"I'll hold you to it. But I don't wanna hear none of that 'I got this' bullshit. I promise you the witch that comes across us is gonna be sorry," Jonah said.

Despite a magician's skill, most of them were afraid to go head-on against a witch. Their powers which were so loosely granted to them, are instant. Because of that, judges from the Society were sent, or they weaved their magic from afar and out of sight. But Titus and Jonah weren't afraid of anything.

Their irreverence was exactly why I chose to make them my Sons and elevate them to Apostlehood so they could receive the Gift from the Holy Spirit and enhance their abilities. It was a pact only a chosen few could make, and it was an honor most coveted of all. No living Christ gathered up all 12 of his Apostles since his first lifetime, but with Titus and Jonah by my side, I had all I needed.

"Levi? Ezra? I know y'all hear me callin'!" Grannie's voice boomed. Her footsteps and the click of her cane drew closer from down the hall.

"Y'all go get changin'" Jonah said.

"I'll take care of this here."

Ezra and I sprinted down the hall going to the other side.

"Grannie! What you doin' walkin' all this way for?" Jonah's voice trailed off.

Ezra gave me one last look before going to his bedroom. "God has a plan..." Ezra said.

"Don't he?"

I looked back at him, clasping the knob of the door tensely.

"Always. Let's just hope it lines up with ours."

CHAPTER 12

Last Supper

God and the Devil were raging inside me. It was true, I played along with the church's rules because I had to. But deep down, there was a voice in my head telling me to break free from His control. Shaddai and I shared a conscience, one mind. I was the only thing able to sustain his essence to walk this earth, any other mortal body would deteriorate. I had a duty, but the witch was right. In my heart of hearts, I knew there was something beyond what was given. I felt like Eve in the Garden who wondered about a world beyond the one she was in. What if the power, status, and safety of being under his rule were all a distraction?

I clasped my head, frustrated. I hated these things, malicious and intrusive. I'd always felt two voices in my head, one telling me it was better to serve and the other saying it was better to reign. I fought the other voice inside me for too long, I didn't know how much longer I could do it. It was said that I once resisted the Devil's offerings of all the kingdoms in the world, but this time it seemed he was offering something else. To be the ruler of my own kingdom. To make my own choices and decisions. There was divinity in choice, and since the day I opened my eyes, I never had that.

The horrible secret I'd kept was envy. I hated the witches for answering to no one, for their absolute freedom to do as they pleased without fear of divine retribution or suffering an eternity in anguish.

Did I really love Shaddai, or was I afraid of him? Serving the God of the Garden wasn't just about faith, it was about loyalty to my family. I was terrified of the disasters he'd bring upon my house and everyone I cared for if I ever turned against him. But up to what point would I continue to live for others?

I faced myself in my bedroom mirror, starting to lose sense of who was looking back at me. Something in my blood was starting to change. For the first time in my life, I felt... like maybe I could be wrong?

A knock came at my door, snapping me out of the whirlpool of doubt I was being sucked into. Standing just outside the door was Titus, snacking on gizzards he'd snuck off the table without Grannie seeing.

"Grannie's waitin' to start," he said.

I huffed, following behind him.

Everyone who'd abused me in some way was there tonight. From the Society that trained my Pops, who, in turn, taught me the art of killing, to the Order members like Father Enoch who delighted in the taste of my flesh and the engorging on my blood on that "Holy Day". Rather directly or deliberately, every laughing eye and stuffed mouth sitting their asses on that chair either cannibalized my body or capitalized on my suffering. Demons in a heavenly place dining by candlelight with the blessing of God.

Bonnie and Rita came in through the door, and shouts of joy and greetings from everyone there clamored louder than the chatter at the dinner table. I looked for Amma possibly trailing in from behind, but she wasn't. I sighed.

Bonnie flashed her straight, white teeth at everyone, but wasted no time to make her way toward Ezra, who longingly stared up at the portrait of Pops.

"Aw, Ezra. Don't you worry. You know they never really leave us," Bonnie said.

She caressed his cheek.

"Yeah..." Ezra said.

A painful lump in my throat formed. I knew it as the tears I was choking back. I could deal with my own pain, but I hated seeing Ezra like this.

"Here, now, look what I've got for you." Bonnie lifted the covering of her basket, revealing bright yellow corn muffins. "I know today's your daddy's day and all, but... I know how much you love them. I just couldn't help myself." She smiled, doting.

"Poor baby," Rita interrupted. "Let's come get you a seat. Take your mind off."

I knew today was supposed to be about my Pops, but having a witch slip from my hands again just brought back all those feelings; helplessness and hopelessness. The desperation to do something despite all this power. Grannie never let me live it down, and neither did Nita. Though Nita never needed a reason to hate me; she did that like she breathed.

I thought when I made her two sons my Apostles, she'd warm up to me even just a little bit. It was like the satisfaction of making me miserable was payment enough. She was lecherous, vampiric; feasting on any light you have inside you until you're just as vacant and dark as she is on the inside. Her mouth was like an open grave, full of rot and foul things bubbling up from the hateful cesspool of where her heart should be. She always seemed less human to me and more a malefic force of nature woven of skin and bone.

Nita pursed her lips at me from across the table, ripping pieces from her biscuit and popping small bites into her mouth so as to not smudge her ruby lipstick. Father Enoch delicately patted his mouth with his handkerchief before turning towards Reverend James and murmuring something I was trying to hear but couldn't make out. Even his lips were hidden from view, and I couldn't read them. No one would think Reverend was responsible for hunting and killing more witches than the Bible had Psalms. Beneath his wide-set hooded eyes and round, welcoming face lay a skillful hunter and true wolf amongst the sheep.

Sheep can't protect sheep.

That's where he came in. It was a philosophy that I could get behind. The scriptures say that the Devil prowls the world like a lion, waiting for someone to devour. But if we're being honest? That sounds more like me than the bad guy. I'm the Lion of Judah walking this world again, waiting for the first pangs of hunger so I can seek out scarlet satisfaction. I couldn't rest until the evils of this world were purged away, and I know one lifetime isn't enough to do it. These weren't just killers; these were the Hands of God.

Sitting at a table of people who were no strangers to blood made me realize something:

God loved to kill. And so did I.

The way poets and artists yearned and pined for love is the way I did for the flow of blood. There was a certain rush of power that overcomes you when you take a life. I already know I'm God, but there's no other time I feel like him most than when I kill. As everyone around me laughed and reminisced in their fond memories of Pops, all I could do was think about the earliest memories I had of him, and they were those of death. Murderous things that horrified me as a boy, but as a man, I look back on in a twisted fondness.

Firm hands slammed against me on the back, shaking me playfully. Jonah's eyes were folded into small creases as his white teeth flashed before a peal of explosive laughter.

"Ain't that right?"

I looked across the table at Ezra, who stared back at me grimly. He quickly averted my gaze and went back to stirring his green beans around his mashed potatoes.

"Huh?" I said.

His voice broke the tight clasp I had around the handle of my knife. Titus and Jonah exchanged puzzled glances. I could see Grannie's scrutinizing glare strike me from where she sat. Her skeptical brow rose over the rim of her wine glass.

"*You better get it together,*" Jonah said, hushed.

"No, I was only sayin', how you was always the first one to check one of them, weak ass magicians that wanna get bold," Jonah announced, louder to the table.

Jonah was a charming guy, but delusional at worst, and this was definitely one of those moments. Everyone else was too lost in their conversations, but Grannie wasn't buying it. Jonah's act was up. And Judging by the twitch in her lip and the clenching of her fist, it was about to be a curtain call on all of us. The wooden legs of my chair slid back as I stood to my feet. Grannie sat back, eyeing me as if standing were the ultimate act of disrespect.

"'Scuse me y'all, I hate to interrupt a dinner like this…'" I said, tensely.

"Then don't," Nita sneered.

Grannie smirked, taking a sip from her wine. I thought I knew how to word myself, but all I could focus on was the portrait of Pops hanging on the wall, flanked with candles on either side and an altar full of his favorite foods, sharing a space with Grandaddy Theodore, Pop's father. He was a quiet man, and taught Pops everything he knew. He was brooding and terrifying in his own way. But not scarier than Granny. She put him six feet under the day he raised a hand to her. He died in his sleep later that night under mysterious circumstances.

But we all knew.

Everyone was savvy enough to know not to fuck with Grannie Tamar. Well, except for Grandaddy, of course. God rest his soul.

"Boy, if you ain't got nothin' to say, then I'd suggest takin' a seat," Grannie said wryly.

Grannie was the definition of *speaking softly and carrying a big stick.* And that didn't mean her cane. Nita rolled her eyes, her jaw slanted as she chewed on her food again.

"I do, ma'am," I began.

Grannie cocked her head to the side with a scowling and skeptical squint in her eye.

"But with all due respect, especially this bein' the day of our Pops leavin' this world and onto the next… what I'm gettin' ready to tell y'all… ain't the best of news,"

My heart could conduct a ceremony with the violent thrashing it made against my chest. All the memories of that night kept flooding back. Seeing firsthand how unforgivingly brutal the witch's magic can be. I was 13 and kneeling with my Pops's intestines laying unfurled from his chest like tendrils of a dead octopus. I averted the ogling stares from across the table.

Crawfish.

His altar was a decadent buffet of all his favorites. He loved that still steaming crawfish smothered in butter despite his high cholesterol. There was shrimp and grits, a ribeye steak with green beans, and sweet potato loaded with brown sugar, cinnamon, and glazed with honey. And that's not even getting into the deserts. It brought back fonder memories of Thanksgivings gathered around the table with Pops cracking jokes. I looked back at everyone still lingering, chattering now amongst themselves. Even my Apostles whispered and spoke in hushed tones, watching me carefully.

The fleeting moments of harmonic nostalgia were dissipating, like Pop's kindness, which, unfortunately, was the exception, not the norm. This moment seemed now a fitting ode to his memory. Pacing back and forth now as quickly as a breath I thought I saw his form, looming tall and disapproving from behind the gathered dinner guests.

Failure.

I could still hear this voice ringing in my ears. The dead eyes of his painting watched me back, not unlike they were in life; cold and unyielding. I knew that it couldn't have been his ghost, because when I learned to ascend to heaven, I saw his spirit delighting in the glory of God and the bliss of leaving behind the sorrows and troubles of the flesh. What I saw was a figment of the past, a lingering and terrorizing imprint of all the things about him I could never find it in me to forgive him for, and yet I allowed him to pass to heaven. This was a ghost of resentment, a wound that you always take to be a scar until you poke it and see it still bleeds. And these were the kinds of spirits you couldn't get rid of; for memories, there were no exorcisms.

"Ridiculous," Nita said, nudging Titus.

Grannie rubbed her forehead, frustrated.

"Sit down, Levi," Grannie said, flicking her wrist.

"Just always lookin' for attention…" Nita said again. "Ain't you tired?"

"Hush, girl," Grannie said, whipping her hand back and snapping her finger at Nita.

"There are witches here, amongst us," I said plainly.

The room boomed with contentious chatter and doubtful whispers. Ezra looked down regretfully at his plate.

"Alright y'all, be quiet and listen good. Me and Ezra caught another witch who we believe is from Summerland. Now, these ain't Magdalene's... these is true to sin Devil worshipin' hellspawn."

"Now—I'm gon' go ahead and stop you right there, brother. Even if witches from Summerland is comin' into our territory, we got God's power, and his strength made whole right here. We can handle this," Reverend James interjected.

I smiled pityingly. "Reverend, understand I say this with all the respect in the world—-but what y'all can handle is what the witches could do before, but you have no idea what they're capable of now."

"*Now?*" Reverend scoffed. "Boy, what kinda nonsense is this?"

"Ain't no nonsense. The witch Ezra captured was able to escape an iron gag and slipped it onto my brother all in the twinkle of an eye... without so much as a spell. And with that, she was carried by the wind—flyin'—dare I even say, and she disappeared in the shadows."

Reverend James flicked his wrist dismissively. Despite his denial, I could tell he was becoming increasingly frustrated.

"Flyin'—Boy, what? And removin' an iron gag? No witch has ever, they're made with metal consecrated by the Order."

"And yet, she did it," I said.

Every sound in the room was extinguished.

"Levi, "Enoch chimed in with a wilted voice, "I believe you."

Nita's skeptical look reflected everyone's unnerved expressions as they turned their focus from me to Enoch, who took the floor. Enoch cleared his throat and reluctantly stood to his feet.

"Levi came to me with a case he was investigating of possession. Only, the spirit that did so claimed to be *Ecstasis*," Enoch said.

Gasps of horror broke out; murmurs became fearful bursts of denial. Grannie slammed the bottom of her staff against the wood floor; the power shook the room, the frames hanging on the walls bouncing with vibration.

"That's enough," Grannie said.

The room quickly fell in line. Although Grannie was old, she was still the Witch Queen of Tophet, and moments like these reminded us all we'd better not forget it.

"Let the man speak and *act* like you got some goddamn sense. Who raised y'all?" Grannie scolded.

Even the grown men at the table became meek, Judge and magician alike. Men respected one thing, power. And there was no doubt Grannie wielded that with an iron fist. Thankfully, she was a Magdalene and was using her power properly and for our side, otherwise, I'm sure the Order and the judges wouldn't allow her to continue to pass on the matriarchy.

"As you was sayin', Father Enoch." Grannie lifted her hand, gesturing kindly.

"Thank you… Yes, now, I believe that the witches are plaguing this town with ancient and malefic forces they ain't got no business tamperin' with, but, as is their nature…"

"So what's all this mean?" The Reverend said.

"It means the rumors are true. On that night three years ago, the witches were able to return the power threefold and tap into the power of Roshana for themselves," I said

Reverend James's large, hooded eyes burst open in a mortified realization.

"Then the Devil was able to walk the mortal coil once again to grant them more power," Reverend said.

"And they were able to tear a rift in the boundary and allow a Primordial spirit to pass through," I said

"We have to stop this," Reverend said.

"If one Primordial can slip through the crack, then…"

"We ain't got much time before the damn breaks, and all hell breaks loose. The witches have come to sow chaos and destruction the likes of which Tophet has never seen," I said. "The one we captured said that there are many of them."

"But why come here?" Reverend said. "They know damn well this is Judgelands. For every witch, there are 12 judges waiting to hunt."

"Reverend, with the kind of things they're able to do at this point, if they're here it's because, knowin' those odds and what they can do now, they're willin' to take their chances."

"We'll take care of this," Enoch said, assuring.

"Everyone here just needs to return to their stations and be on the alert. They're shapeshifters, changin' forms like the moon and just as deceptive. Be weary, my brothers, I saw firsthand what powers the Devil has bestowed upon his disciples," I warned. "This ain't no shit like we've ever been used to."

Nita scoffed. "You expect us to put our faith and trust in *him?*" she said.

"He's the Son of God, Mama," Jonah defended. "Show some respect, what's the matter with you?"

"Son of God," She laughed raucously, "so powerful he couldn't even save his own daddy when it came down to it. Or his Mama from gettin' herself locked up in that nut house."

With a single sweep, I flipped the entire table onto the ground. The plates and glasses came smashing onto the floor in a terrible crash. I leaped over the shattered glass, and in one movement, I conjured a sword bursting with violent flames of holy, white-hot fire. Nita's scooted quickly into the corner of the room, where I followed hotly on her tracks as fervent as the fire that blazed about my sword.

"DON'T YOU EVER SPEAK ON MY MAMA!!" I roared.

Her eyes were alive with a fear I'd never seen before, and yet, a small grin formed across her face. This is exactly what she wanted.

"SIT. DOWN. LEVI." Grannie snapped.

"And what about you, huh? Where were you the night Pop's died? You let me and Ezra sit there with that body 'til the next mornin'."

Grannie's cane smashed into the ground, and I darted across the room with a relentless force that snatched me from my place and sent me slamming into the wall behind me. I fell onto my chest, dropping the sword that burst into a thousand embers on the ground before dissipating. I struggled to get to my feet.

"HOW DARE YOU!" Grannie screamed.

Everyone around us covered their mouths, aghast. No one had ever seen Grannie lose her temper this way before, I was sure she'd bring the entire roof down on all of us.

"HOW DARE BOTH OF Y'ALL! BRINGIN' VIOLENCE ON MY BOY'S SPECIAL DAY!"

The guests cowered against the walls, paralyzed with fear and rigidly watching Grannie as she turned in circles waving her cane and shaking with rage.

"NITA! You pick your bony ass up off the gatdamn floor and you clean this mess up,"

"B—But—-Mama!" Nita protested.

Grannie snapped her hand back, forming her hand into a beak. Her hand trembled as Nita's jaw slammed shut on her. Nita clawed at her neck, fighting to breathe.

"I ain't ask you to talk, I gave an order."

Grannie released her. Nita's head flew forward, gasping for air and feeling her neck.

"Now clean this shit up. Dinner's over," she said. "And congratulations to both of y'all. You ruined this special day."

Grannie turned to me. I knew I should've been six feet under with the look in her eyes right now as she lifted a trembling hand to point at me.

"You... You get out of my sight right now 'fore I make what Nita just said to you sound like a love sonnet," she threatened.

Titus and Jonah went to help Nita to her feet, who watched me with a hateful fire in her eyes. It was the first and only time I'd ever seen Grannie side against Nita, or at least retaliate against her in any kind of way. Maybe it was the sensitivity surrounding her son's death, but whatever the cause for it, I knew Nita never saw it coming. It was years of Nita's cruelty and harassment met with Grannie's complacent silence that assured me that no matter what Nita said to me, I'd be the one to pay for it.

But I was wrong.

Who's ever this happy to be wrong?

I picked myself up from the floor and headed out towards the door, pushing past the crowd of gathered dinner guests still stunned into silence. I dug through my jacket pocket for a cigarette and stumbled out towards the front door. The force of Grannie's magic felt like being hit by a truck going full throttle. No mercy.

The night air was still muggy, and mosquitos promptly tickled against my nose as I struggled to spark the cigarette, marching towards my car. I desperately inhaled the burning smoke as quickly as I could. The lightheaded rush sent the same familiar tingles down my fingertips. I leaned up against the car, staring up at the sky filled with thousands of twinkling eyes watching down on me. Looking up into the black sky always made me feel small, like everything I was angry about didn't matter. Only this time, it didn't work.

"Hey!" Jonah's voice called out.

From the glowing yellow opening of the door, I saw Jonah and Titus's figures fast approaching me. With all the ill feelings of Nita, I always forgot that those are her sons. I knew I'd crossed the line, but that's what she wanted. Nita lived to bring out my worst. And if her sons were here to fight me for that, then I had to be ready to stand my ground.

"The fuck was that?" Jonah said.

"For real, that was OD back there," Titus added.

"Look, y'all heard what she said. And on a day like this? I'm sorry, I know she's y'all's Mama but you know how this shit goes," I said. I took another drag from my cigarette. "It wasn't my most shinin' moment..."

"We get it. She ain't easy. Trust me, we know." Titus said. "But you can't be losin' your head like that, Lee. Especially in front of folks like the Society and the Order."

"I know, I know," I said.

I felt something vibrate against my thigh.

"What was that?" Jonah said, looking around him.

It was a loud, irregular vibration. I dug into my pocket and removed the same small, clear rectangular glass the Watcher agent gave me earlier. The glass now had a blinking, glowing eye that flashed a scarlet red.

"That's wild... what is that?" Jonah said, wondrously.

I held up the glass in front of us, and the blinking eye reduced itself to just a pupil and a winding map that led to the center like a map.

"That looks like some government shit right there," Titus said.

"Because it is," I said.

The Watchers were a clandestine branch of the government, an even more closed case than the FBI. These were the types of hands that organized and operated things like Area 51. It was the most mysterious and secret body of government, which only revealed itself in instances of threat to the planet.

And they were ready to meet with me.

CHAPTER 13

Watchers

Titus and Jonah moved together, forming Hidden Hands as they slammed the car door out of my grip.

I exhaled, digging through my pockets for another pack of cigarettes.

"This got to do with what went down in there?"

"You real funny, cousin," Jonah said.

"Mama ain't got nothin' to do with none of this." Titus scoffed. "You really think we was gon' let you go on down there alone?"

"This is government shit," I said, sucking the cigarette smoke back between my teeth.

"And what that got to do with anything? We blood, cousin. And more than that, *Apostles*. We swore to protect you." Jonah said.

"The same way we've done since the first time they nailed you to that cross. The same ways we was boiled in tar and ripped by lions and made into human candlesticks for you… we'd do it all again." Titus said, solemnly.

Realistically, I could've overpowered both of their magic in one clean sweep, even without transfiguring. But they were right, the beauty of the Apostlehood and becoming the Petram was reconnecting with your original disciples. It was a bond unlike any other, transcending time and ties of bone and blood. Even if I were to fight them off and get in my car, they would follow me, send for angels to locate me, and report back. There would be no way of evading them. We were all interwoven psychically, sharing thoughts at will, amplifying power by being together like iron sharpening iron.

"Alright... only because I know y'all won't stop. Get in," I said, relenting.

I sighed. They released the car from the grip of their magic and rushed inside, slamming the doors eagerly behind them. Jonah rubbed his hands together; his eyes were just two slits in his face from the goofy smile on his face.

"It's about to go down!" he said.

"Relax," I said. "I said y'all could go. I ain't say nothin' about goin' inside."

"What?" Jonah protested. "Titus? You hearin' this?"

Titus rolled his eyes, turning his face away.

"Oh, now. I saw that comin' from a mile away. He gave in way too easy."

I laughed.

"That's cool. Have your laugh. But if you don't come outta there in 20 minutes then, we comin' inside." Titus said.

"How about if I call for you?" I said.

I pulled out of the driveway and made way my way down the shadowy roads lying ahead. I initially had this moment planned out to clear my head, but instead, the entirety of the way was spent arguing about who was staying in the car and how long. Every scenario resulted in Titus and Jonah blasting the door down. I'd say it was my own fault for picking them, but that was a bone to pick with my first lifetime for choosing them and dooming me to 2,000 years of kindred incarnations with this pair.

We bounced on our seats against the bumpy road as my headlights shone into the darkness ahead. There was an abandoned warehouse with a single flickering light post. The fog was starting to set in, wrapping its misty arms around the space in a cold embrace. We trekked across the gravel that crushed and popped beneath our shoes. The white light from the post illumined only a small space. As we stood beneath the light, I could only make out the silhouettes of the buildings behind it.

"This is some really sketchy shit..." Jonah said under his breath, uneasy.

"I won't lie, now seein' this set up I'm glad I didn't come alone," I said.

I squinted, trying to peer into the shroud ahead of me as best I could when I saw embers forming. I jumped back.

"What!?" Titus shouted.

Jonah and Titus leaped back and stood in a fighting stance.

"You smell that?" Jonah said.

"Smoke?" I said.

From the darkness ahead, the embers continued to glow, growing closer, and with it bringing the pungent smell of smoke, and the even more familiar smell of cigarettes.

"Geez," A voice said.

A figure stepped into the darkness, snickering with amusement.

"You guys usually this jumpy when someone sparks a light?"

"It's you," I said, annoyed.

He held his arms out enthusiastically. It was the agent that gave me the invitation to meet.

"Ayyy. Can't forget a beautiful mug like this, can ya?" he asked.

"You know this fool?" Titus said.

"You think I'm foolin' now, wait 'til you catch me with a couple drinks in me," he said.

Titus and Jonah looked at each other, no doubt wondering if they'd be charged for hitting him.
"Sorry, y'all. This is...?"

"Rex," he said, extending his hand. "Like King."

"Man," Titus said, sucking his teeth.

"Yikes, tough crowd. I don't think your buddies like me too much, Mr. Christ."

I sighed, glowering.

"Look, let's just get on with this," I said

"Sooner the better. Unfortunately, the Wonder Twins over there are gonna have to stay behind. This meeting is confidential." Rex leaned in, his mouth now crooked and whispering. "Technically they shouldn't have come at all, but this can stay between us." He playfully nudged my shoulder with his elbow.

"Alright, y'all. Wait in the car. If anythin' goes wrong, you'll be the first to know."

Titus and Jonah were reluctant, but eventually, they dragged their feet back inside the car.

"Showtime, kid," Rex said.

He walked away from the light and speared straight into the darkness ahead. I could barely see the makeup of his shadowy form moving through the night now and towards one of the vacant buildings. The concrete was cracked, and rats as big as small dogs ran across my feet. The place we came to had no door, just a rotting frame leading into an even darker space within.

I followed Rex through, stepping onto pieces of broken glass and pale moonlight shining through a fragmented window.

"Not exactly the settin' I'd expect to meet someone like Hooper," I said.

Rex laughed. He gestured towards the wall.

"Hardly," he said. "You got the map I gave you?"

I dug through my jacket pocket and handed him the thin, square device. He took it from my hands and strolled back to place it squarely on the center of the wall. The glowing eye now had a glowing white pupil, blinking a glaring light.

"What's that?" I said.

"Just focus on the white light. Don't blink for, 3…2…1…."

A sharp ringing pierced my ears, and from the pupil burst a light so bright I was blinded. Everything around me was cloaked in a dazzling whiteness I couldn't see anything in front of me.

"Mother fucker!" I spat. I flailed my arms, trying to swing at Rex, but I couldn't see.

"Just relax," he said. "Let your eyes settle."

The bright white light began to dissipate as blurry images started to come through. Serene colors and a gentle wind swept across my ears. Suddenly I could smell fresh Jasmine, and I could see my feet planted firmly into emerald green grass across a clear blue sky. The light gave way to a romantic countryside view, complete with rolling hills and grass being bent backward by wisps of air.

"Welcome," Answered an unseen voice.

The air in front of me distorted, like reflective ripples of a pond forming the shape of a person. The formless entity extended its hand in greeting. I glanced back nervously at Rex, who only watched on coyly. I shook the hand of the translucent being, and color began to fill the clear spaces until clothes, and a full figure took form.

Belladonna Hooper.

For such a formidable name, she was quite a petite woman. She was lithe and statuesque with mousy and refined features. Her eyes were like honey, but large and protruding. It was an intimidating feature to an otherwise unassuming person. She had thick, black hair that fell in wild curls beneath her shoulders in a hairstyle that, much like her laced, white blouse, seemed from a period long forgotten.

"Pleasure to have finally met your acquaintance, Mr. Beaumont. I take it you arrived here with no trouble?" she said.

Her accent was strange, she reminded me of an old movie with something eerily reminiscent of a transatlantic accent. Coupled with Rex's also rather oddly dated vernacular and dress style, they appeared to be from another time all together. At first, I took Rex's Greaser look as aesthetic, but looking at his worn leather jacket, I wouldn't doubt that he'd owned it since then.

But that would be impossible.

Or... would it?

Neither Rex nor Hooper looked older than 35, and even that was pushing it. They both had this immortal quality to them that I couldn't shake. To say that Hooper's gaze was one that lived a thousand lives would be painfully inaccurate; it was a thousand years old. It was as though she never died.

"What is this place?" I said.

Hooper looked around, smiling vaguely. She shrugged, gesturing carelessly with the flick of her wrist.

"Here and there. Somewhere and nowhere all at once. Come, join me for a walk," Hooper said.

She took the lead and began to walk ahead of me as if my joining her would make no difference at all. By the time I looked back for Rex, he was gone. It was only the two of us, surrounded by rich plains and swaying trees.

"So, to what do I owe the honor?" I said. "Not every day one gets to meet Belladonna Hooper."

"Nor does one get to meet the Son of God. Well, granted, you may not remember me. It's been quite a while," she said.

I laughed. She stared back at me, not even the shadow of a crack of a smile on her face.

"That ain't possible…" I said. "Are you an angel?"

She chuckled now to herself, laying her hand delicately against her chest.

"Oh, no. Angels are quite terrifying creatures. I hope I never have to see one for myself," she said. "But we have watched humanity for some time now, as was our purpose of creation by the God of the Garden."

"If you're not human, and you're not an angel… What are you?"

"My nature isn't of importance, Mr. Beaumont. What is, however, is the destruction of the Great Divide. The Veil between worlds," she said.

"You mean the spirit that escaped?"

She nodded.

"That force is one of many that is beginning to slip through the crack that's been created…. It's one of several ancient, slumbering powers that have lied dormant until now. They are sentient… And we need your help to stop them,"

I kept thinking back to my encounter with the spirit of ecstasy. Even I was powerless to stop it. Nothing I did was able to drive it out, and it spoke with its own authority. I hung my head, shamefully.

"I don't know if I'm the right one to help you with all that... I had an encounter with one that possessed a man that murdered his entire family. I couldn't do anything to drive it out," I said

"Not alone, you can't," she said, unswayed. "When we were created, the mechanics of nature were revealed to us. But beings like this existed long before us, and the nature of the unseen to us is still unknown."

"What can I do?" I asked. "Not even tappin' into Transfiguration, was enough."

"If you don't act quickly, the spirit will continue to wreak havoc, and there will be others... Each more frightening than the last. And, if not them... then something far, far worse will follow before them..."

"Worse?" I laughed, incredulous. "What can be worse than that?"

She looked at me with a sense of discouragement. There was a somberness in her eyes now that I could tell shook her to the core. I didn't know what she was, but it was clear that she has lived long enough to see many things, and if this scared someone like her, then it was something worth considering.

"If the damn breaks and these powers are lost, they will ravish this earth and tear it apart until there is nothing that remains... But if *they* return... It will be the end of everything that we know. And the beginning of a new, horrible reality that the destruction from Primordials will seem like mercy."

"But... who are *they?*"

"My ancestors, the first of our race. The first inheritors of this earth. They were gods in this world, but they abused their power and wielded it in terrible ways, destroying the world around them. They cared for nothing more than power, and the Elohim sent the deluge and destroyed them. Those who survived... we were instructed to watch over humanity and to teach them what they needed to rebuild a world that was left desolate, and void," she said.

"You're... the Watchers from the Book of Enoch," I said "I knew it. They always said y'all was demons, but I knew there was somethin' more to it. There always is."

"What we are called is not important. Gather who you can, and work to figure out who has caused this and put a stop to them. And once you do, close the Great Divide before it's too late."

"You have my word... But answer me one thing," I said. She cocked her head curiously. "You said you knew me in my first incarnation,"

"Well, I wouldn't say *knew*... But I watched you, of course. We all did."

"What was I like?"

"More like you now than you know," she said.

My heart fluttered.

I knew it.

She turned around and walked a few feet ahead of me. The winds began to pick up around us, and her hair blew gracefully in the currents. She brushed one of her long winding curls from her face and gave me a look somewhere between pity and hope.

"We are friends to your kind, Mr. Beaumont. Earth, too, has become our home. Please, do what you must. Quickly."

The world around me began to twitch and lose color until it was hollow. The lights sputtered and flared from the image's projection until the entire system around me collapsed within itself in a glowing grid-like pattern, and the simulation finally shut itself off.

I stood alone in the dark, abandoned room I was in before. They left nothing behind, not even the square map on the wall. Heavy footsteps thumped from behind me.

"Damn, what was that?" Jonah said. "That was some Star Trek type of shit."

I felt like I was spiraling out of control inside. Ever since my encounter with that spirit, everything has slipped from my fingers. I went from the top of the food chain to the bottom of the fucking barrel. And I was losing it. The Witch Queen had the power to raise the dead, Primordial spirits that didn't obey me. I wasn't the best anymore, and it was becoming painfully obvious with each passing moment.

Gerald warned the Order about the power of Roshana returning. He was right all along. The witches had powers beyond anything I'd ever gone up against. I was becoming undone by the second.

Spiraling. Unraveling. But I couldn't let them see that I was slipping or that I was afraid deep down inside. Now more than ever was the time to put a brave face on. I'm a pro at fake it 'til you make it, but this would prove to be my most difficult finesse yet.

"Y'all go get the car up and runnin'. We're gonna go stop and see Craven."

"Craven?" Jonah said. "What for?"

I pushed past them.

"Let's ride," I said

"Hmph," Jonah grunted.

He bolted back towards the car. Titus lingered behind before stopping on the way out.

"You good?" he asked.

"Better than ever," I said

But he knew I was lying. The way his brow lifted and twisted the corner of his mouth.

"Alright," he said.

Titus walked out, leaving me standing in a cascade of moonlight by myself. Hooper said I was more like the first Christ than I thought. A man conflicted. But the Order always said that each Christ served diligently and without question. Why would they lie about that? I've seen all my lives I was allowed to throughout my years of study, but never found anyone like me. Not a single one who doubted, who entertained the idea of breaking away from the God of the Garden.

I could feel the pressure of Gethsemane again. My heart felt like an iron weight in my chest pounding at brittle bones inside, and I couldn't stop sweating. I felt like I could sweat blood. I was going to go to put an end to this, even if I had to shoot blind and go in with guns blazing. But I was still filled with an unshakeable dread. Hooper wanted me to stop these ancient forces from ripping the world apart, but my power alone proved incapable of subduing even *one*. If I wasn't at the top, then who was?

CHAPTER 14

Apostates

The sound of black ocean water crashing against the shores drowned out most of the noise of Titus and Jonah exchanging conspiracy theories about hidden branches of government. But all I could think about was what lay beneath the surface of the church history I so faithfully defended my entire life. I knew this institution was responsible for more bloodshed and suffering than any on the planet; it was a spiritual extension of the brutality of Rome. But still—there was a righteous cause I was fighting for.

At least I thought I was.

I wasn't sure what Belladonna and Rex were, but there was something that reared too close to the uncanny valley for the both of them. They were not quite human, although everything about them looked indistinguishable from myself. Even witches look like the average person, but their presence was a phenomenon that escaped me. In a single moment, she fabricated a reality for us to walk through that was indistinguishable from the world we lived in. All these years working alongside the Watcher Department, I'd never seen neither her nor Rex, but they were an enigma that I'd continue to think of. God was supposed to be all-knowing, but the more I tried to convince myself of my own title, the less I believed it.

I looked back at Jonah, arguing with a whimsical smile his conspiracies that even I could tell he didn't think had any merit. But it was more about his voice being heard in the end. Even if he was dead ass wrong. But I admired his tenacity and his willingness to speak his mind. Titus only listened with a dull stare, nodding and agreeing with Jonah so he would stop talking. They had no idea of what possibly lay ahead of them.

Their faith saved them before. But I was scared to say that could've been the very thing that damned them. I wasn't completely sure I'd be able to come out on top in the end. And what if I didn't want to? The part of my mind that stirred within the quiet hours with muses of doubt returned. Could the church be a lie because the God of the Garden was also a liar?

What if they live to watch me die? Death defeating its final enemy. The Prince of Life himself could die, and there, my followers would watch to see it happen. I'd rise again, maybe in their lifetimes or when their bones were reduced to dust, long after they'd taken their final rest. They looked back at me now, beaming with faithful smiles and ready to conquer and trample the Devil beneath their feet, while I reluctantly entertained thoughts of joining him. If Shaddai wasn't telling the truth, maybe the Man in Black would.

I smiled back earnestly, only hiding the inner evisceration that was happening inside. I didn't have the heart to tell them that I was afraid. That I wasn't sure if I was going to assure them of this victory. Or that I even wanted to fight against the witches at all anymore. I couldn't fight the creeping suspicion that I was being told only what I needed to know. If they had nothing to hide, then why was seeing my first lifetime forbidden?

"Where we goin'? I thought we was headed to Cravens," Jonah asked.

"See? Y'all don't listen," I snarked. "I said we was goin' to *meet up* with Craven."

"Where's he at then?" Titus said.

Their questioning gave room to a reverent silence as they saw the looming figure of the church towering over the rest of the town. The stained-glass windows glowed with an ethereal aura from the moon.

This seemed like a black and mild kind of situation. I dug into the pocket of my coat, and the sweetness of it wafted up toward me as I sparked my cigar.

"You can't walk in there with that," Jonah said.

I slammed the car door behind me.

"Yeah? And who gon' tell me somethin'?" I said.

Jonah laughed, landing friendly punches against my chest.

"You somethin' else," he said.

"What we out here for anyway? What's Craven know?"

Titus asked, stopping in place.

I looked back at him from the top of the church steps.

"Look, Craven and me got a complicated relationship. But at the end of the day, he knows his shit. And I ain't gonna try and take that from him neither."

"So just fuck and make up already. Ain't that what y'all always do?" Jonah jabbed.

Titus tripped up the steps as Jonah shoved him forward as a shield from me.

"What about Enoch?" Titus said, holding his hands up defensively.

"Enoch's got ears everywhere," I said. "I wouldn't be surprised if he knew about Hooper wantin' to meet with me before I did."

"Why would Hooper wanna meet you?" A familiarly condescending voice chimed. From the darkness, Craven emerged with a sardonic smile. His eyebrows curled, showing he was pleased with himself. "And Father Enoch don't need ears everywhere when you talk so damn loud," he added.

"Where you come out from?" I said.

"Boy, I tell you. All these years, and you still ain't aware of your surroundings. Or you forget the garden surrounds this place?"

"See now, I'm tryin' to remember, how it was you got elected Apostle again?" Jonah said cynically.

Craven sneered.

"Because if it wasn't for me, you would've found yourselves claspin' onto the cliffside of the furthest region of Hell when you attempted—

and *failed* at Crossing the Abyss on your own," Craven said, folding his arms.

From behind Craven, was a faint glowing ember and wisps of smoke. A woman was standing in the dark.

"Who's there?" Craven called out.

"I know who it is," I said.

I moved past Craven, Jonah quickly trailed at my side.

"How you know who that is?" he asked.

"Trust me," I said.

The woman stepped forward, revealing the familiar, wily face of Sister Agnes.

"Sister, you seem to live in this Garden," I said. "And in the dark? Things is startin' to seem... strange if you ask me."

She laughed.

"I like to be around nature, you know. One does get awfully tired of all them stone walls and stained glass... beautiful, but man-made. Nothin' beats the real thing, I like to say."

"Sorry... if I frightened you, darlin'. I'm Sister Agnes."

"Sister Agnes?" Craven said skeptically. "I never heard of no Sister Agnes."

"She's from Summerland..." I said. "Ain't that right?"

I looked back at her to see if she would sweat. She was an entertaining person to have cigarette conversations with, but that didn't lift the uncertainty that clouded her. But as badly as I wanted her to give even the slightest display of guilt, she was reposed.

"Yes, sir, indeed," she said. "I know in the church's eyes it's garnered a bit of a... reputation of sorts for the 'dark arts'. But I assure you, the Church maintained a good influence on many. Like the... Wardwell's for instance."

"You knew Gerald?" Craven pressed.

Her eye twitched.

"I did quite well actually... God rest his soul. He was a brilliant man, I was real fond of his theatre."

"What's a nun doin' at a cabaret?"

"Oh, Brother Levi... you and I both know we all have our vices," she said.

Agnes looked at Craven from head to cynically.

"Well, I'd been to the church in Summerland on more than one occasion, *Sister*. And I'm almost sure I don't remember you for nothin' in this world."

"You sure? I've seen you before, you're... Brother Craven. You traveled with Father Enoch many times. Oh! How he sang nothin' but songs of praise about you..."

Craven's eyes scanned her, then began to shift into a fog that now looked to be clouding his mind. He squinted as though trying to re-member a dream.

"Were... you there," he asked, questioning himself.

She chuckled.

"I've been noted for my unremarkable nature. I don't much blame you for not rememberin' me. But I do you, you strived to be the best... at all costs, I remember him sayin'. Wasn't sure if that was a good thing or a bad thing." Agnes said.

Craven's face hardened.

"Aspirin' to be the best ain't nothin' be ashamed of."

"I'm so sorry, darlin'. I ain't mean to offend," she said, gazing into his eyes with inklings of intention. "Don't shoot the messenger." She winked.

"Have you seen Father Enoch?" I asked.

"I'll take you to him," she said. "We was just havin' ourselves a chat out here before y'all came over. He's been pacin' his office all night. Came outside for some air."

"Why's that?" I said.

She smiled roguishly. "It seemed he was disturbed. Troubled very deeply."

"What about?"

"Only God knows... But throughout the years I've known him, he's never been one to scare easily."

Craven glanced back at me gravely.

What would scare Father Enoch?

We made our way through the candlelit hallways and the faint smell of frankincense from earlier Mass. The painted faces of ecstatic and tormented Saints looked down on us, their eyes following us. The magicians enchanted all the eyes of this place and were always watching everything happening within those halls.

The church was usually a place of secrets, but in this one there wasn't room for any. As events begin to unfold, a disturbance reverberated from the depths of me. Even with all these eyes watching, there still yet remained so many things hidden in the dark. Or have they just been plainly in front of me, and I never took the time to really look?

The halls were a cavern of darkness, lit with glowing embers of nearly extinguished candles. The faces of holy saints were deviously twisted by shadows, watching us wander the vacant hall. The sound of grinding stone echoed through the halls, as the statue of Saint Joseph turned his head to face us.

"Who goes there?" it said in a shallow, breathless voice that scratched my ears.

"Where's father Enoch?" I asked.

The statue gestured towards the top of the staircase, pointing towards the upstairs balcony.

"Y'all hang back, I'll come down and get you when I'm done."

Jonah and Titus nodded in agreement while Craven defiantly folded his arms.

"You come with me," I said to Sister Agnes.

She smiled coyly, laying her hand against her chest. We made our way up the twisting staircase. The eyes on the paintings followed us, and the heads of statues turned watching every movement. They whispered and murmured amongst themselves. Before we reached Enoch's office to knock on the door, golden light spewed into the darkened hallway, and the silhouette of Father Enoch stepped out into the shadows.

"Levi," he said, his eyebrows raised with suspicion. "What are you doin' here?"

"I need to talk to you,"

"It's nearly midnight," he said, blocking the door as I approached him.

"And you ain't sleepin'. Let's step inside the office for a minute."

Enoch reluctantly stepped aside, allowing me and Sister Agnes to pass into the room. The room was furnished with fine wooden furniture and flanked with paintings of Biblical scenes. The Assumption of Mary hung behind his desk nearly taking up the entire wall. An angelic lampshade of brass sat on top of his desk, casting a dull light onto an open Bible and other apocryphal texts that lay scattered about. He closed the door behind us and set out small cups, pouring out tea that rose with steam from within the shallow depths of the cups.

"Sister Agnes, I have to say, I wasn't expectin' you to show up at this hour. You should be in prayer."

"I think I've met my quota of recitin' the Rosary for the evenin' Father, and you know how much I enjoy my nightly walks through the garden."

"So you know her?" I said.

"Oh, yes. She was part of the convent in Summerland. Is there a reason you've brought her here?" he asked curiously.

"Mostly to confirm if you knew her or not. Craven didn't recognize her."

"Yes, well, Craven can't see many things from how high he holds his nose… But what is the meaning behind this?"

"What do you know about the Watchers?" I asked, sitting in the red velvet seat. Agnes stood beside me, locking her fingers over her stomach.

"Ancient texts speak of them… They were the first fleet of angels to arrive on earth and guard over humanity… Though I'm sure this isn't a conversation appropriate for Sister Agnes to listen in on."

"Somethin' tells me that she knows a lot more than any of the other nuns in the convent. I sense the power in her. She's a Magdalene, ain't she?" I asked rhetorically.

I glanced back at Agnes, who tossed her hands in the air, amused.

"Cat's out of the bag," she said to Enoch.

Father Enoch sat down, reclining in his chair and closing the Bible open before him.

"One of the few Sisters in Summerland, that is... I asked her to come here."

"Why?" I said.

"There are things that only women are privy to... like the secrets kept by other women. Agnes was our eyes and ears in Summerland... an informant. She was how we knew the plans of the witches and informed us. Without her, Gerald wouldn't have been able to act against them."

"Even though he failed," I said.

Enoch glared at me sternly.

"They could have succeeded sooner and done more damage hadn't she told us. The witches trusted her, she's among the Summerland bloodlines." Enoch said. "And fortunately, we'd won her to our side."

"Father, if I may?" she said. Enoch gestured for her to proceed, calmly turning to take a sip of his tea. "Hadn't we struck an unlikely kinship the other night in the garden, you wouldn't have known I was here. You wasn't supposed to."

"Why?" I said.

"For your protection," she said. "I was the first of my family to turn against the Old Ways. Had you known that you would've treated me with suspicion and not allowed me to help you."

"What help would I get from you?"

"The other witches... they don't know I've become a Magdalene. But I had to. What they're plottin' is goin' to tear apart the fabric of this reality."

"The Watchers have made contact with you?" Enoch said.

I nodded. He sank into his chair, deep in thought and worry plaguing his face.

"Then things must be worse than we thought... The Watchers do not interfere in mortal affairs; they only preside over them. But if they've made contact, then it must be that their fears are becoming actualized..."

"What fears are those?"

"The same I have… that the witches have become too powerful… They threaten to destroy all we know, Levi. When they awakened Roshana, they tapped into a power no flesh and blood beings should ever have been able to. It was a power that was locked away for a reason, to preserve the balance. Power's returned to them. *Threefold.*"

Enoch rubbed his forehead, sighing.

"This is why Shaddai has not relented his throne, He knew that should he vacate, the Horned God of the witches and their whore Goddess would ravish this planet with debauchery and sin not seen since the days of Sodom… We'd already known what they were plotting before you announced their plans at the dinner… We were only hoping we had more time."

CHAPTER 15

Night Woman

In this game of chess, I was the pawn.

"I'm sure this isn't the only secret you've kept," I said. "The leader of the Watchers told me somethin'.... Somethin' that got me thinkin'..."

"And what's that?"

"The first Nazarene, first of my name... Why am I not allowed to see my first life?"

Enoch shifted uncomfortably in his seat.

"Why would the church keep that secret for so long? What are y'all hidin'?"

Enoch let out a long sigh.

"Levi, you are asking frivolous questions. What does that matter? You have the scriptures. Do you really think that would change anything?"

"Fuck the scriptures. I didn't even write those," I said. "You got any idea what it's like to walk around not knowin' who you are?"

Enoch scoffed.

"Why have I never been allowed to access that Immortal Records?"

Agnes and Enoch exchanged uneasy glances.

"What is it you don't want me to know?" I pressed.

"Enoch, you were told all you needed to know."

"*Needed to know?*" I laughed mockingly. "You have subjected me, in every lifetime, to the cruelest tortures, humiliation, and killed me more times than I can count just so you can see me grow more powerful. Like some type of lab rat in a twisted cosmic experimentation."

"That's enough, Levi. You don't know what you're saying."

"Even as a kid… the other boys looked at me as lesser while they drew power on my very name and looked down on me like I was beneath them."

"It was for your own good, Levi. You must trust in God."

"Should I? The person I'm startin' to distrust is you. You and this church, its mission, its intentions… You want me to blindly go and fight in this war when I'm not even allowed to know who I really am."

"Enoch," Agnes interrupted. "He deserves to know."

Father Enoch raised his hand to silence her.

"Look at you… shamefully repeating the sins of Eve, wishing to know more than you were intended to."

I exploded from my seat; the chair flipped backward onto its side. Agnes jumped, covering her mouth fearfully. I wanted to rend Enoch's limbs from off him with my bare hands, and I knew I could.

"Levi," he said with a trembling voice. "I am on your side."

"No," I said. "You're on *their* side. The side that made it okay to use that book to torture, oppress, and enslave. And you're defendin' tooth and nail to preserve that legacy."

"You are out of *line*," Enoch said.

"And all you know how to do is stand in one." I scoffed, pityingly. "Look at you. Pathetic. Hidin' behind a role they gave you to feel important."

"Get out."

"Tell me the truth," I demanded.

He stared back at me defiantly.

"You know all you need to."

I reached over the table and snatched him by the nape of his collar, bringing his nose to mine. I stared deep into his eyes; I could see the white-hot flames in my eyes reflected back through his.

"Tell me right now."

"Shaddai forbids it," he said. "That... That is the truth. Even if I wanted to share with you, to do so would be going against the Crown of Heaven... and He, in turn, will revoke his power from you should you even attempt."

I threw him back against his seat. Agnes watched fearfully from the corner of the room. I heaved, covering my face, and trying to still my breathing.

"You know what makes the witches so powerful?" I said, finally breaking the tense silence. "They know who they are. And where they come from... How do you expect me to win against them when I don't even know myself?"

"His thoughts are not our own. And His ways are higher than ours. We can't understand the mind of Shaddai, only trust in Him."

"Shaddai and I share one mind. And yet, He's kept an entire lifetime from me. What else is He hidin' for the *greater good*." I grunted. "I don't have time for blind faith. I'll let you all blind men lead each other into a ditch. If you won't give me answers, then I will find them on my own."

He hung his head. "You'll damn us all," he said tearfully.

"We already are," I said. I looked at the door, and it slammed open. "I won't go quietly like a lamb to the slaughter. Not again."

I stormed out and flew down the stairs in a rage I haven't felt since my Pops died. I flew past Titus and Jonah.

"Party's over. I'm out."

"Wait!" Jonah shouted, following behind me. "How will we get back?"

"Y'all know the way home," I said over my shoulder.

"Where are you going?"

"Mind your business," I said.

I got into my car and sped away as quickly as I could. I must've sucked the cigarette down to the bud in one breath, exhaling smoke and my frustration through the open window. I've been fighting for a lie. The Devil revealed to his witches the truth, and everything my God has done was shroud me with falsehoods and deception disguised as sincerity. I thought I was a soldier in a holy war, fighting for a righteous cause to blot out the evils from this world. But what if we were the evil ones?

What if the God, whose altar I laid my life on, was built on lies? Could I be the false idol?

Long drives home usually gave people time to cool off. But all I did was simmer, brewing in my anger so badly I couldn't even hold the steering wheel straight. My hands were shaking, my whole body writhed the entire way there. I tried to maybe look at the scenery, but all Florida had to offer was flat lands and plain buildings with about as much excitement as a retirement home. Everything in this town was dead from the people to the land around me. Florida was a strange, deranged place, and this town was the microcosm of the greater insanity that was this state. It was sunny all year, and so, people committed their atrocities in broad daylight.

For me, this was a place filled with lost souls trying to maintain a deluded sense of self-importance while they all went broke trying to look rich. Unlike the transparent waters here, the people were murky and dark; everyone constantly trying to find out what they can get out of me. Hollywood was originally supposed to be here, you know. And likewise, it attracted the same types of people. Those with pipe dreams and heroine-headed hipsters looking for their next dose of aggrandizement. People said they came here for vacation, but they really came to die.

Grannie Tamar said in the old days, this town was the crowning jewel of the coast. But it was now just swamp water and rotting buildings that made the French Quarter smell like a perfume department at a shopping mall. I could never tell if it was the stench of the dirty water or the reeking of rotten hearts and ill intentions of everyone you came across. I'd compare the smell to burning flesh if there were anything left on the bones of these people or the town they lived in; all that was left were skeletal remains of something people wanted to believe were the remnants of something greater, like some lost civilization, only, there was nothing civil about it.

I drove past the theater Grannie used to take me to as a kid that was now a halfway house for wayward people that realized drugs weren't going to help them cope with the fact that they'd amount to nothing, it's more of a funeral house than a place of rehabilitation. When you're that dead inside there's no Lazarus effect, you're just ashes and dust. I'll never know what this was before, only what it is now for as long as I've remembered—a place for wanderers and vagabonds with shattered hopes and expectations, false realities people built in their heads when they moved here only to be killed still standing by a grim reality.

As I drove through the barrier that hid our house, the air around me rippled, revealing our home lit in the dark like a dull lantern. I got out of the car, only to catch Ezra outside puffing away his nerves on a joint that I could smell even before I could open the car door. He turned around, his eyes moving toward me with a hint of alleviation.

"There you are," he said.

I snatched the joint from his hand and took a hit, breathing in those fumes that waked the thoughts in me I tried to subdue the entire ride here.

"Where you been?"

"Handlin' some business," I said. "Where's Grannie?"

"She's on one of her walks, you know how it is," he said with a shrug.

Grannie liked to disappear in the middle of the night to go on evening strolls through the black prairies where she couldn't be found; I think she liked that most. I moved past Ezra towards the door.

"So that's it then," he asked. "No explanation?"

"I don't much feel like talkin' right now," I sighed. "I'll catch you in the A.M."

Ezra didn't fight me, he just squinted with a palpable aggravation as he took another drag from his joint.

The house was dark, the staircase was just barely visible beyond the shrouds that coated the inside. I tripped on my step trying to climb my way back into my room. Like Grannie, I didn't want to be seen right now, I just wanted to be and close my eyes so I could fade into nothing. I closed my bedroom door behind me, catching my reflection in the old mirror that sat on my dresser. Bibles and books I'd bought and kept telling myself I'd get to but never did because finding time to read was harder than finding time to breathe.

I stared at myself, brooding in the dark and mind racing with more questions than anyone had an answer to, or worse yet; they had the answers and refused to give them to me. They said God didn't speak during life trials because the teacher was always silent during the test, but at this point, I wondered if everything they taught me was even true. My hands shook as I clasped onto the dresser, and my breaths only became shallower until the rage boiled up from inside me. I thrashed the books off the table and smashed the mirror with my bare fist. Warm blood filled my fists as I looked back now at my fractured reflection.

That's what I was, fragments and pieces of all these lifetimes woven together into pottery made to be filled with lies and orders from people that I believed my whole life up until this point. They said we had free will, but every major decision had always been made for me. I was just a puppet on a marionette pulled by sadistic lunatics and fanatics that saw my existence as a means to fulfill their agendas.

I was going to be sick.

I lay down on my bed, staring up at the vaulted ceiling that was as high as the hopes I once had for my life. My head became a projection screen playing back the humiliation of not being able to subdue that spirit, and the last conversation I had with Father Enoch. I knew there was, but now more than ever, I wished there was no afterlife. I didn't want light and choirs of singing angels. I just wanted silence, darkness, and sleep in the dust to forget ever being. With eternal rest on the brain, my eyelids grew weary, and I took a long, deep breath. The night that filled the room consumed me, and my body sank slightly more into the mattress. Finally, the cousin of death fell over me.

I was hardly asleep for a few minutes before I felt something cold, slimy, and wet wrap around my shaft. A tried to sit up, but my body was locked in a terrifying catatonic state. I couldn't move anything except my eyes, not even my head was able to turn. Any move I made felt like trying to move while buried neck deep dirt, my own body was useless. My heart was pounding against my chest, no words could escape my lips. I tried to scream for help, to call on flights of angels but no sound escaped my lips. I was paralyzed.

My room grew darker by the second, and I could feel something on top of me, straddling me, and violating me sexually. I was stiff below my belt despite the absolute horror I was feeling, and I didn't understand what was happening to me. A screeching voice filled the room, wild and feral like a bobcat. The voice had traces of humanity, but any semblance of a person was overpowered by whatever dark entity controlled this being. I couldn't even lift my head to see what it was; I was absolutely at the mercy of this creature. I tried to lift my hands, and a dark shadow slapped my hands down and pinned them to the mattress. It had claws that sunk into my skin, slitting my wrists and letting my blood run into the bed and trickle back into my ears.

What was happening?

The creature screeched again; still, I couldn't make out any form except for the talons that clasped at my wrists and held me firmly in place. From beneath my chin, I started to see a form and felt the long, draping sensation of hair prickling against my exposed chest. I was breathless, desperate, and gasping for air when I started to feel myself getting closer to climax. The foul creature finally reared its head, lifting its eyes level with mine, and I gazed upon its dreadful face. It was like that of a woman, with pallid, clammy skin. Her hair hung long in front of her like wet, stringy curtains, and the snow-white, deathly appearance of her skin was contrasted by the bright scarlet blood that covered her body.

Her eyes were inhuman, gaping large golden eyes like an owl. When she smiled, her teeth were like serrated razors, dripping ice-cold blood onto my face. I was still rigidly paralyzed; all I could do was let the blood fall onto my face and purse my lips together and not get any in my mouth. She continued to straddle me, edging me closer and closer to releasing inside her. I tried to hold myself back, my mind racing faster than the wind to remember the words to fend her off. I knew now what she was.

Lilitu.

The Order warned us about spirits like these, the demonic offspring of the first bride of Adam. She was here for my seed to fertilize the hordes of hell that would be born from her. She shrieked again in a horrifying gasp of sadistic pleasure she took in me. She opened her mouth, and a long, slick serpentine tongue slid down from her lips and licked my face. Her snake-faced tongue hissed back at me, flicking a smaller forked tongue from its mouth as I peered into her beady eyes. Mammoth black wings sprouted from her back, stretching wide open and nearly touching the walls. With a single flap, the room filled with rigid winds, and I could feel myself about to give her what she came here for.

My mouth felt wired shut, but despite the resistance, I forced a crack in my mouth and drew breath. She reeked of blood and roses, a fragrant yet repulsive scent that filled my lungs.

I was getting closer.

"S—San——-" My words broke the night air.

She recoiled back, hissing and shrieking something infernal, and slashed across my chest with her talons, breaking open my skin. The scratch tore and burned like there was venom dripping from the ends of her nails. She pinned my hands back down and opened her mouth, dislodging her jaw. Half her face was consumed with the gape of her mouth like a snake with protruding fangs and teeth all around. So wide was the opening she could have swallowed my head whole. Her roar shook the room itself, knocking the photographs from the walls and rattling me down to the bone.

"*SENOY—-SANSENOY—-SEMANGELOF!!*" I screamed, breaking the force that held me down.

Surging, violent winds filled the room as it filled with light as bright as the sun, penetrating through her body. She bellowed and covered her face, flying off my body and slamming with a violent thud into the wall. I stood atop my bed, watching the light and destructive winds burn through her body like burning paper, until ash was left in her wake, floating in the wind like flurries of black snow.

The roaring winds came to a sudden halt, and the light that once filled the room diminished as quickly as it appeared, and I was left alone standing in the darkness again. I caught my breath, feeling the burn of the fresh claw marks that opened the flesh across my chest. They stung to the touch. Wincing, I stepped off the bed and stood in the darkness for a moment.

What the fuck just happened?

The Order said that Lilitu are extremely rare and only came when conjured or sent. Which means the witches must be sending them after me. I slammed the bedroom door open, screaming for Ezra and Grannie. My voice echoed throughout the hollow hallways until a creak split the sound of my voice.

"Yo, what's goin'— What happened to you?"

"Where's Grannie?" I said, dazed and huffing to catch my breath.

Ezra followed closely behind me, shouting for me as I ran for Grannie Tamar's bedroom. I pushed the door open, only to find a still vacant bedroom.

"Lee," Ezra said, stopping me.

"You're bleedin'… What the hell happened here?"

"I need to find Grannie, I need to tell her," I said desperately.

"Whoa, whoa. She ain't back yet, and you scarin' the shit outta me, man. What's goin' on?"

"Just stay here," I said.

I bolted away from Ezra and flew down the steps. He shouted for me, and tried to chase after me for a few steps, but he stopped midway. He cried out for me one last time, but I was nearly out the back door. I couldn't understand why the witches would send a Lilitu after me, especially when they usually took the seed of Adam's descendants. What would they possibly want with that?

The night air cooled the sweat that caked my face, and I felt the wet dew of the grass beneath my bare feet.

"Grannie! Grannie?" I shouted into the void.

The moon was hardly a sliver in the sky, not even a ring of silver on this eve of the New Moon. I couldn't see the hand in front of my face, or even a foot ahead of me. I looked back behind me, and the house was hardly a glow against the heavy drapery of night. Winds howled and crickets trilled around me, but no sign of Grannie. With only the twinkling light of the stars to guide my way, I ran further into the deep darkness that lay ahead. As I ran farther, I heard the distant sound of drumming and the faint sound of a human yipping and whooping.

I stopped, leaning closer toward the direction of the noise but saw only the endless vacuum ahead of me. The pounding beat of the drums became louder, and the voices shouted in a strange tongue I couldn't understand. If I didn't know any better, I would think that Grannie laid a glamour to conceal where she was when she went about on her walks, the same way that our house was hidden from mortal eyes.

There was only one way to find out.

CHAPTER 16

The Madonna

I took a long, deep breath and reached out ahead of me. I parted my hands as if opening a curtain, and to my bewilderment, there was a stilt house, standing alone in the distance across the Serpent's Swamp. I could see blazing torches surrounding the house. I gawked, still disbelieving what I was witnessing.

What was this?

I stepped through the veil, watching it close behind me again, obscuring our home from view, and made my way down towards the small barn. The drums were thunderous and the voices that were inside roared in a language that made my hairs stand on end. There was nothing around but trees and the murky swamp water.

Witchcraft.

I knew it in my bones as I planted my feet firmly on top of the water, careful not to disturb the gators that quietly lay in wait. I carefully walked across the swamp until I stood in the glow of fiery candlelight that spilled out from the crack of the door. I crept up onto the deck, careful not to be seen, and peered inside. There, cloaked behind a veil of illusion, was an unholy site of wickedness and sinful delights and rites.

The pounding of the drums came to a halt. I covered my mouth. The silence that filled that space was so potent I was scared even my breathing might alert them, but I couldn't look away. The people leading the ceremonies were all dressed in white, from head to toe, with their heads tightly wrapped with the snowy fabric. Even within the scarcely lit darkness, their clothes seemed to glow. I saw Grannie emerge from the darkness, holding within both arms two bundles of Wisteria, Foxglove, and Lily of the Valley. Grannie's face was solemn and bore a sternness that would rival stone. The drummers stepped away from their instruments and hung their heads in reverence as Grannie stood at the center. Nita stood behind her holding a silver dagger, glinting against the candlelight with a sharpness that could slice me from where I stood.

The Magdalenes had been lying to us all along. They only pretended to serve the Order and abandon their treacherous ways to preserve their legacy in secret. This was the witchcraft the bloodlines brought with them to Summerland; the virus of wickedness alive and well, thriving in the veins of their adherents; a deadly poison like the herbs Grannie carried in her hands. All this time, it was nothing but a charade, and the woman, as in the days of Eden, gave into her wicked nature and followed the path of the serpent. My cheeks ran sour and watery, and I felt the vomit induced by nerves rise to my throat. All this time, I'd been slaying witches only to have them beneath my roof as family.

I'd been stupefied by vexation, not realizing that around the ring of drums laid bodies of men, rotting and withering at the bone like flowers worn to stock. Their eyes were hollow, and their jaws hung open with frozen expressions of terrors they'd seen before they took their last breath. Grannie raised her hand, and the burning torches and candles reduced themselves to whispers of what they once were, embers now standing in the place of prodigious flames. Grannie looked over the crowd around her, teeming with witches that made up the church choir. With one deep breath, Grannie's voice now became like that of many waters, speaking in a language I'd never heard but terrified me to see that I understood.

The language was hissing, venomous, and reminiscent of the serpent. It felt ancient, like the tongue of devils and the hosts of hell.

"As it were since the days of Eden, and as it has been since the time of the Mother of God, here we have assembled in some secret place; and worshiped the Spirit of her, what Queen of all witcheries…" Grannie began. *"We who have feigned to learn all sorcery and have won its deepest secrets. To us, the true power has been passed on and preserved, and through us, she continues to live on…"*

My stomach churned inside, as from behind Grannie a figure emerged, carried over them in a great, white throne, and covered with a veil woven of lace as white as the lilies in Grannie's arms, contrasted against the ebony form beneath it.

And I knew now what I had the horror to witness.

"And from Mary to Tituba, who came to Summerland following her expulsion and taught the woman the mysteries of the other side… The Goddess has dwelt among her people, a midnight sun from whose power we have drawn on for countless generations…" Grannie continued.

The crowd hissed like snakes. Grannie raised her hand, and they ceased. The figure stepped down from the throne. Nita handed Grannie the knife, who held it high above her head now, brandishing it like a beacon for all her underworld to see. The light revealed strange engravings onto the face of the blade, and it glowed a feverish silver, like the moon moving amongst a bed of burning stars.

"And as blood and water begot the light of God, the Son of Man, so, too, will she be born again; replenished in her youth as the moon restores itself illumined."

They lifted the veil, revealing the radiant face of Amma. Her beauty was beyond the boundless heavens, with skin like the night, glowing with a luminance. She showed not a drop of fear within her deep-set, honey eyes. In her knotless braids were carefully woven seashells, countless in number. She smiled serenely, even as Nita and another woman held her in place by each arm. I clenched my fist, dreading the next moments that followed. I wasn't familiar with their ceremonies, but I knew something awful was to follow.

The ungodly hoard of witches that surrounded them began to hum a mournful dirge. A single, glistening tear rolled down Amma's smiling face as the crowd's voice reached upwards toward high heaven.

"I…" Grannie began in clear English now. "I… will greatly multiply your sorrow… and your conception…"

Amma gently tilted her neck back, proudly exposing her bare neck, muttering to herself with a delirious smile, fixing her gaze on the candles suspended in the air above her, twinkling delicately.

"And in pain… you shall bring forth children," Grannie said.

She slashed her throat.

I watched her eyes lull and her head bob forward, releasing now more fountains of blood onto the ground. Her body gave a final jerk, and the blood that flowed from her body ran dry. Tears ran down my face as I clasped the side of my head, trembling with a terror that rendered me powerless. Nita and the other women held her dangling body, cold and unyielding, with not an ounce of remorse in their actions. I wanted to stop them, but like the paralysis that overcame me tonight at the hand of the demon, my body had given out on me.

I covered my mouth to push the scream down. Grannie held the blade up above her head, then drove the dagger into the ground. She lifted her hands, exposing both her palms to the crowd. She moved now, standing behind Amma's lifeless body offered up in this dark rite. She hovered her open hands now over Amma's head.

"*And she shall be called… 'woman',*" Grannie said.

She forcefully took Amma's head between her hands, and both their heads flew back violently. Brutal and vicious winds blew back all who stood around them, roaring with an unearthly sound, as if all the sleeping spirits had awoken, screaming.

"I… will… thee…" Grannie yelled over the raging winds. "*The power!*"

Grannie flew back with a forceful thrust, caught by the other witches who stood behind her. A second, more rabid wave of gales and winds followed, and Amma slowly rose into the air. Her eyes were glowing ghostly white, and thunder boomed from overhead over a darkened sky. Amma held her arms out to her sides as she climbed into the air higher, and higher. She was glowing, dazzling, and luminous, glowing like a silver flame. She was like the blue-lidded daughter of sunset, the naked brilliance of the voluptuous night sky; Isis unveiled.

She came down, riding on the wind lower to the ground, still hovering with a careful steadiness. The tempered gusts became like gentle breezes, blowing now the garments of her clothing, moving and flowing on their own with a mightiness, like waves crashing against the shore. Her eyes were gleaming, her pupils unseen by the celestial light that poured from her eyes. Nita and the others helped Grannie to her feet.

Grannie looked worn and withered, looking now like a feeble old woman rather than the stern figure she once was. Her cheeks were sunken in, and her skin was heavy wrinkles. Age wore down onto her back, hunching her over as she raised a trembling hand to stand firmly on her cane. It was the life force of their Goddess that sustained Grannie, and now it was gone, living and pulsing through the heart and veins to her successor.

"Behold..." Grannie's trembling voice said. "The Black Madonna... QUEEN OF WITCHES!"

"HAIL!" The witches called back.

The entire ring of witches fell onto their faces in deep reverence, whispering, and murmuring. Nita took the bundle of Lilies and other malefic herbs and laid them down at Amma's feet. From around Amma's body, waves of power emanated, manifesting like a thick heat haze that encased her entire body. Amma stepped onto the blood that ran on the ground, walking into the ring made of dead men's bodies.

"*And man...*" Grannie's voice broke the silent adoration, "*who was formed from the dust of the ground... Received the breath of life... and became a living soul.*" She clasped onto her chest, leaning against Nita, who helped her maintain her balance.

Amma drew in a deep breath, ascending again into the air, and released one long, drawn-out exhalation that echoed throughout the barn, reverberating off the walls and shaking the ground beneath my feet. The ground quaked with a force that made it nearly impossible to stand again, but I hoisted myself up and propped against the outside of the door, keeping my eyes on the fearful sight.

The circle of dead men that lay in a ring around her feet began to tremble, jerking and spasming until one finally lifted his head. I choked.

Even to the witches, the God-given power of resurrection was bestowed upon them. Their lifeless bodies began to take on a vitality, sitting upright collectively and standing on their feet. They looked at their hands and felt their faces. There was a sentience to them. These weren't reanimated bodies, they had within them now the breath of *life*.

Amma gave a quick flick of her wrists, and the bodies moved according to her desire. Now the rigid corpses took the drums for themselves, and with decaying hands and rotting fingers, began to play an unhallowed tune.

The witches began to clap in line with the beat. They pounded faster and faster until they joined now in a frenzied dance, whipping around the circle in a feverish craze, cackling and howling like hounds.

Grannie's eyes locked with mine.

I gasped, jerking back and away from the door. I moved backward, stammering to myself trying to make sense of what I'd witnessed. The Old Ways were alive, and right beneath our noses the entire time. They'd never given up the Devil's ways, just dressed him up and gave him a new name: Jesus Christ. I was just a mask, a facade, and an elaborate rouse for them to charade around as, claiming to be workers of the light who truly only served the darkness within.

I turned around, running as fast as I could across the water and back toward the direction of the house. My soaking feet met the dry land, and I kept going. I didn't know where I was running, all I knew was that I needed to leave after Grannie saw me somewhere I had no business being.

"Goin' somewhere, Levi?"

I stopped, tripping along my feet and falling back onto my knees. I caught myself before my face met the ground. I looked up, meeting eyes once more with Grannie's piercing gaze.

"G—Grannie Tamar,"

Hot tears rolled down my cheeks as I sobbed. There is nothing more powerful than the feeling of betrayal; to know that all you have lived for was an illusion, and all the atrocities you committed for the cause of righteousness were just acts of evil masquerading as a holy calling. I'd killed so many witches, and my Pops before me, all while living in a den of vipers; servants of Satan wrapped in familial skin.

"E—Everyone… Everyone is lyin'…" I said, raspy. "What's even true anymore, Grannie?"

I felt her wrinkled and fragile hands, shaking with a dwindling vitality at the top of my head.

"Oh, baby," she said. "You've done what you was born to do, just like the rest of us… The thing about nature is that it's gon' do what it does. You can't become angry with the clouds for bringin' rain," she consoled.

I clasped her hand, sobbing uncontrollably.

"I came into this world ready to lay my life down for the many. For the truth. But now, I don't even know what that is… I—I can't trust anyone," I wept.

"Come now," Grannie said.

She helped me to my feet. I stood in front of her a hollow and shrunken version of the once proud lion that prowled this world looking for enemies to devour. Grannie laid her hand on my cheek, stroking gently with her thumb. It was the kindest she'd ever been to me.

"Man was made and given free will; the power to choose. No man's life is chosen for him. Even I have made choices that I ain't proud of… But I made them. In this life, we can't blame our actions on any man, or any god."

Grannie fixed her eyes on the open gashes across my russet chest. I flinched at her touch as she ran her hand now across my chest.

"Who'd done this to you?"

I shook my head, sniveling.

"Witches… They sent a Lilitu, and I don't know why. No one wants to give me answers. Just tell me what to do, Grannie. What to fight for! All the power they say I have is ain't nothin'. I'm just the face they use to operate behind, a mascot they can use to just… martyr over and *over* again."

She tutted, shaking her head. "Oh, baby… If I made that choice for you, I'd be no different from the Order or the Society. You must choose on your own. Freedom comes at a price. The price of bein' responsible for your own doin's. You understand me?"

"What if… What if I choose wrong, Grannie?"

"I swear," I said.

She smiled pityingly.

"Wrong or right are things only we can decide for ourselves. Every sinner is a saint in his own mind. What matters is that you have chosen, and in that lies the power."

I stared back at her, dumbfounded and eviscerated.

"Go," she said firmly. "And tell no one what you've seen here tonight. If not for me, then for Amma. You'll only endanger her life if you reveal our secret to the Order."

"I'm not long for this world anymore, Levi… Amma is our Queen now. Protect her as you've protected me all these years… She is… the future of this Coven. Never before in all my days have I seen power like that be poured into a Madonna… Not even me…" She groaned.

"I swear," I sniffled.

"I ain't long for this world no more, Levi… Amma is our Queen now. Protect her as you've protected me all these years… She is… the future of this Coven. Never before in all my days have I seen power like that be poured into a Madonna… Not even me…" She groaned.

"What do you mean?"

Grannie smiled at me, but her eyes swam with fear.

"The Witches in Georgia released a power that awakened with their Madonna those years ago… I saw it tonight in her…"

She hacked and coughed into her hand, frailty consuming her by the second.

"Even stronger than me?"

She smiled pityingly.

"Oh, bless your heart… She ain't who you gotta worry about… It's them Georgia Witches, and the spirits they've unleashed over this town."

"What can I do?" I plead.

"*Fight.*" She said. "Or have you forgotten who you are?"

The metallic taste of blood filled my mouth as I bit down on my lip.

"Go. Go!" She shouted.

With only a quick nod, I ran from her. I looked back, and in her place were only twisting shades of black. She faded into nothing. It came with such a swiftness that if I hadn't known any better, I would think I'd hallucinated the entire thing. Grannie wasn't usually that soft or kind, so her time in this world truly must've been in its last moments. Then it would only be Ezra and I left. The last of the Beaumonts.

I parted the veil that hid their ceremony, revealing again the house sitting on top of the hill, quietly glimmering. I ran towards the side of the house and opened the crimson doors of the cellar on the side of the house. The first few steps disappeared, swallowed by the darkness that led deep into the basement. I descended into the shadows, removing a torch from the cobblestone walls. With a quick breath, the torch burst into wild flames, steadying gradually as I made my way down the steps. The glow was just bright enough to light the next step ahead of me, but the darkness was too great for even its light.

I winced, the searing pain of the Lilitu's scratches burned to remind me they were there. I tried to still my trembling hand and passed it along the wound and muttered in Coptic. The open skin wove itself like an unseen spider was weaving the flesh between the gashes and closing them again. I felt now the raised lumps of keloid scars that remained behind. I choked on the relief, breathing in the dust through my nose with each heavy breath. I had to go on.

I reached the bottom, standing now again on the checkerboard marble floors. I could almost hear the screams of countless witches we'd brought into this basement to meet their end, not knowing I was killing people no different than my own Grannie and Amma. I raised my hand, feeling heat emanate from the core of my palm. The torches that lined the walls were alive with fiery light, illuminating the wide-open space with a ceiling as high as the noonday sun. I searched the room for the Tools of the Arte. No one was going to tell me the truth, only what was true to them. So I had to seek it out myself.

People were fallible, fallacious creatures with only their best interests at heart. I learned that now. Even I was not above living for my version of the truth, the kind that helped me sleep at night and justify every one of my actions. I lived for a version of events that helped me reason my way into torturing and killing countless women, whose sins were no different from the women I held in such high regard all my life. I couldn't rely on a man anymore for the truth, as he didn't know what that was.

No.

Grannie was right, we were created beings with free will, the power to choose good or evil; though we often chose the latter because it was always so much easier to do. But there existed beings that were incapable of telling a lie, and whose only existence hinged on the adoration and mindless obedience to their creator. The heavenly hosts themselves, messengers from the Great Architect formed to follow his every command. Angels.

If I was God on Earth, then they would obey me as it is in heaven.

CHAPTER 17

Queen of Hell

My Pops wasn't a magician, but he devoutly served them and was protected by their power— until he went rogue. It was never wise to attack a witch alone, they were wild and unpredictable like fire in a barn. Ezra went on to be inducted into that ancient Providence and became a Judge himself like my Pops. As the Christ, I was instructed in the ways of the Art Magical, in binding and subduing spirits. Many of the men in our family were magicians, since the time of our Exodus from Summerland. Fortunately, they weren't corrupted by the pact and given the Mark themselves.

Most magicians were made, there were very few born already with the Touch, as Granny called it. My great-great-Grandaddy built this basement as a place where judges could hold their rituals in private. And although the judges didn't have an enchanted history, it isn't one any less noble than that over their Adept Brothers. The history between the Providence and the Order goes back to days most ancient. Magicians were taught by the King of the Magi, that old, wise man Solomon himself, who conquered the Dukes of Hell and all of nature beneath his feet. But the Providence was formed after Elijah the Prophet defeated the whore sorceress, Jezebel, and overcame her pagan magic.

But the woman was insatiable. She wanted power for herself, something that was not given to her or intended for her to use. But that wicked Goddess was cunning and came to teach Eve things which to her were yet unknown. There she came to prove the corruptible nature of women, and so it has continued through the ages. The witches wanted more, repeating the arrogance of Eve to try and become like God; to know both good and evil. But Adam, for his disobedience, was punished. He would forever have Eve at his side, who would spawn more women that desired more than the place they were given.

All things in nature had order. And this was the way.

But witches refused the natural order; they sought to create their own.

This was the first thing one learned as a magician in the Order. Lucifer joined that dark, earthly Goddess, and together they sewed their discord, making a pact through Lilith to continue to birth the spirits of the Fallen into this world.

That's the truth about their power. It was the untold secret of the Summerland Pact. A continued abomination repeated from the beginning of time. It was Lilith who shared the fruit of her body with Eve and taught her the mysteries. And it was Eve who, in turn, would give bodies to the spawns of Lilith who were without form. They were the living spirits of Devils, working miracles. Demons in the flesh.

I stood at the altar, which was laid with the technicolor robe of Joseph, gleaming and shining against the candlelight. As I opened my arms, from the void shone a light behind me, wrapping around me and hanging down my arms shining like the stars, until it became a solid white cloth, and I donned the heavenly robe.

With the wave of my hand, fine sand emerged from the depths of a brass jar, which bore one of the many sacred names of Shaddai. The sand rose, undulating like a snake charmed by the magic that seemed to move it like a melody, and encircled me. I performed the Hidden Hands, and a great seal appeared beneath my feet, glowing a fervent bright gold before dissipating into solid markings on the ground.

I steadied my breaths and approached the altar, and with another wave of my hand, I conjured a golden box, unscripted with sacred writings and laid with precious jewels: jasper, sapphire, chalcedony, and emerald. Inside the box laid a single ring, wrapped in red velvet.

The ring of King Solomon.

With this ring, every power in heaven and earth must obey the commands of the wearer, and only the Christ incarnate was worthy enough to bare it without corrupting him. The mortal magician who bore this ring would be driven mad made drunk on the power of the ring. I slipped the ring over my finger and vibrating waves of power shot through my hands and down to my feet.

It was time.

I hovered my hands over my head and felt the prickling of the golden crown of thorns that now sat on my head. The box vanished, evanescent like the air. A glowing triangle formed around the altar, and from its depths a tall, obsidian mirror rose to the surface in the East, flanked with blazing candles that sat atop golden holders.

I held my arms out towards my sides, and with a deep and vibrating intonation, I spoke the incantation in ancient Aramaic.

"In the name of God, I command you to appear,"

Gusts of wind filled the room, and the surface of the mirror rippled like a pool of water. The ripples gleamed like silver, and the flames of the candles diminished to barely a flicker.

"I command you to appear... MI-CHA-EL..."

I chanted over and over until exhaustion. I felt the globs of sweat running down my face as I continued to repeat the words. The ripples in the mirror became like silver waves thrashing against the edges of its frame, vibrating until a violent roar came from within its depths, and silver-laced black bubbles began to rumble to the surface.

Shining, bright fingers emerged from the black precipice, followed by the entire arm, reaching out for the mortal coil. Before long, Michael's leg stepped out from the portal, emerging in full form and all of his glory. Angels were dazzling, brilliant like the sun, and without proper training can blind a man who is not prepared for their beauty. He shone like the day, nearly translucent, standing over 12 feet tall, and opening his mighty wings. The entire form of his body was engulfed in scarlet and violet flame, that moved like fire but did not devour or burn his form. He was a being made of pure flame and light, taking the shape of a man.

He had no distinguishable facial features, neither eye to see like ours or a mouth. But when he spoke, the sound was nearly deafening.

"*SON OF MAN! WHY HAVE YOU BIRTHED ME INTO THIS WORLD!*"

The ground shook beneath my feet at the sound of his voice.

"I've conjured you forth as you were created to serve me," I said. "As Shaddai has written, 'He shall command his angels concerning you,'"

Michael gave a leering til of his head; I could tell this struck a nerve. The truth was, the angelic hosts yielded to the commands of man and those who could call them, but they had little care for us or our race. To them, we were a lowly, inferior creation, unworthy of their servitude. It seemed that in their heart they joined Lucifer in his rebellion, but their loyalties remained in Shaddai—as that is how he designed them.

"*And what request have you from me, human creature?*"

"I am the Lord, I call you as I see fit,"

"*You are no more the Lord than a wave is a sea,*" Michael said. "*But in his likeness, you were made, and to a Prince, we honor as the King.*"

"I've called you forth to know the plot of the witches. They've conspired against me and sent for me a Lilitu to retrieve my seed! Why are they sending these after me?"

Michael stood there in silence. I could hear the scorching and whirring of the energy that enveloped his form.

"*The Queen of Heaven has come to earth,*" Michael said, a sense of peril in his voice. "*Lo, one whose power rivals even your own. She can command the heavenly armies and subjugate us to her will…*"

"The Madonna of Georgia?" I asked, my heart racing. "Is she the one sending this creature for me?"

Michael turned his face.

"Answer me!" I demanded, waving my fist.

"*Your arrogance will not save you in this fight, Son of Man. Though you are the Lord, the Lady exists, the Mistress of the Kingdom. She who holds the keys to the bottomless pit and stands at the Gates of Life Eternal…*

"A-Are you telling me this woman is stronger than *me*? Me! *I* am the Alpha and the Omega, the first and the last! There is no power greater than mine on earth,"

"Indeed, Son of Man, you are Shaddai on earth, but you were begotten. The one who comes is the Begetter, the Bringer of Life; that dread door that leads the souls through the domain of the Lords of the Outer Spaces…"

"Roshana…" I said, breathless. "Roshana is in Tophet?"

"Yes…" Michael said after a painful pause. *"She and the Brides of Night are with her."*

"Is she the one who's opened the rift? Have the witches opened the gate for the Primordials?" I asked, clenching my teeth.

This was madness. The Witch Queen was more powerful than I thought imaginable. Even Michael himself was afraid to speak against her; even more than that, he was *unable* to.

"Where is she?" I said. "Tell me the location of the Witch Queen."

Michael took a step back, hanging his head.

"Michael. As your Lord I *command* you. TELL ME WHERE SHE IS!"

"I cannot."

"Michael, I will cast you into that place prepared for the Devil and his angels! TELL ME WHERE SHE HIDES!"

Michael hunched over, gasping and heaving. A sound like thunder boomed over me, rattling the ceiling and shaking the walls around me. Michael's limbs shot out from beside him as if he were being restrained by invisible chains that bound him. He struggled and resisted, painful hacking burst from his lips and the light that formed his body was sucked through the black mirror, becoming like streaks of fiery light being pulled through the whirring vortex that became the mirror.

A shrill laugh filled the room, sending a cold chill down my neck. I jolted backward as the same black cat chasing the rooster on our farm scurried past my feet. I recognized its foreboding stare.

"MICHAEL!" I shouted.

Michael roared ferociously as his body was sucked back into the blackness of the mirror. The surface was now like a calm sea, slowly churning like being blown by gentle breezes. I shuddered, moving a trembling foot toward the mirror.

"Michael?" I said, speaking into the mirror.

A voice, icy and seductive filled the entire room, echoing and reverberating through my ears.

"You dare conjure my servants against me?" it said, laughing menacingly.

"Who are you?"

"I have been renowned by men, Artemis and Cerridwen; Diana, Bride, and Melusine. Heaven's mistress, Hell's dark Queen," The voice said, "I am Lady of Phantoms and Mother of Angels…"

It was the Witch Queen.

I'd never witnessed a power of this magnitude, to be able to force an angel of Michael's caliber against his will.

"What do you want? Why're you plaguin' this town?"

Her voice cackled, mockingly.

"Nothin' to me you would give willingly, so I had to take it, though you resisted. Your power is great, Son of God. No magician could fend off a Lilitu by his own power."

"My seed," I said to myself. "You want my seed. Why?"

"Now, now… Who is this that darkens my counsel with words without knowledge?"

"You blasphemous *bitch*," I spat. "How dare you cite the holy scriptures to me!"

"Why… I was there. I watched as the God of the Garden called out to Job from the storm," she said. "It was I who plead with him through the mouth of his comrades to curse your God."

"Whatever it is you want with my seed, you won't have it. I'll never let you take it from me to use for whatever evil you have planned."

She giggled. "Of course not, that's why you will give it to me. Willingly."

"Seems your Master's filled your head with more delusions than I thought."

"You will… If you want to see Amma alive, that is…"

I charged towards the mirror, spitting venomously, flying into a rage.

"YOU HURT HER AND I'LL DRAG YOU TO HELL MYSELF!"

"Oh... the heart. So deceitful above all things, so desperately wicked... who can know it?"

"Fuck you! You don't know what I feel!"

"Oh, come now, Levi. I'd never harm another Sister. Enough blood was shed because of us."

"Then what is it you want?"

"There's a storm brewin'... a titan of tragedy that will befall this town if you choose to do nothin'."

"I'll kill you and put an end to this little storm you desperately threaten me with."

"Oh, Levi... If only you knew..."

"Knew what?"

I felt soft, supple arms wrap around my chest. I whipped around, heaving and ready to slaughter her on sight, but there was nothing but growing darkness behind me.

"That the fate of all you love rests on your choice. You, who's been a puppet for those truly in power, too blind to see who's truly brought these evils into your world. You, who's so blinded by the light that he can't see he is the light itself... Spawned of desire..."

"You're lyin'," I said.

But was she? The most terrifying part about everything was that amidst all the lies and deceitfulness, deep down inside, I knew that she was telling the truth.

"You—You're a liar."

"The truth often sounds that way when you're livin' a lie. You know it, don't you, Levi? Deep, deep down inside... my words prick your heart with the sting of truth."

"The Devil is a lie," I said.

"Don't you want to know the truth about who you are? About your first life on this earth?"

Something inside me snapped.

"FACE ME!"

I circled, pacing and searching the void around me for any hint of her, until lurking in the shadows stood a hooded figure, with locks of gold hanging down over her chest. From my hand, a flaming sword erupted, blazing with all of the fury of Heaven, and I lunged towards her, taking a violent swing.

Nothing.

I whipped back around, using the light from the billowing flames to illuminate the space around me.

"You want to face me?" Her disembodied voice answered.

"YES! YES! COME OUT AND FACE ME!"

I brandished the sword wildly. I didn't care where I swung at this point, only in this blind rage I hoped to have struck her, but to no avail. She escaped me, like wind between my fingers she was out of grasp.

"When the moon has rounded its horns, seek me in the hidden shade, where the phantoms lay to rest beyond the Greenwood glade."

I repeated her words back to myself, trying to make sense of them. I was lost in her cryptic riddle when something rolled from out the black surface of the mirror, hitting my feet. I looked down, and there at my heels lay a supple apple as red as fresh blood. I reached down, holding it now to my eyes, looking back at the mirror.

"The choice is yours." Her voice said.

With a shrieking wind and a mischievous giggle, the remaining lights of the candles and the fire of my sword were swept away.

I saw firsthand the power of their triple-faced, exiled Goddess. She's been the shrieking owl, Lilith, in the wilderness. Or a pale white doe lurking in the darkness. And now, it seemed she acted through the Queen of Georgia.

There I stood in the darkness once more, the way that I came into this world, with my path chosen for me. And yet, I returned, it seemed to the womb, holding now a choice in my hand.

But was I ready to make it?

CHAPTER 18:

The Offering

Secrets corrode the soul. They're a bitter rot; the bloody, beating heart beneath the floorboards that torment you daily. The stench of their decay fills your body, wafting through the cavernous confounds of your chest, slowly feasting on your sanity, your mind. They're maggots, hungry for silence, and continue to dine on your being until there's nothing left inside of you. But the strange thing about secrets is that they're a pain we choose to inflict on ourselves. We feel our silence will buy us peace of mind, not realizing that we're giving that away the moment we seal our conscience behind our lips and bury the key deep within.

Secrets are a strange fruit, a bitter crop harvested by our fears and watered by the tears we wish to shed but harbor inside instead.

And the worst kind? The ones we keep from ourselves.

They hurt, even more, when they're kept from the people you're supposed to love and trust. All my life I've been fighting to maintain the secrets handed down from father to son, from the God of the Garden's lips to my ears. I've kept them all, every atrocity committed in his name and for the sake of protecting my family.

My family was different.

I laughed, choking on the venomous lies I continued to feed myself.

Grannie Tamar was filled to the brim with things untold, but even she wasn't free from the acid that slowly consumed her; that's why she hardly ever smiled. Who could? Keeping all those things inside yourself. Grannie said Mama was locked away because she was driven mad, but I secretly questioned if that was true. What if Mama was also one of them? Only for Grannie to continue practicing the very thing she condemned her for.

In secret.

How could she not hate herself? Or, maybe she did, and that too she kept to herself and used her power as a mask to hide behind. My sins were different, the things I kept to myself were about myself. I had to. Christ couldn't have any weaknesses; you see that's why the church for centuries tried to erase the man behind the god because who would worship a being with fears themselves?

I would say I chose this path, but I didn't. None of us do, really. All of our lives are predestined not by some Great Architect of the universe, but by the design of those around us who believe they know what's best. By those who project and impose their own wills and desires onto us.

Children are just the vicariously lived lives of their forefathers, ideas, and systems held together in place by the weight of expectation and the glue of tradition. Even my chosen disciples, I called them out—I told them that it was their destiny to serve me and the means to my ends, to glorify my purpose. And they believed it. But what if they hadn't? They'd be cast in the cold, outer darkness of failure; of rejection, of lost causes so far gone not even Saint Jude could lift their burdens.

So they agreed, like we all do, bending to the wishes of those who push us in the direction that they would if they were in our shoes, and down a path that they'd walk if they had our two feet.

We suffer for the sins of their fathers because they repeat their actions. The man whose anger destroyed his family passes that down to his son, and that boy grows into a heap of burning coal, cast into the fires of his own rage that are not just his own, but of those gone before him who also had their choices made for them. It was the curse of Helen, to have a face that launched a thousand ships, and yet— had she not been promised to a man who coveted her as a trophy by gods moving her across a chess board of life, would she have found herself at the heart of a war?

Her destiny was chosen for her.

As was mine.

Adam, who "chose" to sin against God did so in a plan designed and set up for him to fail. So was the choice really his? Or was he, like all those pitfall mortal men before him, just a ship in the ever-raging sea being swayed by the waves of a greater fate he couldn't comprehend? And as I reflected on the illusion of choice, I thought back to the decision I had to make presented by the Witch Queen.

If I chose to continue to believe a lie, was a life of charades the fate that was dealt to me? Did the God of the Garden already know which path I was going to take? And if He did, why hasn't he stricken me down yet?

It seemed that Fate, God, whatever you'd want to call it, held in its ineffable hands a set of cards, and no matter which we chose, it always seemed to know which route to send us down.

The illusion of choice.

Grannie said I had the power to choose, but I don't know if that's right anymore. Even the first Christ before me wept in the Garden, doubtful of the plans of his God in heaven, and begged for fate to skip him over, and that dreadful cup to pass from his lips. But they were tears shed in vain because much like me, the choice for him was already made.

His will, or that Heaven? I was faced with the same choice.

So which betrayal would bring me the most joy?

Snap, snap, snap!

"Hello, Lee? You there?" Jonah said.

He cocked his head back, reeling back in his seat. Craven drank from his coffee mug, staring at me intently. Craven knew me more than almost anybody, and I knew that he could tell I was lost in another world. Sometimes my mind was the only safe place for me to be, and my conscience the only thing I could talk to. The sights and smells of syrup, fried eggs, and the smoke of the grill lured me back to my senses, and the ratty, worn-down diner came back to my focus.

"What you brought us out here for?" Jonah said.

"Really, though. You called us out here to meet with you. Ezra said you had some type of crazy night yesterday after you left."

"Yeah, I won't lie, Lee. I've always thought you had nothin' goin' on up in that head of yours, but even this level of spacey is throwin' me off," Craven said.

I cleared my throat, looking down into the coffee that sat still in my cup, reflecting my own eyes, lost in mental darkness as black as its contents. I couldn't put anything into words, so I unbuttoned my shirt, showing the large, raised scars on my chest. They itched now.

"Shit..." Craven said, breathless.

Jonah and Titus's faces flushed pale.

"What the fuck went on? Why didn't you send for us?" Titus said.

I shook my head dismissively.

"It happened too fast. Y'all wouldn't have gotten there in time, anyway."

"What is that?" Craven said, reaching out to touch the wound.

I closed my shirt. "Lilitu..." I groaned. "The Witch Queen sent one for me."

"How do you know it was her?" Craven said, incredulous.

"Because I met her."

Jonah dropped his fork.

"You *met* the Witch Queen?!" he exclaimed.

"Shhh!" Craven hissed, waving his hands.

Jonah covered his mouth, embarrassed.

"Sorry—You *met* her?" he urged.

I clasped the cup between my hands, staring vaguely into the coffee.

"In a way... She interrupted my summonin'."

Craven waved his hands disbelievingly.

"Wait, wait, wait, run that back. You said she did *what* now?"

I shrugged, distraught and now shifting my focus to the window-panes shedding streaks of grey sunlight.

"I don't… I don't know, Cray. She just—pulled him right back into the mirror, like nothin'. Michael wouldn't even—couldn't—speak against her."

"She dismissed *Michael?*" Titus said, his face scrunching with horror.

"She's powerful… I've never seen nothin' like that before. It's like she's got even the angels under her feet and on lock."

"Which means we can't trust them," Craven said. "We can't involve them in anythin' we do, they might report back to her,"

"Or she'll make them," I said. "Y'all I… I don't know how I'm gonna go up against her."

"Lee, don't tell me you afraid of this witch bitch? You're the *Nazarene.*"

"And she's Queen," I said, clenching my fists. "The power of Roshana we thought was just a fable. Old witches' tales of some kind of superpower that could rival the power of Christ. And now we know it's true,"

"So then what's the play?" Jonah said.

"Yeah, what's the move then? Look, if we gotta take her out together then that's what we'll do! But you can't let a stunt like that scare you off, Lee. You forget who you are? All the great things you've done?" Titus said.

"If we're goin' to do this, we need to be smart, goin' in swingin' might not be the smartest move if she's got power like that," Craven reasoned.

"Well, whatever it is we've gotta act fast, it's only a matter of time before the witches allow another Primordial to pass through,"

He grunted, unsure.

"That's the thing… Agh," I rubbed my head, frustrated. "I don't even know if it's them. The last witch we captured said we're doin' their work for them… and the Witch Queen said these things threaten to rip the world apart…"

"Okay… So what you gettin' at?" Titus said.

"What I'm sayin' is… What if it ain't them? What if… it's one of our own? A magician?"

Craven scoffed.

"No one in the Order would be *that* fuckin goofy, come on." he retorted.

"See, I don't know, y'all… I don't think this is as clear-cut as we think it is… What if we've been goin' after the wrong ones?" I said.

Titus sat back, folding his arms.

"This don't sound like the Levi we know,"

"Yeah," Jonah agreed, "why would the Order release somethin' they ain't got no control over?"

"There's a lot I don't know… Which is why I'm goin' to meet her."

"Who?" Craven said, uneasy.

"The Witch Queen," I said.

"Levi… You… You goin' to reason with the Devil?"

"Oh, I ain't goin' to reason. I'm goin' to kill her," I said. "And I'll get what information I can before I end her."

"That's what I'm talkin' about right there," Jonah interjected. "Don't let her psyche you out. Remember that the Devil loves to imitate. This ain't nothin' but a copy of what the God of the Garden is capable of… And his only *son*,"

"Maybe I can talk with Amma, see what she knows about her…" Craven said. "If she's got even close to the power you're sayin' we can't go in on a suicide mission, either."

"What business you got with Amma?" I snarked.

Craven rolled his eyes.

"Get over yourself. You ain't Amma's only friend."

We bickered back and forth when Jonah gasped. His eyes widened, stuttering in a horrible panic as he rapidly patted Titus's shoulder.

"What?" I said.

Craven and Jonah's faces instantly froze over with terror, and they stood to their feet nearly gasping with fear.

"Lee…" Jonah stood up, raising a trembling hand and pointing behind me.

A woman screamed, and the restaurant descended into shrieks of horror and bewilderment. I turned around and fixed my eyes on the television that hung on the wall. There was a woman, standing on top of the roof of the local elementary school, shouting something I couldn't make out over the voice of the reporters frantically babbling into their microphones.

"They're gonna jump," Craven said.

"We'll never make it if we drive," Craven said, panicked.

"We won't need to,"

We nearly knocked the table over with the force we all stood with, rushing outside of the restaurant. We came towards the rat-infested back alley, facing the brick-and-mortar wall that formed the back. I stood in front of them, forming Hidden Hands until a circle began to form, and shining sunlight refracted in gold took shape.

"*Open the gate*," I said in ancient Hebrew.

"Get in," I said.

The gold ring burst a blinding white light, and now, within the confounds of the wall, opened a shining space with ghostly, disembodied voices emanating from within. They called it the Window. It was the way angels could pass into this world when not being conjured through a looking glass, and the way Lot and his family escaped so quickly from Sodom and Gomorrah.

The three of them rushed inside, and I followed behind them. There was a wild whirring, rushing sound like thrashing winds and a churning sea, mingled with voices that screamed and shouted in tongues long forgotten and dead. The world within this portal was like a kaleidoscope, fractured images of not one particular place convalescing into a single image as I began to focus on the scene of the crime. The distorted forms took the shape now of the skyline of the buildings, and the shapeless masses of the woman standing on the rooftop.

We emerged from another back wall, the whir of the portal behind us sending sparks of golden light cascading against the ground before it shut with a thunderous clap that shook the ground. The crowds of people gathered around the school; tears filled the faces of the helpless bystanders as they watched on as the teacher teetered closer to the edge. Reporters flocked towards the front of the school, whisking around the surface like bats cluttered in a cave, desperate to get the best shot of the scene.

We pushed past the crowd, I showed my badge as officers let me through until I reached the front of the crowd, gazing up at the silhouetted figures against the high noon sun. The frizzy-haired teacher held hands with a chain of students locked in arms together, standing at the top of the building edge.

"To heaven!" she shouted. "We're going to fly to heaven!" She gazed up to the sky with a deranged and vacant stare drawn across her face.

"DON'T!" I screamed, rushing forward. She stopped her ramblings and looked down her drooling chin at me.

"To you, O' Lord, do we fly," she said. "To be together with you."

She lifted her leg over the building, as the crowd around me gasped and yelped in desperation. She and the entire class of twelve stepped over the ledge of the building, and plummeted four stories toward the ground, and smashed into the open pavement.

It was like time had stood still, watching their tiny bodies hit the ground and caking the cement with their blood and guts. I knew I was running toward them, but I couldn't even feel my legs. Craven and the others followed closely behind me, shouting in disbelief as they approached the grisly scene. Craven covered his face, and Jonah hid his behind Titus's shoulder.

As I stood before them, helpless and shattered, I fell to my knees. I looked up to Heaven, tears running down my cheek towards the clouds and at God who looked down on this and allowed it to happen. This was his decision, he chose for their lives to come to this bitter, tragic end while I could only stand by and watch.

The parents gathered around me, weeping and mourning, tearing at their hair and screaming in a way that seemed to set their souls on fire with anguish.

A laugh.

I looked up, biting down on my lip. Blood ran down my chin as the world around me plunged into darkness, and the world around me slowed down until everything was still as stone.

"*Savior of the world, where is your salvation?*" A shrill, cold voice spoke.

I wiped the tears from my eyes, trying to speak but my voice was strained by regret so deep I could bury cities. I was blinded by own weeping; I couldn't see where the voice was coming from. The body of the teacher flinched and swayed along the ground as if a snake were inhabiting her skin.

As her body began to stand to its feet, it slunk backward, boneless and elastic, throwing its head forward where it slumped towards the ground, then back again until it gained enough balance to face me directly.

"What... What are you?" I said through a running nose and squinted eyes.

"*I am... the melody that swayed the nymphs and satyrs of old, I am the Curse of Ajax, and passion unrelenting without cause...*" it said.

Its voice was deep, and guttural. The head of the teacher was still dripping with blood, and the sockets of her skull were hollowed out and black with only her eyeballs hanging by the nerve endings attached still to the skull. Its body began to levitate, hovering gently over the ground.

"*Maniae...*" I said, wiping my eyes. "Madness."

It laughed. "*I consume those who know not that they are filled, I am seen only by those without my presence...*"

"What do you want with this world, spirit?" I demanded.

"*Not I, but we, Son of Man...*" replied.

"Why have you been sent here?"

"*We have come to reduce the world to how it began, to create once more what has been corrupted,*" it warned. "*For the earth to be void... and darkness once again to be upon the face of the deep...*"

"Tell the one who sends you that you will not win. I won't let you take this world!"

It opened its mouth, cackling louder and louder until its voice was indistinguishable from the roaring of the heavens as they bolted down streaks of lightning now. The trees around us bent backward, their roots seen from the ground as they were torn from the ground.

As it laughed its head conflated until it expanded like a balloon and stretched out wider and larger than its skull could contain.

I covered my face, screaming as its head now exploded into a rain of skull fragments, gelatinous brains, and warm mists of blood sprayed against my face. With the explosion of its head, the body collapsed to the ground. The light returned, and with it, the world resumed its motion.

"Levi!" Craven said, running to my side.

I was driven wild by the presence of madness, lost now in the craze that consumed me. I was surrounded by mutilated bodies, and the corpse of the teacher now who oozed more blood from the exposed, blown open headless neck. The faces of the children who weren't smashed onto the pavement faced me, laughing hysterically, plunging me deeper into terror with screams still unrelenting.

Craven stood beside me, clasping his head in desperation. Jonah and Titus backed away from the scene, just as powerless to help me as I was to stop this from happening. The sound of crunching bones and bellowing screams rang through my ears as a truck bulldozed through the crowd, crushing anyone misfortunate enough to be caught beneath the weight of its wheels and pinned others against a tree, severing their lower halves from themselves.

"Levi!" Craven shouted, tugging at my arm.

Jonah and Titus pulled me to my feet, still weighted down by the shock. Gunshots fired off, and a barrage of bullets slew countless people in the crowd. Chaos descended onto the crowd, the likes of which I'd never seen before; a ruthless frenzy of carnage and gore. The breath was knocked out of me as I was tackled by a large, burly man dripping warm globs of blood from a smile freshly slashed into the corners of his mouth from ear to ear. He laughed, maddened and depraved as he lowered the knife down onto my face. I clenched my teeth as I struggled to restrain him, the tip of the knife now met the point of my nose.

His jaw was knocked out of place by the force of Titus's kick to his face. The man toppled over with a groan that mutated into shrill laughter, as he searched for his gun amidst the discord of the crowd.

Jonah and Craven helped me to my feet again, pulling me away from the crowd and breaking into a sprint. I looked back over my shoulder, watching people yipping and laughing as they drowned one another in the fountain that stood in front of the school. The crystal waters now ran murky, tinged with blood.

I watched the news reporters' heads being bashed into the ground beneath the weight of their cameras, held by their operators, who were lost in a euphoric and sadistic pleasure that consumed them. We rushed back towards the back alley, and Craven frantically signed the Hidden Hands to open another Window. The distorted coos and echoes that permeated from the portal were symphonic compared to the hellish landscape and caterwauling we were leaving behind. Craven shoved me first through the portal, Jonah followed behind with Titus entering backward and shutting the rift as he entered through.

Evil had descended on the town of Tophet in a plague of violence that claimed the lives of countless people. If innocent lives were brutally taken as part of the grand design, then what were the plans awaiting me?

Maybe there was no choice after all.

Mother Of God

We wove through traffic as carefully as we could back towards the house. Cars smashed into each other, and bodies loitered the freeway like discarded wrappers, bruised and bloodied to a pulp, and freshly cracked open skulls exposing brains through windshields. Car alarms blared in every direction, and thick clouds of smoke from the engines wafted through the air nearly blinding the roads ahead. The sound of distant screaming and chaotic shrieking filled the air, and the hands of death moved through the streets like the delicate hands of a surgeon; cutting and removing the departed souls from their discarded husks.

We drove past the barrier that hid the house and barreled our way down toward it as fast as we could. Ezra must've heard the car grinding against the dirt because he stood outside the door, waiting for us to come in. He had a panicked expression about him, and he waved his arms for us to join him inside.

"Where's Grannie? Is she safe?" I said, charging towards him.

We entered the house to find Grannie sitting in the den, watching the horrors unfold on television.

"Grannie," I said, relieved.

She turned to face me, a blasé expression on her face as she gestured towards the television. I could feel my lip quivering, and as much as I tried to hold in my grievances, I fell to her feet and sobbed.

"I couldn't—I couldn't stop them," I cried. "All those kids…"

"What is all this?" she asked, stoically.

"I—I don't know. Another Primordial entered the world." I sniffled.

She grunted, continuing to knit. She was strangely calm about all of this, but then again, Grannie always wore a face of stone. The only time I'd ever seen her show even an ounce of fear was the day that Pops was killed, aside from rage, that was the only emotion I'd ever seen in her. A calloused, mocking laugh came from around the corner.

Nita emerged, stripping down the skin from an orange and popping the fruit into her mouth.

"Now, let me take a guess… Oh, you wasn't able to stop that one, neither?" she said. Grannie grumbled; she rolled her eyes and looked away from us.

"Go to hell." I said, sniveling.

"What kind of Savior of the world can't save anyone? Not the world… his daddy, his Mama, them children that met such a cruel, cruel end," A wicked smirk curled across her face. "I know the Lord don't make mistakes, but I'm beginnin' to think there's truly a first time for everything."

"Alright, Mama, this ain't the time," Jonah said.

"You shut yo' mouth boy, this don't got nothin' to do with you," she said.

I gnawed on my tongue, digging my nails into my palms. I couldn't let her provoke me, it was like fresh oil to a flame for Nita.

"You're right," I said, calmly. "I couldn't save your husband, either. His heart just gave out at the thought of spendin' another day havin' to wake up next to you,"

Nita slammed the orange onto the ground and charged toward me. "Boy, you—!"

Grannie held out her hand, holding Nita in place with her magic.

"That's enough outta you, Nita, why don't you go on and take your bony ass upstairs. Always stickin' your nose where it don't belong."

Grannie released Nita, who glared at her with knives in her eyes.

"I may have passed on the Power, but I've still got plenty of juice left in me to mop the floor with you. Now, *get*," Grannie said, pointing her knitting needle.

I smiled at Nita, who stomped away now begrudgingly.

"So," Grannie said. "What you gon' do to fix all this mess? These people will rip the town apart before long, so whatever you've got planned, you best do it now,"

"To confront the Witch Queen,"

Grannie laughed heartily, keeping her eyes focused on the pattern she was knitting.

"Oh, yeah? And how you gon' do that?" she said.

"She came to me. And told me when and where to meet her," I said.

Grannie laid down her needles. I couldn't tell if it was fear or disbelief in her eyes, but something inside her stirred.

"The Queen of Georgia?" she said.

I nodded.

"It's true, Grannie. She's become Roshana," I said.

She stared at me for a few moments before raising her brows and returning to knit.

"You know, they say that power rivals that of the Petram, Christ's own power."

I looked down at my feet, painfully aware.

"I know... I've seen it myself. But we have a plan to stop her,"

"So you think she's the one conjurin' up all this madness on the town? *Hmph*, wouldn't be the first time one of them Summerland witches brought terror to this place..."

Craven and Titus looked back at me, quietly urging me for an answer.

"I don't know if she is. She says she ain't, but we both know the Devil is a lie... But we have a plan," I said.

"Oh?" she said, bored. "And what plan is that?"

"I'm gonna kill her. At least, not before she tells me what I need to know."

"You'd be legendary," Grannie said. "But you better act quickly. If another Primordial passes through that veil... there won't be a town left, or a world soon after, for that matter."

"I was born to do this," I said. "Everythin' in my life has led to this moment. You said the other night I had to make a choice... This is mine."

"Oh, baby..." Grannie said, dotingly. "We'll all know when you've made your decision... The whole world will... Let's just hope it's the right one."

There was foreboding disdain in her words like she never really had any faith in me. I looked back at Craven, who gently put his hand on my shoulder. Before I turned to go, I caught the eye of Nita peering from behind the corner. I knew she was listening to everything. And seeing her there made me think twice about what I had to do. A part of me wished saving the world and protecting my family didn't include the likes of Nita. But unfortunately, among the many choices we have in this world, family isn't one of them. She truly was the thorn in my flesh, the Devil's agent used to torment me for as long as I could remember. I liked to think she was here to teach me a lesson, maybe to keep me humble.

I brushed past her, locking myself in the bathroom. I wanted to scrub my mind raw, remembering those kids meeting such a gruesome end, and I practically stood by and let it happen. Where was Shaddai with an answer? How could *He* allow this? I slammed my fists against the walls, pounding until the ceiling shook and tiny debris fell on my head from the crack that formed in the ceiling. My face was hot and wet, slick with tears that couldn't stop falling.

They were innocent.

"Oh, my child..."

I gasped, standing alert at the shallow voice of Shaddai as he spoke. I slid down with my back against the wall, still sniveling and wiping my tears.

"They did nothing wrong," I said

"There is none born without blemish."

"They were just *kids,*" I snarled, slamming my head against the wall, defeated. I wanted to disappear.

"They were my creation. I do with them as I please."

I slowly stood to my feet, backing now against the bathroom door, all the words sucked out of me. My blood ran cold, and my heart felt like it stopped beating altogether. We were just toys to him.

"You know it is I who causes rain to fall on both the unrighteous and innocent alike... Is it not I who sends both prosperity and calamity," he said.

"Stop." I clasped my head, pleading.

"I form the light and create darkness. I, the true god of this world, do these things."

"STOP! STOP IT! STOP IT!!" I roared, shaking in my own skin and clawing at my face. My back pushed against the door, and I fell through and slammed against the wall of the hallway in front of me. My breaths were shaking, and the bathroom light flickered for a moment until it died, and darkness consumed the space. Hollow breaths caught up with me as I stared ahead.

"Levi?" he called out, breaking the silence.

"Do you love me?"

I felt like I swallowed my tongue. I backed away from the doorway, trembling down to my toes. I turned from him, rushing down the hallway, desperate for fresh air.

"Levi..." He called out one final time, a dreadful threat in his voice.

But I didn't care. I had to get away from him. But where in this world or universe could I hide from him? I don't think I loved Him. But now the fear of admitting that, turning against him, was crippling. I rushed past the kitchen, finding Titus and Jonah waiting for me.

"Levi? Hey!" Jonah called out. Titus followed behind him. But I ignored them. I'd damned them again. Just like I did in my first life. I couldn't shake the horrible feeling that I'd been wrong all along. This was a god, but I didn't believe he was who we thought he was. And I feared our Pact with him would cost us our lives. How could I fight against a being that could move heaven and earth?

He seemed to be a kind of egregor, a spirit spawned from the need for hatred and bloodthirsty vengeance. Shaddai was a dark god. Forged in the void of compassion, no different than myself, existing solely to destroy. He devoured souls. The prayers of those too terrified to disobey him sustained his existence; he was a vampiric entity that fed on fear. My original disciples went out and deceived the whole world in his name, but only because they themselves were fooled. And I was his face here on earth. To look at me and know who I was, was to be reminded of one's own gross imperfections. I served as a constant reminder of one's fallen nature.

My face throughout the centuries never changing, but always bringing change. My image always striking fear and horrified submission into those who willingly obeyed. It was in my name that death and suffering truly entered the world. I often wondered how the God of the Garden could be good this world was so evil and violent. I thought it was because mankind was responsible for listening to the wiles of the Devil. But little did I know his words were like scattered voices in the wind. Warnings. Crying, and begging us not to fall, victim, the way he did, to a tyrant. I finally realized the answer to my own question.

Why does the God of the Garden allow evil to exist in this world? It wasn't because of free will or a war for souls.

It was because he liked it.

It was that simple.

He was death. The Pale Rider.

And Hell followed behind him.

I must've spent the entire rest of the day gazing outside my window, waiting for daylight to yield to the blackness of night. I was lost in the swamp of my thoughts for so long that the full moon came peeking over the horizon before I knew it, and the time I'd been waiting for had finally come. Titus, Craven, and Jonah were already waiting at the graveyard for me to get there. The plan was to ambush her, the more of us there the better our chances.

I never thought I'd be put in a position where I had to rely on my disciples to help me defeat anyone, much less the Witch Queen. The Order had long spoken about how to fight witches. Their offense wasn't as strong as their defense. Witches worked best at the art of evasion, so one had to be as quick as lightning and strike with deadly force at the moment of opportunity.

Though I never knew my first lifetime, I knew that I was stronger as my lives carried onwards. Each Christ was made to be killed—martyred in an endless cycle of deaths that mirrored that of the Saints that died for him, and in doing so, he would absorb the power of what killed them, building immunity. I'd been killed so many times I lost count.

No matter how many times I'd been killed, I never got used to the agony that followed right before taking my last breath. And though obtaining dominion of what killed me came with a strange glow of pride, it never made up for the brutal moments I was subjected to just to attain the vaguest semblance of victory.

The last enemy to be defeated is death. Or so the scriptures say. But death wasn't an enemy, it was more like an old friend.

Nita watched me from the frame of her door as I left my room and headed down the hallway.

"Lee," Ezra stopped me. He had Pops's copper-headed axe in hand, clutching tightly to it. "You sure you don't want me to go out there with you?"

I patted him on the shoulder with a weak grin.

"This ain't the type of battle for you. And not against someone like her," I said.

His shoulders that stood at attention slumped, and his determination melted into uncertainty.

"Be careful out there, Lee,"

I looked back at Nita, who glared at me still. I could see the hopes for my failure written in her smug expression. She just wanted another reason to say *I told you so.*

"I got this, don't worry," I assured him. But honestly, I wasn't too sure myself. Although I didn't think he believed me either, but there was nothing that could be done at this moment. As I made my way out the door, my heart beat faster, striking me with flashes of anxiousness like lightning across the sky. I wiped the sweat that started to form in my brow and moved now through the night and headed towards the cemetery.

The town cemetery laid to rest all of the original settlers of the Tophet colony, including those that came from the original Summerland Pact. They had the largest grave markers, with the crowning jewel being the mausoleum of Tituba, the scapegoat of Salem's hysteria. I could see the tall marble pillars in the distance, almost glowing white beneath the silver gleam of the full moon that now illuminated the sky. I approached the cemetery now, standing in front of the disheveled gates that clasped to their hinges only a breath away from collapse. The cool winds brushed against the rusted bars, causing creeks and groans to echo throughout.

The tombstones looked like rows of decaying teeth in the mouth of a ground filled with damp soil. Their headstones were in rows eroded by time and cracked down the middle, sticking out unevenly and resting crookedly. I could see shadows moving in the distance, who I knew was Craven and the others lying in wait for the right moment to strike. Standing on a small hill was the mausoleum of Tituba, with pillars that stood firmly. The left pillar was made of shimmering onyx and the other of sleek white marble. Wavering in the wind, covering the door that led to the inner chamber hung a drapery, patterned with pomegranates, and a triangular roof that bore one word in Greek:

THEOTOKOS

Mother of God.

Tituba was the Madonna of the Florida bloodline, and the first of her kind to pass the power here, where it continued onwards in an unbroken lineage dating back to time immemorial. It was a strange feeling, going up against the Madonna. The earliest we could trace her was Mary being the very first of her kind, the one who begot the first Christ into this world. It was like the God of the Garden, through me, had driven mother against her own son, a sacred bond that should never be broken. But here I was, ready to end the life of the one who first brought my spirit into this world.

But it was a dance as old as the skies, older than the stars in heaven. The disdain for women stretches back to before the first created things. The story was lost to us, how Shaddai supposedly created mankind once before, with the help of an ancient power, the Mistress of Magic, the Goddess of the witches. But since then, Shaddai mistrusted the woman, though she would be necessary in bringing life into the second world that he created; one fashioned where she would remain beneath him, and he would rule over her.

In those days, Mary, the descendant of David, was next line to inherit the divine right to worship at the feet of her Lady, who was of many names but known at that time as Asherah, the Queen of Heaven. And like the angels who looked down upon the daughters of men and saw that they were beautiful, so, too, did the God of the Garden look upon Mary, and he lusted after her. Many times, Shaddai had appeared in visions to the young maiden Mary, pleading with her to lay aside her jewels and garments, and join him in his kingdom.

Such was her beauty that God himself laid down his sword and his crown at her feet and begged for her to let him place his hand upon her heart and abide with him forever. But Mary loved him not, for the God of the Garden caused all things she delighted in to fade and to die. But it was the way of this world, the rule set in motion that he could not stop. It was age and fate, against which He was helpless. It was age that caused all things to wither, but when men died, at the end of time, it was He who gave them rest and peace and strength so that they would return.

And still, it was said she loved him not. But the Goddess showed her cunning, and to save Mary, she sent her to become betrothed, to take the hand of a mortal man named Joseph and spare her from the humiliation of begetting a child without a father. But the lust and resentment festered in the heart of the God of the Garden, and he would have her rather she loved him or not. One night, while Mary slept before the day of her wedding, the spirit of God hovered over the face of the darkness of her room and came upon her in her dreams. He ate from Mary's body as those pious bastards ate of my flesh every

Easter Sunday, and when Mary awoke, she was pregnant with his child.

But not just his child, a baby that would embody his very own spirit, a fragment of his power buried deep within her. A child born of his violence and violation, and one he would use to bring further glory to himself. The pain she felt at birth, the Curse of Eve, was his punishment for her denying him, and he would turn his rejection into edification, a lesson for her to learn. It was an ugly truth and a cycle that was here to be brought to a bitter end.

Through me.

The God of the Garden never let the Goddess thwart him, neither in Heaven nor on earth, and I was here to make sure it wouldn't ever happen again. She couldn't win. I'd do anything I could to stop her, even if it meant dying myself in the process. I was the new Adam. Where the first failed to control the wiles of the Devil through Lilith, I would triumph and Lord over them.

It was *my* time.

She may have had the power handed down from the woman that was once my mother, but it was a counterfeit nonetheless. She succeeded in intimidating me, making me question my ability. But I was the Lion, ready to rend my prey to pieces. Roshana or not, she would bow to the full might of Heaven, to Shaddai who held the throne.

I fixed my eyes on the moon now hanging triumphantly over the mausoleum of Tituba when I saw now a familiar figure standing in the frame between both pillars. A bold, scarlet robe tossed by the wind, and her hair looked like sunshine.

The Queen of Georgia.

She lifted the robe that hid her, revealing her lily-white skin and deep, protruding eyes. She was beautiful and younger than I imagined she would be. She opened her arms, welcoming me.

"And so he appears," she said.

Her voice was like a whisper in the wind, and as she stepped into the moonlight that illuminated her pale skin, she seemed to come alive.

"The only begotten Son of God."

A shiver ran down my neck, and it was plain to see that she was filled with an ancient power, one that emanated from the inside of her very being. She smiled, full of mystery.

"You don't scare me," I said.

"Oh?" she said. She had a prominent Southern drawl, but with a polished and sophisticated quality to it.

"Could that be why you have three Disciples lyin' in wait for me?"

My throat tightened, and my heart felt like it dropped to the pit of my stomach. She laughed haughtily.

"Come now, Mr. Beaumont, that's hardly a fair fight. Why don't we go ahead and... *level* this playin' field..."

CHAPTER 20:

Temptation

With a wry smile, she lifted her arms gently. Titus and Jonah let out tormented screams as rotting skeletal remains shot out from the ground beneath them where they hid. The hands violently tugged at them, pulling their bodies deeper into the fetid soil until only their heads remained poking from the ground, immobile. Craven rushed towards her, quickly forming Hidden Hands and slinging bursts of energy hurling towards her that carved the ground and spewed rock and dirt. She chuckled, gracefully knocking each blast out of her way and absorbing his final blow. She expanded her arms, and a dome of his own energy blasted from between her hands. A wave of translucent blue energy ripped through the ground and burst through Cravens's defense.

"Craven!" I screamed.

He slammed into the tree behind him mercilessly, his legs almost wrapping around the trunk as his back collided against it.

"That's enough, now," she said.

He hobbled back to his feet. Craven screamed as he charged toward her again, now brandishing a copper forged gun and aiming it at her. *Click. Click. Click.*

Craven stopped. He stared back at his gun, stricken with a confused terror that scrunched his face.

"Bless your heart," she said. "That won't do you no good without these, will it?"

In her hand, she held out the blessed bullets, infused with shards from the Calvary cross. She rubbed her thumb and fingers together, and the bullets blew now into the wind as fine sand. "Your head must be in the clouds… Let's get the rest of you there too."

"Lee—Levi! HELP! HELP ME!" Craven cried out into the night.

Craven charged after her, forming Hidden Hands as quickly as he could and muttering his incantation. She lifted a finger calmly, pointing directly at him. Craven's head cocked back as if he'd taken a bullet right to the front of his skull and landed on his back with a painful thud. He shot back up, gasping and desperately tearing at the ground.

"You bitch! What are you doin' to him?"

"PUT ME DOWN! H-HELP!" Craven screamed.

But his feet were firmly planted on the ground. He flailed his arms uncontrollably, screaming and sobbing.

"Just a little flyin' curse, is all. He ain't goin' nowhere, but…" She held her finger to her lips now. "Shhh… he don't know that. In his mind, he's about halfway into the atmosphere."

Everything she did was in the twinkle of an eye, and it took half that for me to fly into a rage. I felt the heat from my body begin to bubble up through my veins, and my breaths felt like magma pouring through my nose and mouth. The ground beneath me fractured, and waves of energy erupted in an explosion that led to me entering my transfiguration. She was unphased, not even a flinch came from her.

"My, my. What a sight," she said. "I ain't come here to kill you,"

"That makes one of us," I said.

"Your fight ain't with me, Mr. Beaumont. This here's a family affair," she said.

Like a sheet, she pulled the darkness around her and vanished.

"Show yourself!" I screamed, turning in circles.

"Blood of my blood," a voice called out.

I turned to face the voice, seeing a figure standing in front of the mausoleum. A woman stood there now, with cheekbones as high as the peak of a mountain and skin as dark as the night, shimmering with power. Her head and body were wrapped in fine, white lace, and she was adorned with beaded bracelets. A deep sense of familiarity filled me, and I knew now who she was.

Tituba herself.

It was the great matriarch of my own family, standing to face me for a battle of the ages. A painful ringing filled my ears. I yelped in pain as the voice of Shaddai pierced through my mind.

"Kill… Kill… My Son… Finish Her…"

The God of the Garden's voice intruded. It was serene, calm, and cold, speaking in ancient Aramaic. Globs of sweat ran down my face as I resisted his pull, fighting against his control of my body.

"I will, I will," I urged back inside.

"Kill her… Kill… Do my will… Do your Father's will… and… kill…"

"My child, you are lost," she said in a thick, Caribbean accent.

"Get out of my way, woman!" I shouted; the rage ravished my body again.

"Kill her…"

"Sweet boy, a battle with me is one against yourself."

I screamed, fighting the consuming compulsion that possessed me. I couldn't resist feeling a bubbling rage against her. She represented something I resented, a primal and ancient hatred that had awoken in me against her figure.

"Kill her… now."

"You're the one who first brought the Devil to my people! *You're* the one who damned every woman that came after you."

Tears of pure rage dripped down my chin, and I shook with a fury that only grew more volatile and violent with each word she said to me. Something in me didn't want to fight her, but I couldn't sustain the resistance. The pull of Shaddai was too great. I had to do his work on Earth.

She held her hands out to her sides.

"You are the light, my son. Accept who you are."

"Step… aside…" I said, through gritted teeth. My hands vibrated with power that was desperate to strike her down. "I won't warn you again," I threatened.

"Smite her. Kill her. Kill her... NOW!"

His power was made complete and perfect in me now. There was no escaping His grasp.

"I warned you," I said regretfully.

Shaddai had possessed me.

Tituba smiled serenely.

"You are mistaken... It is you who should be warned..." she said.

I extended my arms in the air, and snarling, hissing and deafening winds surged around us, bending backward the trees that surrounded us and yanking the tombstones from the ground like corroded teeth from a rotting jaw.

She was unmoved.

Tituba stood with her chin high and her hands folded gently. The airs rushed and beat down on her, howling and ripping through the ground but she remained firmly planted. She slowly closed her eyes and took a breath as deep as the caverns that must've been deep within her. She inhaled the raging sky until the wind was now deep within her lungs. She opened her eyes and exhaled the bottled four winds that blasted through the ground and ripped across the cemetery ground, rushing towards me.

I was punched in the chest from the directed funnel of wind she blew at me, and what little breath I had left in me from its titanic strike was knocked out when I slammed into a column. I was pinned in squarely against my back as the winds raged against me, cutting and slicing my face with razor-like slashes.

I dropped to the floor, flopping onto my stomach as the winds finished slicing and cutting me with the swords of air. I hobbled back onto my feet. With one swift motion of my hands, thousands of gleaming, golden arrows shot out like bullets from the rippling portal of air in front of me. She lifted one hand, remaining still where she stood, and the arrows were reduced to glowing sparks, cascading onto the ground around her like glowing rain.

I choked, speechless.

I released a battle cry, and in my hands appeared the glowing sword of Heaven, shining like the sun and pulsating with swirling energy that wrapped around the blade. I felt my feet come off the ground, propelled by raw power and unwavering anger. I blasted towards her like a human rocket. She came closer into my vision, and as I readied my sword to deal the fatal blow, a shining hand reached out, stopping me in place. In front of me now was Michael, who had no face to bear any expression, but I could sense the guilt and shame in him.

The grip of his hand crushed my wrist; I felt the bones in my hand fracture into hundreds of pieces.

I screamed.

Michael flung me across the air like a rag doll, and I tumbled and rolled against the ground until my back smashed into the Juniper tree behind me, knocking the wind out of me. Michael stood by her side, and in an instant, he bolted back to heaven, leaving behind golden streaks of light that trailed into the sky, fading faster than they appeared.

"*But ever since we stopped… Burning incense to the Queen of Heaven…*" she began, slowly making her way towards me, "*and pouring out drink and offerings to her… We have had nothing… and have been perishing by sword, and famine…*"

I clasped onto the sword that lay at the tips of my fingers, and with the taste of dirt and blood in my mouth, I stumbled to my feet.

"You'll…"

I spit a murky glob of soil and fresh blood onto the ground.

"Be the one to perish by the sword," I said. "And I'll send you straight back to hell."

I lifted my blade again and charged after her. She held her arms out to her side, and the whole of the cemetery vomited its dead, giving rise to rotting corpses and skeletal figures erupting from the ground with awful hissing and groans unmatched by anything I'd heard even in Hell's farthest reach. They surrounded me, waves of undead soldiers enclosed the space around us, and I lost sight of her. All I could see were the hollowed eye sockets and meat falling off the bones of the bodies that met their ends.

And if I didn't act now, I'd soon be joining them.

I swung and slashed my sword, dicing up their bodies that collapsed on themselves, singed at the waist and down across their chest split clean in half. But even as they fell to the ground, they dragged themselves back towards me, biting and ripping at my legs and rending flesh off them. They sprung onto my back, shrieking and oozing an acidic venom from their empty mouths that burned through my skin. As I fought my way through them, I saw her still sitting there with a stoic expression.

She barely moved her arms, and not even a bead of sweat rolled down her brow. She was beating me. I roared deep and primal as I fought off enough of them to clear the space ahead. The sword wasn't working, and not even in my most powerful form could I keep up with them. I was Prince of Life, but they were the promise of death, and maybe that's why they gained a hold over me. God was quiet, like a teacher silent during the tests, and though I barred my eyes to heaven and waited for any kind of help, there remained a painful silence.

It was just me.

I twirled my sword in my hands, and in a burst of light, it vanished. I smashed my knuckles together, and sparks emitted. I had to hit her with everything I had. I let out a battle cry and held my fists out. A rupture of searing fire shot from my fists like a hydrant, lighting the darkness around me and scorching the bodies that surrounded me now. They collapsed on themselves, still flailing their arms until the fire consumed them to dust.

I looked at Tituba, whose dark brown face was now illuminated by the glowing gold of the fire, and a smile of pleasure curled the ends of her mouth. I scorched the earth around me, and the fire continued to flow from my fists until not even one of the bodies remained standing. It was just her and I again, and a wide-open space of fire on both my sides that billowed, sending plumes of smoke and burning flesh and bone up to the inky sky. I panted, slumping over. Salty sweat ran down my face that stung my eyes, but I kept my gaze fixed on her. She clapped.

"Magnificent. The blood is strong within you," she said.

I clapped my hands together, and the sky thundered with ferocity. "I just want to see your blood," I said.

She laughed.

White sparks circulated my arms and fists now, turning into streaks of fiery lightning that consumed my fists. I steadied my fists, setting them on her, and with everything I had left in me, wild and flaring bolts of lightning exploded from my fists aimed directly at her. I moved forward, pushing myself further as more bolts of lightning illuminated the entire graveyard around me, bathing us all in a blinding pale light.

Her flowing white robe was blown back by the gusts of winds and power, and the sky above us thundered and shook the ground, but she stood still. The lightning collided with a barrier that encased her, rippling outwards against a spherical heat haze that shielded her. I screamed, pushing more power, and the ground shook violently, the lightning struck down trees around me and flared off in every which direction as it ricocheted off the shield she had around herself. I was in front of her now, still bellowing louder than the thunder that pounded against the black heavens above me.

Her hair was wild now from the gusts of wind and force of the lightning that blew off her head wrap, but even still, she didn't even lift a hand to me.

How was this possible?

I'd been trained to kill the Witch Queen, but the power Tituba had was unlike anything I was ever prepared for. Any other witch would've succumbed the moment this fight began, but here I was, fighting with raw cosmic power and still losing.

What *was* she?

I finally reached her. I was face to face now, and the lightning curved around the shield, wrapping around her and sending fierce bolts that struck the mausoleum behind her, cracking and blackening the marble structure that should've been her bones. She reached out and grabbed my arm. Her grip was powerful like Michael's and inhuman compared to her build. She redirected my hand, to where now the lightning struck upwards towards the sky, rushing back up toward the clouds becoming thinner. The bolts continued to spew until they turned into a sputter and reduced themselves to heavy flames, dissipating into smoke.

She released my hand, and I fell to her feet, heaving and sweating blood. I gnashed my teeth, trembling like all my bones had become rubber. I looked up at her, a gave a tilt of her head.

I failed.

I lost.

My head hung as I held myself up by my shaking arms, still kneeling on the ground. I dug my nails into the wet soil, clasping dirt in my hands. I gasped for air, desperate to breathe, and my lungs felt like they were about to collapse.

I groaned, clutching onto my side. I could feel the heat in my body fading away, giving room to a frigid coldness that swept over me. The sweat on my face began to dry, but warm, fresh blood still ran down my nose. The fires on my side began to die down, as soft shadows now fell onto her face.

"H—How?" I heaved. "You're just a woman."

She raised a brow, finally breaking her mask of stoicism.

"Just?" she said. "*Dolore nativitas,*"

A wave fell over me that planted me firmly onto my back, and I was instantly stricken with excruciating pain, all-encompassing and unbearable. Sharp pains like searing knives filled my abdomen, groin, and back, and a horrible pulsating in my pelvis felt like I was seconds away from being ripped in half. I screamed in a humiliating way, curling over. I felt like my insides were expanding, a burn that I couldn't escape. The pain was gripping and tightening, and traveling down my back and moving like waves.

Labor pains.

At the same time, I saw flashes of women throughout my mind all throughout the ages. I felt every pain from the fires that burned them alive. I felt the suffocation of being buried and still breathing, every kick to the stomach from every man that denied a child, and the isolation of being confined to mental institutions. Every single suffering that fell upon a woman in every time, tribe, people and tongue, I felt pour into me unstirred and unfiltered. It wasn't that I felt pain. No, I had become it.

"W—WHAT ARE YOU?"

I let out a barking gasp. As the words left my mouth, my lungs felt like they were filled with liquid fire, like there was lava trapped inside them, and gushes of water exploded from my mouth like a fountain. The water filled up towards my throat and poured out from my nose. Any scream that tried to come out was a gurgle. I flopped onto my stomach, clawing at the ground, drowning and choking.

She watched me coldly; whatever heart she had in her was replaced with stone. She showed not even an ounce of emotion. Not even anger. Each breath, I tried to take burned my nose, and my throat contracted, unable to keep up with the water that gushed out of me. The darkness of night was expelled, but a pulsating wave of bright white light started to consume the graveyard. I thought I was dying, and when I looked up, her entire appearance was transfigured.

She laid her hands in front of her chest and began to pull. Flesh tore open, and blood ran down her stomach now to reveal her raw, beating heart.

"I am the Mother," she said.

On her head now was a snow-white veil, with a train that stretched across the boundless ground we stood on, carried by the blazing bodies of heavenly angels, holding proudly the ends of her veil. The clouds at her feet parted, and I saw the whole of the earth at her feet.

Mother of God.

I flopped onto my back, sputtering water and coughing, finally feeling air enter my lungs. I crawled back onto my knees and stumbled to my feet. The celestial vision in front of me remained, and choirs of angels sang in a rough, strange tongue, their own language. The song became more of a chant, pounding and thundering louder and louder.

"What..."

I fell back to my knees, still too weak to stand.

"What do you want from me?"

The angels around her released the train of her veil and began to fly at lightning speed, surrounding us both. More angels gathered, swirling and singing together in a reverberating choir that nearly deafened me. They became now like a vortex like I was standing in the eye of a tornado made of heavenly hosts, gleaming and shining like sunlight. The funnel of their bodies reached into the sky, swirling high into the clouds and encapsulating us both.

She stepped down from the footstool that appeared like a small earth and approached me. She extended her hand to me; her skin was radiant and shining.

"Join us," she said. Her voice was transcendent like thousands spoke through her at once.

The pain she inflicted on me was still subsiding, and tears streamed down my face. I shook my head, resisting. The church warned me that the Devil can come as an angel of light, and here he was through her in all his luminous deception.

"I can't. I won't."

"My bloodline has been tainted… but you can restore it once again,"

I looked up towards the angels that still circled us, these creatures that were once subservient to me, now serving this power. Even though I was no match for her. I was told that I was the ultimate power.

It was all a lie. I knew that now.

"I can't."

"Join us, Levi. And know the truth about who you are. The whole truth."

I looked at her hand again, adorned with a large, ruby ring so polished I could see my terror-stricken face reflected back at me.

"The choice now is yours, truly yours," she said. "What do you choose?"

Seeing the majesty of her power, she could have killed me before the fight even began, right where I stood. And that terrified me to the point that I couldn't speak. I choked on my own words, trying to find a reason to disagree with her. But I couldn't. If I chose to stay by the side of the God of the Garden, I'd die at the hands of the true Queen of witches if we were to battle again. But it would be one in vain; I couldn't match her power. I understood who she truly was now.

My mother.

The thunderous choir of the angels grew louder and more adamant, fiercer than the winds that nearly knocked me back that they were creating with each stroke of their wing.

"The God of the Garden… he'll kill me,"

"The first lie ever told," she said. "Join me and be like God; knowing both good and evil. Join me, and know the truth,"

"Stop this," Shaddai's voice penetrated my mind again. I winced in pain, curling over and trying not to vomit.

I raised a trembling hand towards her, biting down on my lip. I stopped just before brushing the tips of her fingers with mine.

"Do not defy me."

"I—can't," I said, painfully.

"Heed my words, Levi…" Shaddai compelled.

"You were not made to be a martyr," she said. "Don't die as one again."

Her eyes were radiating in ancient knowledge, and strangely enough, a familiar kindness. I felt vulnerable and weak before her but protected. All my life choices had always been made for me. I didn't choose to become the next Christ, or to slaughter witches like cattle, it was a path laid out for me, a road that I was pushed so far down that I didn't even know how to turn back if I wanted to.

In her hand now she held an apple, bright and scarlet red. For the first time, I was truly presented with a choice, something that not even the God of the Garden had intended; something that He didn't plan, and there was a delight that came with knowing that. A place where sin and enlightenment became one.

"You will die," Shaddai threatened once more.

"Did your God know from the beginning the choice you would come to make?" she asked.

I thought for a moment but could only stare back at her in pained silence.

"Then why hasn't he killed you where you stood?"

"*I warn you... Levi...*"

I knew the choice I was about to make. The consuming grip His spirit had over me relented, and as I reached in resistance towards the fruit in her hands, I gained more control. If what I was about to do was not known to him, and if He didn't always know all, then that meant the future was ours.

It was mine to create.

"*DO NOT DEFY ME!*"

I was tired of taking orders. I snatched the apple from her hand before I could change my mind.

And I ate the fruit.

CHAPTER 21

The Fall

Father, I have sinned.

But I ask not for forgiveness, because it felt so good.

It was quiet. Everything around me fell into a mesh of strokes of light, like a living painting. All the worries and woes that people called my name for, who prayed to me in times of distress, came to a blissful silence. I knew the ties had been broken between my mind and the God of the Garden. He'd abandoned me, revoked his spark of life from my body, but I was still alive. I waited for the other voice in my head, the thing I called the Devil. But there was nothing, I was alone with my thoughts. I knew now that it was my self all along. I was the adversary all along.

Finally.

I knew myself.

The prayers and wants from other people that I felt chained and obligated to. I was counted on. I was needed. I had to be what the faithful so desperately needed me to be. But it was all an illusion, a distraction. He knew if I remained focused on the ocean of voices constantly in my mind, on the prayers and hopes of people, I'd fall in line. That I would continue to be the savior I was tricked into believing the whole world needed me to be.

I had eaten from the fruit of knowledge, and I hadn't died.

I had lived again the first lie.

I kept my eyes on her, transfixed as I lifted my lips from the apple. Sweet juice ran down my chin, and she lifted her hands to the sky with a serene and delighted smile. Streaks of light rushed from the funnel of angels that surrounded us and took their angelic form once again. Dozens of their celestial forms rushed to her feet, and a surge of clouds bubbled up from the ground like a boiling cauldron beneath her. The angels lifted her high into the sky, and with a thundering voice, like the trump of an archangel, she called down to me below as she ascended higher.

"I'll send a comforter, a counselor in my name," she said. "And true power, you will know."

She clapped her hands together over her head. The black cloak of night instantly fell over my eyes, and she was gone. A choir of crickets now filled the space where angels once sang, and darkness consumed the light she created. I could hear the wailing and screaming still coming from Craven, who lay in fetal position and clasping his head.

"PUT ME DOWN! PUT ME DOWN!" he shrieked.

Jonah and Titus yelled for help, still buried up to their necks in the earth. I looked down at my hands, still shaking with disbelief. Even the skies were quiet now, and no wrath from Heaven had fallen on me. I was created to be the new Adam, and I repeated his sins. But I wondered now whether he still felt the same guiltless pleasure as me. For once, I finally felt like my life was in my own hands. And even if I'd chosen wrong, I could die in the comfort that I still chose.

I ran towards Craven, turning him over and trying to coax him. He flailed his arms, pounding against my chest and slapping me in a total state of disarray.

"DOWN! HELP ME DOWN!"

I cupped his face in my hands, but he jerked violently from me and continued to writhe on the ground. I pinned him down and held his face between my hands firmly and focused on his eyes. I began chanting in ancient Aramaic, hovering my lips over his and blowing gently into his mouth. His eyes widened, and his chest settled from its vicious heaving. With one deep, long sigh, he released the illusion that had come over him. I cupped his face, looking into his eyes which slowly gained clarity. He reached out, brushing his thumb against my cheek and smiling faintly.

His face was slick with sweat, and he quickly rolled over, backing against a headstone behind him, feeling everywhere along his body.

"I—I'm back?" he asked, incredulous.

"You never left. It was an illusion."

He clasped the bridge of his nose, sighing with trembling breaths.

"It—It felt so real…"

I helped him stand to his feet, and he took notice of Jonah and Titus on the ground. We rushed towards them, forming Hidden Hands together, and the ground that surrounded their necks loosened, forming a small trench that they fell through. We helped them each climb out of the ground, and they dusted themselves.

"What happened?" Titus said. "Did you win?"

"Last we saw were those angles that came down… I've never seen nothin' like that before…" Jonah added.

"No," I said. "But this ain't the end."

"What do you mean?" Craven said, agitated. "You mean you lost?"

"She could've killed me if she wanted to," I said. "But she didn't. She wants something from me, and I'm willin' to bet it's got somethin' to do with my seed she tried sending the Lilitu for."

"Lee, this was our only shot!" Titus said, shaking me. "Now she's gonna release more of these Primordials!"

"They'll tear this world apart…" Craven said, folding his arms. "How could you lose to her?"

"That was the original giver of Roshana. Tituba." I turned to face them. "She began the Summerland pact all those centuries ago."

"That's even worse," Craven spat, furious. "Now the witches are on her side!"

"See now, that's the thing," I said with a tinge of fondness. "After tonight, I think we're all on the same side."

Jonah and Titus gasped.

"She really must've fucked you up bad," Jonah said. "How could you even say somethin' like that?"

I smirked.

"'Cause I think there's more to this picture than we're bein' lead to believe. And I'm gonna find out what it is," I said.

Craven snatched me by the arm before I could walk away from them. "So that's it? You just gonna say some cryptic shit and bounce? You don't got nothin' more to say?"

I yanked my arm back. "'Cause there ain't shit left to say. As soon as I know more, y'all will be the first to know. 'Til then, have some faith in me. Like it was in the old days."

I turned away from them and hobbled out of the cemetery. I looked back at my calf, still missing a chunk from where those creatures bit me. The three of them stood there in stunned silence watching, me go.

"Lee, wait." Craven winced against the pain, quickly gaining on me. "What's gotten into you?"

"I don't know. But you could use some of whatever it is."

"You're about to turn your back on everything. Everything that you are and stood for. On all of us."

"This wouldn't be the first time y'all didn't understand me. But I've made my peace with that. Now I need you to."

Craven grabbed my arm as I turned away and pulled me in for a long kiss. I stared back at him. He still made me feel something. Only, I didn't know what it was. Love? Regret? I wasn't sure. But I didn't have time to stick around and find out.

"I love you too much to see you do this to yourself. I know... I've got trouble showin' how I feel. Sometimes I'm not sure how I feel about you either. But right now... it's all clear. You were born to defeat the darkness... not become it."

I rested my forehead against his and held his hand in mine.

"I know you love me... But I think you were right all along. I only love myself. Amma may be the closest thing, and even then, I'm not sure. Right now, it looks like helpin' myself is the key. Where I'm going you can't follow me... You just need to trust me. And when the time comes, I'll come back for you."

Craven pulled away from me, watching in tearful disbelief.

"I'm not sure I can," he said, painfully, "trust you."

"I guess there ain't nothin' between us then. Not if we don't got that."

A tear fell down his face as he watched me, stuttering and speechless.

"I'll kill you before I let you destroy this world. I won't know where I'll stand the next time we meet," he said, forlorn.

"Then until we meet again." I smiled weakly.

I turned around, glancing back at him one last time as he stood and watched me go. Craven and I have been through many trials throughout the years I've known him. And although we fought and drove each other crazy, this was the first time I was unsure of where he stood. A part of me thought he meant what he said. But there was no way to know. I would tell myself to have faith, but I've had enough of believing blindly.

I made my way back home. I was bloodied, bruised, and deafened, but I felt like a winner. There was a strange calm in what happened the moment I'd eaten from the fruit, a kind of rite of passage.

I never really believed in anything that the Church taught its people, especially blind faith and mindless obedience. To obey was human but to choose was divine. It was something to be cherished and prized. The Bible has been used to oppress and enslave the people of the world for so many generations that the weapon used against them started to become a tool for salvation, or so we believed. If the Devil's power was truly a counterfeit, then how was it able to defeat the real thing? I wasn't happy about the loss, or the humiliation I felt all the way through, but the end result gave me my life back.

I arrived back home, watching from a distance. I tried to listen to the wind, hoping it would give me all the right words to tell Grannie. I'd been so lost in the rush of making my own decisions that I'd forgotten having to face her, and even worse, the scrutiny from Nita. Now she would have a reason to call me a failure.

Before I could take another step, the light in Ezra's room flicked on, and Grannie's screams pierced the night air.

I sprinted towards the house as quickly as my legs could carry me, ignoring the sharp pains in my knees from the battle. I ground my teeth, fighting through the pain until I burst through the front door.

"GRANNIE?" I shouted from the bottom of the staircase.

I bolted up the steps, creaking beneath my weight, stopping in front of Nita, who blocked my way. She flashed a wicked smile, stepping aside.

"You make failure seem like a work of art, boy," she said, shaking her head disapproving. "Why don't you go and see your latest masterpiece?"

Grannie's screams became woeful sobbing and wailing. I pushed open the half-cracked door and saw Grannie Tamar over Ezra's body, moving her hands over him and retracting them as if he were too hot.

"NITA!" she screamed. "I—I can't lift this—NITA!" She turned around, tears streaming down her face. Her eyes twisted into a malignant rage. "What have you done?" she said, breathless. "NITA! Help me lift this!" she begged. "Or call Amma."

Nita entered the room, standing by the frame of the door with her arms folded. "Ain't no sense in tryin' to lift that Mama, can't you see? It's the Curse of Job,"

Grannie whimpered. She closed her eyes tightly, rocking back and forth over his body. "You," she said to me, her voice trembling. "*You* did this!"

I slowly stepped forward, hovering now over Grannie's shoulder to be met with a grisly sight. I staggered back, gagging and gasping. My stomach wrenched inside as I slumped over retching.

"What—How?" I said, covering my mouth now to hold back the vomit.

Ezra's body lay there as he groaned, with horrible lesions and festering boils covering the entire surface of his body. Pus-filled pustules burst a green, foul-smelling liquid that oozed down his arms. His skin was rough like leather, and his jaw looked dislocated. From his face, he grew swollen deformities over his eyes and forehead the size of tennis balls. Streams of drool rolled out the corners of his lips as he groaned painfully.

"LIFT IT!" Grannie shouted at me. "LAY HANDS AND LIFT IT!"

I looked back at Nita, who taunted me quietly and gestured for me to try. My cheeks became sour with watery saliva, still trying not to gag as I approached him. I fought the tears that filled my eyes. I was naive to think that the choice I'd made had no consequences. He was a God of vindication, of vengeance, and held grudges until the end of time. I knelt at the altar of a God who ordered for infants to be dashed against rocks, who sent a plague upon innocent people to rouse the heart of a king, and one who would murder his own son. I was foolish to think that I was above the same reproach, in that He would bring horrors upon my household for what I'd done.

I had a horrible feeling in my gut that nothing was going to happen. Curses that Shaddai laid Himself could never be undone, or so I was told. But my brother lay suffering in unbearable agony, punished for a choice that I made, so it was worth trying anyway. I glanced back at Grannie, who muttered incantations by the bedside in desperation. I extended my hands over him, and laid my hand across his chest, muttering the Aramaic incantation.

Nothing.

"Try *harder*," Grannie urged.

But I hardly had anything left in me since the battle with Tituba. I laid hands on him again, muttering quickly the incantation and passing my hands up and down his body until sweat ran down my brow.

I stepped back, stunned into silence.

"He rescinded His power, didn't he?" Grannie said, barely above a whisper. "DIDN'T HE?"

She turned from Ezra, raising a shaking finger to me. "What did you do, Levi?" she asked. I babbled, trying to find anything to say to placate her. "You answer me, boy! WHAT DID YOU DO?"

A dense silence fell over the room, only Ezra's groaning and hacking cough permeated throughout the space.

"I… I joined the side of the witches," I said, finally.

Nita covered her mouth, gasping in disbelief. Grannie clasped onto her chest, falling back against the dresser and nearly fainting.

"You did *what?*"

"Somethin's goin' on Grannie… I can't explain it. But the witches, all this, I don't think it's their doin'."

"You've damned us," Grannie said, raspy and breathless. "You've damned us all."

"No, no, Grannie," I said, rushing to her side. "I can fix this,"

She screamed, and a wave of her power sent me flying back and smashing into the wall behind me. I fell onto my stomach, my head slamming against the ground.

"Do you have *any* idea what you've done!" Grannie yelled.

"Just like his Mama," Nita said as I struggled back to my feet. "A failure and a traitor from the beginning. I knew you was never worthy enough to be no Petram. Look at you. Spineless, gullible, *weak.*"

"For generations, we've separated ourselves from the Summerland Pact… for ages, our bloodline has served the God of the Garden faithfully," Grannie said.

"And that's where we've gone wrong…" I said. "I see it now, Grannie. I see that we've got this all wrong."

She laughed, bitterly. "Do you know why we separated ourselves, Levi?"

"Go on," Nita said. "Tell her why, Levi."

"Because we'd seen the error of our ways… and used the Dark Gift given to bring glory to the True God," I said.

Grannie smirked, pityingly. "If you knew anythin' about the history of this town, you would've never made no type of agreement with them. They've never cared for us, in fact… they had a hand in the destruction of this place we now call home."

"What?" I said.

"The Order called it the Great Cleansing. The fire that destroyed this town. But do you know how they was able to do it?"

I stared back at her, reluctant to answer. "It—It wasn't the Queen of Georgia who I fought. It was Tituba. Her spirit appeared to me."

Nita's eyes bulged nearly out of her head. She quickly turned to face Grannie.

"*Mama*," Nita said hoarsely.

Grannie lifted her hand to Nita, silencing her.

"Is that right? And what did Tituba say to you, hm? Go on," Grannie said.

"She said the bloodline is tainted somehow and that I can fix it." Nita scoffed.

"You brought this mess to our door, and *you're* goin' to be the one to save us? Please."

Grannie grumbled; her eyes alive now with secrets it seemed she fought to keep from bubbling to the surface; sins of her past dying to come up for air.

"*Tainted*, is it? Hmm..."

"What's he goin' on about, Mama?" Nita pressed.

Grannie smiled, condescending.

"Imagine that. Our great ancestor appearin' to the likes of you to resolve somethin' in the favor of those who laid to ash the work of her own hands."

"I don't understand," I said.

"Of course not, look at you. Seekin' knowledge while blinded by ignorance," Grannie said. She cleared her throat.

"In the old days," Grannie sat down beside Ezra, gently stroking his forehead, "when Tituba, who was the first Madonna, came to this town and laid down her roots... flowers of civilization sprung. This town had buildings as tall as the Empire State, schools, theaters, and ballrooms to dance the night away. It was a haven, not just for Black folks to thrive, but for Black witches to roam freely, just like they do in Summerland to this day..."

She took a deep sigh, wiping the tears that started to fall from her eyes again.

"Until many years and come to pass... and magicians from Salem discovered this town. And it wasn't too soon after that judges soon followed in their steps to hunt us down... The reignin'

Madonna of Florida of that time, my Grannie, Etta Louise Parris went to the Queen of Georgia, Old Adora Scott. She begged her Sisters of the Pact for their intercession, as they was outnumbered and bein' hunted down one by one." Grannie explained. "And you know what happened next?"

I shook my head, a terrible sense of foreboding coming over me.

"Adora sent her away. You see… They loved the power Tituba brought to the girls of Salem and marveled at the might of her magic when she conjured up the Devil in Summerland all them years back, but they didn't love her descendants. They delighted in what was given but didn't love the giver. And so Adora joined old Wardwell Nero, and together they came to Tophet and called down fire from heaven to burn our refuge to the ground. It was a fire unlike the world had ever seen… All because Black folks had no business thrivin' the way we was… She even stole Tituba's Book of Eons that held all the secret ceremonies to ensure we could never rival them again." Grannie went on. She stood back up, hoisting herself to her feet by her cane.

"And we was scattered… those of us left were only able to continue on under the disguise of servin' the God of the magicians, while the descendants of Adora continued to enjoy they freedom. And now here you are, helpin' that line achieve the means to their end at the cost of your own people once again. Now, tell me, boy, who's got it all wrong now?"

My throat was in knots as I stared back at her, robbed of speech by the crushing weight of a painful realization. For the first time ever, I was granted the power to choose.

And I chose wrong.

CHAPTER 22

The Wages Of Sin

My eyes were blinded by tears; the entire room became a blurred mess of distorted faces. I shoved past Nita and ran towards my bedroom, slamming the door shut behind me. I paced the room back and forth, stepping on the shards of glass that remained on the floor, crunching beneath my feet. I pressed my forehead against the wall, struggling to feel against the chipped paint, just to get a fraction of any type of sensation in my body, even the vaguest sense.

I cried that night in a way I don't think I ever have, not even when I lost Pops. At least his death wasn't the result of my own actions. This was my fault. My brother was suffering, cursed by the God that he served all his life because of my actions. And even still, that just made me angry at God. What type of entity punishes innocent people, no less those who have served by his side? It was the behavior of a sadistic ruler, a demagogue instead of a king. He would inflict suffering and burn down the world around him just to hurt one of his own servants.

I slammed my fist against the wall, pounding relentlessly and screaming into the darkness that swallowed my room. Only the pale arms of moonlight passed through the small window, barely a flicker in the vast void that had surrounded my room. I beat and hammered against the wall until my hands gave out, screaming helplessly and sobbing uncontrollably. Regardless of what I felt about the choice I'd made, it still caused suffering to the people around me, to my brother.

Ezra almost joined the Order because he knew the Scriptures the best; even more than me. He could quote the Psalms and recite Revelation with his eyes closed. Yet, he ultimately decided to follow in Pops's footsteps instead.

I slid down against the wall, covering my face with my knees, trying to hide myself from the shame that I felt. I'd been so high on the euphoric rush of making my own choices that I forgot the bargain that came when making them:

Consequences.

No one was free of making any choice without there being a price to be paid. I picked myself up from the ground and lay down on my bed, staring up at the ceiling. I wanted to believe that I had a plan, that I would be able to heal Ezra again and make sense of all the madness that came with that first Primordials, but I didn't. I closed my eyes, and suddenly, I could hear the millions of prayers in every tongue on earth praying to me, asking me for help and to resolve their problems.

But how could I help them when I couldn't even help myself? They prayed for a Savior that couldn't save; for a king with no kingdom, and for answers where I only had questions. I was used to tuning out their voices, but tonight, I felt like I needed to hear them because they were the only ones who believed in me. They spoke power in my name when I felt weak. I was surrounded by a sea of voices who had so much faith in me that they would step aside and let me take control.

But I had no control.

Not even over my own life.

I clasped my head, frustrated, and turned on my side. I rocked myself, pretending I was in the arms of someone who could bring me any type of comfort, even if they were sweet lies spoken just to lullaby me to sleep. I'd take a false sense of peace, a lie in place of the painful truth; maybe that's what made religion so popular.

Rain falls on both the righteous and the unrighteous.

But that was just Bible talk for *shit happens.*

Not even the children who jumped from the top of that school building were spared. Even innocent lives were garbage to him, something to be jettisoned without value or a second thought. I healed my battle wounds and the gashes left by the Lilitu. But there was a part of me that felt I didn't deserve it. I deserved to suffer through that kind of pain because I couldn't do the one thing I was born to do— save.

Every Christ before me had their divinity tested. Moments that proved that they were painfully human and incapable of escaping the very mortal experience of suffering. Maybe this was mine? The God of the Garden loved to test his followers, and I was no different. Ezra was Cursed the same way Job was, which I knew was a message. That even the most faithful weren't above being used for His purposes. But I didn't want to continue to be a device in his hands to achieve his ends. I didn't care what divine plan any of this served, all I knew now was that I had to protect my family any way that I could. And if that included going against the Crown then I'd go down signing. I understood now why Lucifer rebelled.

"Hello, Levi," the voice said.

The hairs on the back on necks stood on end. I sat up, looking in every direction.

"Who's there?" I said.

I backed against the headboard of my bed and reached to turn on the lamp, but there was still only darkness. I strained to see through the thick shades and saw nothing. The branches on the trees scratched against the window, creating a chilling shriek that slipped through the cracks. The moonlight penetrated the shadows in pallid beams, revealing a shrouded figure woven by night.

There in my room stood a tall, shrouded form that stepped forward. The fragments of light were shed on its pale face; rotten and ridden with decay. I could see his teeth through the holes in his cheek, and where his eyes should have been were black sockets and missing a nose. It was a ghastly figure, more skeletal and corpse like than human, dressed in a fine black suit.

"Who—Who are you?"

It laughed, sending cold shivers down my body. It stepped further into the light, and the festering cadaver was replaced seamlessly by a rosy cheeked and raven-haired man. His hair was in a slick curly quiff with hazel eyes and a snarky grin across his handsome form.

"Are you a witch?" I said as my breath frosted in front of me.

He, like the Witch Queen had a deep, Southern drawl. "I'm the Devil," he said chuckling. "And I ain't just anyone, you know." He stood now at the end of my bed. "I'm King of witches."

As he stood now against the pale light of the moon, I recognized him. Time aged the boyhood from him, and he stood now as a man that resembled more of his father, Gerald.

Noah Abertha.

"W—What're you doin' here?"

He gawked, still smiling.

"Ain't you hear? I'm the Comforter that was promised," he said. "I'm here to make you see all this has been worthwhile,"

"Can you heal my brother? The—The God of the Garden. Shaddai. He laid the Curse of Job on him."

"Oh, no. I ain't gonna do that. But you can."

"How?" I said. "He's rescinded his power… I can't do anythin', now."

"Do you trust me, Levi?" Noah said, sly.

"Now, why the fuck would I do that?" I said. "I'd *never* trust the likes of you,"

"That's too bad," Noah laughed. "I was really hopin' we could be friends."

I stared back at him. His eyes glowed, and the smile deepened on his face. He seemed like a carnivorous predator in the sight of a wounded animal.

He stretched out his arms, and my bed violently rocked, bouncing on its ends as long, shadowy arms reached from underneath and wrapped around my body like rope, holding me down. I screamed as more arms replaced the myriad that constricted me. One of the hands covered my mouth, muffling my screams that desperately tried to get out. The ceiling above me looked like it was getting higher and more out of reach, as far as the sky, until I realized I was sinking. I plunged deeper into the bed until I fell through and plummeted into an endless pit, free-falling through the frigid air.

I landed on my back, knocking the wind out of me. I groaned, gnashing my teeth from the pain. I was hoodwinked by the dark, unable to even see even my hand in front of my face. A golden glow approached me, and there stood Noah in the form of a black goat, with a flickering candle flame between his horns. The light from the flames revealed I was wearing a white robe now.

"What is this place?" I said.

"A place the God of the Garden can't see," Noah's voice chimed in my mind. "The place where the first people learned the Mysteries."

"What're you talkin' about?" I spat.

His laugh echoed within me, amused.

"Come," he said. "There's much work to be done."

Noah took off, guiding me through the void with only the light between his horns to guide us. We walked for what seemed like ages, trusting only the solid ground beneath my feet.

"Stop," I said.

He turned around, a mischievous glint in his eyes now.

"Gettin' cold feet?" he asked. "It would be better for you to rush upon a blade than for you to enter this place with fear in your heart," Noah warned.

"And what place is that?" I said.

At my word, dozens of glowing lights appeared in the distance, all wavering in place, and a percussive chant began, rumbling with more fervency and intensity as the moments went on.

"When the first man and woman learned the secret, they was brought to this place... Don't you remember it?"

"Why would I?"

"'Cause, you was brought here too. The first time you walked this world," he said.

I stopped again, staring back at him in disbelief. He laughed.

"You don't ever wonder what happened all those years between bein' a child and an adult in your first life?" Noah said.

"I don't remember anythin' about my first life. I was never allowed to." I confessed, crestfallen.

"You know, the thing about our God is that there is no forbidden knowledge,"

"You say *ours* like he's mine too,"

"Oh, but Levi, don't you see? He *is*. Even in your Mama's womb, he knew you. Been with you since the beginnin'. Just waitin' for the time that you would come back lookin' for 'im."

He gestured towards the sea of lights, and from where we stood now, illuminated by the myriad of torches, appeared more by the number, hundreds by now.

"Who are these people?"

Before me was an endless crowd of faces, holding their torches up high. Men and women, chanting in a strange tongue.

"The Other People," Noah said. "You ever wonder who the *Others* were when Cain was banished to the land of Nod if Adam and their two sons was the only ones on earth at the time?"

"Witches," I said.

"That's right," Noah said. "My people... and yours,"

"I ain't no witch,"

He cackled now, rattling me from the inside with raucous laughter.

"Oh, that is just too good! You mean to tell me your Grannie ain't never told you?"

I was frozen, paralyzed with a sickness that came from a realization I wasn't ready to have.

"Well, seems to me like Grannie ain't told you the truth, the whole truth, and nothin' but the truth so help you, oh, well... I'd say you're beyond *God's* help now, ain'tcha?"

My lips quivered, and my voice shook as I tried to ask the question that had an answer that would rock the foundation of my entire world.

"What truth is that?" I said, finally.

"That your Mama was a witch," he said. I shuddered. "And you was one of the few lucky men blessed to have the Gift."

"No..."

"Come now, Levi... Why do you think you was so much more powerful than all your piers without tryin'?"

"It—It was the Christ power given to me," I said, unsure. "I was born with it."

"Oh, indeed you was. But do you find it a coincidence that He chose *you?*" Noah shook his head, pityingly. "He chose the descendant of Cain, those born of the first witches to spite the Goddess... Just as it was in your first life,"

"I don't believe you,"

"You don't have to," Noah said. "In time, you'll see for yourself. The Christ power was taken away from you by the God the Garden... But I can give it back,"

"How?"

"What He took from you was a key to unlock the door to power... But our Lord holds in his hand a skeleton key. And if you pass through that door into the Lady's domain... power awaits you unlike any you've ever had. Power that runs through your veins, just waitin' for you to unlock it. Would you like that, Levi?"

I was faced with the God of the witches, who spoke through his chosen vessel as Shaddai once spoke through me. I wanted to believe he was lying, but deep in my soul, I knew that he wasn't. If Mama was a witch this entire time, why would Grannie Tamar have kept that a secret from me all these years? And even more frightening, what else could she have been keeping from me? There was only one way to find out, and after my fall from grace, I had nothing else to lose.

"Fine," I said. "What do I have to do?"

Noah stepped aside, gesturing for me to walk forward. I walked ahead until my bare feet were tickled by a warmth that licked against my toes. The human figures who stood with their torches were standing in a murky substance up to their waists. At the forefront of them was an old, black woman, standing nude and with eyes glowing as white as snow. She had her arms out to her sides, and her mouth hung open.

"Take off your robe," Noah said. "And be as you were."

I reluctantly reached over my shoulder, until finally I let my robe fall at my feet. The woman standing inside the warm, murky water extended her hand to me.

"Who is she?" I said.

"You've already met... The mother of the Summerland Pact," Noah said.

"Tituba," I said under my breath.

I stepped back, dipping my foot in, and instantly, flashes of my first life as a child flooded my mind, and I saw myself nursing at the breast of Mary. I staggered backward, heaving in terror.

"What is this?" I said.

"Blood. The river of knowledge of every witch gone before, the living waters of the Lady's womb. Gnosmos. It's life, Levi," Noah said, "and you're about to step into your new one."

"I can't, I can't do this..." I said.

"Don't you want to know the truth, Levi? Don't you want to see what's been kept from you all these years? It's your life. Don't you think you deserve to know?"

I looked back at the rippling, bloody waters and then at Noah. He stood there delighted, urging me silently to take the next step. I took a deep breath and waded through the water towards the old woman standing at the forefront of the Others, whose chanting turned to serpentine hissing as I approached her. My heart raced as I knew this was the final step in my rebellion against the God of the Garden. There was no turning back from this point, no hope for any redemption. To pact with the Devil was to renounce Shaddai and his Kingdom and join the souls who I condemned to his fiery pits.

But I was ready.

The truth was worth dying for. I was tired of living a lie. I was tired of killing for His namesake. I was ready to be my own man, even if there was hell to pay for it. If the God of the Garden laid a curse on my family, then I would do whatever it took to break it. I don't know if the story Granny told me about this town was true or not, but what

I did know was that I was now standing before the Matriarch of it all.

I now stood before Tituba, who radiated and hummed with a palpable energy that emanated all around her. I could feel her power giving life to the Others around her, and even the blood I stood in was alive with an electric sensation, pulsating and almost breathing. It was the living waters of some type of womb, and I was readying to be born again.

As I once stood at the banks of the river Jordan, so I stood again to be Baptized in darkness. I faced Tituba and took her hand. The moment I touched her skin waves of warm, electric power rippled throughout my body like being struck by lightning.

She gently held me by the small of my back, and with her other hand, she laid it over my chest right over my heart. I looked into her snowy eyes before I closed mine and took a deep breath as she lowered me into the blood.

CHAPTER 23:

Original Sin

The deeper I sank, the easier it became to breathe. The waters in front of me started to churn, and wisps of black like ink shot down and started to take form, painting a scene in front of me until ruddy rays of light filled the air, and the blood I floated in became dirt and sky. The inky globs took the form of people, and there I found myself suspended in the air over a crowded village.

"*Remember*," A woman's voice called to me, echoing and speaking in a multitude.

At the sound of her voice, the scene became clearer, and I found myself in a starry night in the days of antiquity, and in the bedroom of a young girl who couldn't have been older than 15. She was backed into a corner, crying and shaking her head as a fluctuating, fiery energy in the form of a man approached her, illuminating the room. It was Mary.

Her nose was pierced with a ring of gold, and her robes were woven into decadent patterns, reflecting the lineage of her family that hailed from King David. Her skin was like burnished bronze, and her eyes were like two jade stones made glassy with tears as she saw the specter enter. The spirit that appeared in her room forced itself onto her. She begged and plead for it to stop, but the spirit lulled her to sleep, and the entirety of his form was absorbed by her body, and her womb now glowed faintly.

"Remember,"

It was the "immaculate" conception. The church always painted this moment as being a triumphant and glorious time in history, but they didn't mention the terror and violence that Mary experienced. When the Spirit of God came upon her, she had no choice in the matter, there was no consent to be had. It was only the God of the Garden forcing himself onto her for His own agenda, for the plans that he had to both humiliate the young priestess devoted to a Goddess He'd long resented.

I watched young Mary weeping that night when she woke, feeling the life inside her that was soon to grow and carry without anyone to help her. It was the plight of every woman who'd had her freedom stolen from a man who thought his owns desires greater than her own; of a calloused God who saw his creation as nothing more than chess pieces in a cruel, cosmic game. Her sobbing made me sick to my stomach, and before I could reach out a phantom hand to console her, the scene around me morphed into the next.

I saw now myself, leaving in the dead of night. My skin was like brass, my hair like wool. I shuddered, finally seeing my first life, a scared little boy fleeing under the cover of darkness with my mother.

"Remember," The voice said again.

Mary covered my head with a veil, and there we stood in front of the mouth of a cave. She handed me an unlit torch, and with a gentle breath, she blew against the wood, and a fire spawned from her breath. She gently placed her hand on my shoulder and stepped aside. I was a man, but I was still boyish in appearance, and I knew then that I was in my teenage years. I entered the cave with my mother beside me, treading through unknown territory.

"He cannot find you here," Mary said. "He cannot see this place."

We wandered through the liminal space when I stopped at the banks of a lake like blood, surrounded now by people that waded in the murky substance and waited for me on the shore.

It was the same cave that Noah brought me to.

A woman emerged from the depths of the bloody waters, nude as the day she was born with a white python wrapped around her neck, hissing. Mary threw herself down in worship and kissed the woman's feet in reverence. I saw myself standing beside my mother and trying to hide the fear that swept my eyes. She spoke in a serpentine-like language, but I understood the woman's words.

"He will kill him when he emerges," The woman said to Mary.

"This is his birthright," Mary answered back in the same tongue.

The woman nodded, and the snake around her neck unwound itself and gave a nod of its head. Mary handed me off to the woman, and I watched as my first lifetime shed my robe-like old skin and followed her into the blood. I knew then that all the years missing in those Gospels where I emerged as a man were spent in this cave, learning the hidden mysteries and knowledge forbidden by the God of the Garden.

But why?

The moment I saw myself step into the blood everything around me changed again when suddenly I found myself sitting at the head of the table at a wedding, my wedding. Mary Magdalene sat beside me, lovingly looking into my eyes. She had thick coils of dark hair and almond-shaped eyes. The Church, for the longest time, denied this history. They said the Christ never took for himself a wife. But with my own eyes, I started to see the veil of lies that they'd carefully woven fall, and the truth was coming to light.

From the wedding now I saw myself again, standing naked, facing Mary, my wife, in our bedroom, and our lips met tenderly. She laid her hand against my cheek; I could see the fear in her eyes.

"Shaddai is readying to kill you and hand you over to the Romans," she said. "The Lady sent me a vision in my sleep of a lamb being led to the slaughter."

I kissed her again, resting my forehead against hers.

"I was born to die," I said. "But like the corn and the grain, all that falls shall rise again. I will return."

"Will you come back for me?" Mary said.

"In every life," I said.

We lied down, and the candles were extinguished, plunging me into the darkness once again, only to be broken by the light of day. I was surrounded now by a jeering crowd, being whipped along the way with a pregnant Mary weeping and following behind me as closely as she could. They nailed me to a cross, and there I cried out in agony to the God that had long forsaken me. As I hung my head and gave up the ghost, the sky went dark in the middle of the day, and the ground shook in a ferocious earthquake.

There was no resurrection. The following scene that played out was Mary, my mother, and Mary, my wife, tending to my body before lying me down in my tomb, where my body would become a feast for maggots and decay. I would live again, but through another life that followed, where the God of the Garden sought to correct the error of the first. Even as the new Adam, I still repeated the sin of disobedience, and Shaddai would carry out his most horrific act yet.

The next thing I saw before me was the Pharisees, their eyes were glowing white with the possession of Shaddai, storming into a nursery where my baby girl was being breastfed. Mary screamed as they yanked her by the hair and dragged her across the room. She begged and pleaded as the Pharisees tore my baby from her arms and took her along the banks of the Sea of Galilea, where crocodiles gathered and tossed her into their den. I screamed, swinging my arms, only to see them pass through the priests, who watched the thrashing of the water turn red and the baby's cries that were extinguished like a candle flame.

My heart was eviscerated, and my throat was raw. I clasped onto my head, begging and crying to make it all stop, and everything around me changed once again, and the ancient times withered to stalk, giving way to a horse and carriage, traveling down a winding, offbeat road. A pale, spindly man with a long, white beard sat across from us in the carriage dressed in a scarlet cassock, watching us closely.

I saw another lifetime of myself now, sitting with what I knew were my wife and five children traveling with us. They were beautiful young girls and a boy, all nestled closely by my wife. Their skin was milky, with eyes like the ocean or lush green forests and loose auburn curls. My wife was a true vision, with almond eyes and defined collarbones, and sunshine hair. We were dressed finely, in suits and gowns that were sewn with jewels. The man in the car watched us tensely, and my wife looked back at me. I smiled nervously, and the sunlight peeking through the window cast an ivory glow against my cheeks.

I didn't know who this priest was, but as I wiped the tears from my eyes from the last vision, I couldn't shake the gut-wrenching feeling I had that something horrific was about to happen to us.

"And you're certain nobody knows where we're going?" My wife said to the priest.

He smiled dryly, and his dead, heavy-lidded eyes twinkled with suspicion.

"You can be sure to trust me, my lady... I'm Joshua's most trusted advisor. I'd never want to see any harm come to him. Especially not the little ones,"

The youngest girl clasped onto my hand, quietly groaning uneasily. My wife looked back at me, silently begging for this to be true. I took her hand in mine, patting it reassuringly.

"Father Dolion has been a friend to me. Don't worry."

"*Remember,*" Chimed the voice again.

The scene of the carriage transformed into a darkened hallway with leaking pipes, and the sound of feet shuffling frantically. I saw my past self again, rigid with fright and moving his family along as quickly as he could. The man called Father Dolion led us, holding a lantern above his head.

"Quickly, this way," he said. "We don't have much time,"

We descended a flight of stairs into a basement, fresh with the smell of rust and slick with grime. There was a small, barred window overhead, and the sound of a train passing in the distance.

"Is that for us?" My youngest daughter asked with doughy eyes.

"It is child," Dolion said. "The train is coming to take everyone to their final destination."

"And we'll be safe there?" My wife asked.

"Where you're going, you won't have a care in the world," Dolion said.

"I can't thank you enough for hiding us all this time, Father. You've proven to be a true friend through and through," I said.

The feeling in my gut grew more painful until I could hardly stand to watch the scene. It was like a horror movie.

"Of course," he said.

Footsteps punned down the stairs, and there, crimson-robed priests emerged accompanied by two soldiers holding guns that I recognized as the judges'.

"Joshua Shepherd?" the priest said.

I stepped forward, my children hid now behind my wife.

"Here I am," I said.

"Miriam Shepherd?" the priest asked again

My wife stepped forward beside me, clasping tightly to the side of my arm.

"Dina, Deborah, Sarah, Hannah, and Amos Shepherd?"

The children held hands, trembling and reluctant to step forward until finally standing behind us.

"We're all present here," I said. "When are we boarding the train?"

Dolion's jagged, crooked teeth came into full view with his sinsiter smile. The priest glanced back at him as Dolion gave them the nod of approval. All the eyes of the priests and suited soldiers eyes glowed white as snow.

"In the name of God Almighty and of the Mother Church, I sentence you to death." The priest said.

The bullets from their guns pierced me through the heart and forehead. I watched myself collapse, lifeless. My wife screamed, and mercilessly, they rained a storm of bullets through her. I watched helplessly, screaming and sobbing again so badly snot ran down my nose. I ran in front of the children to protect them as the priests aimed their guns at them, but they passed through my spectral form and showered them in a flurry of bullets. The shooting seemed to go on for hours as they bounced off the diamonds and jewels that were sewn into their clothing. Finally, the guards grew tired of them and slew them with the ends of their bayonets as the priests held out their hands and joyfully recited the Our Father with tears of joy streaming down their faces. I cried and kicked, swinging my arms in frustration, trying to choke the priests, but my hands passed through their necks.

The bloody scene morphed and blurred, swirling around me and becoming like bubbles rising to the surface of a simmering pot. I reached my hand out to my family that was given as a sacrifice, and the last sight I saw was my wife's cold, dead eyes lying in a puddle of blood, gurgling and gagging before she took her last breath. The next breath I took filled my lungs with a painful burn, like breathing underwater. I slammed firmly against the ground, weeping now on my knees.

I could feel the dirt I clasped onto squishing through my bloody hands, and I knew I was back in my own body and this cruel world once more.

I coughed out tarry, black blood, wiping my face to feel the slick warmth of the fresh blood I'd just emerged from. Cold winds slapped against my back, and I was naked and terrified. I stood now at the top of a cliff, looking over the town of Tophet. As I looked up, the Witch Queen was standing at the edge of the cliff with her deep, red cloak flowing in the wind. I stumbled towards her, coughing and heaving and trying to stop the tears that kept flowing.

Noah emerged from the darkness of the woods behind me, thick with overgrown trees and moss.

"Hello again, old friend. Miss me?"

The horrors that I'd seen, the senseless violence. God truly was an all-consuming fire as the Scriptures say, but it wasn't passion and love. It was deplorable and destructive. It was a callousness, so devoid of empathy and regard for human life that it became plain to see that He didn't love anyone but himself. The God of the Garden would do anything to main his reign and keep those who rebelled against him in line. He would turn on his servants, he would chastise and punish those in the name of love to teach them a lesson. He would torture, coerce, and kill those we loved closest to us and threaten us with the promise of a fiery afterlife if we didn't bend the knee.

It wasn't love that his followers felt for him, it was Stockholm Syndrome and fear for their own lives. All this time I'd been serving at the feet of this God and carrying out the monstrous work of his hands, a paintbrush in the hands of a heartless creator used to color the canvas of the world red with blood. I wasn't a son to him. I was a tool. Watching him take the lives of innocent children all in His name made me sick.

"Why they doin' this to me?" I heaved, wobbling back to my feet and towards her.

"You can't understand history if you don't know it, Levi," she said. "Do you understand yet?"

I shook my head, still weeping bitterly.

"The God of the Garden didn't want your line to continue through the descendants of Mary."

"Why?" I sniffled. "I don't understand,"

"To thwart the prophecy spoken against Him. To stop his downfall," she explained.

"What prophecy?" I said.

A dark expression grew on her face now, and she spoke in hissing tongues like the woman who emerged from the cave.

"From among the pious and the proud, down unto the voices in the shroud, shall rise crimson blood that ascends as high as the Tower, and generations of men shall bend the brow and cower before his horn of power.... And all the while, the wise are led to the slaughter, from the darkness shall flow again my knowledge through the water, and the sword of your Lamb shall pierce the Womb of my daughter; and blood shall restore the balance once brought to totter.

"Then all the earth will behold the Morning Glory and see the sign of the battle won when he that is Vengeance will be brought to justice and bend the knee before my rightful Son..."

I felt like Zeus, destined to overthrow Cronus who threatened his reign.

"This… This prophecy is about me?" I said. "No… No, this was about him. About Noah. That's why Gerald was tryin' to kill you."

"Partially true," Noah said. "The prophecy is a trinity. You should know all about that."

"The Goddess is cunning… Do you think her so simple as to leave all this one person's hands? " she said. "Scores of magicians and judges have tried to stop this from bein' fulfilled… And when you come together with the woman from the line of Mary, you produce wholly divine children, with powers unimaginable."

"My children…" I said, somberly. "He's always taken them away,"

"Ain't you put two and two together yet?" she said.

"I don't understand."

"Why do you think your Grannie don't want you and Amma gettin' together?"

"Grannie said… She said witches and magicians ain't supposed to be together,"

"So Grannie lied." I scoffed. "She been lyin' to me this whole time?"

"In her mind, she was doin' the right thing. But she ain't ever told you the truth, Levi… You and Amma was prevented from bein' together 'cause she ain't want to restore the Holy Grail…"

It felt like a dagger to the heart; the sting of truth. If I return to this life in an endless cycle, then that meant Amma continued to return just like the other original disciples did like Jonah and Titus. Only we were deliberately placed on opposing sides and kept from one another to stop all this.

"The holy bloodline," I said to myself.

She nodded. "It ain't too late to join the right side," she said. "You chose that side in more than one life,"

"And I paid the price for it every time."

"So you're still obedient to fear."

"I don't answer to nobody or nothin'."

"Then prove it," she said.

I paused for a moment, clenching my fist to relieve the tension. "Then answer me this. Why is stoppin' the Holy Grail so important?"

"Because the offspring child would not be human; a creature made entirely sublime. They would help to usher in the final act of this prophecy, and dethrone the God of Heaven," she said.

"It's your destiny, don't you know who you are?"

"I thought I did once," I admitted, jaded. "But now I'm not too sure anymore."

"Rebellion is in your very soul, Levi. Don't you remember? That the fallen angels take mortal bodies through the spawns of Eve, the children of men?" she said. "The Summerland Pact only assured that the woman would receive her cut of the power without question, but the first rebellion of Eve was knowledge, and she paid the price."

"What are you gettin' at with all this?"

"The God of the Garden was blinded in his lust for Mary and in his desire to humiliate the Goddess He overlooked the angelic blood that she carried... and the one that she would pass on."

"Look, I've been through a lot already. I'd appreciate it if you just talked straight and not spin all this cryptic bullshit."

"Who do they say you are?" she asked.

A hollow breeze passed between my silence.

"The Son of God."

She shook her head.

"No," she said. "You are Son of the Morning."

"You mean..."

"You are *Lucifer*," she said.

The hairs on my neck stood on end.

"That can't be..."

"Tell me. All the times you'd been to Hell, you ever see him there?"

She was right. The only thing I'd ever seen were souls suffering in Hell and the angels who rebelled held in chains of darkness crying for eons to be released.

"When the Lady divided herself and brought the Dawn, the morning; the light of day, it was you. You existed long before Shaddai took form."

"No, no, no... that can't be true. If that were, how could Shaddai have taken my power back? I have nothin' to my name."

She smiled compassionately.

"What was stolen was your key. Your power, the true power, comes from the Eternal Flame, the Source of all things..."

"How... How, then, can I get it back?" I said.

"It ain't mine to give," she said. "It's been yours all along... Sleepin' inside you. Waitin' for the moment to wake."

"But how?"

"Who are you?" she said.

"I... I'm Levi Beaumont."

"No... *who* are you?"

I took a deep breath, shutting my eyes.

"*Lucifer*," I said, forcefully.

Rapid, violent gusts of dust from the ground around me formed a tunnel, and I stood in the center, blinded now by the soot and dirt. The ground flew down my throat, suffocating me. I gagged and choked, struggling to breathe.

"And you shall be given power over men and nature, the forces of this world to bend at your will," she said through the howling winds.

I dropped to the ground, able to breathe once more. I clasped onto my chest, heaving and panting for breath, the taste of dirt lodged firmly in the back of my throat. Before I could speak, from beneath the ground bubbled water from the soil, rushing towards me and forcing itself once more down my throat and through my nose. The familiar burn of water in my lungs took over, and I writhed on the floor in agony again as the waters from the earth filled me to the brim before stopping as quickly as they came. I was curled in the fetal position, gagging and coughing up water.

I stood to my feet, looking at the palms of my trembling hands, where the water droplets now moved in rapid circles before rolling down the sides of my hands.

"W—What's happenin' to me?" I said.

"Remember," she said.

My body was instantly engulfed in flames, scorching hot like magma. I screamed in agony, and fire spewed out from my mouth. I could feel the flames burning through my eyes and escaping, consuming me entirely. My feet came off the ground, and I began to climb into the sky, illuminating the darkness around me where the Witch Queen stood. I was like the sun, shining down and expelling every shadow that now fled from my presence. The higher I ascended, the pain lessened until the fires themselves began to dim, and I felt no pain.

I looked down at the ground, my feet dangled, and I was as free as a bird. Gentle winds blew across my cheeks, swirling and thrashing around me, guiding me back down towards the ground, walking on the wind. My feet were finally firmly planted, and I looked back at the Witch Queen, who smiled deeply. I was alive with a power that I'd never felt before, even more profound than entering Transfiguration. I felt like I was truly a living god, and all the earth was beneath my feet. This was the kingdom of the world that I once denied.

"Know thyself," she said. "This is the first lesson we must learn as the Hidden Children. Now, tell me, Levi, again… who are you?"

I was the dragon that waged war in heaven against Michael and his angels. I was that terrible beast that swiped down a third of the stars in Heaven and fell to Earth. I was the one who spoke in whispers, the light of the truth that was snuffed by the true master deceiver. I was the one who fought against the crown of Heaven, against the very throne of the Most High. I was the one who would set myself to be exalted above every name in all the earth and heavenly host. I was the light bearer, the truth seeker, the one who dared to go against the grain. I was the first Prometheus who gave knowledge to man, the peacock angel whose wisdom and knowledge were renowned.

I was ready to take my rightful place once more. I would scorch the sky, turn the wind to gun smoke, and the waters to wormwood.

"Lucifer," I said.

I am Lucifer.

CHAPTER 24

Son Of The Morning

For the first time in my life, I could say that I knew who I was.

It may not have been the identity that I imagined, but it was me. All my life, I'd walked around blindfolded and told who I was and what I was born to do, but now I finally understood why.

Fear.

I tried to control the witches; every man went back to Adam. We said they were out of line and had a power that wasn't deserved. But really, that power was knowledge; they knew who they were and where they came from.

I could feel the power coursing through my body; it was vibrant and electric, alive in and of itself, slowly merging and connecting to every nerve.

"This power…" I said. "It's unlike anything I've ever seen… How does it work?"

"It's connected to thought and emotion. As a magician, you had to form hidden hands. You already understand the foundation… let's just say you have no more need for the trainin' wheels."

She smiled playfully.

"It's your birthright, Levi," she said to me. "You've been denied the truth for long enough,"

"I've only ever served the God of the Garden… That power is all I've known. I've died to protect it."

"Because slavery and fear are what gives Him power. The God of the Garden is a corruption, a mistake created by the hands of the Goddess, who expelled him from the Highest Heaven and the Council of the gods... So he sought to create His own world, one where He would control and could rule without restraint."

"And y'all are here to put an end to this?"

"The first people created were beings of pure light, of spirit. Shaddai imprisoned them in cages of flesh and bone to make them subservient and reliant on him. This is why He loathes Magic, why He'll do anythin' to keep it from the hands of mankind."

"Because then we wouldn't need Him," I said.

She nodded.

"How can I trust what you're sayin' is true?"

"Have I shown you a lie?"

I paused. "I wouldn't know, would I? How can I be sure that all you showed me wasn't some kind of illusion?" I said.

"Why, the truth too painful?" A voice called from behind.

Noah emerged from the darkness of the woods behind me, thick with overgrown trees and moss.

"I thought it was supposed to set you free," he said, smirking.

"You helped me awaken this power in me... But this could all just be to push me into fightin' on your side... Grannie may have lied about many things, but I know she wasn't lyin' about how this town came to be and what y'all did to it."

She and Noah looked away shamefully. Noah rubbed the back of his neck uncomfortably, glancing back at the Witch Queen.

"Look... ain't nothin' in the world can justify what was done," Noah said.

"I'm ashamed," the Witch Queen said. "I couldn't imagine the vileness in our Sisters' hearts that drove them to side with magicians against their own kind. And there ain't nothin' I could say to change that terrible past. If I'm bein' honest, we don't deserve the Gift after those actions Adora took against your Great Grannie,"

"You mean Tituba."

They nodded in unison.

"Didn't your Mama ever tell you?"

"Mama lost her mind when I was a kid. She's been locked away in a mental hospital ever since. Grannie says the God of the Garden cursed her with madness for betrayin' the Magdalenes, and no one can lift His curse."

"Hm. Would God create a rock so heavy even He couldn't lift it?" Noah said.

"What?"

Noah laughed.

"Levi, you've limited and defined your power based on a line that He told you you couldn't cross. Did Adam and Eve die after eatin' that fruit?" he asked.

I hated the feeling in my gut when things started to make more sense than I was ready to handle. It was dizzying and created an aching feeling in the pit of my stomach.

"No," I said, breaking the silence.

"Levi," the Witch Queen said. "Your Grannie's learned to mix the truth with lies all these years, so it would come to a point where you couldn't tell the difference between the two."

"He'll kill them… Or worse," I said. "My family, my friends."

"If He wanted to do that, He would have by this point in time… He must have another plan in motion," she said.

"So it wasn't y'all who set loose the Primordials?"

Noah shook his head.

"Not even close; that's why we came here the moment the Firmament was breached. Although we would be lyin' if we didn't say it worked in our favor."

"How's that?"

"They was the first thing that made you question your power because you couldn't control them."

"It planted that seed of doubt," the Witch Queen said. "And that's all we needed to get through to you. We was never here lookin' for a fight."

"Then why did you send the Lilitu after me?"

"Ain't you hear what I said before? You have to restore the holy bloodline, Levi. The disciples was the original Coven, the one that came together to overthrow the God of the Garden."

"So what did you need my, uh, 'seed' for? Was it for yourself?"

"Not even a little. We were gonna extract the life force from it... But now that you're here, I'd say there's been a change of plans. All accordin' to our Lady's plans."

"I don't understand?"

She laughed.

"Boy, I swear you's dumber than a box of hair. For *Amma*," she said. "Don't you remember the prophecy I just told you? '*And the sword of your Lamb will pierce the womb of my daughter*'... That's you and Amma. Christ and Magdalene returned."

"How... How am I supposed to do that?"

"It's called the Great Rite," Noah said. "A sacred act that generates life. But because you are divinely made, and Amma's got the same power flowin' through her, you'll bring Hidden Children into this world... The first witches, created by Shaddai and the Goddess."

"Shaddai created people with this Goddess?"

"Oh, yes," The Witch Queen said. "It's the reason He resents us the way He does."

"I still don't know if I could trust you," I said.

Noah winced. "That's fine, but I reckon you'd trust your Mama, wouldn't you?"

"But the curse," I said.

"Don't mean nothin' no more. You're greater now than you was then," The Witch Queen said.

"We know it ain't much, but we was hopin' one thing could convince you that we're on the same side," Noah said.

"What's that?"

The Witch Queen gave him a solemn nod. Noah held out his hands, palms facing up as if he were holding something unseen. The sound of fluttering pages reverberated from between his hands and revealed themselves, falling into place and now forming a large book. The book was bound with what looked like human skin, aged, and with a spine made of bone. The book's cover bore a skeletal face with a gaping, black mouth. I shuddered at the sight, stepping back.

"What the hell is that?"

"The Book of Aeons," Noah said. "Tituba brought it to the New World before she showed the girls of Salem, who in turn brought it with them to Summerland,"

"Stole it," The Witch Queen corrected. "It was supposed to be shared amongst the 13 bloodlines of the Summerland Pact. But after Adora's actions, it's remained with the Summerland Coven. It carries the signed names of every witch gone before,"

"The Devil's black book," I said, barely above a whisper.

She nodded. "It rightfully belongs in Amma's hands and her coven here. This was where Tituba made her home, only fittin' that it should be here."

"What am I supposed to do with this?" I said. "I don't want that,"

"This book contains Rites and rituals long lost to the Tophet Coven. If you show this to Amma, she will listen to you."

"Why would I do that?"

"Because I want to speak with her," she said. "This is the most sacred book that exists for the Bloodlines. There is no book with deeper magic and history. In it is the truth of creation itself, and every secret between highest heaven and the deepest regions of Hell."

"What business y'all got with Amma?" I said defensively.

"We need to be united. The God of the Garden will use someone to continue to conjure these Primordials and let them tear this world apart before He allows it to fall back into the Goddess's hands."

"So if y'all ain't behind none of this, then... who is?"

"Well, now," The Witch Queen said. "Why don't you ask the man you call 'Father'?"

"What?"

Noah gave a wave of his hands, and billowing, dusty winds pushed me back into the reaches of the forest behind me until I stumbled backward against the dirt and vine beneath my feet, piercing my soles with sharpened twigs and thorny branches. I stumbled until where they once stood was obscured with darkness, and the leaves and prickling trees beneath my feet were now hard wooden floors, cold and firm. I tripped over myself, landing on the ground now and facing my bedroom's plain walls and flowery wallpaper.

I was back home.

I clutched the book firmly against my chest, wrapped around my arms like cradling a newborn. I caught a glimpse of my reflection in the shattered mirror in the corner of my room. I was covered in dried blood and dirt, looking fresh out of the womb, a newborn creation forged in true sin and a decadent corruption that caused an inner glow inside. Obedience was instilled in my mind as virtuous, something to aspired to and be rewarded for, but I saw now that it was just verbal shackles on our feet to keep us from taking what rightfully belonged to us. God rewarded the obedient because He wanted slaves, not children or equals.

I hid my book underneath my bed and headed toward the shower. I ran the water and stood beneath the hot current, watching the blood run down the drain.

They said that blood and water ran from my womb when I was stabbed with the spear of destiny. It felt poetic and like all had come full circle as my own destiny now caused me to bleed under running water. God supposedly gave us free will, but as I've learned, this was only the illusion of choice; fate and predestination determined everything. We get to choose the characters we become, but only from a roster of carefully crafted possibilities already laid out for us.

The murky, red water finally ran clear; with that, it was like the mental fog was lifted from me all at once. How could we be liberated from the chains of spiritual enslavement only for many of us to tighten the shackles again and call it religion? Humanity worshiped a man that sat in the clouds, waiting to punish every wrong move one made in the name of order, law, and love. It wasn't faith; it was madness. It was a profound delusion, and I wasn't free from this either.

I cut the water and let myself air dry, lost in my own thoughts, before I heard a knock at my bedroom door. They were delicate at first, subtle enough that I almost dismissed them until a heavier pound followed. BANG, BANG, BANG.

I wrapped the towel around my waist and went to open the door, only to find Grannie's eyes scrunched with tears she pat dried with her handkerchief.

"You got a visitor," she said.

"Who?" I said.

She glared.

"Mmhmm…" She grunted, walking away.

She seemed to be leaning against her cane more than usual. The night I saw Grannie after Amma's ascension to the matriarchy, she looked as though the very essence of life had been drained from her, like that power was the only thing keeping her alive. She said she was not long for this world after that, but now it started to become plain to see. I wanted to chase her down the hallway and ask her a barrage of questions and accusations, but at this stage, she looked like it took all her energy to knock on that door.

I quickly threw my clothes on and hurried downstairs into the living room. Along the plastic-covered couches and standing near the Grandfather clock was Amma, watching in horror at the soft glow of the television. News reporters on every channel, even in Georgia. Gallowsville straddled the border between there and Florida. And our madness was their media. They reported the chaos happening in our town.

"Amma?" I said, coming off the final step. "What're you doin' here?"

Her eyes twitched as she shook her head, mouthing prayers of denial to herself.

"The whole world's lost its mind," she said finally.

The television showed images of the aftermath left in the Primordials' wake. There were cars on fire, lootings of every store in sight, and people sitting at the street's curb, pulling their teeth out with pliers and laughing deliriously. Madness and ecstasy have driven everything they touched into an apocalyptic wasteland. There were mass suicides, murders, and deplorable actions of every shade and variety.

"Grannie send you?" I said.

She nodded. "Miss Tamar asked me to come see you... She told me what happened to Ezra and said to talk some sense into you."

I laughed sarcastically.

"As if I'm the one needin' sense talked into 'em."

"Where is he? Ezra?"

I gestured vaguely.

"Upstairs,"

"I wanna lay hands on him," Amma said. "I reckon Grannie couldn't much do nothin' on the count of her passin' the Power to me. So I'm sure I can do it,"

"Not if you callin' on God's name to lift it," I said.

She scoffed, incredulous.

"And by what other name would I do it?"

I stared back at her, my silence speaking an answer that caused her eyes to swell.

"Oh, Levi." She gasped. "Tell me it ain't so."

"It ain't what you think, Amma... We got it all wrong."

Amma shook her head.

"No wonder Miss Tamar asked me to come to talk with you. Boy, have you lost yo' mind? No wonder all this evil came into the world; you brought it to our door!"

"No, no," I rushed to her side, cupping her face.

Amma tried to pull away from me, but I held her tight.

"Amma, please... You think I'd do anythin' to bring harm to my own family?"

"Well, from where I'm standin' right now, it's hard to think anythin' different."

"What if I told you His power ain't nothin' but a spark?"

"Levi, you're lost... I can't believe I'm hearin' this. You—You supposed to be the Son of God."

"No," I said. "I'm much greater than that."

"And what would that be?" she said.

"A god."

She pulled away from me, incredulous.

"Let me prove it to you," I said. "I'll take you to my brother."

She stared at me for a moment, her eyes wide and breaths racing. Her mind was rushing with questions filled with fear and doubt. But her nature, the Eve-given inspiration, provoked her curiosity.

"Show me," she said.

I held out my hand in waiting until I felt the soft brush of her fingertips against my palm and took her by the hand upstairs. We made our way upstairs, stopping outside the door. Ezra's painful and quiet wheezing seeped through the door.

"How bad is he?" she asked, nervously looking back at the door.

"Enough to make Job pity him," I said.

I pushed the door open. Tears immediately slid down Amma's face as she covered her mouth and recoiled in fear. She approached his bedside, reluctantly reaching down to touch and reeling her hand back immediately.

"Oh, poor baby… What's happened to you?" Amma said, her voice trembling. "Why did this happen?"

"To punish me," I said. "For agreein' to work with the Queen of Georgia."

She closed her eyes, globs of tears running down her cheeks as she clutched onto her heart.

"How could you do this to him?" she asked.

"The God we've agreed to serve did this to cause us pain, yet somehow you're turnin' this on me?"

"If you would have just *obeyed*, Levi." She sniffled.

Amma laid her hands on Ezra's forehead. He gurgled, looking up at her with tears running down his face.

"We'll work tirelessly to lift this curse," Amma said. "I promise." She leaned down, kissing his forehead gently.

"If you heal him by Shaddai's power, I'll repent right here. But if *I* do it… you'll have to at least listen to what I gotta say,"

Amma glared at me, begrudgingly nodding in agreement. She pulled up a chair, sat at his bedside, and laid hands along his stomach. Ezra reached a trembling hand and laid it over Amma's, clasping her desperately.

"P—Please..." Ezra groaned.

Amma wiped the tear from her eye with her free hand and smiled bitterly.

"Through Him, all things are possible," she said.

Amma cleared her throat and closed her eyes, focusing her power. The room was filled with a vibrant hum, pulsating from Amma as she began to generate energy.

"*They cried to the Lord in their trouble, and he saved them from their distress. He sent out his word and healed them,*" Amma muttered, reciting the Psalm. She chanted the last portion again and again as gentle breezes ran through the room, catching our clothing and the bedsheets in its caress.

"*He sent out his word and healed them,*" Amma repeatedly chanted until she was out of breath.

She whimpered, slowly recoiling from Ezra's grasp. She sat quietly, watching him lie there unaffected, inflicted still with the suffering that even she, as Madonna, couldn't lift. Fresh tears trickled down her face as she gasped with a painful realization.

"Nothin'," Amma said.

I placed my hand on her shoulder, quietly gesturing for her to move over. I helped Amma stand from the chair, and she sat behind me now as I took her seat. I took Ezra's hand in mine, patting him reassuringly.

"Don't worry, my brother... I got you," I said.

I closed my eyes, focusing everything in me the same way I'd have healed anybody else. I took one deep breath, and words suddenly came to me in a hushed serpentine whisper, and I repeated them aloud:

"*I remove this Curse,*" I said.

Amma shuddered.

"H—How do you know the Hidden Tongue?" she asked.

The festering boils that consumed his body began to vanish, climbing up my arm instead and filling my chest. I chanted the words repeatedly until I couldn't breathe anymore. Gradually, the same in-fliction crawled up my skin, and suddenly, I was covered from head to toe in painful blisters and leathery skin. Ezra's body was now in pristine condition, radiating with newness.

He was healed.

I was relieved. I looked back at Amma, whose mouth hung now in disbelief. I laughed, only for the sound to be snuffed out by Ezra's crushing hand wrapped tightly around my neck.

CHAPTER 25:

Fruit Of Knowledge

"Ezra!" Amma screamed, running to my side.

He shoved Amma off of him, slamming her against the dresser. The more I tried to break from his grasp, the tighter his grip around me became. Ezra stood up from the bed, heaving and with blood-shot eyes. He lifted me off the ground, my feet dangling and kicking desperately. My vision was blurred, and I dipped in and out of consciousness as he choked the life out of me. Ezra rammed me against the wall with flared nostrils, his brow digging deep into his forehead.

"You did this to me," he growled.

My hands helplessly beat against his broad chest, but it was like landing strikes against the stone. Ezra was as big as a bull and twice as temperamental.

"*You* brought all this onto us!" he said.

Tears ran down his face now.

"How could you do this? HOW!" he bellowed, tightening his grip.

Amma stood from the ground, and with a wave of her hand, she catapulted Ezra across the room, flinging him against the wall and pinning him in place by the force of her magic. I collapsed, fighting to breathe as I rubbed my raw throat. Her eyes were beady and black, emitting a heat haze that distorted the air around her arms.

"That's enough."

"HE'S JOINED THEIR SIDE! HE BROUGHT EVIL INTO THIS TOWN!" Ezra screamed, trying to fight the grip of Amma's magic.

He struggled to lift his wrists off the wall, but the crushing pressure of her hold overpowered him. She held him in place until he stopped resisting and finally settled back onto his feet. Amma ran to my side, helping me up. Ezra glared at me from across the room. I could tell he wanted to lunge at me to finish me off, but he knew Amma would stop him before he even lifted a finger.

"I…" I said hoarsely. "I didn't do this. Your God did."

Ezra scoffed, stomping towards me. Amma held her hand out to him again, and he froze in place, backing away like a scared dog.

"It's *my* God now?" Ezra said. "You one of them now, ain't you? That's how you was able to heal me,"

"Anythin' I've done, it's been to protect my family. Anythin' that can do that to you…. I don't want no part of,"

Ezra took a step towards me, pointing at me. If he could've spit venom at that moment, he would, but instead, he choked back on his own words.

"You're dead to me, you hear? Pops would be rollin' in his grave," Ezra spat.

I hide my face, fighting the shame.

"Ezra," Amma said, gasping in disgust. "He is your brother."

Ezra shook his head.

"Not no more he ain't," Ezra said.

He walked by us; Amma stood in front of me, shielding me now. Ezra stopped at the door.

"And if I ever catch you at this house again… I'll kill you with my bare hands."

Ezra spat at the ground, slammed the door back open, and stormed down the hallway. Amma rubbed my shoulder.

"You doin' alright?" she said softly.

I looked down as the deformity I absorbed from Ezra in my arms began to fade away.

"I can't be here no more," I said tearfully.

I pulled away from Amma and charged back to my room.

"Levi," Amma said, following behind me.

She closed my bedroom door behind me. I furiously packed clothing into duffle bags, pacing back and forth between the bed and my closet.

"He ain't mean it," Amma said.

"He does," I said. "The Providence swore to kill anyone that works with witches. And that means me now."

Amma watched me in stunned silence.

"But how'd this happen?" She said.

"Turns out the Christ power ain't everythin' they told me it was."

"Who all told you that?"

"Ain't nobody told me nothin'. That's the problem. It took me gettin' a smack down by Tituba herself for me to realize." I grunted. "And trust me, gettin' my ass beat by a woman wasn't never part of the plan."

Amma raised an eyebrow.

"No offense," I clumsily added.

"Y—You met Tituba?" Amma asked. "The Great Mother?"

She sat on the bed, staring down at the floor, incredulous.

"*How?*"

I shrugged.

"She came to the aid of the Queen of Georgia."

Amma scoffed dismissively.

"Miss Tamar ain't never told you about what they'd done to us? How they burned this town to the ground?"

"And stole the Book of Aeons?"

Amma gawked.

"How do you know what that is?"

I reached under the bed and grabbed the book, placing it in her hands. She shuddered with fluttering breaths, and her eyes glossed over. She gently ran her hands across the face of the book; I could see the hairs on her arms standing on end.

"H—How? How did you get this?" She laughed in a stupor.

"The Witch Queen gave it to me tonight. She said it rightfully belonged to y'all."

Amma stared down at the cover, sniffling. She glowed with a disbelieving smile, too stunned to speak.

"Why?" she finally said.

"She said it's the least they could do for all the damage caused by the Madonnas before her."

"I don't know what to say," Amma said. "Why would she trust you with this?"

"If we're bein' real right now? I wouldn't want nothin' to do with them after what Grannie told me. But they were the only ones who was willin' to show me the truth."

"What truth?"

I sat down beside her with a heavy sigh.

"They showed me my first lifetime, and another after that… I know now why I keep comin' back here, and it ain't to serve the God of the Garden."

"Then why?"

I turned towards Amma, taking her hands in mine and looking deep into her questioning eyes.

"It's to keep findin' you."

"Me?" she said, curious.

"Amma… Do you know who you are? Who you really are?"

She paused for a moment.

"I feel like if I said yes… that would only be half the truth, wouldn't it?"

"There's a reason why the Petram and the Madonna ain't supposed to be together. And it don't got nothin' to do with witches taintin' the bloodline," I said. "It's because it will create *the* bloodline. The Holy Grail… Amma, if I'm Christ reincarnated, then what do you think that makes you?"

"Mary." Amma covered her mouth. "Mary Magdalene."

I nodded.

"Together, you and I are supposed to usher in a new era, where the God of the Garden will no longer rule this world."

Amma stood abruptly, pacing now back and forth.

"No, no," she began. "I don't know what ideas she's puttin' in your head. I don't even know who you are anymore."

"Lucifer," I said.

She gasped, stepping back.

"I'm Lucifer,"

Amma shook her head, moving farther away from me, clasping the Book of Aeons tightly against her chest.

"No, no, you're the Son of God."

"I'm Son of the Mornin'," I said "See... Shaddai wanted me to think I was just his son. But I'm a god in my own right. The other half of your Goddess, the darkness."

"No," Amma argued. "We don't bend to her. We serve Shaddai."

"If that's true, then why do y'all need those Rituals to pass the Power along?"

Amma's eyes ping-ponged; I could tell she was searching desperately for an answer.

"Because your power don't come from Him, it never did... Y'all have the blood of fallen angels runnin' through them veins... I know it, and so do you," I said.

"The Devil is a lie," Amma said. "I won't hear none of this."

She ran for the door. I waved my hand, and the door slammed shut. She tugged at the handle, but it wouldn't give.

"Let me out before I blow this door down," she said firmly.

"After what their Madonna did to us... I wouldn't want to help them, neither. But Amma.... There's somethin' greater at play here."

"They opened a portal to Primordials, and you wanna turn around and help them?" She laughed mockingly. "You've sunken to a new low, Levi. Your Mama would be ashamed of you."

"My mama was one of you," I said. "Just like you, like Nita, and Grannie."

Amma rubbed her eyes, frustrated.

"They're destroyin' this town. First, they used fire; now, they're usin' Primordials. You're helpin' them with our extinction."

"It ain't them, Amma."

"No, then who is it?"

I shook my head, doubting the answer, even myself.

"I think… Father Enoch,"

Amma gasped, recoiling in disgust.

"Father Enoch would *never*. Listen to you!" she retorted. "You lettin' them fill your head with all these lies. Turnin' against me, against your family. And you come with this book and expect me to trust their word? Where was they help all them years back? They get to walk around they town, holdin' Sabbats and parties, worshipin' in the Old Way without fearin' for they lives,"

"Ain't that what you want too?" I said. "Don't you want to stop hidin'? To stop pretendin'?"

Amma tugged at the door again.

"You could've healed Ezra too. If you'd just called on a different Power."

"I would never," Amma said.

"Because you don't believe? Or are you too afraid?"

Amma pushed passed me again, tugging at the still-locked door. I reached forward, opening the door for her and holding it.

"Amma, please listen."

"I've loved you all my life," she said. "But to ask me to join you and risk the lives of my Coven?"

"Their lives are in danger already," I said. "It's only a matter of time before the God of the Garden punishes them too."

"Then stop this. Shaddai won't stop until you repent. He'll come for us all."

I turned away from her.

"Levi? Please. Levi?" Amma plead.

"He can only punish you if you submit to Him. You have to Renounce Him and join the Pact again."

Amma shook her head in horror.

"I would never betray my God," she said.

"Then I guess you won't be needin' that book then," I said.

I held my hand out. Amma clutched the book tighter to her chest.

"This don't belong to you," Amma said.

I smiled. "You know the truth deep down. I know that's why you won't give me that book."

Amma glared at me. "I do know the truth. I hope you open your eyes and see it before it's too late."

"Amma, please. Speak with the Deborahs, and y'all decide together."

She looked away pensively. "Goodbye, Levi," Amma said.

Her braids swung behind her as she quickly turned away and stormed down the hallway, stopping firmly in front of Nita. Nita looked down, her mouth cracked open with shock as she looked down at the book in Amma's arms. Amma pushed past her and made her way downstairs, slamming the front door behind her. Nita stood now facing me in the hallway, obscured by the darkness that covered her face. Only the whites of her eyes and the embers of a lit cigarette were visible now. Nita stepped into the moonlight shining through the windows, puffing out a thick cloud of smoke.

"Now where'd you go on and find that Book?" she asked.

"None of your business," I said.

Nita laughed. "You've really gone and done it now. Even takin' that book is an act of rebellion. I know it, and she knows it too," Nita said.

"Yea? And what're you gonna do about it?" I said, stepping forward.

She smirked. "Why don't you go on and pack up your shit and get up outta this house. 'Fore your brother come in here and ring yo' neck." Nita said, giving her back now as clouds of smoke clung to her.

"Don't you worry, like they say...two can keep a secret if one of 'em is dead," she said, chuckling to herself as she vanished into the darkness ahead.

I turned my bedroom door behind me and grabbed the duffle bags off my bed, facing the wall now. I signed the Hidden Hands, and the whirring portal with sparked edges opened, illuminating the entire space and casting a long shadow of everything caught in its light. I took one last look at my room. It was the last time I'd ever return here; I knew that now inside me. Ezra was so far gone that I had no doubt in my mind that he'd kill me if he had the chance. The worst part of all of this was the crushing feeling of loneliness. I felt like I had no one to turn to or to console. Noah and the Witch Queen were the closest things to allies I had, and I was too scared to risk losing Jonah, Titus, and even Craven.

I knew I couldn't keep this secret forever; they would eventually know what I was hiding from them all. The last time I saw my disciples, they almost lost their lives for me, something not historically foreign but still undesirable. Like the countless martyrs and saints whose deaths I matched to take a share in their power, they were all too eager to die. But it wasn't me they were dying for; it was an idea. Jesus Christ lives enterally in the imaginations and the hearts of blind believers; I was many things to many people, and even still, none were less dying for than myself as I stood now. I was arrogant and entitled and thought I had the entire world wrapped around my finger until I faced something that even I couldn't control.

God wasn't who He said He was, and I wasn't what I thought. I didn't know anything about these ancient entities that the witches have come to call the Lord and Lady, except for what the Order had always said of them; that they were devils masquerading as gods and performing wonders. The name Lucifer struck fear into the hearts of believers, but for me, it only echoed pity and wallowing. Lucifer was shunned and exiled from the grace of God and cursed to wander the cosmos in solitude, seeking refuge wherever he could. The darkness was cold and bitter, and his brothers continued to bask in the light of heaven's glow, surrounded by the comradery of each other, but who did he have?

The Scriptures tell us that it was for his arrogance that he fell from grace, but now knowing that he was a God in his own right, what if it was envy? He was most beautiful among the angels in Heaven, whose words could sway the cosmos and inspire poets and sinners across the ages to follow one's own ambitions. What if the God of the Garden feared his influence, and for that, he was banished? The plight of Adam and Eve was taking fold in my own life, and where once I saw myself in the dutiful man, I was slowly becoming the serpent who tried to sway the faithful away from the God of the Garden.

And the worst part?

I'd secretly known it all along. It wasn't difficult to sway me because, in all truth, I was tired of serving in Heaven. Maybe it was better to reign in my own personal Hell. I didn't want to be told what to do anymore, how to think and act. I didn't want to parade around and pretend I was a meek lamb, looking for the next person to forgive and love when I was a ravenous wolf waiting to tear someone to shreds. I was born with rage inside me, a deep resentment against piety, and those who blindly served a being that did nothing for them but absorb their energies and dictate their lives.

I stepped through the portal I formed, thinking of only Titus and Jonah. Call it wishful thinking, but I wanted to believe they would follow me from the ends of the earth or straight into the fiery pit if we failed. At this point, there was no trying; it was either successfully aiding in thwarting the King of Heaven or meeting a bitter end. I didn't have a third of the angels in Heaven this time; I only had my three closest friends, and even then. There wasn't a guarantee I had them either. The kaleidoscope of a world fractured and morphed around me, giving way to a flickering porch light and cracked steps beneath my feet. The window behind me closed with a thunderous clap. A light inside flicked on.

Shuffling and muffled voices murmured from inside. Titus opened the door with a joint dangling from his lips.

"Lee?" he asked. "You good?"

Titus popped up from behind him. Wisps of pungent smoke wrapped around them like tentacles from behind, flowing out the front door now.

"No," I said. "I don't think anythin' ever will be again."

CHAPTER 26:

Rebellion

Nita's husband's house had been around long before I took my first steps. It was one of the first homes built in Tophet, and their great-great-grandfather helped found this town alongside the descendants of the Summerland bloodline. They owned their land and grew their own food, and back in the day, the farm was filled with every type of domestic animal, from horses to pigs and roosters. Farming has been a lost art to the Hawkes family, especially once all the sons became judges and magicians alike, then the focus shifted towards scholarly education and deep, mystical learnings.

Titus and Jonah were top of their class alongside me, much to the disdain of our classmates. Even before they knew I was the one Chosen, they stuck to me closer than brothers. People always said soulmates had to be romantic, but I know they were mine. They've seen me in every moment of weakness, at my lowest, and even seen me shed more tears than I cared to admit. If I made a bad choice, they were the first ones to chew me out and set me straight, and that's how I knew they were my true friends. I didn't like 'yes' men; those kinds of things only ever lead to trouble. The day it was confirmed they were my original Disciples, I felt pieces of my heart come together; we were a family, who met, knew, and loved each other again.

Everyone thinks the disciples died for the faith, but it was something much deeper than that—Loyalty. They knew me in that lifetime, and when the time arose that it became them against a world of people who claimed to know me and distort my message, they fought with their lives. They sat with me at the feet of the broken, sick, and dying. They also sat with me as I lay dying, stealing my body so it wouldn't be desecrated after it was carried down from the cross. I didn't have to be raised from the dead to live forever; the memory of me and the bond we shared ensured that I'd have life eternal in their hearts and in their most cherished times of remembering.

I sat down on the edge of their bed. Everything was original wood. As much as I hated Nita, even a broken clock was right twice a day. She maintained the house as beautiful as the day it was built. She spared no detail; everything from old oil family portraits to intricate teapots and silverware shone as bright and new as if they were just used by the people who walked this home over 200 years ago. Titus and Jonah's room used to belong to their great-grandmothers, so everything from lace curtains and floral wallpaper remained intact, the only difference was the second bed added for Titus. Jonah kept his grandmother's bed complete with a velvet canopy. Jonah always had that extra extravagance, so it was only fair.

"You're not lookin' too good," Titus said.

"If… I told y'all… I made a choice that went against everythin' we was raised to believe… would you still stand by me?"

Titus and Jonah exchanged worried expressions. Jonah sat down on the ground, bringing his knees close to his chest.

"We've stood by you even when our lives was at risk," Jonah said. "There ain't nothin' in the world that would keep us from havin' your back."

Titus sat down beside Jonah, nudging my leg.

"Yeah, Lee. So tell us, what's goin' on?" Titus said.

I clenched my fists into tight balls and told them everything from going to the cave, my identity, the lives that were hidden from me, and even the word from the Witch Queen that Father Enoch was behind it all. I poured out everything I knew, all things I was unsure about, to find some sense.

"And... I tried talkin' to Amma, but she ain't havin' none of it. She did take the book with her, though."

Titus and Jonah rubbed their foreheads before standing up and wandering the room back and forth.

"So you're a witch now?"

"Not now... Looks like I always have been. The God of the Garden just ain't want me to know who I was... And anytime I found out or went too far, He ended me. And everyone around me."

"So we're next?" Titus asked, frustrated.

I cringed, shutting my eyes as tightly as I could hoping I'd disappear.

"I'm sorry... I thought I could turn to y'all. I shouldn't have brought this here. I just couldn't keep fightin' and killin' for a lie," I said.

"Oh, no," Jonah said. "We're mad you ain't tell us sooner. But we're still behind you. I don't know what Shaddai's gon' do to us, but we've faced worse."

"Is there a way to stop Him? From hurtin' us, that is."

I shook my head regretfully.

"Y'all ain't part of the Summerland bloodline... So you don't have power received from that Pact."

"So, we're just sittin' ducks then?" Jonah said. "How are we supposed to help you if He's gonna rain down fire and brimstone onto us any second now?"

"Well, there is one way."

"I'm all ears for not turnin' into a human torch." Jonah scoffed.

"Grannie said the witches of the Pact wasn't affected by the God of the Garden 'cause they renounced them and swore allegiance to the Lord and Lady, and they protected them," I said, "What if, just like the Magdalenes pledged obedience to the God of the Garden, y'all did the same thing with the Old Ones?"

Jonah looked like a pufferfish as he exhaled the tension.

"Alright, and... how would we go about doin' that?"

"You sure that would work?" Titus said.

I shrugged.

"It's worth a shot."

"But how?" Jonah pressed.

"Amma would know… Even though they ain't allowed to practice those ways, as the Witch Queen of Florida, she would know the process."

"Well, Sunday service is tomorrow, and the Deborahs are singin' for Reverend James; he's doin' another Miracle Crusade, so I hear," Titus said.

"Yeah, the only problem is she ain't talkin' to me," I said, defeated.

"You said she took the book. Because she even got that in her hands, the judges would kill her for it. If she held onto it, that means a part of her might side with you, right?" Titus said, looking to Jonah for reassurance.

"If Amma's got that book, then the battle is half won. Maybe seein' us on your side might do her some convincin'." Jonah added.

"What about Craven?" Titus said.

I groaned.

"He's the one I'm worried about most… He's just as bad as Father Enoch when it comes to followin' tradition."

"And you still think he's behind this?" Jonah asked.

I threw my hands up, frustrated.

"Maybe? I don't know. All words from the Witch Queen, all the history between us. I don't know if I could trust her or her Coven after all they'd done to us and this town."

"Not even bringin' that book back is enough to undo all that damage done, but the real question here is… are you doin' all this to help her or us?"

I smiled. There was a bitter-sweet tinge of truth to that question, and one that I hadn't thought about until Jonah asked.

"If this was troubles that they was facin' on their own then I'd let 'em die… That's the God honest truth. After all they'd done, they made their bed, and they can lie in it. But these Primordials… even the Queen of Georgia seemed afraid of 'em. What's worse is that it's happenin' in our town, and I'm afraid if we don't do somethin' these things are gonna wipe us off the face of the earth."

"So this threatens all of us," Titus said. "Maybe that's why she's here."

"She's here to save the skin off her own ass, that's for sure... But whichever way you spin it, the trouble's arrived on our doorstep and ain't discriminatin'. This is comin' for us all. Even the government's afraid of all this, probably why they sent those two Watchers," I said

"Then why tell you all this extra shit, then? About you bein' Lucifer and all this about restorin' the Holy Grail." Titus said.

"I couldn't stand a chance against this believin' the power given to me was all I had. The first Primordial didn't give two shits about me. I couldn't bind it or get it to obey. She helped me remember who I was, and this power just awakened through me."

"Fine," Titus said, frustrated. "Fine. But before this gets any further, you need to talk to Amma. Otherwise, we'll be struck with lightnin', smallpox, or worse at any point."

"Shaddai is a god of vengeance... If He ain't done nothin' by now... Somethin' tells me He's got somethin' much worse in the works," I said harrowingly.

Titus shuddered.

"Then let's hop on it. I ain't takin' any chances," he said.

Titus took the duffle bags from the bed and walked towards the door.

"You'll stay with us for the time bein'. If Ezra says he's gon' kill you, I'd take him at his word," Titus said.

Jonah followed behind him with the rest of my bags, giving me a tough pat on the shoulder.

"Better rest up. We got Sunday Service in the Lord's house tomorrow," Jonah said with a cringing smile.

They both vanished from view. I plopped down onto the bed, staring at the ceiling that seemed to spin with my thoughts that whirred around my head. I smiled vaguely. I wasn't alone after all.

We got up at dawn the following day to ensure we were on time for the Sunday service. The crowd was bustling and teeming with excitement when we made it through the door. They flocked and gathered around Reverend James, who flashed a doting white smile and finely pressed suit with a cross pin through his tie. Reverend James was an unassuming man; he wore kindness like a costume, but deep inside him was a bloodthirsty and calloused leader who led the Providence with an iron grip. He donned a streak of grey through the waves of his hair, and his beard was trimmed down to a pencil-thin goatee wrapped around his duplicitous grin.

I anxiously scanned the crowd for any sight of Ezra; fortunately, he wasn't anywhere to be found. But Grannie's icy glare from across the room was. She was dressed in lavender, her favorite color, wearing a wide-brim hat decorated with hydrangeas and a hummingbird broach pinned to her jacket. The crowd parted for her as she hobbled toward me with her cane. They murmured and whispered amongst themselves. The once poised, and statuesque Tamar Parris was now hunched over, struggling, and depleted of her youth.

Her reign was over.

She began straightening my tie, pursing her lips tightly together. Her hands trembled, barely able to grasp the fabric.

"Just 'cause you no longer in the house don't mean you've got an excuse to look raggedy," she said. "Far as anyone knows, we're all one big happy family. You hear?"

"I came to find Amma," I said.

Grannie rolled her eyes, stepping back.

"That girl don't want nothin' to do with you. It's best you leave her be. I don't know what mess you went and got yourself wrapped in or what lies they been feedin' you, but you keep that to yourself."

"See, what's crazy to me is the one I've found to be lyin' was you," I said.

She cocked her back, biting down on her upper lip.

"What you said to me, boy?"

"You've got a lot that needs explainin', Grannie."

"I don't gotta explain *nothin'* to you." She scoffed. "Look at you, a damn shame. Your daddy would've never talked to me like that."

"Guess I get it from my mama," I said, snarking.

She stopped, looking back at me with a deathly stare.

"You stay away from Amma. Nita told me about her gettin' that book of Devils, and you're lucky the Providence or the Order don't know about that either," she said.

Rita came to her side, gently putting her hand on Grannie's shoulder.

"Come on Sister Tamar, right this way."

Grannie looked back, glaring at me as she was led away into the crowd.

I caught Amma stepping onto the stage, followed by the Deborahs behind her wearing cerulean choir gowns. Amma's gaze met mine from over the crowd, and she quickly averted her eyes from me. I pushed past the Sunday crowd toward the stage. I looked back at Jonah and Titus sitting in the back pew, mouthing something I couldn't make out, but the dread on their faces didn't look promising. Sitting amongst them and walking past me were members of the Providence, many of whom I wasn't used to seeing outside of their own gatherings.

"Levi," Reverend James said, stopping me before I reached Amma.

Grannie sat down at the organ on stage, flipping through the music sheets and shooting me threatening glances from a distance.

"Reverend James, how are you doin'?" I said, distracted.

"Good to see you again. I haven't seen Ezra in a couple of days; has he been well?"

I laughed uneasily.

"Ezra's been just fine, just a little under the weather."

Reverend James chuckled, patting me on the shoulder vigorously.

"Glory Be, Glory Be," he said.

"Reverend James, what're all these judges doin' here today? I ain't ever seen so many attend a service before."

"Oh, we have somethin' special planned today."

"Special?" I said, weary. "What kinda special we talkin'?"

"To help us demonstrate the righteousness of the Lord, and how He works through the community," he said. "Go on, take a seat and relax."

Reverend turned me back around and gave me a nudge toward Titus and Jonah. As I walked down the aisle towards my seat, beads of sweat started to roll down my hands and grease my palms. I used to feel at home here in this church, away from the prying eyes of the saintly statues and the hierarchy of the Cathedral. But now, there was a deep sense of terror, something lurking beneath the surface of the dark waters that I could once walk across.

"You seen all these judges here?" Titus said in an urgent whisper.

I sat down between them, wiping the sweat onto my pants.

"I don't know what Reverend's got planned," I said. "But somethin' don't feel right to me."

"Alright, alright now, settle on down, everyone," Reverend James said, standing behind a silver, cross-adorned pulpit. The congregation chattering died down to a silence so deep you could hear the mosquitoes enter the room.

"How merciful is our Lord? Can I get an 'amen'?"

"*AMEN!*" The crowd shouted back.

Women nodded their heads in unrestrained agreement, fanning themselves from the blistering Florida heat sealed inside the room. They tried to open windows, but that only let the humidity in, and now there was a thick blanket of wet heat, muggy and suffocating. Reverend James patted the sweat off his forehead with his handkerchief, smiling like a politician ready to deliver a speech that would deceive and divide the masses.

"Saints, I know y'all have seen the madness that has torn this world apart outside. But the Lord shall always preserve the faithful. The testament of all you present here today proves true."

"*YES!*" they shouted, standing and clapping praises.

Amma joined in their applause, looking away from the Reverend with uncertainty in her eyes. Reverend James lifted his hands, silencing the crowd again.

"We are preserved through the madness and wickedness of this world while those around us reap the consequences of their faithlessness," Reverend said.

The women around us stomped their feet and lifted their hands in affirmation.

"*Yes, Lord!*" A woman shouted from somewhere behind us.

My heart started to race. Reverend James looked around the room, smiling with Hell behind his eyes as he fixed his sight on me.

"Now, Church, let me ask y'all... Who can tell me what the Lord values most here among the faithful?"

The crowd murmured amongst each other, leaning in and exchanging answers.

"Faith!" one man shouted.

"Love!" called an elderly woman.

"Hope!" said a woman, bouncing her baby in her arms.

Reverend James smiled, shaking his head.

"Faith, hope, and love are all valuable in the eyes of the Lord. But you see, only one thing is most important to Him. One thing that seems to be lackin' here in this congregation... somethin' that has brought evil straight to our doorstep and even here onto this stage," he said, turning around to face the choir.

Amma stepped back from him as the Deborahs shot panicked expressions. I slowly stood from my seat as Reverend James now kept his eyes on me.

"*Obedience*," he said. "Disobedience was the first sin of man... And the Lord promised to Adam and Eve one thing should they disobey him..."

The judges scattered around the pews and jumped to their feet, and the sound of their loaded guns filled the room. Their loaded guns were aimed at Amma and the Deborahs.

"*Death!*" the crowd jeered.

Ezra emerged from the entrance's double doors, holding a rifle dripping with blessed water.

"Death." Reverend James said.

CHAPTER 27

The Mark

Bullets spewed from their guns. I hit the ground, crawling out from behind the pew just enough to poke my head through and see the stage. I screamed for Amma, but she didn't need them. Her eyes flickered solid black, and she waved her arms. Before the bullets could land on the wooden stage beneath her, that stage tore up from the ground and curved around her and the choir. Clouds of dust exploded from the impact of the bullets, and in a whirling motion, the suspended wall of wood and planks turned on their sides and shot out from her like disks.

The judges who didn't duck were decapitated, spraying blood from their exposed necks into the air, casting mists of their blood, and staining the church seats before collapsing. Grannie found a corner of the wall behind Amma just dark enough, hurriedly made her way into its crevice, and vanished into the darkness. I caught Ezra's eye, who crawled back onto his knees after dodging her defense. He drew Pops's axe and charged onto the stage. The rest of the judges followed suit, shouting war cries and lunging for the Deborahs.

Amma stomped her foot onto the ground, and the wooden planks of the floor shot up from beneath them in thick, jagged spikes, disemboweling the judges that got close enough to her and impaling them in place. Their feet dangled, and blood ran down the jagged wood fragments, gurgling and cursing her with their last breaths.

More judges seemed to pour in from every direction of the church, aiming freshly drawn guns back at Amma and the choir. She held her arms out, and the bullets that would've rained down on her stopped in midair, hovering just over the skin of her palms. She pushed her arms back out, and the bullets shot back at the firing judges, popping each of them directly in the forehead, dropping dead on sight.

The last surge of judges ran for the stage, Ezra leading them. He roared with a ferocity I'd never heard come from him, inching closer to the stage and running past the impaled bodies surrounding where Amma stood. She raised her arms in the air, her arms now distorted by a rippling energy that consumed her. I extended my hand, feeling a surge of power rush down my arms, and with the force of my magic, I yanked Ezra back, sliding him onto his back and rolling across the pews.

Amma clapped her hands, and a thunderous boom shook the foundations of the church, and a wave of golden, translucent energy tore through the room, vaporizing all the judges that remained. In a hot flash, like a nuclear detonation, I saw their skeletons through their skin before they were turned to bloody dust and bone.

An eerie silence fell over the church; only Ezra's screams of defeat echoed through the room as I held him in place with my power. Amma caught her breath, looking at me with a pained expression. The cremated dust of the judges' bodies rained down, slowly caught in the rays of sunlight peeking through the stained-glass windows.

With a swift motion of her arms, the dust assembled in a whirling vortex tinged red, circling Amma and the choir.

"Wait!" I shouted, still pinning Ezra down.

With a graceful wave of her hands, the cyclone of dust that surrounded her expanded, exploding outward. I dug my feet into the ground, covering my face from the harsh winds and ground, stinging my eyes from the debris. I leaned over, coughing on incinerated human remains and blinded by the tears from the dust caught in them. As I caught my breath again, there was nothing but an empty stage.

She was gone.

All that remained in her place was a line of bodies bleeding out onto the ground and impaled carcasses lining the curvature of what was left of the stage on jagged pieces of wood. I should've been disturbed by the grisly scene of the aftermath, but somehow bloodshed fit the church perfectly. That was its history, after all.

Christianity has always been a death cult. Death and martyrdom were the highest of honors coming at the greatest of prices. All their rituals revolved around the death of their savior and commemorated the event by ceremonially drinking his blood and eating his flesh. The God of the Bible was a god of death and destruction. Suffering was how you reached the heart of God; it was through conscious torment that one could draw close to him.

It took me long enough to realize it, but I was once the hands and feet of history's most prolific mass murderer, acting as the agent of death and mortal torment and dressing it as something holy and re-vered. I looked up at the cross that hung up on the wall, hanging upside down from the violent winds and bullets that loosened its stable hold.

For centuries, people even gathered around the instrument of my execution, wearing it on their necks as a testament to their faith. But faith in what? How can one celebrate and take heart in a father de-manding the blood of his own son? Of all the acts I'd performed in my first lifetime, it was only the brutal death that was remembered. And celebrated.

But never again.

Ezra tripped over his own feet, hoisting himself back up with his axe.

"You... You did this," Ezra said, spitting webs of blood onto the floor. He looked around, laughing incredulously.

"You've brought death on us all... Turnin' us against each other in the Devil's name," Ezra said.

"Ezra, I saved you for the second time now. You would've been turned to dust or worse," I said calmly, not trying to provoke him.

"No," he said, pointing the end of the axe at me now. "No."

"Ezra, please... I'm your brother," I plead.

I'd never been looked at with so much scorn and disdain from Ezra like this before. Sure, as brothers we fought growing up. But the way that he looked at me now was different. He truly wanted me dead; I could see a supernatural hatred consume his eyes, growing like a fire. Each breath he took fueled the rage he'd built up against me.

"You ain't no brother to me," he growled, "and if Pops was around to see what you'd become he'd kill you himself. But he ain't no more, is he?"

"Ezra, please."

"There ain't no mercy for you no more. You're lost," he said.

He picked up his axe and darted towards me full speed, raising it above his head, ready to take a swing. Titus and Jonah quickly formed Hidden Hands and propelled Ezra through the air like dead weight. He slammed into the wall, forming a deep crack, and tumbling to the floor. Chunks of debris crumbled and fell on top of him.

"You good?" Titus said.

I stared back at Ezra in disbelief. In the brief moments, I stared off, all the memories from childhood came flooding back to me. From fighting over Christmas presents to talking to him about girls for the first time or teaching him how to throw a football and memorizing scriptures together after Grannie took the TV out of our rooms as punishment.

"We gotta go," Jonah said, tugging me by the arm.

Ezra's arms shook uncontrollably as he tried to hoist himself up again and shot me one last glance of absolute malice.

"I *hate* you," he said. "I HATE YOU!" he screamed, spitting and hissing as he gnashed his teeth trying to stand again.

"We have to find Amma," I said, turning away.

I wiped the tears from my eyes, feeling the tightness in my throat compress as I tried to fight the urge to cry. Losing Ezra hurt more than anything I'd ever felt before, including the numerous barbaric deaths I'd been put through.

All I could think about was how many families were torn apart and ties severed all in the name of religion. They say I didn't come to bring peace, but a sword, dividing mother against daughter and father against son. I see now how truly painful those words were, and how devastating such a sentiment was in practice.

The scriptures say that the Devil would deceive the entire world. Who would've thought the real Devil would be the God of the Garden, who won over the masses with promises of redemption in exchange for their souls that they so willingly forfeited?

"How would we even know where she went?" Titus argued.

"The same place witches have hidden in for centuries," I said. I took one last look at Ezra, who was almost standing again. "The woods."

I formed the Hidden Hands, and a blazing window portal opened in midair. Through the glowing ring, the gentle breeze of trees became clear, and I stood facing it.

"You'll pay for this!" Ezra shouted from across the room.

The rift shut quickly behind us, with Ezra's slumped silhouette still visible before closing. The seismic sound of the portal closing plunged now into an eerie silence, wind-swept trees in its place.

"God damn it, why'd they have to come out here?" Jonah said, trembling.

Sheol.

Despite being seasoned and trained magicians, Sheol was a forest that even angels feared to tread. The tall, ruddy trees blotted out the sun with their leaves, coloring everything below them in red shadows, like being in an infernal Hellscape. The forest connected all the deep South, starting from the tip of Florida, where we were. It helped to hide the witches as they traveled and dispersed, hiding from the likes of judges who hunted them down but were too afraid to pass through the terrain themselves.

The judges in Alabama had initiations revolving around treading the forest, even marking it out so they wouldn't get lost, but there came a certain point where even they wouldn't go past. It was a haunting place, gloomy and foreboding like stepping into the underworld. People went missing every year around here, and the disembodied voices of wandering specters could be heard if you listened close enough or were caught alone.

The local magicians used to take dares to see who could go the farthest out, but one Summer, much like the one we're in now, one of the magicians in my class never made it back out. They'd searched everywhere, only to find his severed head placed firmly onto a slab altar, covered with strange markings that none of the Magisters could decipher. The witches found him before we could and offered him up in some kind of blood ritual,

And not knowing is the most terrifying part.

I paced back and forth, trying to think of where to move. I knew Amma and the others must have come here. The barn where they held rituals would be too obvious. Once again, history would repeat itself in this town, and they were now driven into hiding. Nazarenes before me hunted and searched for them through these very woods, and now I was seeking their help instead.

"So where is she?"

"I—I don't know," I said.

"You mean to tell me you dragged us into the middle of this creepy ass forest and don't even much know where we goin'!" Titus shouted.

"I can't focus much with you flappin' your jaw the way you doin' right now. So why don't you let me focus?"

I stepped away from them, hanging my head in frustration. I exhaled sharply, looking down at my feet to see strange tracks in the ground. The dirt was protruding, like something beneath it was traveling.

"What?" Titus said as I pushed past him, analyzing the ground.

"I think I know where they are," I said.

The tracks left in the ground had a swaying nature to them, like a serpent traveling underground. According to the old legends, the Devil guided the Salem descendants on their way south into Summerland by taking the form of a snake beneath the earth. If the Coven needed to hide, Grannie said that the Devil would appear to guide them to safety… if the witch accepted.

The Devil was never one to push His ways onto anyone. There was never any coercion, it was what he was presenting alone that was so tempting. Grannie said that's what made the sin of the Summerland bloodline so great, that they willingly served the darkness. But could it be that the Devil was actually a being of free will? The God of the Garden forced us to obey Him, and if we didn't, there were always horrific consequences that ensued from our disobedience.

"Follow me," I said.

Titus and Jonah hesitated, but as they saw me vanish further into the trees, they chased behind me.

I felt like the Israelites, cursed to wander the barren desert for 40 years, but instead, it was wandering through trees that all started to look the same. And soon enough, I plunged into a madness driven by leaves and bark.

"We've been at this for hours," Titus complained.

"Can we at least stop for somethin' to drink?" Jonah added.

I wiped the sweat off my eyebrow, keeping my eyes on the swaying track beneath me. As much as I wanted to keep going, they were right. We'd been wandering this place for hours with no sign of an exit in any direction. There was no clearing, no difference in the trees around us; it seemed to be a deliberate maze constructed to confound and confuse anyone who dared wander in and not know which way they were going.

"Fine," I snapped. "But wrap this shit up. We're losin' sunlight,"

Titus stepped forward and forming Hidden Hands, a stream of water burst from the trunk of the tree, running into the ground. Even the dirt beneath us had a rusted tinge, and when the water hit the ground, it looked like the tree was bleeding from its base. Titus and Jonah both crouched down, slurping as much water as they could. They wiped their mouths, panting.

"You should have some too," Jonah said.

I grunted, kneeling at the base and trying to catch the water with my tongue and drink as much as I could. The tepid water rolled down my cheek when I looked at the ground, seeing the serpent-like track wind around the tree we knelt at and coming to a dead end. I wiped my mouth and crouched through the hanging branches of shrubbery nearby, horrified at the drop-off.

"It's gone," I said.

"What's gone?" Titus said.

"Oh, no, no. I don't know what you're talkin' about, but that don't sound good."

"The tracks, but..."

Whispering and chattering broke our quipping amongst each other.

"*What are we supposed to do?*" a woman chimed.

I shushed Titus and Jonah, holding my finger to my lip and slowly crouching toward the direction of the chatter. I parted the trees obscuring the direction of the voices and saw the dark blue robes of the choir gathered around a stone slab, the same one we'd found the magician's head mounted on all those years ago.

"We can't go back there, they'll try to kill us," Amma said.

We'd found them.

I stepped through the trees. Titus and Jonah emerged behind me. Shrill screams erupted from them as they saw me approach, all moving behind Amma to protect them. Her eyes shifted with disappointment, but there was a sense of relief in her gaze. Deep down, I could tell she was happy to see me.

"It's alright," Amma said. "We can trust him,"

"Ain't he the Petram? He's workin' with them!"

It was Bonnie. She stood firmly beside Amma, even if the fear in her eyes when she saw me was instant, knowing Bonnie, she would fight me to the death. Her brows were furrowed, stepping now in front of Amma and holding her arms out. I raised my hands towards her, stepping back.

"Come on now, Bonnie, you know I wouldn't hurt none of y'all,"

"How do I know that?" she asked. "It ain't like you defended us when them judges attacked us."

"That's because he ain't need to," Amma said. "I was there. I could protect y'all perfectly fine alone."

Bonnie stood back.

"I got this," Amma said.

"What're y'all doin' here? How'd you find this place?"

"We followed the snake tracks," I said. "Looks like y'all accepted the Devil's help."

Amma lowered her head.

"Listen, things… changed once you gave me that book. It was like nothin' else in the world mattered. That is the Book of our people, of our ancestors, and all their knowledge that was lost to us for centuries. I couldn't give that away. And when the time came to protect my Coven or face death, I chose my Coven. I'm the Queen of Florida, and it's my duty."

"So then we're on the same side, now," I said.

Amma glared at me, pensive.

"What I don't understand is why the judges would just turn on us on a dime like that? We've served them for centuries."

"They must've caught wind of you gettin' your hands on that book. Amma, you know even havin' that book is unforgivable in their eyes. You might as well have signed your name in blood."

"But who… who would do somethin' like that? Hadn't I acted as fast as I did, we all would've been dead by now," Amma said.

"You know I would never rat you out, especially now that we on the same side."

"I ain't got much of a choice," Amma said.

I folded my arms.

"Right. Well, think, who was the last person beside me to see you with that Book?" I asked.

Amma scanned the ground for a moment, thinking. Her eyes widened in disbelief, looking back up at me.

"No… No, she wouldn't."

"It was Nita," I said, "and you know it. Who else here knew about that Book besides me and you? And she saw you with it in your hands."

"But Nita wouldn't betray her own Coven like that, we—we could've died."

"And I'm sure she was countin' on that. Don't you know enough about Nita by now to realize that the only person she cares about is herself? Besides, Nita always said you didn't deserve the Crown…

Seein' you with that Book in her hands was just the motivation she needed to get you out the way."

"Because then the Power would pass to her…"

"She was next in line, at least, accordin' to Grannie."

Amma sighed, painfully. She pinched the bridge of her nose.

"So what now?" Amma said, frustrated.

"It's only a matter of time before the God of the Garden acts against us. You saw what happened to Ezra," I said. "I've already made my bed. But all of y'all are targets."

"The only way would be to formally renounce the God of the Garden," Amma said, reluctant.

"Then we'll have to do it," I said.

Titus and Jonah looked back at each other, tensely.

"Receive the Mark of the Beast…" Amma said, shuddering. "That would need a male to conjure the Devil."

"Tell me what I need to do," I said.

CHAPTER 28

Sins Of The Mother

Bonnie snatched Amma's arm in a tight lock.

"You lost your mind?" he retorted. "You have any idea what Shaddai will do to us?"

"You got any idea what He'll do if you don't?" I snapped.

Bonnie stepped aside, casting her gaze down on her feet now.

"All our lives we've faithfully served the God of the Garden."

"Out of fear, Bonnie. Just as Grannie and I did, and all of us goin' back generations. All this time, we've denied ourselves power that's rightfully ours in service to a God who only wants to see us submit. This religion, this way, it's the way of our oppressors. Do we really wanna continue to uphold that?" I said.

"You doin' the Devil's work now, Levi. If you wanna damn yourself, then you go right ahead, but it don't mean the rest of us should burn with you," Bonnie retorted.

"If by the Devil's work you mean reclaimin' our power, our identity, and free will? Then yea, Bonnie, I'm doin' his biddin' with no regrets. But don't make me start havin' them by allowin' y'all to be cursed and tortured into submission," I said. "Those days are over. Our time is now."

"He's right, Bonnie," Amma interjected. Bonnie shuddered. "We've been lyin' to ourselves. The power that flows through our veins wasn't given to us by Shaddai, it was the man in black. Even the way the power is passed from Madonna to Madonna ain't got nothin' to do with His power."

"Miss Tamar said it was the way it's always been done," Bonnie said.

"And you ain't ever ask yourself why that was?" Amma scoffed. "I'd be lyin' if I said this decision was easy to make. But I'm the Queen of Florida, and my duty is to serve and protect this Coven. And if that means takin' the Mark of the Beast, then so be it."

Tears streamed down Bonnie's face as she shook her head.

"We'll go to Hell for this," She panicked. "I— I can't do this,"

Amma gently stroked her cheek.

"Bonnie... that's fear talkin'. Ain't you tired of bein' afraid?"

Bonnie covered her mouth and receded into the choir of women who stood behind Amma.

"As Madonna and Queen of this Coven, I ask you, my Sisters, to make your own choice. Here, right now, in this moment. Will you side with the God of the Garden? Or reclaim your original place in the Summerland Pact?"

A solemn silence swept over the space as the Coven exchanged worried glances and chattered amongst one another.

"I swore fealty to you, my Queen, and I'm tired of servin' somethin' that only loves us as long as we're in chains. I'll take the mark," Rita said, stepping forward.

Rita came from a long line of Handmaidens who served many previous Madonnas. She was petite and had thick eyebrows and a heart-shaped face.

"So will I," another woman said.

"And me," added another.

Within a few seconds, the entirety of Amma's coven surrounded her in a circle, with Amma at the center and a small parting in the middle, awaiting only one.

"Bonnie," Amma said, extending her hand. "Please. I need you here by my side."

"If we do this..." Bonnie said, stepping forward. "Do—Do you promise we'll be safe from Shaddai's fury?"

"You have my word,"

Bonnie extended a trembling hand to Amma, finally taking her hand. Amma pulled her into a tender embrace.

"I trust you with my life," Bonnie said.

"It won't be unfounded. I promise."

I clapped my hands together.

"So, we're all on board," I said. "What allyou need from me?"

"Titus, Jonah, will y'all be takin' the mark too?" Amma said. They nodded. "Come," she said.

Titus and Jonah joined us. Amma went around the circle, gently tapping the foreheads of all who stood around her.

"What are you doin'?" I asked. "Passin' the spell to them. Stand back." I took a few steps back. Titus and Jonah glanced back at me with anxious expressions.

"Get ready," she ordered.

I wanted to argue, but the stone gaze she shot at me struck a newfound fear in me. I'd never seen Amma's power displayed even a fraction of its full potential, but I was about to. I saw Tituba moved Heaven, and by the look in Amma's eyes, I knew she was going to summon the very forces of Hell.

The Coven focused, closing their eyes. Titus and Jonah followed suit, but with more shyness and reluctance. They unified their voices in one pitch, singing a singular note that vibrated beneath our feet and caused the stones and dirt to rise. We all stood together now, hidden by the twisting trees underneath a violet sky. I stood outside the circle with my back south, and Amma centered herself. She held her hands under her breasts and stood with her feet close together and her head held high. When she opened her eyes again, they were as black as the ocean depths, with a lustrous shine to them.

Amma gathered us around. Her frightened hands shaking, and the bravery of her actions locked fingers with mine in a firm clasp. Everyone around us held hands, Titus and Jonah joining us with bleeding lips that dripped with the tension of the moment, of their decision. This was it for them and everyone else. I'd already made my peace with turning against the thing I feared the most, and now the decision was theirs. Amma and her coven exchanged glances, kissing each other's hands with tears streaming down their faces.

They smiled and nodded nervously, I could tell this was all the courage they had in them. This here, this moment was holy. More blessed than any pompous and ceremonial ritual I'd ever participated in. There was more love amongst them than I'd ever seen in any church; there was no wall. For them, to turn against Shaddai meant to challenge death itself. And as scared as they were, they persevered. It was the spirit of my people once again, defying any odds and choosing to survive. And it wasn't me who led them, it was Amma.

I felt diminished by her, extinguished by her humility. Amma, at this moment, was willing to do anything to save her coven and this town. I forgot what that felt like. I was told the first Nazarene did it, but I've never known it myself. And if I did, I don't think even then anything could come close to what Amma was doing. Faith is a powerful thing. And I saw all that poured into Amma and felt it myself as I placed it in her too. I don't think even my own disciples ever looked at me the way they did her.

Amma and her coven have thrived throughout the centuries, risking even their afterlives if this fails. But they didn't care. For their people, our people, it was a gamble they were willing to take. They swore never again to have any master on earth. Heaven should be no exception. It wouldn't be. Like Eve, Amma looked the God of the Garden in his eyes and defied him. I saw the glory of what she was doing. The purest act of true love, I saw it through her. That was the light I'd been searching for. That was God.

"Are y'all ready?" Amma said.

"We're ready. *Iya.*" Rita smiled.

"What's that mean?"

"It means *Mother.*" Amma's eyes watered, lifting her chin proudly.

She turned and gently blew in Bonnie's face. Bonnie gasped, her mouth hanging open.

"I give you the breath of life, the breath of memory and knowledge. The wisdom of the ancestors," Amma said.

Bonnie turned to Rita and passed on the gentle breath to her and from Rita to the next. The coven's eyes flickered solid black, and they started to sing. Every hair on my body stood on end as I started to slowly understand the words they sang in ancient Yoruba. I realized now why I understood this language the way I did the hissing tongue of the witches. Because it was in me all along, it was in my blood.

Amma and the coven sang, and I felt my body possessed by the soul of music, to the sound of drums pounding in the distance still obscured by darkness. Titus and Jonah followed me, and together the coven danced, our feet carried by the spirits of ancestors long forgotten. The music started to build, and Amma and her witches roared with song to call the spirits down.

The trees rustled, and guttural groans permeated from the darkness beyond the leaves. Towering figures emerged; monstrous black shadows that looked like people surrounded us. The coven stopped, Amma clapped and shrieked at them, hailing their arrival. The coven followed in similar cries and shouts in the Hideen Tongue. The heads of the goliath beings were obscured by the treetops, we were like grasshoppers compared to them.

"Sing the Song of Ages!" Amma cried out in ancient Yoruba.

The shadow men surrounded us, enclosing us in a ring. Cylindrical shades appeared in their arms, forming what looked like a drum.

"Begin," she said.

The beings pounded against their drums, and the circle around her was divided in two, one moving clockwise and the other counterclockwise. They began to move slowly, before quickening their pace with a percussive chant:

"TA-HA-MUT! TA-HA-MUT!"

The tops of the trees swayed, and gusts of wind swept through the space, bending the trees by their trunks in a wind-swept circle. The power built, and the ground shook with a great force. I could hardly keep my balance. Dirt and rock whirled around the circle as they chanted with more vigor, and infernal whispers poured into the space.

Amma held her hands up, her palms facing the waning crescent moon that started to take form in the sky.

"I call upon the Lord of the Wellspring, ruler of the Abyss!" Amma shouted.

"*Descend on us Father, intercede on our behalf!*" the circle shouted back, circling her faster and faster with an inhuman speed.

"I call upon the Lord of raging storms by blackest skies!"

"*Descend on us Father, intercede on our behalf!*"

"I call upon the Lord of blazing fire by powers of scorching sun!"

"*Descend on us Father, intercede on our behalf!*"

"I call upon the Lord of fury and love by the womb of the earth!"

"*Descend on us Father intercede on our behalf!*"

"NANNA!"

"*Descend on us!*"

"SHAMASH!"

"*Descend on us!*"

"NERGAL!"

"*Descend on us!*"

"HORNED ONE WHO REIGNS UNSEEN!"

"*Descend on us, Father, intercede on our behalf!*"

Amma's arms flew to her sides as she held her head back in a tribal, warring shriek. The gusts of power exploded from the circle, sending the trees nearly snapping backward in clean halves from the magnitude of the energy. Out of Amma's mouth, a blazing fire as black as midnight erupted, spewing uncontrollably with a clear handle protruding from inside. Amma pulled the sword from her mouth and held it up high towards the sky.

The circle danced in an ecstatic frenzy circling Amma, still chanting, "TAHAMUT!"

Her eyes now glowed as white as snow, gleaming like shimmering stars in her face. With both hands, she held tightly onto the sword.

"*By the power of the Mother of Darkness!*" Amma shouted. Her voice was legion, as if thousands of voices all meshed together in different pitches and tones.

"I call forth the dread Lord of Shadows, bringer of life and giver of life! I invoke thee, thou ancient serpent, by the living waters of her womb! Descend into the body of this thy servant! TAHAMUT! Wake ye unto life and come forth from the abyss, I birth your presence into this space, awake now from thy slumber! TAHAMUT! Descend into this body! TAHAMUT! Lay on us the mark of freedom and knowledge!"

Cold shivers ran down my body, and suddenly, I had no control. I convulsed with gut-wrenching pain. I fell to my knees, clasping onto my stomach, and a searing burn swept over me. Something churned from the inside, rising rapidly up my throat, scorching like magma as it made its way. My head was thrown back from the force as globs of black tarry energy burst from my mouth. The substance had a horrific sound, like hissing serpents and chariots rushing into battle. The black energy cut through the ground, at a lightning speed, slicing through the dirt and circling the Coven. The energy whirred around the air, climbing higher into the sky, darkening it in a monstrous black energy, neither solid nor liquid. Within seconds, all light was blotted out, and the black mass formed two arms and a torso; protruding horns sprouted from its head.

I fell back, watching in a terrified wonder at the creature that snaked around the Coven and made its home amongst the clouds. The torso, in a wisp, formed back down in a circling cone around the Coven, encasing them in its presence. The being opened its eyes, and they glowed bright red. Amma quickly clasped the blade with her bare hand and slid her hand down, slicing open her hand. She held the sword in one hand up high, with the wound in her palm facing the once lumbering god that now hovered high in the sky.

"Dark Father, I summon and stir thee!" Amma cried over the howling winds. *"We renounce the God of the Garden, we reject the trinity of three devils, and turn to you! Lay your mark upon us and shield us from the false god's wrath! Lay your mark on us all and make us yours, and may the power be made known to us, the descendants of your Promise!"*

The being growled and raised its arms further into Heaven and dispersed again into a thick plume of smoke until it was dissolved into spiral tentacles of power and shot back down into the space. The black energy forced itself into the mouths of everyone who stood in the Circle, lifting them from the ground as they convulsed and spasmed, levitating in the air and being filled with the dark presence. My mouth hung open as I watched the gruesome scene. They were violently shaken in the air as the power passed into them until finally, the sun peaked again through the trees.

Silence.

Not a bird chirped, or a single leaf rustled in the wind. Amma's eyes flashed with a bright white light, and she extended her arms to me.

"Behold," she said. "He makes all things new."

It was done.

Amma reinstated the Summerland Pact and renounced the God of the Garden. They were agents of the Devil now, and there was a palpable energy in the air, a dense and heavy presence rocking me back and forth like trying to stand still in a churning sea. The circle clasped onto their chests, feeling their bodies, erupting into giddy laughing and exasperated surprise.

"I feel so alive!" Bonnie shouted. "Oh!" Bonnie's feet suddenly came off the ground. "I'm flying!"

The Coven laughed, reaching for Bonnie's hand, and she carried them off the ground. The Coven now started to fly, circling Amma like a wild flock of birds, whipping and dashing through the air shouting in a strange tongue. Amma raised her hand, and they all slowly returned to the ground behind her. Titus and Jonah were the last to join the group, ecstatic as their feet were now firmly planted in the ground. They ran to my side, shaking me and shouting joyfully and in disbelief.

"Did you see that!" Jonah shouted.

The Coven fell into an ecstatic frenzy, still high on the euphoria and rush of their newfound power.

"Well done." A voice called out from the wilderness. I turned around, and there stood Noah and the Queen of Georgia. The coven gasped, whispering amongst themselves as they saw the scarlet-robed figure appear. "And welcome, Sister," she said.

"Amma Putnam, so lovely of you to finally rejoin the Pact. I was beginnin' to worry," Selene said. "And you know the Devil's name... Why, color me *impressed*."

Amma sneered.

"Now...Who all do you think taught your girls that name in Salem?" Selene pursed her lips.

"The first Madonna, Bridget Bishop."

Amma laughed harsh, and derisive.

"Bishop she says!"

Amma's coven jeered.

"Tituba and the Three Marys gave her that power so y'all could survive. Or did y'all forget who *really* taught you what you know?" Amma snickered.

Selene sighed, frustrated.

"Besides...Since when did y'all ever care about anyone but yourselves? Unless...You want somethin', that is...Don't you go thinkin' we've forgotten what Adora did to us."

"We've come only to help." Selene said, clenching her jaw.

"Baby, don't nobody need your help. Now, you and *Great Value* Marlon Brando can get to steppin' and best be about your way. Whatever needs to get done I'll handle from here."

Amma laughed.

"No, we need *your* help. The Primordials that have come to this town will destroy this place and move onto the next. Not just Georgia, even our sisters in Alabama. Then South Carolina next, no doubt. Unless...You help us fulfill the prophecy." Amma laughed. "Go on and run home, lil' girl, I already done told you nobody needs your help."

"Not even for the rest of our sisters?" Selene plead.

Amma's eye twitched, pensive.

"There ain't nothin' in this world or the next that I could do to erase the pain and the sufferin' that our clan caused you. We don't deserve your forgiveness, and frankly, I don't have it in me to ask for somethin' like that." Selene said. Amma squinted her eyes at her suspiciously. "But what's come to us is even bigger than you and I. I know the judges have turned on y'all, as they did on us over three years ago now. But prophecy must be fulfilled, and without you, we can't bring it to fulfillment."

"Pfft." Amma rolled her eyes, tossing her hair behind her shoulder. "And why would I do that?" she asked. Selene pursed her lips, frustrated. "I understand you're angry."

"Understand?" Amma snapped. "What do *you* understand? While our town burned to the ground, our aunts, sisters, and grandmothers was killed, and all the work they'd done to build a life and future for us went up in smoke, scorched from this earth by the women of *your* clan. We suffered, tryin' to heal through the generations and rebuild somethin' that y'all destroyed because you couldn't stand to see us be beautiful, powerful, and independent of the likes of *you*. Now, tell me again, what is it you understand?"

Selene hung her head, humiliated. "You're right… You're right." Selene looked up at Amma now, teary-eyed. "But I was hopin' re-turnin' that book might help to mend the bridge that we burned."

Amma cackled.

"Save your tears, so many of us have died as your people have shed them. You think returnin' somethin' that rightfully belonged to us is goin' to change anythin'? Look at you, strollin' through here with your *color me impressed* as if you'd done somethin'. Look how proud you look, waltzin' into our territory like you have anythin' to offer us, except for somethin' you stole. Thieves don't get a reward for re-turnin' somethin' stolen."

Selene flushed red, stuttering. Every time I'd seen her before, she was always composed and in control. Now she was crumbling beneath the weight of Amma, and I was happy to watch it happen. The mask of composure she'd worn all this time was quickly unraveling, and I'd never found Amma more powerful than now. The legendary Roshana, the Queen of Georgia, was like a scared child, shaking in place with nothing to say to save herself.

"I heard you went to the other side to learn the mysteries of the Womb," Amma said, circling Selene now like a shark. "But we've already learned them. I bet you've come to try and show them to us. To come save us all from our ignorance. Do you think that Tituba didn't know that book like the back of her hand? When she was the one who brought that knowledgeto the girls of Salem, *your* ancestors who was readin' egg yolks and lickin' toads and callin' it witchcraft."

"I… I know. The Madonnas before us hated to admit it, but it was Tituba who brought magic to our ancestors from overseas. I won't deny who brought us the Power."

"Oh? So no more, 'first Madonna' Bridget Bishop?" Amma gawked. "That's a big admission. Y'all have come so far." She rolled her eyes, walking back towards the coven. "You can leave now, Miss Bishop, don't nobody here needs anythin' from you."

"These Primordial forces will rip the world apart," Selene said. "We want to help you."

Amma stopped, her back facing Selene. Amma turned her face. "Help?" Amma's nose crinkled as she laughed heartily. Selene's confidence was deteriorating by the second. Her shoulders drooped, and she furrowed her eyebrow, an uncertainty became etched into her face. "*You* want to help *us*? Do you hear that, Sisters? She's come to save the day," Amma reeled in maniacal laughter, hunching over and clasping her stomach.

"Amma, you have every right to feel the way you do. But if we don't work together, it'll be the end of us all. The God of the Garden will destroy this world before He allows the prophecy to be fulfilled—!'"

"*Don't* you speak to me of prophecy," Amma said, raising her hand. "Our foremothers were there when those words were first spoken. *Iyami*. The Other People. The *first* witches. But your people? Ain't exactly known for doin' nothin' new."

"We can do it together, with the power of Roshana—"

"Oh, Roshana, is it? Yes, that's what I'd heard. That power was a means of defendin' the matriline in dire times, but Tituba didn't trust it in the hands of just anybody. Especially not one single person.

That's why she designed it so difficult to attain, and yet... So, *so* easy to take away."

Selene stepped back; I saw her throat tighten as she gulped. She clasped at her chest.

Amma laughed. Bonnie, Rita, and three other women circled Selene, slowly approaching her while chanting beneath their breath with glowing eyes.

"Checks and balances need to remain, and one person couldn't be left alone to wield that power and abuse it. So, it was left to the Madonna of each land to know how to revoke such a power. Did you know that?" Sweat ran down Selene's forehead. "Of course not," Amma said. She hovered her hand over her chest, hissing and muttering in the Hidden Tongue.

"S—Stop. What is this? What are y'all doin'?" Selene shrieked.

"Selene!" Noah said, rushing towards her. He slammed into rippling air, falling onto his back as he struck the wall of Amma's magic.

"Why don't you take a seat, boy? And let the grown women handle this." Amma said.

Selene screamed, falling to her knees and clasping her stomach.

"STOP THIS!" Noah shouted.

"The power of the Dark Counselor can never turn against His Queen. And here I was thinkin' y'all was comin' to try and teach us a thing or two," Amma sneered.

Selene writhed and squirmed on the floor, her honey hair faded quickly to white, thinning out into strands and exposing her bare skull. Her ivory skin washed over grey, and the youth was sucked dry, leaving her a masse of skin wrapped around bone. Her face was gaunt, sullen, and sunken, as she lifted a trembling hand to cry out.

"*I rescind the power*," Amma said in the Hidden Tongue, her eyes glowing white again.

Selene screamed as flames burst from her chest, and the hilt of a sword emerged. Noah watched on hopelessly, looking back at me for help.

I smiled.

Amma wrapped her hands around the handle. Selene shrieked.

"I could take it from you. Right now. Then who would be helpin' who?"

With a violent gasp, the color returned to her hair, and her skeletal form regained life and vibrancy. Noah rushed to her side, trying to help her to her feet as she struggled to stand. Her legs were like rubber, shaking and falling back to her knees like a newborn calf.

"You ain't as important as you think. Now kick rocks," Amma said.

"Amma," Selene said, her voice strained. "You'd have every right to take the power back from me, but you'd only be hurtin' yourselves,"

"Oh? But you're so powerful, Roshana. And with your King? Why don't you end this for all of us so we can marvel at your greatness, hm?"

"I only hold the power of Mary the Mother. But you, you are Mary the Magdalene returned. You are the *true* Holy Grail of Immortality. If you and Levi come together, you will birth a child that not even Shaddai can touch, and not only would our kind never taste death, we'd be one step closer to allowin' the Lord and Lady to physically enter this realm. And when that happens, nothin' could ever harm us again. The God of Heaven will be removed from His throne, and the Queen of the Abyss will rule again, usherin' in an age of magic and power unlike the world has ever seen."

"Amma, please," I said, stepping forward.

"If you won't do it for them, do it for me. For all of us. I told you there was a reason you and I was kept apart… but we're meant to be. This is what we're here to do."

"Christ and his disciples were the original Coven. The first child Mary gave birth to was killed to stop the prophecy from beginnin'. But now, if you and Levi do perform the Great Rite, we'll only have one portion left to fulfill. And Shaddai will fall."

Amma paused, giving us her back again.

"Amma, please…" I pleaded, running to her side. "I can't do this without you. Forget about them. Do it for your coven, for *our* kin. If we don't do this… we ain't got no chance at winnin' this war. This is our only shot."

Amma heaved, looking back at Selene and then at me again. She cupped my face in one of her hands, gently stroking my cheek.

"Fine." Amma glared at Selene. "But I ain't doin' this for you."

"Then we need to act quickly," Selene said, regaining her balance and leaning on Noah.

The clouds darkened, and an earth-shaking thunder erupted from the blackened heavens. From the center of the sky, the air rippled, and a terrifying shrilling screech pierced our ears, and everyone clasped their heads.

"Another Primordial," she said.

CHAPTER 29:

Judas

A monstrous roar tore through the sky, and the air was rancid, like rotting flesh, and burned our noses with each breath we took. The Coven screamed, huddling together and keeping their eyes fixed above them.

"How do we stop this?"

Noah stepped forward, trying to hide the fear on his face, with a swift hand through his hair to look cool and composed. I would want to also, especially after that level of humiliation.

"You need to find the one who opened the rift, and then only together will we be able to close the barrier again," Noah said. "We can't do it alone, not even with the power of Roshana and myself combined,"

"Why not?" I said.

"These is raw, cosmic forces of creation… I can command all created things, but these things existed long before the universe came to be. They ain't created, they always was. They had a hand in creation. I can't contain that alone," Selene said, looking to Amma now.

"All four of us standin' here together can do this together."

Amma folded her arms.

"And you really believe this is Father Enoch?"

"The Eye of Lilith showed me. He's doin' the conjuration. But he ain't actin' alone," Selene said.

"But why?" Amma pressed.

"And who would be dumb enough to do somethin' like that?" I said.

"It ain't got nothin' to do with intelligence, but obedience." A painful quiet came over Amma and me. "If y'all can get your hands on him before the Spring Equinox, then you can offer him up," Selene said.

"Why would we do that?" I asked.

Amma lowered her eyes to the ground.

"There are things about this Tradition that y'all wasn't meant to know. If the Providence or the Order knew what we was doin'. they would've killed us off a long time ago," Amma said.

"What are you goin' on about, Amma?" I asked.

She groaned uneasily.

"The Gift... has to be maintained. The Power handed down through the Pact requires blood."

My heart started to race.

"What kind of blood?" I said.

"The blood... of a Salem descendant."

Titus and Jonah backed away from her. My mouth hung open in a stupor.

"Every year we abducted one of the judges or a magician from the Order that had ties to Salem. And we offered 'em up to the Devil in the woods. It was supposed to be a secret, and although we turned to the Lord, it was the only way we'd be able to continue the circulation of the Gift to our descendants."

"And how long before y'all would have come for me? Or Ezra?"

"Never," Amma said. "We took only from those who wanted to hurt us, like judges."

"Ezra's a Judge,"

"*Other* judges. Grannie Tamar ain't only ever been nothin' but good to us. We'd never hurt her family."

I stepped away, facing the sea of trees and trying to compose myself. I knew that the witches had their ways, but I never thought that they were sacrificing people to maintain this dark Gift that they seemed hellbent on preserving at all costs.

"How… How could y'all do things like this and continue to serve the God of the Garden?"

"We do it out of His sight, same as the rituals to pass on the power of the Madonna," Amma explained.

I laughed, exasperated.

"Bullshit," I said "This is His world, He sees everythin' that's going on."

"Not everythin'," Noah interjected. "Remember the cave?"

"There is a place where the first of the race of man were taken to learn the secrets of the art and to copulate. There are other places, such as this very part of Sheol,"

"I ain't never heard nothin' like that about these woods," I said, disgruntled.

"It's true, Levi," Amma added. "Adam and Eve was the second attempts at makin' man because the first creation went behind his back. My Grannie used to call 'em the Hidden Children, the first witches birthed by them. It's an incantation that places you in the womb of the Queen of the Abyss."

"I can't believe this…"

"It's a place of darkness. When our female babies are born, we hold rituals there and pass them through the fires, and they're never burned. Instead, they're filled with the light of knowledge."

Jonah and Titus's eyes twitched. They covered their mouths, speechless. They looked at me, silently begging me to say something. I could tell they wanted me to make sense of all this, but I was just as horrified and confused as they were. The rumbling thunder stopped me from descending too deeply into doubt. What was I really helping in here?

"Fine," I said, frustrated. "So we stop Father Enoch, and then what?"

"You and Amma must perform the Great Rite," Selene said. "And you'll create the Holy Grail."

"What is that?"

"It's always been a legend," Amma said. "The witches from even back in my Grannie's time talked about it. They said someone called the Bringer would come."

"The Bringer?"

"A woman wholly divine, made of quintessence, she'll not be flesh and blood. This would allow her to host the Queen of the Abyss forever, and She will walk among us with her Consort and rule the Earth again." Amma said. "But I've always been told that's just a story."

"The witches who changed allegiance needed to create that belief to keep the Magdalene and the Christ from creatin' this child. It's the most important part of the prophecy."

I turned to Titus and Jonah. "Then we'd better get goin'," I said.

"I'm comin' with you," Amma said. She faced her Coven now, calling Bonnie forward. "I need you to cover the Coven with darkness and lay tricks all around you. Make sure anyone who enters into them woods searchin' for us is confused or terrified by whatever visions y'all create. You understand?"

"What do you need from us?" Selene said.

"To stay in your lane," Amma said. "We'll handle things from here."

Amma raised her hands, and the bushes curved at the whirling force of black mass that formed inside their leaves as she conjured her portal of darkness.

"I'll go with them," Noah said, approaching the portal.

"I ain't ask you to come with us," Amma quipped.

"I know," he said, digging his hands into his pockets. "But trust me, an extra hand ain't ever hurt nobody."

Amma glared at me, cocking her head as if to reprimand him. I shrugged.

"The enemy of my enemy, like they say."

I waved Noah to join us, and we stepped into the portal.

We traveled through blowing winds and crushing darkness until a light appeared at the end of the void we walked through. Burning candles and stained glass came into focus, and the polished, marble floor of the church extended to our feet. I was the first to exit the portal, stepping into something slippery, and gushy.

"Ugh," I recoiled back.

Amma and the others stepped out from the shadow of the crevice of the wall. A torso with missing limbs was laid out in front of the pool of blood where its exposed entrails leaked. From within the darkness of the church was a sickening gnashing and grinding sound, wet and fetid. Two priests in black robes ripped apart the limbs of a body that lay on the ground across from us, chewing on the intestines and tearing through his flesh with their teeth.

"Jesus Christ…" Jonah whispered.

One of the priests cocked his head and faced our direction. His eyes were large, flushed in a pale blue with skin as ghostly as death. He stood to his feet, dropping chunks of human flesh from his hands. Fresh blood ran down his chin as he slowly approached us, growling.

The other priest crawled on all fours, his back curving and breaking through the material of his robes like a feral animal. Blood and saliva dripped down from his mouth and onto the floor in putrid globs, flashing us teeth stained red and oozing.

"What the fuck kind of Primordial is this?" Titus said, backing away slowly.

"Hunger," Noah said.

Growls approached us from behind, we huddled together now as more priests drenched in blood and twisted faces approached us. They screeched lunging forward at us. Noah's eyes flashed pitch black, and he hissed in the Hidden Tongue. The ravenous priests faced each other and started tearing into one another, gauging out one another's eyes and ripping chunks of flesh from their bodies. They fell on top of each other, shredding and eviscerating one another and consuming the meat they tore from their bones.

The priests in front of us charged toward us, leaping into the air. I stood in front of the group, but before I could even move my hands, the two priests stopped in their tracks, rigid and catatonic. They shook, trembling, and screeched like banshees, and their skeletons in their entirety were ripped out of their skin. Their flesh, intestines, and organs fell at their feet like robes, and their skeletons collapsed onto the ground, scattering in every direction. Another figure emerged from the darkness. The feminine figure sparked a cigarette, blowing out a plume of smoke.

"Sister Agnes?" I said, taken aback.

I could see her shoulders bouncing as she chuckled.

"Aw, shucks," she said, her voice now more youthful. "Call me Melinda. Melinda Scott."

She stepped into the light, revealing a beautiful woman, with milky skin and raven black hair, with wine red lipstick.

"Good to see you again, Mama," Noah said.

Noah embraced her.

"Wait a minute," Amma said. "Melinda Scott? Then you must be Noah Abertha."

"That's right, sugar," Melinda said.

"So we've got the son of a plantation owner and the great-great-granddaughter of the woman who helped burned this town down and drive us into hidin'. Levi, how could you trust these people?"

"Listen... Now, you got every reason to treat me with suspicion and contempt, I ain't gonna hold that against you. It's well within your right. What our ancestors did to y'all was unforgivable... But that ain't gonna stop me from protectin' this Coven, and that includes you. Adora may not have seen y'all as sisters to her, but I damn sure do," Melinda said.

"You're right, I don't trust you, not 'til y'all show me somethin' different," Amma said. "But we have a common goal."

"So... y'all mind explainin' to me what the hell's goin' on here?" I said.

Melinda shrugged, holding the cigarette between her lips as she fixed her hair.

"Ain't nothin' but a little glamour, darlin'," Melinda said. "And Sister Agnes made the perfect image to impress on."

"Why?" I asked.

"Oh, Agnes was what we'd call a Williams witch. She was workin' with magicians to help get us killed. Besides, I needed someone trusted to come in and spy. A familiar face, you know how that goes."

"What was y'all tryin' to find out?" I said.

"Who in here was responsible for openin' up that portal. Turns out I was right; it was Father Enoch. I followed him one night. Did you know there was an entire cavern beneath this church?"

"Trust me... I'm painfully familiar," I said.

Beneath the church was where the outgoing Christ was crucified, allowing the next one to enter the world. It was also where I'd spent every Easter, allowing the Pope and the clergy to drink my blood and eat my flesh, killing me all over again. It's where I'd remain dead for the following three days until I was able to return again.

"And where's the real Sister Agnes?"

"Oh, she's bein' held. I figured with Spring Equinox comin' up and the like, she'd make just the *perfect* offerin' for the Pact. Wouldn't you agree?"

"Let's not talk about that."

"Oh, please, Levi," Amma said, annoyed. "You snub your nose at us, but how many times have you allowed yourself to be eaten alive? Besides, ain't nobody ever told you the history of how this church came to be?"

"I don't think I'd ever heard about that before," Jonah said.

Amma sighed.

"This church was once ran by women... not a priest in sight. Many of the Nuns was also witches, usin' the cover of the church to practice their craft without fear. But then the magicians came," Amma said, watery-eyed. "At first, the women was afraid that they would be violated, so they cut their noses off to make themselves less appealin', but little did they know that they would be doomed no matter what they did."

"Jesus Christ," Titus said.

"That's right. The magicians then bound them, they was outnumbered. The magicians nailed them against the walls and then laid stone over them. Their screams fueled the magic as they was buried alive behind these walls." Amma laid her hand gently against the wall. "They hang here now for all eternity, their very souls was given to feed the spirit of this place."

"I'm sorry... I didn't know."

"My great-great-grannie was one of them. So think twice about why we give the blood of our enemies to sustain us. There's a poetic justice to that, wouldn't you agree?"

"Ooo," Melinda said, giddy. "I *like* her!"

I took Amma's hand, coaxing her. "I'm sorry, okay?"

Amma pulled her hand back and folded her arms.

"So, the question of the evenin'," I said, "where's Father Enoch?"

Melinda shrugged, taking another puff of her cigarette.

"Beats the hell outta me. He saw me catch him that night, mutterin' that incantation. He ran away from me after that, opened a portal into who-knows-where." Melinda said.

"We don't got a lot of time," Noah said. "They're eatin' each other alive out there. Who knows what Primordial comes next. You sure you don't know nothin', Mama?"

"I think I know someone who might," I said.

"Who would've warned the judges about Amma havin' that book?"

Amma's eyes darkened with anger.

"Nita," she said.

CHAPTER 30

Thief In The Night

Melinda grimmaced.

"Another witch who betrayed her Coven? Well, now that's a damn shame."

"She has to die," Amma said.

"You don't gotta tell me twice," I grunted.

I signed the Hidden Hands, and a window portal opened in the air with a distorted image of Grannie's house plain to see.

"Titus, Jonah, you stay behind and search with the others anywhere you think you could find Father Enoch. Amma, you can come with me."

"The Providence might be hidin' him," Titus said.

"But it'll be a suicide mission goin' in there. It's crawlin' with judges and magicians no doubt waitin' to ambush us,"

"Then reconvene with the Coven. We'll take the Providence after we find out what we can from Nita,"

Noah nodded, gathering them together and opening a dark rift in the corner of the church.

"I'll hold down the fort here," he said.

Amma locked arms with me, facing the whirring portal ahead. We stepped inside.

The portal closed behind us, and Amma and I stood underneath a dark sky illuminated with stars. The house was like a lantern on a hill, glowing just enough to be seen from the cloak of night that shrouded even our hands in front of us. The grass was wet with evening dew, and crickets chirped by the thousands all around us. Amma took a first step, sending up emerald green fireflies dancing through the sky around her, lighting up the area around us.

"You think Ezra's inside?" Amma asked, trekking through the field.

"He's likely with the judges by now tryin' to figure out a plan. You took down more than they was suspectin', that's for sure."

"Well, peaceful don't mean harmless. Somethin' I don't think they've ever understood about us," Amma said.

We stood on the porch. My stomach was in knots being back at the home I was told to never return to. It was just as much my house was it was Ezra's, even if we weren't on the same side anymore. But standing at the threshold of the door, unsure of what I'd see on the other side, drove me to near madness. The only way to satiate my fears was to go through the door. What if Grannie was dead? Or Ezra driven so mad with hunger that he was feasting on Grannie? They may have seen me as the enemy, but I only saw them as kin who lost their way. But there was no love like Christian hate.

"You think she's in there?" Amma asked.

"Only one way to find out."

The door creaked and groaned as I pushed it open, watching our shadows stretch out across the floor from the moonlight behind us. Candles dripped wax onto the floor nearly down to the wick around the house, casting twisted shadows along the walls and giving the family oil paintings life enough to feel their eyes on us. It was as silent as the grave in that house, except for the faint sound of a distant pining.

"Nita?" I called out. "We know it was you. Why don't you come on out and face me since you're so bold?"

The whimpering grew stronger as we approached the den, where a figure was slumped over in the couch facing an antique mirror, lined with a chipped gold frame. The fireplace was crackling, and the paintings of all the Madonna's gone before lined the walls, almost consoling the lone, weeping woman that sat in the chair. A foul odor hung in the air around her, like decay.

"Grannie?" I said, cautiously approaching.

She sobbed inconsolably, blubbering and coughing. Amma gently held me back, gesturing towards the floor where a large puddle of blood and saliva laid with a small pile of teeth and hair that gathered. The top of her head was balding. The hair that was left formed a ring around the spot exposing her scalp. Grannie raised a trembling hand, and as her fingers passed through the strands of hair, she removed handfuls that peeled off her scalp. She wailed, dropping the hair onto the pile of teeth and blood.

"You," she heaved, "you did this…"

My eyes watered, too afraid to turn her around and see. I slowly reached for her shoulder, and she turned around to face us. Amma gasped, staggering back. Chunks of flesh fell from her face and into her lap, leaving gaping holes that exposed her back teeth. She sniveled, pointing at us with a trembling finger after removing another tooth that loosened, dropping it onto the ground.

"You brought the Devil into our home," Grannie cried.

She looked at her horrid reflection in the mirror, shrieking and covering her face again. Vanity ran deep in this family, and even in her old age, Grannie was a beautiful woman. That was the very thing that Shaddai weaponized against her. Grannie used to spend so much time looking in the mirror, and now she could hardly stand to see herself in it.

My heart shattered into pieces seeing the state she'd been reduced to, and the worst part was that it was all to get back at me. I could never forgive the God of the Garden using those around me to hurt me, only a coldhearted and sadistic tyrant would do something like that. But since He couldn't harm me directly this time, he went for everyone I cared for.

"Grannie, please let me heal you. I did it for Ezra," I said, rushing to her side and taking her hand. Grannie yanked her arm away from me.

"NO!" she screamed bitterly. "I knew you was born corrupted. Even after tryin' to stop your Mama, you still turned into this,"

"What?" I said, recoiling from her. "What did you say?"

Grannie hung her head, still peeling off the hair from her scalp and sobbing.

"Your Mama was born with the darkness in her," Grannie said. "Hell, we all was, but your Mama gave into it."

"Grannie," I said, tightening my fist. "What are you tryin' to say?"

Grannie tried to rub her cheek, but her fingers protruded through the flesh, and she hollered in pain, scraping another chunk of flesh from her face and dropping it onto the floor. She looked and wreaked like a walking corpse, as if she was rotting from the inside out.

"Your Mama once she found out what you was, what you was destined to be, wanted to take you to the River Gnosmos and baptize you in the blood and teach you the Old Ways. But Shaddai chose you, and we couldn't let her corrupt you,"

"*We?*" I said, angrily.

"Your daddy and I agreed that she couldn't be in the picture anymore, so I called on Shaddai to inflict her with madness and put her away."

"You mean… all this time…" I could barely get the words out of my mouth, my heart raced so quickly I thought it would fail at any moment. The room around me started to spin, and I felt lightheaded with a dizziness brought on by a rage I hadn't felt in my entire life.

"All this time you kept tellin' me my mama was crazy and not to see her 'cause it would only break my heart. But really, it was all because you was tryin' to keep me from findin' out the truth…"

"I knew you would try to heal her," Grannie said. "Your daddy and I both knew it, and you might have succeeded, but we couldn't take the chance. We tried to save you and look at the thanks we get. Now he's dead and buried, and I'm one foot in the grave right behind him. You make me *sick*."

My eyes seared as globs of tears ran down my face. I dug my fingernails into my fist so deeply I drew blood, and I was shaking uncontrollably.

"All these years," I strained, fighting to get out the words I kept choking on. Amma laid her hand on my shoulder pityingly. "You made me believe you cared for me and that you loved me."

"I could never love you," Grannie said, almost amused at the thought. "Every time I looked into your eyes, I only saw that woman. Now, here you are, doin' the Devil's work like she sought out to do all them years ago."

I hated her. A woman I'd idolized my entire life, writing essays about in school, believing she was the backbone of the family. I praised her endlessly about how she raised my brother and I and loved us as her own, and it was all a lie. Grannie never loved me, and she hated herself even more. I realized then that because my mama and I became comfortable in being what we were, Grannie always hated herself and thought the more she served God, the happier she would be; and it was the greatest deceit ever told. There was no happiness, no love or light within Grannie because she didn't know it for herself.

All these years, I believed it was just tough love, that she was only looking out for us because she wanted the best. But little did I know it was resentment in the front seat of her mind and steering all her actions. Grannie was now as ugly as she was on the inside. I was only ever a trophy for her, something to wave around in people's faces to convince the world and herself that she was holy, how God had chosen *her* household to dwell in. And now that I no longer served that purpose, it was easy for her to discard me; toss me aside like trash with no use. I never meant anything to her.

It was my mama that paid the ultimate price. Now I saw Grannie and the God of the Garden as two sides of the same coin, terrestrial and celestial; both as cruel and vindictive with reactions that lived to serve the means to their selfish ends. Mama was never able to be controlled by the fear the church instilled in her for so many years. She knew she was a witch. And that scared Grannie and gave her no other choice but to cut the fat off and cast her to the fire, inflict her with a disease of the mind so that Mama wouldn't know who or what she was.

Growing up, all I ever wondered was where she was and if my mama could even remember having me. I cried so many nights, just wanting to be held by her, only to receive disdain and resentment from Grannie, who could barely even look at me more often than not.

Even worse than that, Grannie used to tell me my mama wanted to abort me, and it was her who convinced her not to do it. The one who never wanted me to exist until she saw a way to use me for her own glory was Grannie. In the end, she only cared about herself and her own reputation. I always thought family was supposed to be the shoulder to lean on, the only people in the world I could trust. But I learned now the most painful lesson of all; not all skin folk are kin folk, and sometimes water made better for drink than blood, no matter how thick it was.

"You took my mama from me…" I said, broken.

"And I'd do it again." Blood ran down Grannie's chin as she forced a smile on her face.

I screamed until my voice was hoarse, snatching her by the neck.

"Levi!" Amma yelled.

"Where's your God to save you now?" I asked through my teeth.

She gasped, kicking high above the ground where I pinned her firmly in place. I raised my fist towards her, and it caught fire in a blazing ball of sparks and embers. She screamed as the fire scorched the open wounds in her face.

"I DID IT TO PROTECT THIS FAMILY!" Grannie yelled.

"YOU DID IT TO PROTECT YOURSELF!"

Her eyes lulled to the back of her head. "You," she coughed, straining, "are just like your Mama. Plain evil."

I winced.

"And you have no heart," I said.

With the flaming hand, I smashed through her chest. She opened her mouth to scream, but nothing came out except gurgling and fresh blood drizzled down her chin. I reached into the flesh of her body and wrapped my hands around her beating heart and ripped it straight from her chest. Her body dropped onto the ground with a loud thud, and I looked down at her pulsating heart in my hands. Amma covered her mouth, aghast and shaking her head. Grannie's vacant-eyed and lifeless body now laid at my feet. And the worst part about it all? It felt good. To quote Grannie, *I'd do it again.*

I looked towards the fireplace and cast her heart into the flames like an old love letter, listening to it crackle and sizzle in the fires that now consumed it. Maybe the flames would purge her of the evil and hatred she'd carried in her heart, but even I wouldn't expect such a miracle. A curdling scream came from the other end of the room, and there was Nita.

"MAMA!" she cried out with tears running down her face.

"*YOU,*" Nita growled.

I smirked at her, lifting my bloody hand towards her, beckoning. Her head shook before she screeched ferociously, and her feet rose from the ground carried by a sudden surge and rush of torrential air. She bolted towards me, howling louder than the winds that gathered inside. She slammed against me, nailing me down against the wall digging her knees into my pelvis, brandishing a copper knife that I knew was used to kill witches and sever the ties to the Pact. Her eyes bulged from her head with rage as she held the knife over her head.

"BURN IN HELL!" she screamed.

Nita brought the knife down onto me. I raised my hands in front of my face and felt the dagger puncture straight through my hand. She unsheathed it again from my palm and stabbed again, puncturing through my other hand. I screamed, pushing back against her as she brought the blade down closer towards my heart. Her hair was wildly blown in the wind, and streams of saliva whipped around from her mouth and against my face.

"I'LL KILL YOU!" she screamed.

Nita was ripped off me, and I collapsed onto the ground near Grannie's body. Nita rolled across the floor from the force of Amma's magic. The paintings of Madonnas past whipped across the room, smashing into the walls and against the floor. Amma motioned her hands, and a translucent wave of energy shot across the room and split the couch in half, spraying cushioning that now whirled across the room. Nita pushed back waves of energy. Amma deflected them, sending them behind her, where they smashed into the wall, tearing chunks and sending them into the vortex of air that consumed the room.

My eyes could barely open from the violent winds. All I could see was Nita sending blasts of energy towards Amma, who continued to deflect her attacks. Amma whipped around and motioned her hands quickly, and a piercing screech tore through the cold air. I clasped my ears from the sound, but by the force of Amma's magic, Nita's face was ripped clean off. Nita covered her face, hunching over and hollering in pain. Nita looked up at Amma with a face made of now pure muscle and tendon, and her eyes like two golf balls protruding from her skull. She looked more like a skeleton with moving eyes than she did a person.

"YOU'LL PAY FOR WHAT YOU'VE DONE TO THIS COVEN!" Amma shouted.

Nita raised her arms in the air, screaming as thick vines burst through the windows behind her. Amma yelped in pain as shards of glass sliced through her skin, and vines from the trees outside continued to surge through the room from behind Nita and towards the both of us. They picked me up and slammed me into the wall beside Amma and wrapped us up in their thick embrace. They crushed my bones as they tightened their grip around me, and I yelled out, my voice drowned out by the wind and glass that slashed across my face.

"YOU'LL BURN FOR THIS!" Amma screamed, fighting against the hold.

Nita's skeletal smile consumed her face in an ear-to-ear, mischievous snarl. Her feet levitated off the ground, and her dress whipped and blew in every direction with her hair.

"Catch me if you can," she said.

An echoing, raucous laugh filled the room, and she cackled, darting out the gaping hole in the wall where the vines had entered. The winds were instantly hauled, and the vines curled off of us and retreated back along the walls and slithered back towards the trees they came from, reeling backwards across the floor. I ran, limping and following behind Amma out through the smashed wall and into the field. Nita whirled around in the air, cackling before stopping again. She was barely a shadow against a backdrop of stars behind her.

"YOU BETTER GET TO YOUR MAMA BEFORE I DO!" Nita yelled from on high. "'CAUSE I'M FIXIN' TO RETURN THE FAVOR!"

Nita gracefully twirled through the air again, and then shot off into the night out of sight. I clasped onto my side, the adrenaline giving way to the pain as I fell back onto my knees. Amma hoisted me back up, putting my arm over her shoulder.

"So much for findin' out where Father Enoch was," Amma said.

I groaned, collapsing from my injuries again. Father Enoch was the primary objective, but right now he was the furthest thing from my mind. I needed to get to my mama.

And I was running out of time.

CHAPTER 31

Mortal Sin

$\mathbf{M}$y hands trembled; I couldn't move my fingers, and trying to close them felt like having the blade thrust inside all over again.

"You ain't gonna help nobody with your hands like that," Amma said.

"I'll be fine," I grunted.

Amma took my hands in hers and brushed her finger across the open wound. I watched the nerves and skin join together instantly when the wound closed. I closed my hand, opening it again and feeling no more pain than a dull ache. But I could move them again.

"Thanks, Amma," I said.

She smiled at me with large eyes and a deep stare. I could feel the love between us that withered and died so long ago start to bloom again. I cupped her face, and she laid her hand over mine.

"I don't deserve someone like you," I said.

Amma smiled, weakly.

"I'm here now, that's all that matters."

I looked deep into her eyes again, trying to resist the urge to kiss her. I wanted to savor something other than pain, but I wasn't going to use her lips as a crutch for the turmoil I felt. I knew I loved Amma, but I didn't want to use this moment to prove that to myself or her. I signed the Hidden Hands, opening another window portal.

"You ready?" I said.

Amma smirked, stepping through the portal first, and I followed behind her.

The rift closed behind us. We stood in a hospital that was in shambles. The dingy lights flickered above us, and blood stained the walls and doors. People half alive begged to die from their injuries, writhing in pain as others feasted on each other and any trace of life they could find around them. Hunger swept through this town like a plague, and everyone caught within its grasp was reduced to a bloodthirsty animal, prowling for another life to consume. The way the people around us moved was in strange, erratic turns and gestures, like they were creatures driven more by an insatiable impulse rather than a single thought.

"Stay close," I whispered to Amma.

I dreamed so many times of coming to this hospital to see Mama. Saint Hildegards was once a hospital of repute for women in need of mental recovery, but now there wasn't anything left to recover. There were patients scattered on the ground like discarded wrappers, oozing out blood and laying with bone exposed to become feasts for flies. Amma covered her nose from the pungent smell, and we tried to move as quietly as we could.

I went towards the back desk and found a computer screen with blood splattered across the screen and half the torso of a woman still clinging onto the mouse, as if she was ripped in half before she had time to respond. I took the mouse, shaking off the hanging limb that collapsed to the ground and entered her name: June Beaumont. The registry quickly pulled up a photo of her. My heart leaped, as it was the only time I'd ever seen her outside my memories. Grannie destroyed any pictures that remained of her, and I barely had any memories of Mama to fall back on or remember fondly.

"You look like her," Amma said kindly.

My eyes burned with the tears that formed, and I had a lump in my throat too large to swallow no matter how hard I tried. I brushed my hand against the computer screen longingly. I couldn't shake the pain that consumed me. There was a bittersweetness in seeing her photo here, the only one I'd ever laid my eyes on. Anxiousness filled me as I knew I was only moments away from seeing her in real life. I was living a dream in a nightmarish scape strewn with blood and mangled bodies, and yet it was the happiest I'd felt in so long.

"0701," I said, pointing at her room number on the right corner.

I took Amma by the arm, rushing down the darkened hallways and stepping over corpses. The smell was unbearable, Amma and I trekked through the abysmal hall, covering our noses until we reached a door at the end the hallway. I held my hand over the doorknob, trembling with angst.

"I'm right here with you," Amma said, bright-eyed and reassuring.

"Well, ain't this sweet?" An all too familiarly disdainful voice said.

Nita stood at the end of the hall, the exposure of her skull now dried with blood and her eyes bulging and peering directly at us. I stood my ground, raising my arms and ready to fight.

"Looks like y'all beat me here. Look at that," she said, stepping closer towards us.

Fortunately, we got to Mama before Nita did, but I knew she wasn't prepared to make this easy.

"Why?" Amma shouted. "How could you betray your own Coven?"

Nita laughed hoarsely.

"Why? 'Cause you didn't deserve that crown. I should've been crowned Madonna of this Coven. And who all does Mama pick? You. I was next in line, Mama chose me as her successor."

"I perfromed the 13 Pillars in front of the elders. *Me.* The spirits chose me, Nita. When they cast the cowrie shells, the ancestors made their decision."

Nita's skull face gnashed its teeth.

"They did, didn't they?" Nita said. "Well, why don't we take you to join them while we're all here?"

"I *outrank* you. You don't have the power it takes," Amma retorted.

"I told Mama you and Levi would be the end of us all… and here we are, the end of the line."

"It's only the end for you," Amma said

"Is that right?" Nita said. The wholes of her eyes turned solid black.

"*Wake up, sleeper,*" Nita said, her voice now slick and snake-like, echoing down the hall. The bodies that lied on the ground trembled, and before Amma could react, a headless corpse snatched her by the ankle, knocking her onto the ground.

"*Rise from the dust,*" Nita said, lifting her arms out to her sides.

The cadavers that lied on the floor sprung to their feet, hobbling and darting towards us in a frenzied attack. Amma waved her arm, blasting the dead body that clasped to her feet off her. Nita stood at the end of the hall, heckling shrilly. I helped her to her feet; she raised a wall of energy that rippled and distorted the air in front of us. The bodies bounced off the wall of energy, sliding across the floor, only to stand back up and lunge at us again.

"I thought only the Madonna can raise the dead!" I said.

Nita may not have been chosen to be Madonna, but she was a force to be reckoned with and came from a powerful line of witches. The blood of Tituba still ran strong through her.

"There ain't no life in them," Amma said, panting, "but that don't mean she can't make them bones dance."

Throngs of mutilated bodies barreled from behind Nita towards us.

"Fuck this," I said.

I rushed out from behind the barrier she raised. Amma screamed, trying to pull me back inside. I took a deep breath, feeling a scorching heat rise from my throat. I opened my mouth, releasing a blast of raging, crimson fire roaring like thunder and surging down the hallway. The bodies caught in the flames were incinerated, others caught in the flames collapsed again, turning to ash as the fire consumed what was left of them. The flames surged towards Nita, who brought her hands in front of her like a clap, parting the flames down the middle, sending the fire up towards the walls like Moses splitting the sea.

Her silhouetted figure stood, illuminated by the flames that climbed into the ceiling, sending plumes of thick, black smoke into the air. Nita looked as she was standing at the gates of Hell, still firmly planted on the ground undeterred. I hated to admit it, but Nita was still a deadly, formidable enemy. As the fires raged around her, she looked more like a demon with her skull face and protruding eyes. Amma stepped forward, and with a quick motion of her hands, the ground beneath Nita's feet erupted, shooting out jagged, thick rocks from two ends. Nita leaped in the air, missing the colliding rocks that would've snatched her legs.

Nita whirled her arms around her, and the darkness behind her rushed forward, and she wrapped it around herself like cloak of shadows, vanishing into thin air.

"Mama," I said, turning back towards the door.

I pulled on the handle as the fires blackened the walls and itched closer towards us. The door was locked firmly in place. I jiggled and tugged the handle to no avail. I took a step back, and pushing forward, I released a burst of power that blew the door off the hinges, slamming into the wall through the darkened room.

"Mama?" I said, rushing inside.

"She's right here," Nita's said.

Amma and I stopped dead in our tracks as Nita held her with the copper blade firmly at her throat. Mama sniveled, tears streaming down her face. She was crying, babbling in confusion but had enough awareness to know she was in danger.

"Nita…" I said, stepping closer.

Mama screamed as she pressed the knife deeper against her throat. Blood ran down her neck now.

"Take another step, and your Mama'll be joinin' the souls in Hell where she belongs," Nita warned.

My heart burned with the overwhelming desire to brutally and violently kill her, but I knew if I stepped too soon, she'd kill Mama, and with that blade in her hand, Mama was destined to meet an end in hellfire.

"You killed my mama, the woman who raised you. And you stood around while witches took my brother away from me, and you didn't even have the power to bring him back," Nita spat through clenched teeth. "You don't deserve what was given to you,"

I held my hand out, pleadingly.

"Nita, please put the blade down, Mama don't got nothin' to do with this."

"Oh, June's got everythin' to do with this— bringin' you into this world so you can destroy this family, takin' after her. She wasn't supposed to be with my brother, you know? She wove her magic 'cause she just had to have him herself."

"That ain't true," I said.

"You wouldn't know the truth if it bit you in the ass, boy," Nita said venomously.

"You're right, I wouldn't. This whole family's been built on lies."

Mama screamed as Nita pressed deeper into her throat with the edge of the blade.

"*An eye for an eye*," Nita said. "You took from me, now I'll take from you!" Nita gasped, as her hand started to shake uncontrollably. I looked back to see Amma's eyes, glossy and jet black.

"W—What are you—?"

"I've entertained your treachery long enough, Nita," Amma said.

Nita forcibly removed the blade from mama by Amma's magic. Mama collapsed onto the ground and scurried backward into a corner, covering her face and muttering frantically.

"As you was sayin', Nita. *An eye for an eye.*"

Nita struggled against her own body, bending to Amma's will, and with a pleading scream, she drove the blade deep into her eye, screeching in agony.

"NO!" Nita screamed as she yanked the blade from one socket and drove it deeply into the next. She dropped the blade onto the floor with a loud *clink!*

Nita clawed at her face, seething and crying as she backed herself against a wall, swearing and screaming down curses on the both of us. Nita reached back out, swinging and clawing the air blindly. She threw her head back in a bellowing squawk as from the center of her chest, a burning ring of fire appeared, charring the edges around her skin like the lit end of a cigarette. The room was filled with the smell of burning flesh as Nita convulsed from the fire that consumed her from the inside out. When Nita opened her mouth to scream again, fire spewed from her mouth.

"I told you you'd burn for this," Amma said coolly.

"NO!" Nita screaming hoarsely, embers spraying from her lips.

She quickly reached her arm towards Mama, and she was ripped from where she stood, flying across the room back into Nita's grip. The room around us was consumed with twisting black shadows, whirling around Nita in a vortex of shroud and shadow. Through the streaks of darkness, the room transformed into the twisting trees and hummed with sound of cicadas.

Nita restrained Mama, the flesh still searing from the fire that burned inside her.

"Tag. You're it!" Nita hissed.

She waved her arm, and with one leap into the air, she was swallowed by the darkness.

"NO!" I screamed.

I lunged towards her, reaching for her but gripping only the fleeting shadows that slid through my fingers.

"W—Where did she go?"

"Serpent's Swamp," she said. "Hurry!"

Amma lifted her hands in the air, bringing down the darkness once again upon the room and opened a vortex of twisting shade. I ran through the darkness with Amma quickly trailing behind me. I rushed through the darkness, feeling now thick leaves and vines stinging my face as I rushed past them. The bending darkness took solid form now of trees, and the whipping air beneath my feet gave way to slugging, cold water. We stood waist- deep in the middle of the swamp.

The smell of Nita's burning flesh still lingered, I knew she wasn't far. I trudged the water, pacing back and forth.

"Where is she?" I said, desperate.

Amma lifted her hand to me.

"Stop," she said.

Nita's cackle echoed around us, and the trees swayed gently now in an eerie breeze. We waded in the water, searching frantically for any sign of Nita.

"You found me," she said voice called from above. She was silhouetted against the moon behind her, gracefully descending from the air and hovering over us. "Well, look at you!" she chirped.

"WHERE IS SHE!?" I screamed.

Nita chuckled. The pale light against her skin revealed her seared body and skull face with the smell of her corroded body wafting from the smoke that faintly permeated from her.

"About to be dinner," She sneered.

Nita snapped her fingers, and Mama was fully revealed beside her, dangling upside down now, slowly descending towards the water. Vicious hissing crept behind us, and the glowing eyes of ravenous alligators swam past us towards Mama, whose hair now brushed against the surface of the murky water. The gators thrashed, quickly rushing towards her.

"MAMA!"

I signed Hidden Hands and sent a blast of translucent red energy towards her. Nita rotated her hands, the blast colliding with her and, with a swift motion, she dissipated the attack, laughing. Amma shot her hand out towards Amma as the alligators were just inches from her, and Mama was yanked out of the air and barred across the swamp into the muddy shore, tumbling across the ground, slamming back first against a tree.

Nita screeched, raising her arms in a fury. Slimy, wet vines sprouted beneath the water and wrapped their thick, slugging tendrils around my neck and arms, forcing me down onto my knees and pulling me into the water.

"LEVI!" Amma shouted.

The vines tore at me forcefully, tightening their grip around my neck as I desperately gasped for air. I fought their pull, watching as the alligators quickly rushed towards me now, then pulled me under water. I writhed beneath the muddy water, desperate for air as I felt the seconds quickly going by until I ran out of breath and the serrated teeth of the gators met me. I opened my eyes, and through the streaks of moonlight that penetrated the water, I saw the gaping mouth of the alligator ready to swallow me whole.

A powerful current swept me, yanking me away quicker than lightning. The churning waves pushed up against my chest, ripping from the clasp of the vines that entangled me and tore me from the beneath the surface of the water like a fish on a line. I slammed into the mushy ground of the bank, coughing out brown, bitter water.

Amma glanced back at me and gave me a quick nod. I heaved, catching my breath and locking eyes with Mama, who was curled into ball, stammering and trembling. I rushed towards her. Amma rose from the water with her arms wide open, hovering now over the water. Rapid winds gathered around her, and the trees around us bent and swayed by the power of the rushing gales.

Nita shrieked like a banshee and bolted across the open air towards her. Amma waved her arms quickly, and the thick branches of the trees slammed into Nita, sending her tumbling into the water. Nita quickly came up for air and began to rise from the water. Amma cocked her head calmly, deadly focused. Thick vines bulleted from the trees and wrapped around both of Nita's arms, hoisting her into the air. Her feet now dangled over the water.

Nita struggled, kicking and struggling against the tightening grip of the vines and branches that locked her in place. Amma's feet came down onto the surface of the water, where she stood now with the same monstrous alligators, circling around her, obedient to her will. Their glowing yellow eyes flashed in the dark as they dipped in and out beneath the water, churning the swamp beneath her feet.

"You," Nita grunted, "you will *never* be worthy of the crown!"

Amma titled her head, amused.

"And you'll never wear it," Amma said.

Amma hissed in the Hidden Tongue, and instantly, the alligators were driven to a frenzy. Their tails thrashed against the water as they rushed towards Nita, who dangled helplessly.

"No, no, no…" Nita begged.

Her screams echoed across the water and the gators raised their ravenous mouths towards her and everything below her waist was swallowed by their bite. She yelped and screamed as the alligators ripped her apart. They severed her torso by the hips, ripping her lower body clean off. Intestines dangled and blood spewed into the water, flowing from the gaping hole left of her body. Her screams were weakened until the gators leaped from the water, ripping her arm and leaving her last bit dangling by the other.

They tore chunks from her, shredding her body to pieces, and ripped off what was left dangling of Nita on the vine.

There was only the sound now crickets over the stillness of the water.

Nita was finally dead.

It was a horrible thing to say, but I dreamed long of the day that would happen. I always believed that it would come to her in old age, but I was happy to see she went out in the way she lived her life, violent and full of pain and with no remorse. Nita was the cruelest human being I'd ever known. For someone who preached God and the goodness of the Gospel, she was full of a seething hatred that I never understood.

I used to think maybe because she was family, I'd feel some type of remorse the day that she came to pass, but I felt nothing. After all the early years of mocking, mentally abusing, and torturing me, she was finally just a pile of ash. Something that had been and no longer would be. I buried the thought of her the moment her bones collapsed to the ground.

Amma glided along the water, reaching the banks of the swamp and rushed to my side.

"You alright?"

"Yeah…"

I looked back at the dark swamp water, taking a twisted peace in knowing that Nita's grave would be in the belly of gators.

"So much for Nita," I said.

Amma smirked.

"Yeah, well, now she can be the shit she always thought she was."

I laughed bitterly. I looked down at Mama beside me, trying to comfort her.

"Mama?" I called out, itching closer towards her.

She was curled into a ball now, rocking back and forth. I slowly reached out, grabbing her shoulder, and she screamed, shaking her head and tugging at her hair.

"She ain't in her right mind Levi," Amma said. "The madness is still runnin' through her,"

Tears ran down my face as I reached over and held her by the chin and looked into her eyes for the first time. She was frightened, and shaken beyond words, but she was finally here.

"Let's get her home," I said.

Mama was safe now. I felt the delicate rays of hope's warmth cast its light on the darkness of disparity that loomed in my heart, but it wasn't enough. Mama may have been safe now, but not even half the battle was won. I had a hand in Nita's death, and I killed Grannie with my own hands. As vile and disgusting human beings they were, they were the only family I had. Now there was only Ezra. A friend loved at all times, but a brother was born for a time of adversity. I couldn't bring myself to kill Ezra, yet there was a chance, and that thought plagued me. I fought this long for the freedom to choose, but what if he took that from me when the time came?

What if I had no choice?

CHAPTER 32

Lamentations

Mama looked around in an awestruck wonder, still trapped in the madness of her mind as we passed through the window portal and back into Grannie's house. Shattered glass and debris loitered the house, and the power was out leaving us to wade through darkness. Amma blew, and the flickering flames on top of candles around the house danced alive again. There was a warm glow permeating through the darkened home, creating a damp heat that stuck to my skin.

"I'll go set up wards outside and then send my etch out to bring the others here. This can be our base instead of out in them woods," Amma said.

I nodded, looking back at Mama. Amma pursed her lips pityingly, leaning against the edge of the wall.

"I'll give y'all some room," she said.

She turned around, walking out the front door. I sat Mama down, holding her hands. I couldn't stop touching her, as if trying to prove to myself this wasn't a dream. It was real. I spent so many years creating imaginary conversations in my head, all the things I would say to her once I saw her, and now that she was in front of me, I drew a blank. My mind was swimming with mixed words and incomplete sentences, there was nothing that could have prepared me for this moment.

I squeezed her hand and knelt in front of her.

"I can fix you, Mama," I said, whimpering. "You'll be back in no time."

I closed my eyes, focusing until I felt the warmth of my energy slither up towards my spine and travel down through my arms. I didn't know where the words came from, but I hissed a spell in the Hidden Tongue.

"*Be healed*," I said.

Mama's mouth slowly hung open, and her head titled back. Her body twitched, shaking lightly and she groaned. She looked back down at me, her skin was like amber against the glow of the candlelight, and her honey eyes became clear and in focus. She wasn't looking past me; she was looking at me now. A gentle breeze entered the room, and there was a lightness in the air now, and around her energy. She sat straight up, no longer bogged down with the weight of madness.

"Mama?" I said.

She titled her head slightly, raising her brow curiously.

"Wh—Who are you?" she asked.

"It's me, Mama," I said. "It's Levi." Tears ran down my cheeks un-ashamedly as I pulled lightly on her arm.

She furrowed her brow pensively, muttering to herself.

"Levi... But... No, that can't be..." she said, looking up at me confused and horrified all at once. "My Levi's just a baby?"

"No, Mama," I pleaded. "Look. It's me."

She stared at me for a moment, and her denial quickly came to a painful realization. She laid her hand against my cheek, looking deeply into my eyes.

"It's you," she said softly.

I wrapped my hands around her waist and wept. I cried bitterly and painfully in a way that a grown man shouldn't, but I didn't care. I felt her hands gently stroking my back, shushing me quietly.

"I thought I'd never see you again," I sobbed.

She wiped the tears from my eyes, smiling vaguely. Her eyes were glossy, and crystalized beads of her sorrow trickled down her thick eyelashes.

"I'm here now, baby, don't you worry," she said. I clutched onto her tighter, sobbing and heaving. She let me keep crying, embracing me serenely with a love that I could feel permeating from her being.

"How old are you now?" she asked.

I looked up at her, sniffling and wiping the tears from my eyes.

"33," I said.

She gasped quietly, looking away from me. I could see her eyes drowning in regret as she scanned the house around her.

"33 years she's stolen from me," Mama said vaguely. She laughed bitterly and stood up. She wandered around the front of the house, feeling the walls and looking around the room.

"33 years... and it almost feels like no time has passed at all," she said.

"And Ezra?" she asked.

She looked fragile, as if any wrong word would shatter her into pieces. But there was no easy way or any lie I could come up with to tell her. And after so many years of lies and deception, I needed the truth. No matter how painful it was.

"Ezra... sided with the judges, he damn near wanna kill me at this point." Mama cast her gaze on the ground, closing her eyes painfully as she clasped at her chest.

"She's taken everythin' from me... I couldn't even be a mother to my two boys and now they're at odds with each other,"

"That ain't true... You'll always be my mama. There wasn't a day that went by that I didn't miss you," I said.

"Where is she?" Mama asked.

"Who?"

"Tamar, where is she?"

I leaned against the wall, shrugging blasé.

"She's dead. Killed her myself when I found out what she'd done,"

Mama gasped, exasperated.

"And Nita?"

"Dead."

She grunted, staring down the hallway for a moment.

"And Tamar's... body. It's here?" Mama said. "In the house?"

I nodded. I knew she was eyeing the living room where Grannie's body still laid. Mama walked down the hall and entered the den. Cold winds surged through the exposed wall. Mama stopped, gasping at the sight of Grannie's body lying on the floor. Most of the blood was between dry and coagulating, and the stench of her already was enough to suffocate. Mama stepped up to her body, pushing her corpse over with her foot, flopping her onto her back.

"That woman never cared about anyone but herself," Mama said. "She tried everythin' she could to stop me and your daddy from gettin' married. Even told everyone I'd given him a Love Potion." She scoffed. "And your daddy?"

I cleared my throat.

"He's gone too,"

"I knew she'd give him up as sacrifice for the Spring Equinox."

I hunched over like I was punched in the gut.

"W—What?" I said, shaking my head, disbelieving.

"Every year, the Coven gives a tribute to the Man in Black, so that he can—"

"Mama, I know what that is," I said, stopping in front of her. "But... What are you sayin'?"

"Your Grannie gave him up as a sacrifice," Mama said regretfully. "There was whispers in the Coven before she cursed me. I tried to warn your daddy, but he wouldn't listen to me... Your Grannie had already turned him against me by that point."

"Why... How could she do that?"

"The same way she used everyone else in her life to get ahead... The truth was, Tamar was never supposed to ascend to Mother Superior. But she was always greedy for power and status, and she promised the Man in Black his blood on the Rite of the Spring Equinox on his 33rd year around the sun... a perversion of the sacrifice of Christ on the cross."

"How do you know all this, Mama? You was locked away for years."

Mama sighed.

"There was a time when Miss Tamar really was fond me, Levi. She trusted me. Truth was, she was the one who set me and your daddy up. She said she saw herself in me, and in hindsight, that ain't no compliment... But at the time I was so flattered. Miss Tamar was a powerhouse of a woman, a true act of God. In all the worst ways, it would turn out."

"How you mean?" I said.

"One night, I stayed behind at the church, and I heard her cryin' like someone died. She begged at the waist of God to break the bargain she'd made. She caught me and confided in me to never tell a soul..."

"And why didn't you?"

Mama turned away, ashamed.

"If you think your Grannie was scary at this age, you should've seen her at her prime. Back when I was growin' up..." Mama finally faced me, emboldened and scared all at once. "She would've killed me, Levi. Then on the night of my Annunciation, Grannie found out and I was forced to marry your daddy. She wanted to ensure and so-lidify her place as the greatest Madonna, to have a God livin' in her home. She was great. Terrifyin', even, but a wonder to behold. Even if I denied her, she would've made me wish I was dead."

"I believe you... I've seen that side..." I said, painfully.

I dug my nails into my knee, trying to shake off the rage that started to build up inside me.

"Her trusting me so much when I was younger meant I knew too much, and when you're hidin' a secret that big, the ones who know the most need to go. I knew too much, Levi."

"No..." I said, my throat tightening. "This... This can't be real..."

"I tried to stop her, but she struck me with Madness before I could do anythin' about it,"

"Why would she do that?" I said, exasperated.

Mama shrugged, pensively.

"When she did what she did, she tried to invoke the Queen of the Abyss, the old Goddess of the witches, to reverse what she'd done. And she was ignored. She made her bed, and she had to lie in it.

The Goddess don't take too kindly to the selfish... there's an old story about it. And Tamar knew it well. But she acted in self interested anyway... And, well, she faced the consequences. After that, she resented her Gift and thought it to be a curse." Mama groaned. "Ever since then, it was like she'd tainted her bloodline."

Tituba's words.

Tituba said at the cemetery that her bloodline was tainted, and now I finally knew how to make it right, by creating the Holy Grail. Grannie made her bloodline unworthy of being Queen, and now Amma rightfully wore the crown.

"But Pops was killed by a witch," I said.

"His blood was spilled," Mama said. "The deal was made, he ain't need to lie down on no altar. Your Grannie wove a spirit of obsession into him, which lead him to trackin' down a witch, but little did he know that it would be your Grannie wearin' a glamour to disguise herself as another..."

I clasped at my head, horrifying flashbacks came rushing back to me. Painful images of Pops's death coursed and surged relentlessly through my mind.

"It was Grannie. The witch that got Pop killed that night... I knew it. I knew somethin' was wrong, he was so *fixated* on her. He— He never hunted alone, but that night he did, and... and..." I covered my face, fighting the tears that stung my eyes. "But he... He was her *son*."

"Killin' children ain't nothin' new for the God of the Garden. Neither for your Grannie. They just two sides of the same damn coin if you ask me. That's why I wanted to take you away. The night that of my Annunciation I knew I had to get you away as far as I could."

"To protect me from what?"

"From a lifetime of service to absolute evil... the Coven served Him on the surface, but there were many of us who never believed in those ways. Unfortunately for me, I had been chosen. There was nothin' I could do, but I'd be damned if He used my baby boy to further His evils on this world..."

"What do you mean?"

Mama shook her head shamefully.

"The Blood of witches feeds him. The God of the Garden feasts on sufferin', that's why Hell is paramount to His existence. Without the conscious torment of His enemies, He ceases to be. He's a God of vengeance, not of love. Without objects of his vengeance, He will be reduced to nothin'…" Mama sighed. "The night He came to me, it was under the disguise of your daddy. I thought it was him, he felt and kissed me just like he did. But when I saw your daddy again, he never remembered a thing. And I knew somethin' was different about you the moment I had you."

"Well, I know the truth now. I was taken to the River Gnosmos and bathed in it."

Mama gasped with joy, covering her mouth.

"Oh, *praise* the Lady," Mama said. "Tell me, did you at least get Ezra to take the Mark of the Beast?"

"Shaddai already laid the Curse of Job on him, but I'd healed him already. Was no use, either. Ezra just woke up and swore to kill me for turnin' on him,"

"Please," Mama said. "Don't kill him, Levi. You can't."

"Mama… I've been battlin' with myself tryin' to figure out what to do, but if Ezra tries to kill me…"

"Don't. Your brother's the only family in this world you got."

I had pains in my stomach, the nausea was painful. I was so angry I could hardly breathe. Just when I thought Grannie reached the height of her malicious nature, her venom only proved to be more deadly. Grannie stole something for me I could never get back: time. She robbed me of a mother, of precious hours that could have been spent learning from her and experiencing hardship and feeling less alone.

I felt like I was made into the monster she wanted me to be. I was taught to kill instead of love, to survive instead of enjoy, to crave blood over affection. Without Mama in the way, I was clay left to be molded into the image of *her* God, using Pops's hands to get dirty instead of hers. All these years, I'd been living and dining with the devil.

Grannie was an absolute evil of the worst kind, who did so because she could. Now I understood Nita. And even more painful?

I finally understood myself.

Footsteps pounded against the floor. Amma turned the corner, her chest rising and falling as she panted.

"Levi! You have to hurry," Amma said.

I ran after her out towards the front porch. Mama trailed quickly behind me.

"Levi, what's goin' on?" Mama cried out, shaking.

In the distance, two headlights of an old truck sped down the field, revving in full speed towards the house. It was Ezra's car. Plumes of smoke spat out of the engine as I slammed on the gas, barreling faster towards us.

"He's goin' to hit the barrier," Amma said.

CRASH!

The whole hood of the car crinkled, smashing clean into the barrier Amma laid in front of the house. The barrier rippled and shook in a translucent blue energy, sending waves across the once invisible dome that encased the house. The barrier vanished again, leaving the car alarm blaring and smoke pouring from the front of the car.

"EZRA!" I screamed, running towards him.

"Levi, no!" Amma said, snatching me by the arm.

The driver door opened, and the large mass of Ezra's body plopped out of the car and onto the ground. He coughed and heaved, struggling to his feet and facing us on the porch. He pulled an axe from his car. It Pops's signature, a copper blade with fragments of the Calvary Cross. He dragged it from its head towards us, pointing.

"YOU KILLED HER!" Ezra screamed hoarsely. He coughed again. "THE MAGICIANS SHOWED ME WHAT YOU DID! YOU KILLED GRANNIE!"

We were facing each other now, only an invisible wall separated us. It was the closest I'd stood in front of Ezra, and I knew if it wasn't for the barrier between us, he would've taken the axe to me without thinking.

"I had to," I said, coldly.

"YOU—"

"Ezra," Mama said, stepping down from the porch.

Ezra staggered back in disbelief.

"M—Mama?"

Mama approached the barrier, moving me aside and stepping in front of Ezra. She held out her hand compassionately. Ezra raised a trembling hand towards her, laying his hand over hers. The barrier illuminated again, glowing a translucent hue again before vanishing again.

"How?" Ezra asked with a shaking breath.

"Your brother lifted the curse," Mama said.

"Y—You're on his side?"

"Baby, please join us. You're fightin' the wrong fight. You're fightin' the people who love you most."

Ezra sniffled. "I loved Grannie most. And he killed her."

"Ezra, please… I love you,"

"You was never here," Ezra said, pulling his hand back. "Grannie said you would've given us to the Darkness,"

"The only darkness was in that woman's heart," Mama said.

"DON'T YOU TALK ABOUT MY GRANNIE! SHE WAS THERE! YOU WASN'T!"

"Baby, your Grannie was the one who did this to me!"

"LIAR!" Ezra screamed. "God punished you for choosin' evil. You strayed from the light, Mama… You could've chosen us, but you chose yourself. Like Levi. And now look what he's done to this family,"

Tears streamed down Mama's face.

"Ezra, now," Mama pleaded. "Please. You've got it all wrong."

Ezra backed away, raising a pointed, shaking finger at me.

"You on his side, now. Which means you ain't for me. You ain't for the light."

"Ezra…"

"Y'all won't win this…"

Mama sobbed. She wrapped her arms around me, crying into my shoulder.

"YOU WON'T WIN! YOU HEAR ME, LEE?" Ezra bellowed.

"She's clouded your mind, Ezra, we love you," I said.

Ezra shook his head, his lower lip quivering.

"I'm all alone now 'cause of you. You won't get away with this," Ezra said. "I swear it."

He climbed back into his car, speeding away.

Ezra buried me that night. And worst yet… I didn't know if I could keep the promise I made to Mama.

I might have to return the favor and bury him too.

CHAPTER 33:

Gnosis

I had a pit in my stomach, watching Ezra drive off into the distance. I knew in my heart that the time would come when I'd be put against my own brother, and there was nothing I could do to change it. I used to get into fist fights in the early days for everyone who picked on Ezra because of his weight. He was always a stocky guy, but I didn't care. I would take any number of bloody noses and bruises before I let anyone bad mouth my brother. The past didn't matter anymore, especially not to Ezra. He was so blinded by his fealty to the God of the Garden and to the Providence that he was willing to repay kindness and love with hatred and blood. I looked back at Mama, who was on her knees now, clasping the dirt between her hands and weeping as if she were at the feet of death.

Amma leaned over, gently stroking her back and whispering to her. Mama kept shaking her head, pushing Amma away from her. I couldn't imagine the pain Mama was going through, to have 30 years stolen from her life, only to return to see the two things she cared about most in this world on the verge of slipping from her fingers again. As fucked up as it all was, she was probably happier in her state of constant madness, blissfully unaware of the reality that was quickly unfolding around her. I almost regretted bringing her back to sanity. As I watched her tug at the coils of her hair, I wondered what she thought about all those years, or if she had any thoughts at all.

"Mama," I said, kneeling to her. I tried picking her up from the ground, but she fought me. I held her hands down in place.

"No! No!" she kept screaming.

"Mama, let's get you inside, please," I said.

I hoisted her off the ground. Her feet just dragged behind her, all the way up the porch and back inside. The house was in disarray, the place that memories and generations had stayed in. It was only fitting. It reminded me of all the lies that were undone, and the only thing keeping this house together was a foundation built on deception and moral corruption. Now the house was exposed for what it truly was; wreckage stripped of the disguise of togetherness.

For generations, this house was founded on the idea of hope and safety. Grannie did all she could to maintain its luster, but that only reflected how hard she worked to keep up appearances. Grannie was a wolf in sheep's clothing, putting on the costume of caring and love when there was nothing but an insatiable hunger for selfishness, and an eternal pining to destroy anything that went against her. She was truly like her God, loving those who obeyed and listened to her without question, that's why I was always at odds with her. In her final moments, she rotted from the inside out, finally becoming as hideous as she was deep down inside, and now the house reflected just that.

From the shadows of the house, limbs emerged, giving way to faces that followed soon after. The Coven one by one emerged from the depths of darkness, Titus and Jonah stepped out from it as the last amongst them.

"Holy hell," Titus said, looking around at the carnage left in the wake of the battle with Nita.

"Is that... June?" Jonah said, approaching Mama, who hid her face, silently sobbing still.

"She ain't doin' well," I said, putting my arm around her and trying to hide her from everyone who now surrounded us.

"What happened?" Titus asked.

Amma and I glanced back at each other.

"Nita ambushed us."

"Where is she?" Jonah said.

"I…"

"I killed her," Amma said. "I'm sorry. It had to be done…"

Titus sniveled, and his eyes welled with tears before he stormed off into another room. Jonah followed behind him. I felt awful. As venomous as Nita was, she was still their mother. I hung my head, ashamed. Amma rubbed my shoulder.

"They just need some time," Amma said. "I'm… sure they'll come around. As evil of a bitch Nita was… that was still their mama."

"There was judges already searchin' the woods," Bonnie interjected.

Amma smirked. "Bold to be makin' it out that far," Amma said.

"The illusions worked; they ran off screamin' and hollerin' before they got too close."

"Never mind them for now, everyone can stay here. Amma's already laid up a barrier so there ain't nothin' gettin' in this house," I said.

Jonah reemerged, sullen and glassy eyed. He sniffled.

"We… can't hide forever, any luck on findin' Father Enoch?" Jonah asked.

"Who said anythin' about hidin'?" I said. "And I'm willin' to bet that son of a bitch is hidin' out at the Providence."

"And how long we gonna let him do that for? The world is damn near ripped apart outside, I can hardly tell the difference between earth and hell out there no more," Bonnie said.

"Not long… Tomorrow, first thing, we'll go," I said

"There some kind of game plan I should know about?" Bonnie asked.

"They'll ambush you out there," Amma said.

"Then we'll let them think I came alone," I said.

"How?" Bonnie said.

"I can cloak us, catch 'em by surprise, but they have to think you came alone," Amma said.

"That's good thinkin'… I'll make 'em think I'm turnin' myself in. Maybe that'll be enough to lure out Father Enoch. You know he loves to see himself proven right," I said

They all exchanged uncertain glances.

"Tomorrow? It's the Spring Equinox," Bonnie said.

"Which is why y'all will make preparations while we get this handled," Amma said. "Tomorrow night I need you to take the Coven back to the woods. Noah and Selene will be there to help."

"But the judges might come lookin' again," Bonnie said fearfully.

"The enchantments are still in place," Amma said.

"But Amma…"

"Do as I said," Amma said firmly. "As your Queen, I command you."

Bonnie stepped back. "Yes, my lady," she said.

"What about your Mama?" Rita asked.

In my madness to come up with some kind of plan, I'd forgotten where Mama would go.

"I want you and Bonnie to watch after her,"

"There's Miss Etta. She and a few other Elders stayed behind and went into hidin'." Rita said.

"Then it's settled," I said. "Everyone rest up, tomorrow's gonna be the darkest day of the year."

"Good Friday," Amma said.

"Let's hope I don't gotta repeat that same end tomorrow 'cause there won't be a resurrection."

"I'll check on Titus and fill him in on the plan."

I nodded, turning to nudge Mama, and leading her upstairs.

Tomorrow, for the morbid of faith, was one of the most beautiful times of the year. It was a remembrance of the day that I was brutally mutilated and tortured for the sake of their sins, or so they thought. The truth was that I was killed for rebelling against the God of the Garden and his plans, and so it would be again two thousand years later. What's done in the dark is always brought to the light, and as the son of the morning, I was destined to shed light. The last enemy to be defeated was death, and that was Shaddai. This time, the dwelling of God was with men, and I would shepherd my people into a new promised land.

I brought Mama into my room and sat her down on the bed. Her face was glistening with dried tears as she looked up at me.

"I've lost everythin'," she said.

"That ain't true, Mama. You got me," I said, kneeling in front of her. She sniffled, stroking the side of my face.

"But for how long? I… I couldn't handle it if I lost both my boys…"

I held her hand on my cheek, kissing it tenderly.

"Until the end of time, Mama. And after that, after everythin' I'm doin' now, I promise you'll be with me again in paradise." She scrunched her face, sobbing again.

"I promise I'll do everythin' I can to win Ezra back to us," I said. I lied.

Maybe hope was really just deceit disguised as a promise of something better to come. There was no winning Ezra back, even I knew that. There was a fine line between Faith and delusion, an act of God that caused them to believe a lie.

"I swear, Mama… I never meant to get caught up in none of this…"

"It had to be this way," Mama said bitterly. "You was destined to carry out the Great Work. This is bigger than you and me all together… You're just bearin' the weight of it all yourself."

"That ain't nothin' new," I said. I stood up, pacing the room and facing the window outside. "If this would've been an issue of the Summerland witches, I wouldn't help them. After all, they'd done to us, they deserve to get wiped off the face of this earth," I said, rubbing my forehead, frustrated. "But now it's on our doorstep, and I have to act."

"You're wrong," Mama said.

"What?"

"This came to our door because Spring is here," Mama said.

"What are you tryin' to say?"

"Our Sisters woke up and realized the error of their ways… Greed is an evil mistress, and only death ever follows."

Mama patted the bed, gesturing for me to join. I went and sat down beside her.

"The struggle between us… Is a tragedy as old as time, but not one without redemption… If they do the work. Not even the Witch Queen may realize, but her comin' to you now is just like the story my mama used to tell me."

"What story?" I said.

CHAPTER 34:

Soil & Snow

" *L*ong ago, *The earth was abloom with flowers of every shade, and hummingbirds drank freely from the nectar that dripped from the pedals. In those days, the darkness remained beyond Heaven, and the cold hand of death was not even a dream in the heart of the earth. Sunlight danced upon the face of the greenery, and there was warmth on all the days of the year. The lion walked with the lamb, and the Children of Men tended to the garden of earthly delights. The Goddess created the earth in her likeness; fertile and full of life, giving birth to worlds of beauty, and life eternal.*

"The daughter of the earth was called Ayé. No beauty rivaled hers, with skin like the rich soil and flowers that sprang at her feet. Her voice was like the song of birds, and in her heart was wisdom and compassion, she nurtured the world and all things that lived in her bosom. One day, the Cold looked down at the warmth and longed to feel the sunlight and walk upon the riches of the earth. The Cold grew lonely and knew of her sister that dwelled in the world beneath her. This sister was called Egbo, and she becameenvious of a world unknown to her.

"'The riches of Ayé are vast,' said Egbo. 'She is clothed with life and fragrance, and my lands are frigid and unyielding.' So she plead with the Goddess to descend to the world that blossomed, so she, too, could taste the sweetness of life and know the kisses of sunlight.

"'Yes,' decreed the Goddess. 'But on the Earth, you cannot remain forever, for darkness and light cannot share one dwelling.' Egbo, agreed and quickly

made her departure from the darkness and descended upon the earth. Shadows crept upon the sky that day, and a great terror overcame all that was living in the earth's abode. Ayé went to the source of the darkness and watched as a visitor from the sky above made its way into her home. With Egbo came frozen rain called 'snow', and it was icy to the touch of Ayé.

"'Who is this that darkness my council with coldness?' said Ayé.

"'It is I, your sister, Egbo, and I wished myself to feel the fertileness of your green pastures.' Ayé had never seen a creature such as she, for she was beautiful indeed, but her skin was as white as the foam of the sea, and in her presence, the flowers beneath her feet withered and died. But Ayé welcomed her sister with open arms and sought to show her the joys of life, to share with her the riches this world provided. Together Egbo and Ayé strolled the pastures, and Egbo tasted of every fruit on each tree and drank for herself the sweet waters that flowed in her stream.

"'This world's treasures are numerous, and I've never seen such beauty. The land I come from is as cold as I, and there nothing dwells but remains forever in sleep,' said Egbo. 'May I bring my children to share in these wonders and show them the beauty that I have come to know?' Ayé was uncertain, but she trusted in her sister, and she knew no hatred in her heart.

"'Very well, my lands are boundless, and I have more than enough to share with the children of my sister,' said Ayé.

"'Tomorrow I will return with my children, and together we will delight in all the wonders of this place,' said Egbo, and she returned to the darkness that hung above the firmament of the blue skies. Ayé had agreed, but as her sister returned to heaven, there was a feeling that overcame her that was as alien as her sister, and this was called doubt. The next day Egbo returned, and with her rained down frozen rain that slowly covered the green earth, consuming it with blankets of ice that caused the greenery to wither.

"'Isn't this beautiful,' Egbo said to her children. 'Go and take whatever you'd like for yourselves, for the splendors of this world are vast.'

"'Sister,' said Ayé. 'Your children are many, and I cannot satiate their hunger for this world'

"'Nonsense!' Said Egbo. 'Let us stay a little while longer, and when we're finished, we will leave you in peace. Don't let greed be the divide between us.

Are we both not sisters? Are we not children of the Goddess Most High? Then what is yours must surely be mine also.'

"But greed was at the heart of Egbo, and she brought down more children from the sky onto the earth, and they ravished her world of all it had to offer. Of every tree, every fruit, and animal that lived on the Earth, they took for themselves, their hunger for this world becoming more consuming. As time passed by, the world now was coated with snow, and the branches no longer yielded leaves, nor was there any longer any fruit. She'd been robbed naked.

"Ayé herself had become depleted, and as the world she nurtured was stripped of every splendor, her once rich, fertile skin had become grey, and there could no longer sprout any flowers at her feet from the snow that now covered the ground.

"'You've overstayed your welcome, sister,' said Ayé. 'I no longer have anything to offer you in this world; your children have covered my face by the multitude, and all that remains are skeletal trees and the bones of animals once fat with flesh'.

"'We love this place more than our home,' said Egbo. 'Here we will remain, and there is much room for all my children.'

"'And my children are numbered,' pleaded Ayé. 'If you stay any longer, we will be no more.'

"But Egbo didn't care, and she continued to bring down her children from the darkest place in Heaven and poured over the earth. Death entered into the world now, and the land that was once vibrant with life was now a rigid corpse, frozen solid with the snow that now covered every inch of the world. The children of Ayé cried out for their mother, but she could not hear them. Ayé was quickly buried by the snow, and the earth was dormant beneath the cold.

"With the last of Ayé's strength, she sent a powerful sleep to all that walked the frigid landscape, and into a deep hibernation went all things, sleeping away the starvation that would have come onto them. Egbo welcomed Death into this world and made her the sister in place of Ayé. But Death, called Ikú, was a crueler mistress than she, and she wanted to devour more of the life on earth.

"'We have consumed this world, but I'm still hungry sister,' said Ikú to Egbo. 'Where is Ayé, so that I can feast on her myself and satisfy my hunger?'

"*'Ayé sleeps in the belly of this world' said Egbo. 'She was once fertile, bringing to life all things in this world. Surely, she must have more to offer that she is keeping for herself!' And so Ikú and Egbo searched the land for their slumbering sister and found her nestled in a bed of frozen flowers. Ayé was wrapped in fine, white silk, with crystals of ice enveloping her lashes and coating her dried lips. Even at the brink of death, Ayé's beauty was overwhelming. Ikú saw the rising and falling of her chest, and the cold winter breeze skirted across the land, rippling the silk fabric that wrapped her body.*

"*'She is still alive,' said Ikú. 'Let me place my cold hand over her heart and feast on the life force that remains'*

"*Egbo looked around the earth now with cold winds, coated with her snow children, remembered how beautiful the green pastures were, and saw that they were no more. Egbo recalled the kindness Ayé had shown her, and her frigid heart now felt the spark of compassion, tinged with regret.*

"*'Stop,' said Egbo. 'Ayé had given me everything. And I have taken advantage of her kindness. I cannot allow you to feast on her life.'*

"*'Get behind me!' Said Ikú. 'Or I, too, will feast on you.'*

"*'Mother!' Cried Ayé. 'My sisters have betrayed me and robbed me naked of all I own, and now seek to kill me. Rise up and defend me before I am no more!'*

"*The darkness that loomed in the sky yielded now to the golden rays of the sun, and the face of the Goddess was now in the sky, beaming down upon the cold lands and bringing with her a forgotten warmth.*

"*'Wretched sister!' the Goddess spoke with a voice like thunder. 'Did I not tell you that in this world you cannot remain? You have exchanged kindness for thievery and allowed your children to take what was not theirs, and now the earth that was once my footstool no longer teems with life. Your own greed had caused you to take more than what was offered, and now your sister is on the brink of death! Now I will extend my hand, and you will no longer be. It is I now who will rob you of the life you were given.'*

"*'Mother!' Egbo wept. 'I have taken of my sister and her children, the bloom, I have killed. Take pity on me Mother, as I have felt the pain of compassion. Melt away my children, so that they can replenish this land until the end of time. Use the blood of their waters to fertilize the Earth so that it* can grow mighty. May I melt away every year to strengthen my sister. If it is pleasing to her, may I return for a time to walk with her again, and when I depart, I will give my children to her again to grow strong.'

"'In my forgiveness, there is no forgetting,' said Ayé. 'But I will accept your sacrifice, and may your children water this land so that I can rebuild it stronger than what it was.'

"'Very well,' said the Goddess. 'Bid farewell to your sister, until she will have you again.'

"The sun beamed down on the land, and the children of Egbo cried out in pain as they melted away, sinking into the ground beneath them. Egbo, too, began to deteriorate, and her tears fell in snowflakes that melted away.

"'For three months I will allow you to seek out the treasures of this world. For deep within the coldness of your heart, there lives compassion, and to-gether we will rebuild the world. But you will repay me with your children,' said Ayé. 'For your greed, you will continue to pay for eternity, and when you come to this world, I flee from you, as the bitterness of the cold will remind me always of what you'd done, but may your waters remind me of what you have the potential to be.'

And it was so. Ikú fled from the earth, as there was nowhere for her now. Egbo melted into the ground, watering the body of Ayé herself. From this water, the earth bloomed and teemed with life, and the buzzing of bees and sweetness of the fragrant flowers once again reigned over the world, and Ayé blossomed once more. From where once death and cold abided, together they worked now to restore the warmth and light. For the first time since Egbo came to earth, Ayé sang again.

And this was the first Spring."

CHAPTER 35

The Forsaken

I scratched my head, stirring in thought, trying to find the meaning behind Mama's story.

"Don't you see?" Mama said. "The Queen of Georgia is Egbo. We are Ayé. There ain't no forgettin' what was done to us, but together we can rebuild a world better than the one we've left behind."

"So you want me to just forgive and forget?" I scoffed. "I mean no disrespect, Mama, but you sure I lifted all the crazy off you?"

Mama laughed. "No, never that. You wasn't understandin' the story. They've admitted to their wrong, and though it won't erase the past, it gives us a chance to build a better future. All things happen at the right time. The Nazarenes across the centuries would've swept this all under the rug, as did all the Madonnas that came after Adora. But the Queen of Georgia is lookin' them all dead in the eye and admittin' it was wrong. Words is just words, but she's puttin' action behind them."

"I… I don't know about all that, Mama…" I sighed. "I don't think I can just put all that behind me."

"You're already doin' the work,"

"For us, for our people, so we can thrive." I said.

"That is Ayé. Never forget. But don't pass up the chance to *bloom*."

I heaved, standing up.

"Have a goodnight, Mama," I said, stopping at the door.

"Levi?" Mama said. "Promise me that no matter what happens, you'll spare Ezra? Please. I'm beggin' you."

I bit my bottom lip, frustrated.

"I'll do everythin' I can," I said

Mama nodded reluctantly, as fresh tears rolled down her cheek again. This time I was telling the truth, and I truly meant it. Killing my brother was the last thing that I wanted to do. I didn't know what I would do if my life was about to end at his hands, and that terrified me to the point that I couldn't even say those words out loud. In my heart, I wanted to believe my brother would spare me. I wanted to believe that Ezra wouldn't have it in him to end my life. But the way God hardened the heart of Pharaoh, I feared that Ezra's heart of flesh was replaced with stone against me.

I wanted to forge a new world, one better than the one we now stood on like Mama said, but how could I put behind me the centuries of cruelty and oppression that the Queen of Georgia represented? She may have extended an olive branch, but what good is a branch from a tree that sprouted on the backs of our people? Blooming with flowers that only her descendants were able to enjoy, and bask in the shade of comfort that it provided while we suffered? We toiled the ground that the tree grew from, and they were wanting to start over again.

I wanted to believe in a world beyond the evil they brought into it, but I was afraid that we were just a tool that they needed to bring peace back into their own lives. What if this was a terror that would only destroy this town while sparing their own? Would Selene have interjected and offered her help anyway? It was hard to say, but maybe I should give it a chance?

Chance, after all, was something that our ancestors weren't afforded. Maybe this was the Spring that was promised to us.

"How is she?" Amma said, approaching me.

I closed the door behind me, sighing heavily.

"She's fine," I said, "she told me some story about the Soil and Snow,"

Amma smiled warmly.

"My mama used to tell me that story before bed,"

"Do you think there's really a chance?" I said.

"I don't know. But I do know that this is an opportunity to better us all. To create a world where we don't gotta hide no more or live in fear." Amma groaned, pensive.

I leaned in and kissed Amma on the forehead. "Maybe that's enough for me," I said

"Titus and Jonah are in on the plan… they just need some time to grieve their loss." I sighed, understanding.

"Levi," Amma said I stopped, halfway down the hall to the guest bedroom. "No matter what happens tomorrow… I'm here for you."

I smiled weakly.

"I know," I said.

I turned around, glowing with the promise of Amma's devotion, and closed the bedroom door behind me.

The morning sun rose over the horizon, and Amma and the others gathered downstairs. As I descended the steps, their muttering and barrage of voices quieted, and all their eyes fell on me. Titus and Jonah, I could tell were fearful, but there was an air of valiance that surrounded them. I never would've chosen them as my Sons of Thunder if I couldn't rely on them for the toughest battles, and now this would be the final test of their strength. If they could survive this battle, only eternal glory awaited them.

Titus stepped forward, his eyes still glossy.

"I'm sorry," I said.

Jonah embraced me tightly.

"We know. We know," he said.

"We understand…" Titus said.

I sank into his embrace, patting him on the back.

"She would've killed me," I said. I clasped onto him tighter. "Please… Forgive me. I'm sorry."

"We understand…" Titus said.

I pulled away from Jonah, still too ashamed to look them in the eye.

"Ready?" I asked, cutting the tension.

"We'll follow you even to death," Titus said.

"Remember that," Jonah added.

"The Coven is preparin' for the Equinox tonight," Amma said, rubbing my shoulder and giving me an affirmative nod.

"We'll be there to see it done. All of us. You hear?" I said, reassuring.

Titus straightened up, and Jonah pounded his hand against his palm. We headed out the front door and down the steps of the porch. I stopped.

"What is it?" Jonah said.

"Look," I said, pointing at the ground.

Long shadows formed at our feet. I looked up towards the sky, and a cold chill fell over us. The moon quickly moved in front of the sun, blotting out the sun in a total eclipse. The world around us plunged into twilight, casting orange hues and reddening the sky.

"Another Primordial," Amma said.

"Darkness," I said.

I looked behind me and saw Mama leaning against the column of the porch. Bonnie and Rita approached from behind her. Rita put her arm around Mama.

"Mama," I said. "I *promise* you, when this is all over, I'll come back for you. Then we'll have an eternity to make up for all that lost time. I promise."

Her eyes were filled with dread, and all I could do was give her an assuring smile. Another Primordial quickly moved upon us, and I knew time was running out before Shaddai destroyed this world. I turned to Amma and gave a quick nod. She lifted her hands.

"*Occultare*," she said.

Invisibility draped over them like a fabric, and they instantly vanished. I signed the Hidden Hands, and opened a window portal, seeing the foundation of the Providence shimmering on the other side. I took a deep breath, clenching my fists, and stepped inside.

The portal shut behind me as I emerged from the other side. I could feel their bodies crowding around me still, as we stood now at the base of the Providence. The building looked like a large white temple, with an all-seeing eye adorning the peak of the building's pyramid capstone. Great columns stood on either side as we ascended the steps. The building was designed to look like Solomon's Temple, a prodigious and beautifully crafted testament to the might and wealth of the Providence. I pushed past the double scarlet doors, entering the temple.

The floors were checkerboard, and the ceiling was painted cerulean blue with golden stars as far as the eye could see. A red carpet led from the front door down the great hall, where paintings of past Magistrates hung on full display. At the end of the carpet were flanked two great pillars with a golden sun at the top of the right and a moon on the left. At the very end of the hall was a marble carving of the crucifixion, and another all-seeing eye depicted with golden rays shining down on the scene. On the left of the hanging Christ was a roman soldier, stabbing into his side with the Spear of Destiny, and another soldier standing guard holding a shield.

I looked up at the vacant balconies on either side, searching for any sign of anyone.

"Father Enoch!" I yelled. "I know you're here!"

I walked down the hall until I stood in front of the crucifixion scene, eyeing the diamond tears that ran down Christ's face.

"Levi," A voice called out to me from behind.

There stood Craven, trembling with anger I could tell he tried to keep contained.

"Craven," I said. "I know Enoch is here. Where is he?"

"He is," Craven admitted. "Levi… Why are you here?"

"Enoch's the one that released the Primordials,"

"I know. I'm the one who helped him,"

I cocked my head back.

"What?" I spat. "How could you do somethin' like that?"

Craven dug his hands into his pockets, slowly stepping closer to me.

"Enoch had a vision of the Lord. He told him that there was darkness in your heart, and you would turn on him. So He asked Enoch to part the Veil and release these spirits to test you. And you…you failed, Levi. Instead of leanin' on the Lord for strength, you turned to the Devil,"

I knew Craven didn't care about my failures as Christ. He only wanted to prove to himself that he had the power to help conjure up a spirit of that caliber and to watch me fail. That was the real reward for him. And standing now facing him, I was afraid. My throat tightened anxiously.

"I know," I said. "That's why I'm here to turn myself in… I want this all to end."

Craven tilted his head, unbelieving.

"Are you?" he said. "That's too bad because it's too late for that, Levi. You're beyond forgiveness. Now, this world will suffer the consequences of your disobedience."

"Then if that's the case," I lifted my hands, standing in a fighting stance, "I'm goin' down swingin'."

Craven laughed smugly.

"Is that so?"

From behind Craven emerged now dozens of magicians from the Order, and armed judges, and in the previously vacant balconies were slews of judges aiming their guns.

"It was a mistake comin' here alone, Levi," Craven said.

"It was a mistake to think I did."

Amma pulled back the invisibility, revealing them now standing behind me. Craven stepped back, shocked as he locked eyes with Titus and Jonah.

Craven recoiled in disgust.

"You. All of you… You've taken the Mark. I can feel the corruption flowing through your veins from here."

I smirked.

"It should be all too familiar, then."

"I ain't nothin' like you!" Craven snarled.

"You got that right," Titus said.

"You Judas bitch," Jonah snarked.

Craven's head trembled with rage.

"KILL THEM!" Craven screamed.

Bullets sprayed from the balconies towards us. Amma raised her arms and enclosed us in a translucent dome, rippling as bullets bounced off the surface. With another wave of her arms, the barrier exploded, sending the mists of bullets towards the judges in the balconies. Craven screamed in a war cry as he quickly signed the Hidden Hands, and a blast of golden fiery energy barreled down towards us. I stepped forward, quickly forming Hands on the ground, and a thick, earthy wall rose between us, rumbling and shaking. The heat of his blast split between the wall, scorching the ground on both ends.

Titus and Jonah charged behind us. Bursts of energy slung across the air at the magicians and judges, back and forth. Judges charged at us from every direction. Amma motioned her hands, chopping at the air. Every judge caught in her direction was sliced in half, spilling blood and intestines. Blood splattered across my face from Amma's relentless attacks at the judges that lunged at her. Titus and Jonah blocked and repelled the streaks of energy sent out by the magicians, blasting them backward and dowsing the walls with their blood upon impact. Craven and I exchanged swift bursts of energy. Shockwaves rocked the ground as the energy slammed into the walls around us, tearing off chunks and forming deep craters.

"SHADDAI NEVER SHOULD'VE CHOSEN YOU!" Craven screamed as he slung more waves of energy toward me.

I laughed mockingly. Craven clenched his jaw and doled out feats of magic that almost leveled Sorcery. The walls around me coalesced swiftly, the rubble at my feet swept me up in the current. Quickly, in a sweep of my arms, the torrent of ground exploded outward, blasting Craven back. He slid backward on his heels, holding his ground.

My quickened breath burned with each gasp, and heaving forward, I whisked the crystals from the chandelier hanging over us, firing like shimmering darts at Craven.

With quick Hands, the crystal shards liquidated and became a molten whip that he struck at me like a cobra. I clapped, and the waters collapsed to the ground, and I directed it, rapidly wrapping and searing Cravens's body. He screamed as his flesh, burned and bound by the current, coiled around him in a firm grip. I gnashed my teeth, struggling to maintain the hold.

"I RELEASE THE SNAKE THAT BINDS ME!" Craven screamed in ancient Aramaic.

He started to sign Hands; the ground cracked under his feet. A blinding flash of light and heat seared my arms as I covered my face. Craven laughed wickedly as flaming bodies of fire took form.

I reached towards the walls on either side of me and tore at the air. Water from the pipes burst towards us, rushing towards us. The waters whirred together, forming bodies woven of their churning currents around me. Craven and I quickly formed Hands, and the bodies of water and fire battled, engulfing us instantly in a thick cloud of steam.

I parted the mist, dispersing it like smoky waves that collided against the walls and spread, climbing upwards.

Craven aimed his hands at me, shouting, "BA'AL, I SUMMON THEE!"

I quickly muttered the same incantation, but too late before the burst of glowing green plasma shot from his fingers like lightning, booming with a roar that shook the walls. The unbearable heat hit me squarely in the face, pinning me to the wall as endless waves of its power burned deeper into me.

I flopped onto the ground, gagging and holding down the vomit from the pain.

"Go on! Transfigure! Go ahead and use that Christ power on me!" Craven shouted, wobbling like a drunk man barely strong enough to keep his balance.

"BA... BA'AL I SUMMON THEE!" I screamed.

Sapphire blue energy surged from my fingertips, colliding now with Craven's attack. A wave of translucent energy exploded outwards, vaporizing magicians and judges standing too close. Howling winds raged against us as our power struggled against the other. Bolts of lightning shot from the center, striking chunks of the wall out from around us.

I could feel his betrayal, pain, and rage pouring from him. It's what was driving him even though he hardly had anything left to feed it.

It was pure scorn that kept him going. He was truly Craven until the bitter end.

With one last, bellowing roar, I gave a final push. Craven screamed as my power overcame him, and he rolled across the ground like a rag doll, writhing as the final rounds of the energy that entangled him finished burning his already raw skin. His legs wobbled as he stood, his shoulders bouncing as he heaved.

I walked towards him.

"That… Christ power?" I said, panting. "Turns out I didn't need it."

Craven quickly formed hands, slinging bursts of translucent energy hurdling toward me. His eyes were bloodshot, and his face was sunken and pale. But he raged against me. The ground under our feet cracked with each step we took, and the air around our bodies rippled like a heat haze from the energy that burned from the fire within us. Our energies clashed in constant bursts of light.

I deflected his last blow, redirecting it at the wave of judges who approached and were incinerated instantly from the impact.

"And you'll always be second best," I snarked.

Craven screamed, firing more intensely at me. I deflected again, pushing out my fists and blasting him with hot lightning that exploded from my hands. Craven slammed through a pillar, sending a cloud of soot and dust and bringing down a balcony collapsing on its weight. The judges at the top fell over. Jonah rolled across the floor with deep burns on his arms, sizzling with smoke from the impact of a blast from another magician.

Titus screamed and charged towards him, dodging the bursts of energy until he pounced on the magician and snapped his neck.

Jonah staggered to his feet, sending more blasts of energy as quickly as he could. Craven tried to lift himself again as I approached him, holding my fists and panting.

"This what you wanted, isn't it?" I said.

I kicked another blast of energy, slamming into Craven again and pummeling him into the wall behind him. He fell flat on his face, smacking his head against the hard ground.

"The only thing that hurts most is once trusting you," I said.

A slew of golden arrows of light formed in front of me, locked and aimed at Craven.

"I guess there ain't nothin' between us then," he said with a re-membering smile.

Craven flinched, readying to be flayed with arrows. I screamed as the blunt end of something struck me across the head, and I rolled across the ground. Ezra now stood there, heaving and wielding a bat-tle hammer in his hands.

"You ain't got nowhere to run now," Ezra said as he approached me.

I clasped onto my head; his words were muffled by the loud ring-ing in my ears. My stance was wobbly, but I still held my hands up toward him.

"Ezra, you don't gotta do this."

"No," he said. "*You* didn't have to do this. I made a promise to fight for Shaddai. And unlike you, I intend to keep it,"

Ezra swung his hammer again. I dodged out of the way and sent a wave of energy that knocked him onto his back. The hammer slid across the ground.

"I promised Mama I wouldn't hurt you," I said.

Ezra leaped back onto his feet.

"And I promised I'd kill you," he said. Ezra pulled out the axe strapped to his back. I shuddered at the copper head that glinted at the edge.

"And I intend to keep that promise."

Ezra brought down the axe against me. A shield forged of golden light quickly formed around my arm, blocking the blow, but I was still sent me staggering backward from impact.

"I don't want to hurt you!" I yelled.

"That makes one of us," Ezra said.

I opened my hand and an energy sword formed, glowing with a blazing fiery substance.

"Ezra, please!"

Ezra swung again, and the end of his axe met the blade of my sword, sending rippling energy across the floor that cracked the ground beneath my feet. I looked over my shoulder, Titus and Jonah still screamed and grunted, fighting ferociously against the onslaught of judges around them.

Our sword and axe clinked and flashed as I deflected and clashed with his axe. Amma screamed as she slammed into the wall behind her, surrounded now by a group of magicians.

"Amma!"

Ezra brought down his axe again, I dodged him; the end of his weapon slammed into the ground.

With the fierce swiftness of her magic, Amma ripped limbs off the judges and magicians that surrounded her. Curdling screams echoed in the hall as she ground their bones and snapped their spines in half. Blood and intestines dyed the floors a murky red as she decimated their numbers. Everybody that fell became a puppet in her hands, used to deflect and disembowel her attackers. Their reanimated bodies were like toys in her hands, gutting and slashing until she discarded them.

"FINISH THE WITCH!" a freshly wounded magician screamed, flailing the one arm he had left.

I pushed out toward them, and a blast of an unseen force blew back the magicians that circled them, sending them bouncing off the ground and in every direction. A magician flew across the room, slamming into Ezra, and the wave knocked me onto the ground. I scraped my body against the jagged protrusions as I slid across the marble floor from the wave of impact and saw gusts of wind quickly gathering around Amma.

"WITCH?!" Amma yelled.

Her eyes glowed bright white, and her hair began to whip around in every direction. She slowly climbed into the air as violent gusts ripped across the temple. Amma slowly rose into the air, the howling wind became deafening as she slowly ascended in the air.

"I AM THE GODDESS OF THIS EARTH!" Amma roared.

The ground shook violently, knocking everyone onto their feet. Ezra tried to stand, but the wind quickly knocked him back down. The temple walls rumbled, and the roof above us blew off like a lid, where Amma climbed higher into the sky, surrounded by thick, black storm clouds, flashing with lightning and peeling with thunder. Her voice was louder than a roaring sea now as she spoke.

"I AM NUIT, NEPHTHYS, WADJET! I AM YEWA, OBA, AND IBU KOLE!" Amma roared. She extended her hands, and funnels of tornadoes rushed down to the earth beneath her, tearing and ripping apart all four walls of the temple. We were surrounded now by twin tornadoes circling us in a violent vortex, ripping through the ground around us, and sucking in the tiles of the temple floor we stood on. Titus and Jonah snatched Craven too wounded to move.

"I AM MAMAN BRIGITTE, FREDA, MANBO ZILA, AND EZILI MAPYAN! I AM AYÉ MADE FLESH!"

The magicians and judges around us screamed as they were whisked away by the force of the winds that surrounded them, flinging them in every which direction mercilessly. Ezra forcefully walked across the winds, slipping each time but making his way toward me.

"EZRA!" I shouted over the raging winds. "STOP! IT DOESN'T HAVE TO BE THIS WAY!"

Ezra inched close enough towards me and leaped on top of me. He quickly drew a copper blade from his boot and drove the tip of the knife through my chest before I grabbed his arm. I struggled against his hold, but I was physically outmatched by his brawny arms. My arms shook as I tried to stop him, screaming as I felt the blade drive deeper into my chest.

"DON'T DO THIS!" I yelled.

"THIS IS FOR GRANNIE!" he said.

He drove the blade deeper into me, seconds away from going straight through my heart. I looked across from me and saw the Roman soldier statue still in place with the shield in his hands. Ezra and I both screamed as I closed my eyes and flicked my other wrist, whisking the shield from the statue's hand and catapulting it across the air and straight across Ezra's neck, decapitating him.

I shrieked desperately. His head toppled onto his side, and his headless body spewed blood. His body squirmed for a moment before slowing down. The blade was just within his reach, but his hands fell over my face. I felt the tips of his fingers brush against my cheek, before falling to its side. His body collapsed on top of me, crushing me beneath his weight like a boulder. Blood gushed and spewed from his neck onto my face, running down my neck. I tasted the iron from the warm blood that caked my face now. His body jerked violently until the nerves died, and his corpse laid still.

Ezra was dead.

CHAPTER 36

Keening Of The Three Marys

Amma shot down from the sky, riding on a cloud that dispersed into a mist and dark shades of grey as she touched the ground. I cleaved to Ezra's corpse, trying to bring him back to life, but it was hopeless. I sobbed, and snot ran down my face, coughing and heaving as I clung to his body screaming. Speckles of blood coated my saliva, and my throat was raw. Amma tried to lift me from him, but I shoved her away, shaking and crying and clutching onto him as hard as I could. Titus and Jonah climbed out of the ditch in the ground with shimmering rings of light binding Craven's wrists in front of him. Amma laid her hand on my back despairingly.

"He's gone," I said, looking up at her.

Tears streamed down her face. I looked around me and saw only jagged bits of what remained of the entire temple. We stood on the small fragment of tile floor that remained, and all that was left was dirt and windblown dust, not one stone of the temple left on top of the other.

"I know, baby," Amma said. "Come on."

"No!" I said, clinging to his body again. "I ain't leavin' him," I wept. I wobbled to my feet, trying to lift him myself but collapsed to the ground with a heavy thud. I covered my face, clawing back down my cheeks, digging deep into my face with my nails, screaming and gnashing my teeth.

"Let me bury him," I cried. "Please."

Amma nodded, looking back at Titus and Jonah.

"What you wanna us to do with him?" Titus gestured to Craven.

"I have just the place for him," Amma said. She held out her hand, and two shovels appeared. "But for now, help him dig."

Titus threw Craven onto the ground, slamming into the pieces of tile left on the ground headfirst. As they dug a grave for Ezra, all I could think about was what I was going to tell Mama. What would she think of me then? She'd grieve and mourn as Eve did when Cain slew Abel, mourning the loss of a son she never even had the chance to know herself. The only memories of him she had were giving birth to him and watching him disown her, both times including tears and pain unimaginable. She would be in a twilight between joy and sorrow, relief and distress. That's all that would remain in her.

Between Titus, Jonah, and myself, we lowered Ezra's body into the grave we'd dug and covered him back with soil and dirt. Each shovel full of dirt that covered his body brought him closer to no longer being with me until finally, I saw nothing left of him but a pile of dirt. I thought about how he always screamed for no reason, about how different we were but always bonded over our same twisted sense of humor, all the inside jokes between us, and the grievances we shared. How we'd sneak off to smoke weed behind Grannie's back or sneak alcohol into church services in a thermos. Ezra was now only a memory and one that was too painful to remember right now.

I wanted to be angry at God for driving him to the point where he felt like he had no choice.

I had a choice.

And I chose myself.

I was angry at myself for not allowing him to just kill me; it would've been better than living with the irrevocable guilt that plagued me now, cursed to forever remember the moment I took my own brother's life. Doomed to be haunted by the knowledge of choosing myself over him. I was such a shitty Christ. I was supposed to stand for others when all I could stand for was myself and my own ambitions.

Did I let my rebellion against the God of the Garden go too far? There was no sense in beating a dead horse; I'd already gone far past the point of no return. I had to own it. Death was the work of my own hands.

"Amma," I sniffled, wiping the sweat off my brow. Titus took the shovel from my hands. "

"Would you mind?" I asked.

She shook her head.

"Please," I begged.

Amma reluctantly closed her eyes, and from the darkness ahead, Rita and Bonnie passed through the shadows.

"Amma!" Bonnie said, rushing to her side.

"We heard your call," Rita said.

Amma gestured in our direction. I wiped the tears from my face, and without a word, she knew. Bonnie and Rita wailed with a scream that split the sky. I hung my head, wallowing in guilt I couldn't shake. Tears filled Amma's eyes again, and they gathered around the small grave we'd made for Ezra.

They wept together until the well of their tears had dried up. There were no more tears left to cry. Finally, Bonnie cleared her throat and held hands in a ring around Ezra's grave. And she sang. I'd watched Bonnie and Rita lead countless funerary services, but the way Bonnie sang eviscerated me inside. I didn't know until then, the quiet love that she'd harbored for Ezra over all these years. Amma and Rita joined her song, harmonizing together in a sorrowful sweetness that both dazzled and disorientated me.

Streaks of light radiated from beneath the dirt, and Ezra's tall, broad form made of golden light stood now. He looked at me, striking me with a tormenting regret that I'd gladly trade death for. Without a word to me, he lifted his head toward the dark sky above him, and his shimmering body began to dissipate. I tried to fight the tears again. And failed.

"Ezra!" I cried, rushing towards him.

I reached out for his quickly depleting form and grabbed only air. I couldn't breathe. My legs gave out on me, and I collapsed to the floor. I clasped the dirt from his grave in my hands, releasing the screams I tried to keep inside. Titus and Jonah knelt down beside me, coaxing me.

He was gone.

For good this time.

Where do I go from here? I didn't know. I'd lie down and die there with him if I could. But I had to keep going. If I stopped now, Shaddai would win, and all of this would've been in vain. He couldn't win. I won't let him win.

"Let's go," I said, standing and wiping the snot from my nose.

Since Darkness had fallen over the land, the rest of us traveled by shadow through a hedge of trees not far from ruined remains of the Providence. We arrived through a darkened shadow on the wall at the house, where Mama laid with clasped hands on the couch, eagerly waiting for us. She bolted to her feet as we passed through the shadows and into the house, following behind Amma. She looked over us, keeping her eyes on the darkness, a hope in them quickly fading when she saw Ezra wasn't with us.

"And Ezra?" Mamma said, finally.

I couldn't bear to look her in the eyes. I clasped the bridge of my nose, sobbing again and shaking my head. Mama fell to the floor, clutching onto her heart and wailing. It was more painful to see the torment I'd brought on her than I imagined. I thought I was prepared, but the sounds she made were distraught, whimpering crying. Amma helped her back to her feet, shushing her gently and leading her back upstairs.

"You deserve everythin' you've got," Craven said.

His face was bloodied and bruised, with one eye swollen to the point it couldn't open. I stomped towards him and grabbed him by the throat, tightening my grip around his neck. He hacked, smiling through the pain.

"You may not see it now, but you're done for. God has won. After tonight, there won't be a world left for you to save. No witches. No people, no you. He's gonna wipe the slate clean and start again."

I dug my fingers deeper into his neck, watching his one good eye bulge.

"If Amma didn't need you, I swear to the God you still serve that I'd rip you apart with my bare fuckin' hands, you worthless piece of *shit*."

"Tonight, it all ends," Craven said, laughing.

"For you it does," I said. "Lock him in the basement until it's time."

Titus and Jonah dragged him away out of sight. I went back to what was left of the den, watching Grannie's rotting corpse now collect flies, her body soon to become food for worms and maggots that would find more substance to her than she ever had in life. I looked down at her for a moment, pulling out a cigarette and sparking it, taking in the brisk menthol and drawing in a heat in me that I needed from how frigid I felt inside. I could hear the muffled and faint whimpers of Mama's crying upstairs. I closed my eyes, trying to drown out the sound, but the more I tried to ignore it, the worse it got.

I tossed the finished butt onto Grannie's cadaver. If she was good for anything now, it would be an ashtray. Let that be her greatest contribution. I followed the groaning upstairs, passing old family photos that lined the walls, stopping at one of Ezra and myself in our younger years. I sighed, stroking the surface of the painting. A photo would be the closest I could ever get to him now, and I was reminded again of my own doing. Amma approached me quietly.

"She hates me, don't she?" I said.

"No," Amma whispered, coming to my side.

"I failed, Amma…"

Amma caressed my cheek dotingly.

"You did the best you could…"

"My best ain't good enough. My best couldn't save him."

"There was no savin' him, Levi… You need to make peace with that. If you let him kill you, what would've happened to the rest of us? To this world you'd have left behind?"

I hung my head in a shameful, pained silence. "Craven said everythin' ends tonight. He must be releasin' the final Primordial that's gonna finish us off."

"Don't count yourself out just yet If one night's all we got, then you be that light of the new day. They called you Son of the Mornin'. Be that."

I smiled, weakly. Amma stood on her tiptoes and gave me a light peck on the lips, the sweetness of her kiss still lingered in a tingling that left me craving more.

"Take your time," Amma said.

After Amma left me, I must've stared at Grannie's body for hours. Lost in her cold eyes. I remembered Titus and Jonah trying to talk with me, but I didn't I hear anything that they said. Their words were muffled, distorted and distant. I drifted further into the pool of my memories, replaying killing Ezra repeatedly in my head, reliving every last visceral detail nonstop. Nita's death, Grannie's, those didn't phase me none.

They were family, but not really. Not truly. People always said that *family was family.* But that was just a crock of shit. Blood relatives used that excuse to inflict pain and abuse onto you and expected you to just sit back and take it. They believed after all the years of cruelty that you'd still somehow love them back in the end. Maybe that's why mine served the God of the Garden so diligently. I remembered when Grannie had me go out to a tree and pick the branch she'd use to beat me until I bled, then sat me down and told me she did it out of love. And the fucked up part of it all? I believed her.

Even the day was darkness, and that only made it all the easier to lose track of time.

"Levi?" I heard Amma call.

Her voice broke me out of the trance I was in. I followed her call that came from downstairs and found the entire coven with Titus and Jonah dressed in white, silky robes. Amma's body was woven with a long, deep red gown beneath a cloak of dark blue, with silver studs forming a starry pattern. She wore bangles of silver, and an Adé, a dazzling crown that draped over her face a curtain of strung diamonds, obscuring her face. A hissing, thick python was wrapped around her neck, and in one arm, she carried a bundle of fabric.

She delicately extended her hand to me, covered in jewels and rings with stones more precious than gold.

"It's time."

I stripped down on the staircase, standing bare in front of everyone, and slipped the white robe on. I couldn't take my eyes of Grannie's body.

"Let her go, Levi. Let it all go." Amma said.

I took a deep breath, and with one long exhale, blazing fire fanned into flame, covering Grannie's body. As I took in the smell of her burning body, the fresh scent of searing flesh, I could feel a twisted smile forming on my face, and I felt like Shaddai again. To take delight and joy in fires consuming your enemies. Maybe a part of him never left me.

And maybe it never will.

"I'm ready," I said, watching the pummeling smoke rise to the ceiling.

The coven parted, and Amma took me by the arm, leading me toward a whirling, shadowy portal in the wall. We passed through the portal, the hardwood beneath my feet becoming branches and grass, as we entered into the mouth of Sheol. The Coven held torches high, illuminating the darkness with warm glows as we passed deeper into the forest. In the distance was a flickering glow, and the percussion of erratic drums pounded.

We followed the light and beating of the drum until we came to a clearing. In a ring that danced fervently were the witches of Summerland clad only by night, yipping and shouting ecstatically with wreathes of sunflowers in their hair. Selene stood in the distance in the nude, wearing a silver crescent moon crown, and Noah stood beside her with a horned headdress. In front of them was a throne, woven of tree bark and blooming with flowers. Towering behind them was a golden statue of Ba'al, with his hands out and palms facing up, ready to receive offering.

The Coven behind me shrieked in joy, rushing to join the dancing circle. Bonnie and the other women removed my robe and draped over my shoulders a violet robe, fine and smooth. Bonnie held over my head a golden crown of thorns. She firmly laid the crown over my head, puncturing my skull. I winced as fresh warm blood now ran down my face. Amma gestured ahead, pointing towards the East. I made my way to my place, and the percussion of the drums stopped as Amma took her place before the throne. Women gathered around the circle, those who weren't dancing nestled newborns close against their chests.

Amma undid the bundle in her arms, revealing the rigid corpse of a stillborn baby. Amma lifted the baby before the crowd.

"Tonight," Amma began in ancient Yoruba, "what was dead shall live again! As testimony of our power from now, until the end of the Age!"

Amma lowered her face and cradled the baby in her arms. Her lips met the corpse of the baby, giving a gentle kiss. Amma lifted the child again in the air, and the baby's chest rose with a violent inhale of air and screamed with the wake of life. The coven erupted into yipping and shouting. A woman approached Amma, throwing herself on the floor in reverence, slobbering and crying. Amma handed her the crying baby to the mother, whose tears of anguish now became joy. She screeched, holding the baby in the air before the crowd, and they roared with praise and danced with the baby, passing it through the arms all held high in the air.

Amma took her seat. Noah sounded a horn, blasting through the air that shook the ground, and all fell silent.

"Children of the hidden shade!" Noah called out in the Hidden Tongue with a voice that boomed like a trump.

"Tonight, we gather with our Sisters for the first time in over a century. Together, on the eve of the Equinox, we prepare to feast together on life, renewing the vow our ancestors once made together!"

The Covens shouted joyfully and the drums pounded again in unison.

"Bring to us the sacrifices," Noah declared.

Titus and Jonah dragged Craven to the center. He kicked and writhed within their grasp, but the cuffs around his hands seared deeper and tighter into his flesh. Craven screamed, and they tossed him to the ground, where he fell to his knees. Melinda dragged the real Anges across the floor, kicking and screaming. She threw her to the floor beside Craven. Agnes looked up through her messy, dark bangs, red-faced as she begged for her life.

"PLEASE! PLEASE! SISTERS! DON'T DO THIS!"

"You gave up the right to call us Sisters long ago," Melinda said, smiling wickedly.

"NO!" Craven screamed in rabid protest. "I WON'T DIE FOR YOUR GOD!"

The Coven jeered, laughing and heckling. Noah snickered.

"You ain't dyin' for our God tonight. You die for yours."

Tears streamed down Craven's face. I almost pitied him.

Almost.

He sobbed, struggling to break free.

"You won't get away with this!" Craven cried, but there was the tinge of doubt in his voice. Even he knew it was the end.

"Oh? Will your God save you then? Call on Him."

Craven hung his head and began to pray frantically. He turned around, looking to me. He silently plead with me as tears dripped down his chin. I closed my eyes, painfully turning away. I had to make my own difficult decisions, and Craven made his. It pained me to let him go to the flames, but it was a bed he chose to make for himself.

Amma rose from her throne with a regal poise and held her arms out in the air. Now her beaded necklace and jewels glowed against the flickering flame.

"*Horned One! You, O' Ancient of Days, who was of old called many names; but whose true name is written in our hearts, we call on you this night to honor the Pact that was made by our ancestors who called on you many moons ago!*" Amma began in the Hidden Tongue.

The women of the coven raised their infants in the air towards the statue of Ba'al that loomed behind her.

"Ancient serpent, bringer of knowledge and spirit of rebellion! We invoke thy spirit to descend upon us! Spirit of the hoof and horn, raise thy scepter, light be born! And from the land, the darkness cast, unconquered sun to reign at last!"

Amma turned to me now.

"O' thou Queen of the Abyss and keeper of the Eternal Flame! Who was the darkness formed and divided herself and spawned the day! Upon your consort unto the East, birth thy light again, and on power, we feast!"

A rushing heat surged through my body, and gashes opened in my palms like stigmata, bleeding out onto the ground, flowing from my hands like a fountain and watering the ground. A wafting heat seared behind my head, and countless rays of light beamed from behind me, as if I had the sun itself radiating on the back of my head in a glaring halo. The Coven knelt down, extending their arms to me as the beams of light fell onto their forehead, and all their eyes glowed white as snow. Their hair waved and whirled around them as if they were submerged beneath the waters of a current of energy that surged through them now.

The beams of light that permeated from behind my head receded, and the blood from my hands ceased to flow. The Covens plunged into hysterical frenzy, and the drummers slammed on the drums, pounding erratically, possessed by the spirit of raw power that fell upon them.

"And now, in blood, we repay you, Dark Father!"

Amma lifted her hands again. Craven and Agnes screamed as they were swept up from the ground and suddenly encased a massive, golden bull, towering high above the ground. The horns reached the tops of the trees. Craven's screams were muffled from the inside, and dull bangs of him slamming against the idol reverberated. Witches cackled, swooping over the ground like birds in flight and soaring high up towards the bull. They layered over its horns a large wreathe of sunflowers, so large it was carried by four witches. They draped the crown over the bull's horns and dipped back down towards the earth below, touching the hands of the other witches that reached on high, holding their babies in the air.

"TAHAMUT!" Amma called out. "ACCEPT THIS OFFERING! AND BRING US CHILDREN TO THE CRAFT TO MAKE US MIGHTY!"

Amma took a deep breath and blew forcefully. The wicker that was under the bull ignited in flames, rising towards the belly of the giant idol. Their screams sounded like the grunting of a bull, and the smoke of their torment permeated through the nostrils of the massive, golden idol. The smell of their burning flesh was aromatic, like a sweet incense wafting out from the nostril of the bull. The louder they screamed, the more the bull seemed to come alive, grunting and panting through the smoke from its nose. The Coven lifted their hands, yipping, and instantly, a wall of fire erupted from around the statue of Ba'al, climbing high from the ground and flickering over the top of its head.

The Pact had been renewed, and I had shed my blood in a New Covenant. The witches who had their babies laid their infants over the fiery hands of Ba'al. But the fire didn't burn them; the eyes of the babies shimmered a solid black, and they laughed in delight as power passed to them. One after the other, the women passed their babies through the fire, sealing them with the Pact that continued to thrive, more powerful than ever with my blessing. The witches flew in circles around the bull, and others danced in a large ring around it, cackling and babbling like raving maenads.

As the frenzied scene played out, everything started to slow down. Their laughing and the music was drowned out by a whirring buzz, and everything around me started to spin.

"*Levi...*" A hushed, alluring voice called to me.

"*Levi...*"

The voice called again. I felt a gripping compulsion around my heart, and I faced the woods. I couldn't stop my feet from moving, and I slowly made my way towards a deeper mouth of the woods, transfixed beyond my will.

"Levi," Amma's voice pierced through the calling, "where're you goin'?"

"Gather the Coven at the hidden chamber in the church and wait for me there," I said. "Titus and Jonah will show you where,"

The creeping realization came upon me, and I knew without a shadow of the doubt who called me forward.

It was Shaddai.

The God of the Garden himself.

CHAPTER 37

The New Covenant

I held my arms out, and pure white light encased my body, draping down my arms and forming a white robe, which was tied around me, and I trekked towards the forest. An eerie glow from the eclipse cast a red hue on the trees, and I stood now in the overwhelming darkness. I circled the clearing but found only shadows.

"*Levi,*" Shaddai called again.

I turned around, and obscured in the trees was the form of bare feet with the ends of a robe draped over them, opaque and resting on a dark blue cloud that enshrouded the rest of his body.

"*You've defied me for the last time, Levi,*" he said.

"And you've destroyed everythin'. You took my family, my brother,"

"*Your family died by your own hand,*" he said.

His voice was hollow, with an eerie, serene tone like a wilting breath. But familiar. Like an abominable conglomeration of the voices of everyone I've ever known in my life in a hushed growl.

"You hardened my brother's heart against me... You set all of this in motion,"

"*I did,*" he said calmly. "*And I will stretch out my hand and smite Tophet and this world for your transgressions,*"

"You won't win," I said defiantly.

"*You will lose... everything... There will be no Christ again after you.*"

There ain't nothin' left for you to take."

"*You will fail.*"

"You sure about that?"

"*I will bring this world will to an end.*" he said.

"Not if I have anythin' to say about it,"

He laughed.

His form vanished like a wisp, fading again into the darkness. Thunder boomed in the distance, and as I looked up, the clouds began to peel with lightning and funnel over, gathering over the shore of the ocean. Bolts of lightning shot down onto the earth, and cold winds gathered and swept my robe over me. I signed the Hidden Hands and quickly opened a window portal, watching the seashore on the other side and waters churning violently.

I stepped inside, and as the portal closed behind me, my feet were now firmly planted on the grainy sand. Torrential winds skirted across the sand, and the ocean was tinged from the light of the black sun, red like wine. I saw Father Enoch standing on the shore, the words of his incantation carrying over the distance between us.

"Enoch!" I yelled.

Father Enoch turned around, his robe windswept and a crazed look in his eyes. They were glowing white, with a shining carving on his forehead in Hebrew:

EL SHADDAI

The destroyer.

He smiled ear to ear, laughing raucously. His voice was a myriad, louder than the crashing boiling waters of the sea.

"*Enki!*" he called back. "*You've come to join me!*"

Shaddai was possessing his body, speaking through him. Enoch's body shot into the air, hovering over the face of the dark, churning waters with his arms at his sides.

"I've come to put an end to you!" I said. "You know the body you possess can't s ustain you on earth. It'll deteriorate."

Enoch cackled again.

"It's too late! The final Primordial will engulf this world, and it will be no more! Then I'll have no need for this sack of flesh. I will release the flood gates as in the days of Noah, and here will enter into this plane... The Deep!"

"Why are you doing this?"

Enoch laughed, tauntingly.

"Lucifer! Don't you yet see? This is our dance across the eons, since before the world began!"

"What is this?"

"We have shared this body through the ages! Knowledge is mine to be had. You will never usurp me!"

I shuddered. Now the final truth had been revealed, and everything was made clear as day. Shaddai killed me anytime I got too close to learning the truth, to knowing more than he did anytime I lived a lifetime of learning the mysteries of the Goddess, his sworn rival. God and the Devil were waging a contest, and Shaddai was willing to snuff me out anytime I got too close to beating him. All the conflict I've felt inside me finally made sense, two cosmic polarities raged inside me, and I was tricked almost every time to only serving one.

A man cannot serve two masters.

"Levi," A voice said to me.

I saw before me, thousands of men surrounding me, each laying their hands one on top of the other, forming an endless chain that finally reached me and rested on my shoulders. It was my first lifetime, the Nazarene. I fell to my knees before him, clasping at his robe.

"Kneel not to me," the Nazarene said. *"Arise, it is yourself you see, Levi. Yourself you see in me."*

In Shadadi's rage against me, when he revoked his Spirit from me the day I ate the fruit, he left me open to connect back to myself. There was no longer anything inside me that could stop me from connecting back to my root and finding the truth inside me. His connection and binds were removed from me by his own hand, and I was now the thing He hated most: free.

"Remember who you are, Levi," he said. *"Remember… who we are."*

I looked across the myriad of lifetimes surrounding me now. The figures around me starting shine in a dazzling brilliance, and they rushed towards behind me, blasting toward my back and filling me with a terrifying and fearful amount of power. I clasped onto my sides, gnashing my teeth and losing control of my body.

"I… I'm Lucifer," I said.

I closed my eyes and felt my eyes searing with white-hot energy.

"I am Lucifer…"

"Son of the Morning,"

I screamed, and my sides tore open from prodigious wings, sprouting from my side and woven of pure light. They were three sets of peacock wings, and the six of them began to flap, summoning and stirring all every power of the element, shining like the sun rising over the East. They beat their wings until I was entombed in a dome of rushing winds and sand. The wings extended themselves, and in a blinding flash, they dissipated. Father Enoch screeched, hiding his face.

I felt myself become weightless, and then my feet came off the ground. I screamed, and the dome exploded, sending ripples of sand and gales of wind in a ring around me. I opened my mouth, spewing with glowing silver fire, and drew a sword from my mouth. My entire body was radiating and shining, no longer flesh and blood but shining gold like the sun itself.

Shaddai shook with rage I could feel even from where I stood, and he raised his arms up towards the sky. The clouds twisted and molded into what looked like the face of a snarling dragon with gaping nostrils. The beast in the sky roared, and the nostrils of cloud flared, and from them, two twisting, fiery barrels of light came rushing down from heaven above him, shooting past him on either side. It was the entire fleet of archangels, charging to war towards me. Shaddai cackled; his laughter rumbled the ground beneath me. I took a deep breath, channeling all the power within me.

Cracks formed along the ground, and from beneath me twisting and screeching, raving mad shadows burst. All the souls of hell were released at that moment, and with my sword, I directed them toward the scores of angels that charged against me.

The damned and discarded struck back with the fury of an eternity of rage against the God of the Garden, colliding in a violent explosion of embers, carving craters from the impact waves that boomed a deafening noise as they collided with each other. The sheer force crystalized the sands, blowing ferocious storms of sharp glass and sand against me, slicing me all over my body until I was covered in blood. The torrent of angels and the souls of the damned collided, incinerated until there was nothing left of dust. Shaddai's face darkened, and I could see the outrage etched clearly onto his face. The fury of heaven was equally matched by the rage of Hell and all the souls damned by his own hands. They were all eviscerated, now nothing but ash.

Soot rained down from the sky left from the impact, a black snow that coated the ground in the ashes of the wicked and righteous slaves who served Shaddai's purpose. I clasped the blade in my hands and shot through the air, rushing towards him. I lifted the sword, inches away from dealing a blow.

Enoch punched me square in the chest, knocking the breath out of me and sending me barreling into the churning water. I held tight to the sword as I plummeted deeper into the ocean. From beneath the surface, I saw the iridescent red glow of the sky, and I swam as quickly as I could. I poked my head from under the water, choking on the salty globs. I rested my arms on the wave, feeling it flat like a tabletop beneath my weight and hoisted myself up from its depths. I stood now on the face of the ocean, dripping with water and burning eyes from the salt. The sky rumbled again and flashed with lightning.

I leaped as high as I could, shooting into the air in flight when a thick rod of lightning scorched across my chest, just barely missing me, striking the water and sending a web of electrical currents through the waves. Enoch laughed mockingly. Hundreds of bolts of lightning quickly struck the ground, and I dodged them as quickly as I could. Another strike came down, hitting me directly, sending unbearable heat and wrapping me in tentacles of electricity. I screamed, feeling the current moving through my body and extended my arm, redirecting the lightning back at Enoch.

The bolt zapped across the air, illuminating the sky as it rushed towards Enoch, striking him in the arm, blowing a gashing hole directly through his chest. Enoch looked down at his body and smirked. He raised his hands and smacked them together in a thunderous clap that nearly knocked me out of the air, and the ocean parted in an earth-shaking rumble, deafening as the waters shot high into the sky, clearing a ring around in the ocean floor. The waves climbed high into the clouds. Enoch swooped down below, landing in the clearing.

I rocketed towards him, and he slung his arms, sending blasts of ocean water toward me. I swerved and maneuvered past the torrent of water, feeling the energy coursing through me. I waved my arms, watching the water curve from around me, blasting craters into the ground and sending up sprays of sand. I landed on the ground and pulled from the wall of water around me, firing at Enoch. He extended his arms, holding them together like a spear, splitting the water into two violent streams that sprayed now behind him.

I twirled the sword in my hand and shot across the surface, sending spikes of sand beneath me from the force of my flight, and swung the sword. Enoch grabbed the sword with his bare hands, and in his clasp, he shattered my blade, sending fragments of embers through the air, snatched me by the throat, and slammed me into the ground. I struggled on the floor, gasping desperately for air. From the funnel of the sky another light flashed, and I dove to the ground as another bolt of lightning collided with the earth, just missing me again.

"*It's here! The Deep has come!*"

The ground rumbled at my feet, and through the lightning glinting in the sky, it illuminated a massive, serpent-like creature bigger than the highest tower, wrapped around the ring of water that enclosed us, growling. It was the Leviathan.

"You think that…" I said, grunting. "When you gave me the power to defeat you."

"*I AM THE LORD!*" he roared. The Leviathan behind him shrieked, quaking the ground beneath me. "*THERE IS NO ONE LIKE ME!*"

"Except for me."

Like a blow to the head, I remembered Father Enoch's words to me when I went to see him at the church. The power that was passed down to Peter.

"What I bind on earth will be bound in heaven, and what I loose on earth, will be loose in heaven. Those who have seen me have seen you also."

"*NO!*" Enoch roared.

He extended his arms, and the wall of water began to part, and the beast reared its head from the depths of the ocean. Its head was like a snake; it opened its mouth and roared ferociously, blowing me back and curving the wall of water behind me. Enoch lifted his head triumphantly, laughing maniacally. I rolled onto my back from the harsh gusts that emitted from the Leviathan's roar. I struggled to stand my ground as the Leviathan slowly emerged further from the surface of The Deep. I signed the Hidden Hands, and a glowing seal inscribed with Hebraic letters and mystical symbols stretched out from beneath Enoch's feet.

"I OPEN THE DOOR TO THE BOTTOMLESS PIT!" I screamed. "APOLLYON!"

From beneath Encoh's feet, a monstrous trench opened, a void of darkness that expanded hundreds of feet in a ring around him, cavernous and contained by the seal. Thick, black chains shot from beneath the earth, wrapping themselves firmly around Enoch. They strangled around his neck, binding him and chaining his arms to his sides. A look of horror filled Enoch's face, when he saw he couldn't resist the onslaught of chains that continued to wrap themselves around him.

"*THIS ISN'T THE END! I AM KING OF KINGS!*" Enoch screeched hoarsely.

"Now bind him and cast him into the outer darkness," I said.

"*NO!!*" Enoch roared.

The Leviathan recoiled back into the water, and the opening in the wall of churning waves sealed again. With a final scream, Enoch was yanked into the pit beneath his feet, his last cries echoing until his voice was no more, and the seal contracted, shrinking until it shut closed, and with it, the earth that swallowed him. Drops of water started to come down on me like rain, and the water from the bottom rushed towards my feet as the wall of ocean collapsed, rushing towards me in an awful sound.

I leaped into the air, moving past the crushing walls of water as the waves collapsed upon themselves, crashing together and exploding into the air in one final crest. I descended on the sea, planting my feet firmly on the face of the water, feeling the cold ocean churning beneath my feet, and the waters calmed. The clouds formed into eyes and an open mouth, bellowing and raging with rolling thunder and flashes of lightning against the sky. Shaddai wasn't defeated, but His vessel on earth was in the furthest trenches, lost in the void of the bottomless pit.

Shaddai was gone. Banished to the darkness, as it was in the beginning. The settling peace reminded me now of my own mind. I was free from his voice, his reign, and compulsions. Maybe now my body and mind would become my own, no longer a puppet in his hands to slaughter, coerce, and deceive. All the rage I felt inside me was gone, lifted from my shoulders, and finally, a soothing peace had come to me, a bliss that I hadn't known before. His voice was gone forever, no longer filling me with the violent need to kill, and the relentless pursuit of blood and conquest through death.

The God of the Garden's presence was finally outside of me. I exorcised myself of a demon that was devouring my essence, riding my body to accomplish its own sadistic means and maintain its own power. It was a spiteful spirit of vengeance and scorn, and it was no longer free to command me. I was now my own King.

I looked across the sea and saw the cathedral tower in the distance. Everything would end where it began.

The church.

CHAPTER 38:

Apocalypse

As I flew towards the Cathedral, storm clouds gathered and funneled over the towering cathedral. I landed on its steps, looking up towards the raging sky. The ground shook as hail the size of school buses streaked down onto the earth, smashing and blowing off chunks of the cathedral, blowing holes into the ground around me. I took a deep breath and raised my hands high above my head. A tidal wave of energy shot out toward me, encasing a dome around me.

The hail that rained down struck the shield I conjured, incinerating and blowing me back with a violent thud against the church door, now reduced to snow. I coughed up globs of blood, the scarlet stained the pale clumps of snow on the ground. I dusted myself off as the hail relented around me, pieces that struck the shield were turned to more clouds of froth and ice, blowing into the wind around me.

The sky grumbled, and again, the furious visage of Shaddai appeared in the clouds. The ground beneath shook violently, unbearably. I fell against the pillar and clasped it to keep me from losing my foot. The ground began to crack open with an awful sound, and the earth beneath me fragmented, separating in serrated chunks, and the church began to drift apart as the mouth of the ground opened into a cavernous bit, separating the church from the chunk of land now that was the rest of Tophet.

I ran down the steps and towards the edge and was blasted back by a vicious heat that seared and burned my skin. I fell onto my back, looking up in astounded horror as molten magma blasted out from the crevice of the ground, higher than the clouds. Flaming chunks of magma and rock rained down on me, blasting through the church and tearing it down in flaming chunks of cement and glass. I heard the wicked, rumbling laugh of the God of Heaven, as now the wall of magma surged back down towards me. I choked on the vaporous, poisonous gases that rose from the crevice of the earth, sweating profusely as the magma rushed towards me in a molten tsunami of fire.

I took one last deep breath and signed Hidden Hands, and with the wave of my arms and the very essence of what power I left in me, the roaring fire and trembling blasts that shook the ground with all the fury of heaven seemed musical. I looked up, and over the dome of the sky, I saw a flash like a grid, and everything around me vibrated in a kind of song, like a choir of different octaves.

Music.

I looked down at my hands, remembering now that I was a spirit of music. And the universe was made of vibration, of sound; therefore, I commanded the universe. All these years, Shaddai was able to control me because He made sure the sound of His voice drowned out my own music. Waves of hot, electric energy rushed through me as the final piece of who I truly was had come to me. I'd rediscovered my song. The song of myself.

I roared; I quickly signed the Hidden Hands. And with the wave of my arms, I looked like a conductor now, playing the forces of nature like an orchestra. I now commanded the rushing magma. The lava that rushed towards me parted like the sea and whipped around me, following the direction of my hands. The lava whirled around me and the church in a surging vortex of liquid fire and picked up the sea of snow that was once the hail, cycling faster by the second.

The snow merged with the whirling lava, casting me into a blinding haze of pure steam. The snow danced around me faster than wind, and the magma slowly began to turn to rock. I screamed, blinding by steam and nearly unconscious from the heat around me, and with one final push, the barrier of snow reduced the flowing lava to rock, frozen in place. I slumped over, heaving. The sky roared again, and I smiled haughtily. I turned around before the next onslaught and sought cover inside.

I pushed past the door of the church, walking alone now as the statues of saints twisted their heads, screaming curses down at me from on high as Shaddai filled their stone tongues with threats and scorn. I moved past them, sliding the door open that lead to the hidden chamber beneath the church. As I descended the steps, the sound of chanting filled the darkness, and deeper into the earth I went. Finally, I arrived at the scene where it all began, where my torment and suffering were born, and where every Christ before me was executed to pass along the spirit of the living Fraud.

The Coven gathered around the upside down cross, still dry with the blood from the last Christ that passed along the power to me. The black waters on either side of me were still, carrying the voice of their chants and reverberating off the walls that enclosed us. Outside boomed with thunder and roared ferociously. The air was sweet with incense, and hundreds of candles lined the ground floor. Selene and Noah stood at opposite ends, annotating a vibration that rumbled the jet surface of the water. Amma was clothed in a white robe and veil, like Mary. She held her hand out to me, beaming with pride as she saw me emerge victorious.

The roof of the church was blown off, and surging winds filled the space we stood in. I looked up, watching as tornadoes formed around the church, ripping the building.

"We have to move fast!" Selene said.

"What about the Primordials?"

Selene smiled, her hair blowing wildly against her face now. "They're the key ingredient. We saw Enoch would do this." Selene winked now.

"Y'all did the work for us."

Father Enoch, so eager to serve his God and prove his devotion, brought these forces into this world at Shaddai's orders. And now the witches were going to add to the power of this spell sevenfold, all because of the window of opportunity they saw in the rage against his most ancient rival.

"It was my idea," Amma said.

"A—Are you sure?"

Amma took me by the hand and pricked her finger against the thorns on my crown.

"It all ends tonight," she said.

The ruby drop of blood rolled down her finger, and she held it out to me. I licked her finger, swallowing the tip and sucking the blood from the open wound, taking her into myself.

"Blood of the New Covenant," I said.

I kissed her deeply. The spectral forms of the disfigured convent emerged from the walls, shimmering in a grey translucence, chanting together now fervently with the Coven. The spirits of the entombed nuns appeared, lending the full force of their power to the magic of the ritual.

All four walls of the church above us exploded in a billowing eruption. Scathing and wrathful winds consumed us in a furious storm. All at once, clouds of dirt and stone exploded from above us as the winds ripped through the ground above and exposed the hidden chamber hiding us deep within the womb of the earth.

Of the entire Coven, Rita and Bonnie's voices carried nearly over everyone else's as they fought with all their might to raise the cone of power. They fought for their survival in their final test of strength against the God of the Garden.

A shimmering dome of translucent energy vaporized the falling rocks that tumbled over us, protecting us. A spinning sphere of protection encased us, cutting and slicing through the ground. Protected and buried deep within now I saw was the Great Mother. Stars fell from the sky, followed by monstrous rods of lightning that barreled down from the sky, pummeling down against us in streaks of white-hot fire and exploding into fiery embers, and electric webs that rocked and rippled the shield that encased us below.

From the ground beneath, streaks of black shadows exploded from the ground in a spray of rocks and stone, rising high above. Tall specters woven of pure shadow towered dozens of feet above, forming a chain of locked arms around us.

Stars, lightning, and the full rage of the elements slammed relentlessly against the dome that encased us, strengthened now by the shadow agents of the Underworld, handmaidens of the Abyss that they served and rose up to protect us against the relentless rage of the God of the Garden. Sheets of rain, thick hail, lightning, and fire from the stars poured down on us, but the protection of the Ancient Ones prevailed against the onslaught. Like an enraged and spoiled child thwarted at his own game, the God of the Garden flipped the game board and slung the pieces in defeat. But it wasn't tiny, hard plastic; it was the elements of the very reality he had a hand in creating, the forces of nature.

"*KARAZA! KELAMOZ! SANANAG! AIDARA!*"

I heard Rita and Bonnie, roaring with ferocity that came second only to Amma's, who led the entire Coven with a thunderous shout.

"FILL ME WITH THY POWER!" she cried out.

The scorching powers and forces of the elements that once stormed down on us came rushing into Amma's body, absorbed into her stomach. She laid her hands over her womb, trying to contain the rush of wind, rain, fire from the stars, and the monster hurricane that once plagued the skies. Waters, fire, and lightning rushed towards her; all being pulled in by vacuous energy that Amma started to gain more control over with each passing second. She roared as blood ran down her nose, and she fought to contain the forces of nature within her.

Every raging force was instantly absorbed into Amma, the very forces of nature thrown into the cauldron of her being, forming within her a titan worthy of terrible greatness; the elements soon to be born as a living soul. The Garden had been thwarted by the Goddess of the witches, who, in her cunning, used His rage against him once more and outwit him. The very Primordial forces Shaddai allowed to pass into this world to destroy us, now only enhanced the magic that was being woven. What He sent to destroy, She now used to create.

He was the Great Architect of his own undoing.

The sky above us was clear once more, and all that remained was the blackened sky, devoid of even the stars that once shone above it.

"*DESCENDERE!*" The Coven shouted in unison. A ripple of darkness came from beneath us, encircling the entire coven, and everything around us vanished, swallowed by darkness until all that remained in my sight was Amma lying beneath me, her eyes twinkling as she stroked my cheek tenderly.

The Coven was obscured with darkness, but their voices echoed all around us, vibrating off a floor I couldn't see it. It was like we'd entered a void, somewhere outside of time and space, and in the distance appeared a glowing, white doe with horns protruding from its head forged of crystal.

A feverish passion consumed me, and Amma and I kissed each other passionately, feeling the build of something that shook me to my core, shaking my entire body as if trying to escape. I laid my hands over her stomach, looking deeply into her eyes. I could feel our spirits merging, joining and becoming one flesh.

She clasped onto my back, and we vigorously breathed in and out into each other's mouths until we reached an ecstatic state. The Coven's chants crescendoed over the sound of our gasping breath and Amma's moans. I felt myself reaching a climax in my heart until I couldn't contain myself.

With one final scream, my body quaked, and a spectral form burst from my body, glowing in shimmering gold, and shot straight into her stomach. Amma's head flew back in a cry of ecstasy. Light shot from her mouth and through her eyes, and she was ripped apart from me with a violent force and into the air.

"*EKSTASIS!*" Selene and Noah shouted over the Coven.

At their word, a translucent wave of energy came barreling into the circle and sucked into the glow that now surrounded Amma's stomach.

"*PARAFROSYNI!*"

Another surge of energy came screeching into the circle, sucked straight into Amma.

"*PEÍNA!*" Selene and Noah roared.

"*SKOTÁDI!*"

"*VATHIÁ!!!!*" They finished together.

All of the Primordials once summoned were absorbed into Amma, and she screamed in a manner between pain and pleasure.

A halo burst brightly, appearing behind Amma's head of silver light, casting a pale glow that illuminated now the Coven standing around us in a circle. The black cloak of the abyss we were in twinkled now with stars all around her, and she held her hands gently over her stomach. Within seconds, her stomach began to grow until it was full and as round as the moon. The shimmering light from the halo behind her silhouetted the Coven, and their chanting ceased to give way to a smile as they fixed their eyes on Amma hovering above them.

"*UNTO US A CHILD IS BORN!*" Amma's voice called out in a myriad. "*UNTO US A DAUGHTER IS GIVEN!*"

Tears slid down my face, and I laughed, awe-struck. We'd reached the Holy Grail of immortality, of life eternal. Now we would be ageless, and death would be no more, neither mourning, crying, nor pain amongst us ever again. Shaddai said that there would be no Christ after me, and so it would be. The Great Rite was completed, and the Holy bloodline would be born again. I'd lost everything I had to gain a kingdom that would never pass away. I forged anew, made in my father's image. I was the dragon and the adversary, born with the seed of rebellion. I warred against heaven and took home the crown, rivaling the creator of this very world. I lived long enough to see myself become a living god.

I didn't know what life would bring me next. I looked around me and found myself in a circle of witches, where priests and church elders once stood. The Devil likes to ask difficult questions, and I learned that appears to us as doubt. The master deceiver will always weave in the truth with a lie until they merge to become something indistinguishable. And not knowing was worse than an impulsive decision. It was a gamble, a stab in the dark if the traditions that were taught to us turned out to be the right ones.

How sure can you be?

The people around me who were absolutely sure were who I feared the most. They believed they had the absolute truth, and I wasn't sure I ever did, which lead me to discover it. The witches taught me that sometimes the things we hate most, we desire to do ourselves. I wasn't going to let fear continue to keep me in the dark. People thought the light was safe, but I learned that even that can be blinding.

I thought all the murderous rage would melt away once I exorcised Shaddai from my body. But it was still there. I thought it was his influence, but really it was inside me all along. The blood lust, the violence, and all the parts of myself that I thought would die with him. But they were begging to be fed. Gnawing, clawing, and ravenous. Where once I reserved those emotions for witches, now I would turn it on the servants of God who would sooner tear this world apart than deny his will. They worshiped a malevolent Maker, so I will become the destroyer, the devourer of his disciples.

I followed the orders of a being I believed was good because he told me so. It was the monster boasting of his beauty, and there I was, taking him at his word. He was a lion who permed his mane and convinced the flock he was a sheep. He was the real beast, and he was the one the entire world would follow blindly. What kind of creature *was* the God of the Garden? I'll never be sure. But I wondered now, was the Garden of Eden actually paradise, or was our expulsion really an escape? Until now, I followed in the image of Adam, when I should have been like Eve, less asleep and more awake.

She was the first to choose, and so was I, and on that day, I learned the secrets of good and evil.

I'm the Alpha, and the Omega, the first and the last, the beginning, and the end.

Though I knew there was much work to be done, I have wrestled with God and won.

THE END

Made in the USA
Columbia, SC
21 January 2023

10815703R00233